# *Jasmine gasped with joy and need . . .*

arching wantonly into his bold touch. The liquor had smashed all her inhibitions, and now even her pain was just a dull, aching memory. She wanted to obliterate it, utterly! She kissed Jared back with reckless passion, opening her mouth wide to him and stroking his hot tongue with her own . . .

Yet after a moment, he paused, pulling away from her. "Jasmine, no," he said brokenly, his hands trembling on her shoulders, a haunted quality in his bright blue eyes. "We must stop this. You're a lady."

But Jasmine wasn't thinking straight. She only knew she would die here and now without Jared's wonderful strength. She wanted to lose herself in him, to forget all her problems and savor the power and magic of her rescuer's embrace. "Yes, I'm a lady," she told him. "But tonight you've made me feel like a woman for the first time in my life. Please don't spurn me, Jared. I need your comfort."

"But you don't seem to understand," he said in an agonized voice she was beyond hearing. "I think I'm in love . . ."

Jared swept Jasmine up into his arms and carried her to his bunk . . .

\*      \*      \*

*Mississippi Madness*

T3-BPD-365

**Also by Eugenia Riley**

*Laurel's Love*
*Sweet Reckoning*

Published by
WARNER BOOKS

# Mississippi Madness

## Eugenia Riley

**WARNER BOOKS**

A Warner Communications Company

WARNER BOOKS EDITION

Copyright © 1989 by Eugenia Riley Essenmacher

Cover art by Don Case

Warner Books, Inc.
666 Fifth Avenue
New York, N.Y. 10103

 A Warner Communications Company

Printed in the United States of America

First Printing: June, 1989

10 9 8 7 6 5 4 3 2 1

With love to my brother, Philip—
he'll be mad for this one.

The author extends special thanks to
Kathy Smitherman of
the Judge Armstrong Library
in Natchez, Mississippi.

It is a common calamity;
we are all mad at some time or other.

—*Johannes Baptista Mantuanus*—

# ⋆ Prologue ⋆

The moon was full . . . And from the moment Jared Hampton saw the beautiful woman struggling for her life in the black depths of the Mississippi River, he knew he was in love. He had come out on the deck of the *River Witch* to get a breath of fresh air and to scan the waters ahead, when he spotted her flailing about in the churning waters, screaming for help. He found he could not take his eyes off the captivating mermaid who had just so dramatically appeared in his life.

In the treacherous waters beyond, Jasmine Dubroc Boudreau was, indeed, fighting for her life. She had fully expected to drown before she saw the gray hulk of the side-wheeler steam into view. Then she had spotted the tall gentleman standing on deck, staring down at her in amazement. Heedless of the fact that she wore only a shockingly thin, torn nightgown, she found her instincts for survival—and even more acutely, her thirst for revenge—taking over. "Help me!" she screamed out as the steamboat drew nearer. "For God's sake, help me!"

Jared Hampton removed his Panama hat and looked down in astonishment. "Love, whatever are you doing down there in the river?" he called out in a cultured drawl.

"Drowning!" came the terse reply.

1

"However did you land in such a predicament?" he demanded.

"That's a long story!" she snapped.

And that was enough for Jared Hampton! Pausing only to remove his boots and to order the pilot to reverse the engines, Jared climbed the railing, then plunged headlong into the waters of the Mississippi to rescue his floundering goddess, calling out to her in a laughter-filled voice, "*This* I've got to hear!"

# ★ One ★

Natchez, Mississippi
Summer 1850

*Only two weeks past, old Ephraim had come to her at the orphanage. "Yo' daddy done passed away, Miz Jasmine . . ."*

Jasmine Dubroc sat in the parlor of St. Mary's Orphan Asylum with one of her charges. She was quite fond of six-year-old Maggie, who sat companionably close to her on the threadbare settee. Jasmine often used part of her luncheon break to tutor the girl, who was rather shy, and had great trouble reading in class.

"That's *tomorrow*, darling," she now gently corrected, as the little girl stumbled over a word. As Maggie trilled on, Jasmine glanced through the window and saw her family servant, Ephraim, come limping up the flagstone path. His head was downcast, and his lower lip was trembling.

"Darling, go find Sister Philomena," Jasmine murmured to the child, automatically patting her head to reassure her. Maggie obediently closed her primer and left the room.

Jasmine brushed a loose strand of wheat-colored hair from her eyes, and hurried for the front door, her faded muslin skirts trailing on the scarred floor. Ephraim would never fetch her from the orphanage at this hour, she thought, unless something was wrong.

3

She flung open the heavy oaken panel. The barest breeze stirred the heavy summer air, sweeping in the cloying aroma of nectar.

The gray-haired slave removed his tattered hat with unsteady fingers and wiped his sweaty brow on the sleeve of his faded jacket when he saw her.

"Yo' daddy done passed away, Miz Jasmine," he said in a cracking voice.

In the small cottage on Pearl Street, Jasmine hung her bonnet on a peg, then went into her father's room. The summer heat inside the small bedroom was oppressive. Her father was, indeed, dead. His face—with the prominent nose, tight mouth, and bushy brows—had already taken on a grayish pallor, and his hand was cold.

*Cold.* Cold old Frenchman, that's what she had always called her father privately. So distant, so unreachable, so undemonstrative. Her father had never loved her—that's what she had always thought. Still, the pain twisted in her heart right now.

She heard Ephraim shuffle into the room. "What happened?" she asked, turning to him helplessly.

Ephraim blinked back tears. "It was his heart. He called out fo' me, and when I come a'runnin', I foun' him holdin' his chest. Then he fell back on the pillow and he jes' pass on, Miz Jasmine."

"At least he didn't suffer long," she said hoarsely, her fist clenching her damp handkerchief. "The doctor always said his heart was weak . . ."

Suddenly Ephraim seemed unusually nervous, "Oh, no ma'am, Miz Jasmine. Yo' daddy didn't suffer long at all."

And despite his limp, Ephraim hurried from the room.

They buried Pierre Dubroc three days later, at a graveside service held in Natchez Cemetery. The priest from St. Mary's, Father Grignon, conducted the service. It was a muggy, overcast morning; the scent of camellias, magnolias, and wisteria was heavy on the wet air. Jasmine stood beneath the sheltering arms of a tall oak as the priest intoned the service. Her father had been a well-respected silversmith in Natchez, and representatives of some of the city's most venerable families were present today.

Jasmine felt touched that her father's memory had been honored by this good-sized showing of mourners. However, she found her attention drawn by a single woman who stood off from the others. The woman was wearing black, yet both her gown and bonnet were tawdry, fashioned of black satin interlaced with small dyed feathers and dark, flashy sequins. Her hair was a bright, unnatural red, and Jasmine was sure she glimpsed rouge on the woman's veiled cheeks. Jasmine wondered who she was and why she was there. When the first clods of dirt thudded down on the plain wooden casket, Jasmine was sure she saw a tear trickle down the woman's face.

Two days later, Jasmine was summoned to the office of her father's attorney, Richard Gates, for the reading of his will. Ephraim drove Jasmine to the Franklin Street office, and waited outside in their small buggy while his mistress went inside.

As Jasmine entered Mr. Gates's dusty, cluttered inner sanctum, her nostrils were immediately assailed by the odor of cheap perfume, and she was astonished to see, once again, the woman who had mysteriously appeared at her father's funeral.

Richard Gates, a tall, slim man, instantly sprang up from his desk chair to acknowledge Jasmine's entrance. "Good afternoon, Miss Dubroc," he said, coming around his desk to greet her, even as the scarlet woman inclined her head in Jasmine's direction, and raised a dark eyebrow.

Courtesy demanded that Jasmine return the nod before she took the lawyer aside. Her first words were low but straight to the point: "Who is this woman, and what is she doing here?"

Gates looked extremely uncomfortable. Nodding toward the woman who sat beyond them, he said, "Miss Dubroc, meet Miss Flossie La Fleume."

Flossie La Fleume! Jasmine was stunned. Who in Natchez

had not heard of the infamous riverfront tart from Natchez-Under-the-Hill? There had to be some mistake.

Not knowing what else to do, Jasmine numbly took the seat the lawyer indicated and nodded perfunctorily to Flossie. Gates quickly returned to his desk and sifted through some papers in front of him.

In the following moments, Jasmine learned that she was to receive from her father's estate the house on Pearl Street, as well as custody of Ephraim. She was feeling rather relieved, knowing that these were the only true assets her father possessed, when Gates turned to Flossie La Fleume. "It seems that the remainder of Mr. Dubroc's estate—including all the money in his bank account—shall pass to you."

"I beg your pardon, Mr. Gates," Jasmine cut in, mystified by this announcement. "What bank account?"

Gates nervously removed his spectacles. "Your father had fifteen thousand dollars in an account at Natchez Bank and Trust. The money now passes to Miss La Fleume, unless she dies before this provision is executed. In that event, the money would pass to you, Miss Dubroc."

Jasmine was so stunned she couldn't even speak. "But, Mr. Gates, that's impossible!" she sputtered at last. "My father never had any money! That's why I worked at the orphanage after he became ill."

Gates grimaced as he nodded to Jasmine. "I'm sure the money comes as quite a shock to you, Miss Dubroc. Perhaps your father sought to put aside a small nest egg for a rainy day—"

"A small nest egg?" Jasmine repeated with bitter amazement. "Mr. Gates, by your own admission, we're talking about fifteen thousand dollars! Are you telling me my father had that money secreted away all those years while we suffered?"

"So it appears," Gates conceded with a tight frown.

Jasmine shook her head in bewilderment and went on speaking, almost as if the other two were not present. "Oh, my God! How could he have done this to me? To think how I worried myself sick over his doctor bills! And I nursed him every night! Now he's left all his money to this—woman?"

Gates took out a handkerchief and mopped his brow. "Miss Dubroc, please. It seems your father and—er—Miss La Fleume shared a special relationship."

"I'll just bet they did!" she said.

"Now, to get on with our business," Gates continued, consulting the document in front of him. "As I was just saying, the bulk of Mr. Dubroc's estate passes to—er—"

Jasmine abruptly stood, squaring her shoulders with as much dignity as she could muster. "Our business is concluded, Mr. Gates." She glowered at Flossie La Fleume, hating the hot tears that stung her eyes. "I refuse to remain for one more moment in the presence of this—this thieving hussy!"

Jasmine fled the room, struggling to keep from breaking down entirely. Surprisingly, it was Flossie La Fleume who caught up with her in the outer office. "Miss Dubroc, please!" she begged in a surprisingly cultured voice.

Jasmine turned to glare at the woman who had stolen what was rightfully hers. Flossie's round face was so heavily rouged that it was difficult for Jasmine to gauge her age, yet her deep brown eyes hinted of a sad wisdom that Jasmine found quite odd. Catching a steadying breath, she said, "I have nothing to say to you, Miss La Fleume."

The woman sighed. "I just want you to know, honey, that your father didn't suffer at the end—"

"You were *there*?" Jasmine hissed incredulously.

Flossie glanced at the young law clerk, who was watching the two women with his mouth agape. As he blushed and lowered his gaze to the law book he had been consulting, the redheaded prostitute turned back to Jasmine and whispered, "Yes, I was often there with Pierre during the day. Your father and I were friends, Miss Dubroc. And I just want you to know that Pierre thought quite highly of you—"

"But obviously not as highly as he thought of you," Jasmine finished.

The woman offered Jasmine an open-handed gesture. "I'm sorry, Miss Dubroc. Pierre just wanted us both provided for."

The words hit Jasmine like a potful of boiling water. All those years, *she* had provided for Pierre Dubroc! She had slaved at the orphanage for wages during the day, nursed him at night, scrimped and stretched their every penny. She had gone without new clothes in order to provide for her father! And then to learn that all that time, her father had used her and hoarded away all his thousands, that he'd left her a ramshackle cottage and had cheerfully given his fortune to a riverfront tart—that he'd died in bed with a whore!

Flossie La Fleume's cajoling voice cut into Jasmine's outraged thoughts. "Miss Dubroc, if it's the money that you're concerned about, perhaps we can—"

"Actually, Miss La Fleume, it's not the money, it's the betrayal it represents," Jasmine cut in. "But then, you know all about betrayal, don't you? Tell me, was it difficult for you to convince my father to leave you all his money?"

As the other woman tried to protest, Jasmine held up a hand in warning and coldly sized her up. It was to Flossie La Fleume's credit that she feigned at least a token display of guilt for robbing Jasmine of what was rightfully hers. Yet Jasmine did not believe for one second that this prostitute from Silver Street would share one dime of her father's fortune with her! "Keep your inheritance, Miss La Fleume," she at last told the other woman, in an embittered voice. "I'm sure you earned it."

Jasmine fled the office, a red haze of rage blinding her as she boarded her buggy and sat down next to Ephraim. "You knew, Ephraim!" she said. "You had to have known that my father and that woman were . . . And you never told me!"

"Yes 'um," was all Ephraim said before he clucked to the horse and drove them home.

At the door to the cottage on Pearl Street, Ephraim offered helplessly, "Miz Jasmine, we still gots each other."

"Leave me alone, please," was all she could manage to say to him as she fled inside.

Safely inside her bedroom, Jasmine fell to her knees and cried. She doubted the pain would ever stop.

Damned old Frenchman! Damned old bastard! He'd never given a thought to her! He'd never loved her! He'd only used her! And now from his very grave, he had flung his heartless will at her like the cruelest, cheapest joke! He had told her in the most brutal terms that he valued a prostitute from Silver Street much more highly than he valued his own daughter!

She was twenty-three years old, alone and penniless, with nothing but the bitter memory of her father's betrayal.

It was all over. There was no tomorrow!

# ★ **Two** ★

*Only a week later, Jasmine met Claude Boudreau.*

Jasmine went back to the orphanage the Friday following her father's death. Her initial pain and rage at Pierre Dubroc's betrayal had died down to a dull ache. She simply felt numb, empty, and dead—*worthless*.

She would have taken herself to the river to put an end to her miserable, useless existence, yet she could not quite bring herself to do that to the girls at the orphanage.

The moment Jasmine arrived at St. Mary's, young Maggie rushed into her arms, her precious little oval face tense with fright, her blue eyes wet with tears. "Miss Jasmine, I thought you'd left me forever!"

Jasmine stroked the child's pale-blond hair and wiped her own tears with her free hand. "Darling, my father died."

"I know. Sister Philomena told me."

The child's voice shook, and her frail arms trembled about Jasmine's waist.

As Maggie clung to her for dear life, Jasmine suddenly thought about adopting her. She realized that the trustees of the orphanage, as well as the Natchez Orphans Court, would doubtless prefer having a married couple take her on, but there were so many children in need at the orphanage, and so few prospective parents to adopt them. Jasmine decided to speak with the head of the orphanage, Mother Martha, about the child. After all, she no longer had the responsibility of an invalid father to care for.

Late that afternoon, Jasmine left the orphanage and boarded her buggy to drive home. Ephraim usually drove her to and from work, but this morning, the old slave had been so stiff from rheumatism that Jasmine had insisted he spend the day resting. Her horse, Sugar, seemed unusually agitated. She was usually such a docile animal, yet today she was rearing and whinnying, refusing to obey Jasmine's commands. "Easy, Sugar!" she called, pulling back hard on the reins.

The horse suddenly bolted, and the buggy raced out of control through the busy streets, heading in the direction of the bluff at the edge of town. Pulling back on the reins seemed only to enrage the horse more! Jasmine could feel sweat breaking out on her upper lip, and her arms and hands soon ached from her exertions as they veered onto the hill.

Jasmine gazed frantically down the two-hundred-foot expanse of bluff at the gray Mississippi below. The trail was hopelessly narrow and twisted here; one misstep by Sugar, and they would both go hurtling to their deaths in the river below!

Jasmine was beginning to despair of her fate when suddenly, a stranger on a black horse galloped up beside her. "Whoa! Whoa, there!" the man called to Sugar as he grabbed a handful of her harness and pulled back on the leather straps. In a few minutes, he managed to bring her to a complete halt. Dismounting, he stood for a moment talking to the snorting, lathered horse, then examined the harness straps carefully with his gloved fingers. Only when the horse was completely subdued did the stranger turn to Jasmine. "Are you all right, mademoiselle?"

Jasmine stared in astonishment at the Frenchman who had rescued her. Tall, broad-shouldered, and slim, he was dressed in a fashionable brown wool frock coat and buff-colored trousers tucked into shiny black boots. He moved closer to her, and she studied his face beneath the brim of his white

Panama hat. She saw strong male features, deeply tanned skin, and eyes so black and intense that for a moment, she found herself fighting a shudder. Then the man smiled at her, revealing even, white teeth in a wide, sensual mouth, and her unease swiftly faded.

"Yes, I'm fine," she managed to tell her gallant rescuer. "And thank you, sir. It seems you have saved my life."

"It is an honor to have been of assistance, mademoiselle," he said, bowing modestly. He nodded toward Sugar. "Your horse—does she often take her head this way?"

"Oh, no," Jasmine assured. "She's normally so docile— I was stunned when she bolted." She frowned. "I can't imagine what could have caused this."

Her rescuer shrugged, brushing a piece of lint from his elegant coat. "Horses are spirited creatures. Perhaps she saw a snake in the path."

"That could be true," Jasmine acknowledged.

The Frenchman smiled, his dark gaze fixing pointedly on her. "Mademoiselle, may I see you safely home?"

"Oh, no!" Jasmine replied with embarrassment. "I wouldn't dream of imposing!"

"Since when is it an imposition to escort a beautiful lady to her residence?" he inquired charmingly.

Jasmine felt color burn her cheeks at the compliment. No one had ever called her beautiful before. Actually, she felt dowdy in her plain black muslin frock and fraying bonnet. "Please, it's unnecessary," she pleaded, all too conscious of the black eyes that held her in such frank regard.

"Ah, but it is necessary," her rescuer returned. "What if your horse should again bolt?" Looking straight at Jasmine, the Frenchman added, "Obviously, she needs a firm male hand."

Jasmine was rapidly losing herself in her dashing rescuer's smile. "I suppose you have a point, sir."

With a grin, the forthright Frenchman turned to tether his horse to the back of the buggy. Then he moved to Jasmine's side, obviously ready to join her in the conveyance. "By your leave, mademoiselle," he said with that same, disarming smile.

Jasmine could not be so rude as to refuse. "Of course, sir."

Jasmine scooted over and the Frenchman climbed in beside her. She immediately caught a lungful of his scent—leather, tobacco, and an alluring male essence. Her heart was hammering as he turned to smile at her once more and said, "Claude Boudreau at your service, mademoiselle. I apologize that, given our circumstances, formal introductions are not possible. Nevertheless, I would consider it a distinct honor to know the name of the lovely lady I am escorting to her home."

"I'm Jasmine Dubroc," she replied unsteadily, enchanted.

Since Boudreau was driving, Jasmine pulled off her gloves and flexed her sore hands. Her palms and the insides of her fingers were throbbing from her exertions with the reins. Her rescuer glanced down at her bare fingers with interest. "Since you wear no wedding ring, mademoiselle, may I be so bold as to assume that you are *Miss* Dubroc?"

Jasmine blushed again. "That is correct, sir."

He tipped his hat to her with gloved fingers. "I am enchanted to have made your acquaintance."

They wound back down the trail toward Natchez proper.

In the main business district of town, shopkeepers were locking their stores. A lamplighter was starting to light the gaslights on the public square. After a moment, Boudreau remarked to Jasmine, "Pardon me if I sound indiscreet, mademoiselle, but I couldn't help but notice that you are in mourning."

"Yes. My father passed away only a week past."

"My heartfelt condolences," he said.

"Thank you," Jasmine returned stiffly.

"If you will be so kind, then, as to direct me to your residence."

Jasmine was embarrassed to direct her rescuer to the plain Natchez side street where her small house sat. Her concern was misplaced, however, for as soon as the Frenchman pulled the buggy up before Jasmine's vine-covered bungalow, he remarked sincerely, "A most charming cottage, Miss Dubroc. I can smell the honeysuckle even from here."

Jasmine felt her pulses racing as Claude alighted from the buggy with lithe grace, then assisted her down. As her feet touched the ground, his strong hands lingered for a moment about her small waist, and Jasmine felt a peculiar quiver in her belly.

He took her arm and led her up the path. She was grateful for his support; she felt rather unsteady in his arousing presence. She marveled that Claude had noticed the honeysuckle vine. Now, she drank in all the essences of this lovely summer day—the deep grass, mossy trees, the sweetness of Ephraim's prized roses—and most of all, the alluring scent of the man beside her.

He escorted her to the door and they paused in the dappled light. Finally, Claude frowned. "Tell me, Miss Dubroc, have you a protector—someone to oversee your needs?"

Jasmine lowered her eyes. "There is no one, except for our family manservant, Ephraim. I mostly take care of myself." She ventured a glance up at Claude, no longer able to contain her own frank curiosity. "You're not from these parts, are you, Mr. Boudreau?"

"No, mademoiselle. I am from Louisiana—St. Martin Parish. I own a plantation there."

"I suppose you have family there—a wife," Jasmine remarked, with a boldness that shocked her.

Surprisingly, the Frenchman smiled, his dark eyes glittering. "I have neither, Miss Dubroc. It seems we are both sadly without suitable relations." Shaking his head, he went on, "You know, it's a pity that I shall be in Natchez for such a short time. My business here shall be concluded in a week."

"I see," Jasmine replied dully. She was thinking that she might never see him again.

"I cannot help but wonder . . ." the Frenchman continued with a pensive frown. "I know it seems forward of me, Miss Dubroc. After all, we have not even been properly introduced. But could I possibly attend you again before I take my leave of your charming city? It seems to me that you have had quite a nasty shock today, and I would very much like to reassure myself that you have emerged from the frightening incident without any lasting ill effects."

Jasmine was stunned that he was interested in her. "Sir, I would be honored to receive you," she managed to force out.

"Considering our limited time together—may I escort you to mass on Sunday?"

"Yes, that would be fine," Jasmine found herself saying.

Claude took Jasmine's hand and raised it to his lips. She could feel gooseflesh breaking out on the back of her hand as his warm breath scorched her flesh and his sensuous lips pressed against her soft skin.

"Until Sunday morning, then," Claude Boudreau said, bowing with fluid grace before he turned, smiling, to retreat down the path.

Jasmine went into her bedroom, removed her bonnet, and stared at her reflection in the mirror. Claude Boudreau had called her beautiful today. She had never thought of herself as even remotely attractive, but now, as she gazed into the looking glass, more than ever she saw her beloved mother, who had died of yellow fever when Jasmine was five years old. Jasmine picked up the miniature of Camille Dubroc that sat on her dresser, and tears blurred her vision. She was staring at her mother, yet she was also looking at herself— at large, deep-set eyes that were a vivid green; at a classic, finely boned nose; at a shapely long face with graceful feminine angles, including strong chin, high cheekbones, and a full, wide mouth. In the miniature, Camille Dubroc wore her rich, honey-colored hair down, and Jasmine now found herself pulling at the pins that restrained her traditional chignon. Shiny, wheat-colored tresses cascaded to her shoulders, the heavy silken waves outlining her oval face and the slender column of her neck.

Yes, she looked just like her mother. She even had her mother's figure—the willowy curves, the generous hips and breasts. She had always thought of her mother as beautiful —yet she'd always thought of herself as hopelessly ugly. Why?

Her father had reinforced that conception, she supposed.

Nothing about her had ever pleased Pierre Dubroc—not her looks or mannerisms, the way she spoke or dressed.

Since Jasmine had matured to biddable age, other men had seemed to reinforce her father's ill opinion of her, mostly through their studied neglect. Only once had Jasmine been courted—when she was nineteen, by a shy, awkward store-keeper who was thin and balding. When George Tilson had learned of Jasmine's obligation to care for her father, he'd stopped calling on her, to her immense relief.

And now, to be courted by this enchanting, wealthy stranger! It seemed almost too good to be true. Perhaps he'd only offered to attend her on Sunday out of courtesy, she told herself, in a moment of terrible self-doubt. Perhaps he would not even show up to escort her to the appointed mass.

One thing was for sure, though, she decided vehemently. If Claude Boudreau did return, she would never, ever tell him of her father's betrayal. No one, other than her lawyer and Flossie La Fleume, need ever know of the shame and degradation her father had heaped on her!

On Sunday morning, Jasmine dressed for mass early, and Claude Boudreau appeared at her door long before she could gather doubts that he might show. Jasmine smiled as she saw him on her porch.

"*Enchanté*, mademoiselle," was Claude's comment as he tipped his hat to her. He smilingly surveyed Jasmine in her best black silk gown and matching bonnet. She had worn her hair boldly down about her shoulders, and his dark eyes lingered on her thick, glossy tresses with an admiration that brought becoming color to Jasmine's cheeks.

Claude drove Jasmine to mass in a shiny black carriage drawn by two matched grays. She felt like a princess as they wound through the shady streets. They caught the glances and smiles of other church-bound couples and families, who moved past them in their own fine conveyances.

During the service at St. Mary's Cathedral, every eye in the sanctuary was turned toward the intriguing couple seated near the back of the church. After the service, several venerable Natchez dowagers, who had rarely before deigned to speak with Jasmine, came forward demanding to be introduced to her handsome escort.

After they left the church, Claude insisted on taking Jasmine out for dinner at the genteel City Hotel. They laughed and chatted over their meal of fricasseed chicken and stewed vegetables, discussing the curiosity of the nosy matriarchs at church.

"In their minds, I'm sure they all already have you married off to me," Claude commented with a bold grin, reaching across the starched white tablecloth to place his hand on Jasmine's. As she stared at him in mesmerized amazement, he winked at her devilishly and added, "Not a bad idea, I must say."

Jasmine lowered her eyes and Claude gently removed his hand, sensing that Jasmine was momentarily overwhelmed by his dauntless wooing. Yet moments later, when he teasingly asked her if she'd care for more sugar for her tea, she again found herself laughing and gaily conversing with him.

Jasmine felt at home with Claude. He was bold and forthright as he flirted with her, and she loved it!

During the next few days, Claude was at Jasmine's side almost constantly when she wasn't at the orphanage. In fact, Jasmine found herself begging Mother Martha for some extra time off, so she could spend more time with her handsome suitor before he returned to Louisiana.

Jasmine and Claude went shopping together, and attended a concert given by the City Band, as well as a local theater performance of Shakespeare's *Twelfth Night*. Claude brought Jasmine lovely gifts—English toffee and sprays of exquisite roses. Despite her protests, he even hired a craftsman to repair some leaks in the roof of her cottage. They spent long evenings together sipping tea on her gallery, while he told her all about his Louisiana plantation. Jasmine found herself falling deeply under his spell.

The afternoon before Claude had to leave, he asked her to go walking with him on the Old Spanish Parade Grounds, a popular spot out on the bluff. Arm in arm, they circled the large clearing, beneath the shelter of century-old oaks. Both were in a serious, reflective mood.

"Jasmine, you have made this visit to Natchez so special for me," Claude remarked, a catch in his voice.

"Yet you must leave tomorrow," she added, her tone hinting of her own despair.

He paused and turned to her, a dark, almost haunted light in his eyes. "There is something you must know about me."

"Yes?" They were standing beneath a huge, moss-hung tree, and Jasmine looked up at Claude with her heart in her eyes as the warm, fragrant breeze tugged at the back of her skirts.

He hesitated a long moment before he spoke. At last, in a pain-filled voice, he said, "I have loved only once, dear lady. My family came over to this country from France fourteen years past, bringing along my young fiancée. Gabrielle was but fifteen years old when we emigrated." Claude paused, then went on hoarsely, "Not three months after we settled in Louisiana, there was a scarlet fever epidemic. I lost my entire family, as well as my beloved Gabrielle."

"Oh, Claude!" Jasmine burst out, gripping his sleeve. "How terrible! I'm so sorry!"

He turned away from her, his shoulders trembling. "The guilt has haunted me ever since."

"Guilt?" Jasmine cried. "Why should you feel guilty? It wasn't your fault!"

He turned on her almost savagely. "Ah, but it was! You see, I was the one who insisted that Gabrielle come along with me to this country—even though she wanted us to remain in France. If she hadn't emigrated with me, she would be alive today!" Passionately, he continued, "I swore on her grave that I would consign myself to a life of bitter loneliness as my retribution for her death, hoping I might one day join my beloved in the heavens." He stepped closer, gripping Jasmine by the shoulders as he went on in a cracking voice, "That was fourteen years ago, and not once has my resolve wavered in the least—until I saw you last Friday."

Jasmine was overcome with joy. "Claude! Do you mean . . . ?"

His strong fingers dug into her shoulder blades, almost hurting her. "Yes, my dear. I want you as my wife. And I think even poor Gabrielle would agree that I have suffered long enough. End my torment—come back with me to Louisiana."

Fighting tears, Jasmine looked up at Claude in wonder, even as he claimed her lips with his own. His boldness set her heart to racing. His lips were hot on her tender, virgin mouth, while his tongue probed deeply, drinking of the sweet nectar within. Jasmine was so transported she clung to him. When Claude's lips moved to her tear-streaked cheek, she gasped for breath and found she was barely able to think. His arms were tight about her small waist. His hard form pressed crushingly against her softness, squeezing her breasts. "This is—rather sudden," she managed at last.

"It's not that sudden, my dear," he pointed out. "We've learned much about each other these past few days. Besides—when I saw you last week, I knew you were the one for me."

She stiffened, asking in a small voice, "Do I remind you of her?"

He drew back to smile at her, and brushed a tear from her rosy cheek. "No—never concern yourself with that! Gabrielle was small and dark. As for you—you are the love of my life I never dreamed I would be blessed with again."

"Oh, Claude!" Jasmine breathed, as the Frenchman's hot, sensual lips descended on hers once again.

After a long moment, they reluctantly parted. "Will you come with me?" Claude asked, his black eyes reflecting his fierce need. Watching her frown and bite her lip, he added, "Dearest, what is it?"

"Claude, I'm in mourning," she said helplessly.

"Darling, there are times when convention need not— should not—be honored. Mourning is a cruel custom indeed if it prevents two people from seeking their greatest happiness together."

"But—are you sure?" she asked in a voice stark with her tumultuous feelings.

"Are you?" he countered, a sudden, dark pain glazing his

eyes. Bitterly, he inquired, "Do you fear I'll bring ruin to you, too, my lovely, as I did to poor Gabrielle?"

"Oh, no!" Jasmine hastened to reassure him. "I'd never fear that. I simply must know that you won't regret—I mean that you are sure—"

"Quite sure," he said. With a tender smile, he added, "You must forgive my rushing things a bit, dear Jasmine. But there simply is no time. Soon, I must return to my duties—and I trust it will be with you at my side, as my bride."

Jasmine bit her lip, her insecurities still coming to mind. "I'm twenty-three years old," she told him in a small, trembling voice.

He grinned. "And I, beloved, am thirty-four. Do my advanced years cause you distress?"

At these tender words, Jasmine wept with joy, and Claude embraced her again.

Drawing her closer, he spoke huskily. "It honors me deeply that you have waited so long to bestow your most precious gift upon a man, and that I am to be that man."

"Oh, Claude. You are so dear."

"I am the one for you, Jasmine."

She hugged him tightly to her, feeling the loneliness flow out of her life, as if all the hurts inside her had miraculously been healed in this special moment. "Oh, yes, Claude! You are the one!"

## ★ Three ★

*Jasmine was caught up in a whirlwind.*

Claude postponed his return to Louisiana for three additional days, so that they could obtain a marriage license from the courthouse. The following morning, he escorted Jasmine to the orphanage to explain to the directress, Mother Martha, that Jasmine would soon be leaving with him for Louisiana as his bride. He asked the nun to keep the news of the imminent wedding secret for now, pointing out that, with Jasmine in mourning, an announcement might be ill-received by the Natchez community. Jasmine was not surprised by Claude's request. Earlier that morning, he had explined to her that he felt they should marry with all discretion. "Otherwise, every dowager in town will come calling on you, and you'll never get packed by Monday. We will, of course, publish an announcement in the local newspaper later on." Jasmine had felt touched that Claude had wished to spare her any possible annoyance by local gossips. And even the normally stern Mother Martha seemed to find the Frenchman's charm disarming. Despite the unpropitious timing of Jasmine's marriage to Claude, the nun wished the couple all success and happiness in their coming nuptials.

Before they left the orphanage, Jasmine took Claude aside in the downstairs hallway. "Claude, there is the matter of a child—" she began shyly.

"A child?" He quirked a dark eyebrow at her.

She blushed and explained awkwardly, "There is a young girl here at the orphanage—Maggie. We've grown quite close over the two years she has been here. I want to adopt her."

Claude frowned at this announcement, and something dark and unfathomable flickered in his obsidian eyes. For a distressing moment, Jasmine was reminded of her involuntary urge to shudder when she first viewed Claude's black eyes, and his brooding expression now hinted that he was displeased with her. Yet the distressing quality quickly faded, replaced by a mellow gleam. "A child," Claude repeated. "You are too kind."

"Don't you like children?" Jasmine asked.

"Of course I like children, but perhaps I prefer to father our own."

Jasmine felt all color drain from her face. "Oh—I hadn't thought—"

Quickly, Claude stepped forward and took her hand,

amending tenderly, "Of course, we'll adopt the child, and love her as one of our own. Forgive the selfishness of my remark just now. It's simply that I desire to have you all to myself for a time. Would it be too self-centered of me to ask you to wait a few months?"

"Oh, no, Claude!" Jasmine cried, embracing him warmly. Shyly, she added, "But when . . . ?"

"We shall return to Natchez before Christmas to fetch the child home with us," he promised magnanimously.

"Oh, yes, at Christmas! That will be wonderful! May I tell Maggie, Claude?"

"By all means. At once."

After they left the orphanage, Claude and Jasmine went by St. Mary's Cathedral to ask the priest, Father Grignon, to marry them on Monday. The portly, middle-aged man raised an eyebrow when he learned that Jasmine planned to marry Claude so soon after her father's death. But when Claude politely explained his circumstances, Father Grignon agreed to perform the service.

As Claude and Jasmine left the church, he explained to her that, after they were wed, they would take the riverboat *Mississippi Belle* to his plantation home in Louisiana. Jasmine was in heaven, dreamily envisioning the prosperous estate Claude had already described to her.

Before returning to Jasmine's cottage, the couple made a stop at a clothier's shop downtown. "Indulge me," Claude pleaded as they stood glancing through the window at racks of ready-made garments. "I wish you to wear white for me."

Jasmine blushed. "But, Claude, I am in mourning." With tears in her eyes, she went on, "You must think me terrible, to marry you at such a time, with no dowry, no family to provide for our nuptials—"

"Jasmine, I am your family now, and do not forget it," he said firmly. "We have no need of such conventions between us. No mourning, no dowries, my sweet. We have each other, and that is as it should be."

"Claude, you are too good for me."

In the clothier's shop, Jasmine selected a simple white

eyelet frock with an underdress of finest white batiste. Claude wanted Jasmine to wear a showier garment, but when she reminded him of the simplicity and secrecy of their planned nuptials, he relented, adding, "On our first anniversary in Louisiana, we shall reaffirm our vows in the presence of all our friends, and you shall be dressed as my queen."

Jasmine felt she was floating on a cloud when she and Claude drove home to her cottage. Then she frowned, spotting her lawyer's buggy parked in front of her house. "That carriage belongs to our family attorney," she explained to Claude nervously. "Mr. Gates must have come to discuss my father's estate."

Though Jasmine managed to smile bravely at her fiancé as she spoke the words, she felt far from serene, since she had not told Claude of her father's betrayal. She prayed Mr. Gates would not reveal Pierre Dubroc's perfidy now. Nothing would shame her more.

Claude was quiet, his expression strangely unreadable as he approached the house with Jasmine. The moment they stepped inside the door of the cottage, Ephraim sprang up from a nearby wooden bench. "Miz Jasmine, yo' gots gentl'-man comp'ny," the old servant announced fretfully.

"Thanks, Ephraim."

Nodding to his mistress, the slave left the room. Jasmine turned toward the parlor, even as Richard Gates stood to acknowledge her presence. "Miss Dubroc, there has been a change I must inform you of." Then Gates's gaze shifted quizzically to Claude.

Jasmine stepped forward, with Claude following close behind her. "Mr. Gates, this is my fiancé, Claude Boudreau," Jasmine announced.

A shocked expression flitted across the lawyer's dark, intelligent eyes. Then he quickly recovered, clearing his throat and stepping forward to extend his hand to Claude. "Pleased to meet you, sir. It seems congratulations are in order here."

"Indeed," Claude remarked with a benign smile, appraising the other man intently.

"Won't you take your seat, sir?" Jasmine inquired of Gates, walking over to settle herself on the horsehair settee.

As the two men sat, Jasmine asked Gates, "What is this business you speak of, sir?"

Gates glanced from Jasmine to Boudreau. "I had thought to speak with you privately, Miss Dubroc, but since this man is your affianced . . ."

His voice trailed off, leaving no doubt as to his curiosity about Jasmine's sudden, astonishing engagement. She chose to ignore the lawyer's veiled query, saying to him instead, "I want Mr. Boudreau to hear whatever you have to say, Mr. Gates." The words came out smoothly, despite Jasmine's misgivings about what Gates might reveal.

"Very well, it shall be as you wish," Gates replied. Clearing his throat, he went on awkwardly, "It always pains me to try to explain to someone how another's misfortune has become his gain. Miss Dubroc, as I told you during the reading of the will, your father left most of his estate to a— er—Miss Flossie La Fleume."

"Yes, I'm aware of that," Jasmine murmured, her eyes downcast. She felt miserable as she absorbed Claude's dark, confused gaze through the corner of her eye.

"After meeting you," Gates continued, "I think Miss La Fleume had some misgivings about accepting her inheritance."

Jasmine's head shot up, and for a moment she forgot Claude's presence. "She did?" she asked guiltily.

"Yes, indeed," Gates said. "After you left my office so abruptly, she expressed those misgivings to me. But, ultimately, we decided that Pierre's wishes must be honored. I requested that Miss La Fleume return in a few days' time to sign the final papers, but she never did. This morning, I went down to Silver Street to make some discreet inquiries, and I've received some rather distressing news."

"Yes?" Jasmine inquired tensely.

"It seems that last Friday evening, there was a brawl at the—er—Scarlet Slipper, were Miss La Fleume was employed. She was hit in the head by a stray bullet."

"She's—dead? How awful," Jasmine gasped.

"At any rate, Miss Dubroc," Gates continued, "since Miss La Fleume passed on before claiming her inheritance, the money is yours now. It is merely a matter of your coming to my office and signing some papers. Perhaps this afternoon, if you are free . . . ?''

Jasmine was so stunned, she could barely reply. At last she managed to ask plaintively, "Could we make it on Monday, Mr. Gates?'' Jasmine dared to glance at Claude, inwardly wincing as she spotted the dark anger in her fiancé's eyes. He had evidently guessed a lot. She turned back to Gates. "This has been—so sudden, such a shock,'' she explained, getting to her feet.

Both men also stood. "Of course, Miss Dubroc,'' Gates said. "I shall see you on Monday, then.''

Feeling numb, Jasmine saw the lawyer to the door, then returned. Claude was scowling at her, his brow furrowed.

He strode over to her and demanded furiously, "Why didn't you tell me what your father did to you?''

"It—was my great shame,'' she stammered helplessly.

"*Your* shame?'' he repeated, his fingers digging into her flesh. For a horrible instant, Jasmine feared he would strike her. Instead, he shook her soundly, and her head snapped up as he said fiercely, "It is your father's shame. Now, tell me everything that scoundrel did to you.''

"Oh, Claude!''

Jasmine was so relieved, she burst into tears. When she finished the account of her father's betrayal, Claude released her and began to pace, his fists clenched at his sides. "That bastard! Were he not dead, I would call him out!'' Jasmine was shocked at the venom in Claude's tone as he continued, with an angry gesture, "We'll take his ill-begotten inheritance and fling it to the depths of the Mississippi.''

"Oh, no!'' Jasmine cried. "Claude, please, it's quite a sizable amount. I want us to have it.'' Suddenly, she smiled. "It can be my dowry!''

He shook his head adamantly, and folded his arms across his chest. "I want no dowry from that reprobate. Anyway, your gift of self outshines the most priceless jewels.''

Jasmine was quite touched by his words, but she was determined to be practical. "Let's keep it for Maggie, then,'' she suggested. "You were so kind as to agree to adopt her. It can be her dowry when she comes of age."

The Frenchman paused, gazing at Jasmine. Then a thoughtful smile pulled at his mouth and he shrugged. "Why not? You do have a point there, my love. We'll keep the inheritance for Maggie, then." He reached out and pulled Jasmine into his strong embrace. "And now, go put on something pretty for me."

"B-but, I can't," Jasmine stammered. "I'm in mourning. It simply isn't done."

"Do it," he growled, "or I shall be compelled to attend to the matter myself. And I promise you, if you so force my hand, I may well consummate our wedded bliss before the fact." As she gasped and blushed to the roots of her hair, he added, with a disturbing streak of violence in his eyes, "I'll not allow you to mourn that bastard—or his whore."

He brought his mouth down fiercely on hers, and when she left the room to change, her lips were bruised and throbbing.

# ★ Four ★

*The moon was full . . .*

Jasmine and Claude stood near the rail on the boiler deck of the stately steamboat *Mississippi Belle*, sipping champagne as they studied the dark mirror of the river below them, the enchanting trees, hung with silvery moss, on the shoreline beyond. In the dark forest, owls hooted. The night was warm and balmy, thick with the sounds of steam escaping the riverboat's boiler, and the lapping of the paddle wheel as it plowed the mighty river.

Downstairs, most of the other passengers were finishing dinner in the main cabin or visiting in the aftercabin, but Jasmine and Claude had wanted to be alone on their wedding night.

"To, us," he now said to Jasmine, raising his glass to his bride. The crystal clinked in the night, and in silence the two drank to each other. Tears of happiness welled in Jasmine's eyes as moonlight glinted off the wide gold band now on her left hand. She was Mrs. Claude Boudreau! For the rest of her life, she would hold her head up high! It was so wonderful, it could hardly be believed! It was paradise!

"The river is so wide—so lovely," Jasmine murmured.

"The perfect setting for our honeymoon," Claude responded with an endearing grin. He glanced up at the wide sky above them and added quietly, "The moon is full tonight. Have you heard, Jasmine, that the full moon can bring on madness?"

Jasmine's heart skipped a beat, and, for the first time since she had married Claude earlier that day, she felt a twinge of unease. She realized that there was still much she didn't know about this man she had wed—that, in some ways, she had entrusted her life to a stranger. "I don't know what you mean," she stammered at last.

Claude laughed, and Jasmine smiled her relief, realizing that he had only been teasing her. He took the empty glass from her hand and tossed it, with his, over the side. "I know the full moon brings on madness," he whispered in a voice almost frightening in its intensity. "I am utterly mad for you tonight."

Claude kissed her and Jasmine eagerly melted against his hard warmth. "Darling, I grow hungry for you," he said huskily. He nodded at the door to their cabin just beyond them. "I will allow you a suitable time to prepare yourself for me."

"Yes, Claude," Jasmine whispered obediently, her lips trembling beneath Claude's possessive parting kiss.

Claude turned to stroll down the deck toward the stern of the boat, and Jasmine retreated to their stateroom to dress for bed. Inside the cabin, by the light of a lantern, she undid the buttons on her traveling frock, her fingers trembling badly. She was rather apprehensive about the night to come.

Jasmine's only knowledge of the marriage act had come from one of the crusty dowagers at St. Mary's Church. When Jasmine was sixteen, old Mrs. Peabody had taken her aside and described the vulgar ritual men demanded of their wives. The dowager had also made clear to the girl that it was a wife's duty to submit to her husband's lusts. To Jasmine, it had sounded unpleasant, and most assuredly hurtful. She knew that, by all rights, she should be terrified of what would come to pass between her and Claude later tonight.

Jasmine did feel a bit disquieted, recalling how on Friday, when Claude had found out about her father's betrayal, he had kissed her so hard he had bruised her mouth. Afterward, her breasts had also throbbed from his crushing embrace. Yet surely, she had rationalized at the time, that was simply the nature of a man's passion. Claude had been angry—and justly so!

Thus, tonight, Jasmine vowed that she would trust her new husband. After all, Claude had been good to her in so many ways; he had brought her a joy she'd never known before.

As she undressed, she relived her exciting day with Claude. That morning, they had taken care of her business in town, both with the lawyer and at the bank. Claude had told Jasmine that, since she would not again live in Natchez, her inheritance funds would have to be transferred to his bank in Louisiana. Jasmine had paid little heed to the details Claude discussed with the banker, Mr. Elroy, and had later cheerfully signed the papers he had proffered.

Claude had then taken Jasmine back to her cottage so she could dress for their wedding ceremony. While he waited for her on the front gallery, she had taken Ephraim aside, to tell him that she and Claude had decided he should stay on in Natchez and care for the cottage until they returned at Christmas. Even as Ephraim protested this news, saying he wanted to come with Jasmine to Louisiana then and there, she had given him all the cash she had on hand and had told him of a separate decision she had made in his behalf.

"Ephraim, I want you to know that I spoke with Mr. Gates today about drawing up a manumission paper to give you your freedom. By all rights, my father should have freed you in his will, but he neglected to do so. This will be my gift to you for so many years of loyal service to our family. Please consider the money I've just given you your wages to care for my cottage until Claude and I return. I want you to wait until then to decide whether or not you want to come live with us in Louisiana. Of course, I'd love for you to come, but this should be your decision. After all, you're a free man now."

Jasmine smiled as she recalled the tears of joy in the old man's eyes as he accepted both of her gifts. Freeing Ephraim had also been Jasmine's way of telling him she bore him no hard feelings for not telling her about Flossie La Fleume.

After she had bid Ephraim farewell, Jasmine left with Claude for St. Mary's Cathedral. They were married in a quiet service at two o'clock. Sisters Philomena and Scholastica had come from the orphanage to serve as witnesses. The two nuns had dabbed at tears at the end of the service, when Claude tenderly kissed his new bride. Afterward, Claude had left Jasmine at her cottage to finish packing, while he went back to town to conclude his business. Then he'd fetched her and they'd boarded the *Belle*.

Jasmine smiled at her happy memories. She had stripped naked now, and shivered briefly before hastily pulling on a thin, handkerchief-linen nightgown. She wished she had something more elegant to wear for Claude on their wedding night. Yet she knew Claude wanted *her*; the trappings mattered not to her new husband.

Jasmine stared at herself briefly in the looking glass on the cabin wall, noting the bright flush of anticipation on her cheeks, the glow in her eyes.

Then the cabin door opened and Claude appeared in the archway, outlined by the moonlight behind him. Jasmine's heart increased its wild tempo as she surveyed her husband. Claude looked so dashing in his white suit, with the lamplight gleaming in his thick ebony hair and glinting off his deep-set black eyes. Jasmine trembled as those dark orbs swept over her with a startling animal hunger. Yet another emotion lurked there—something quite odd. Was it puzzlement, perhaps?

"You're lovely," Claude said at last, in a voice hoarse and strangely full of surprise.

He drew a step closer, and she blushed and said, "Claude, please, the door! Someone will see us!"

He chuckled then, and the familiar sparkle returned to his eyes. "I shall see to it shortly. But first, a more immediate concern draws me."

Claude blew out the lamp and came to Jasmine's side in the darkness. She gasped with pleasure as he leaned over and swept her up into his strong arms.

For a long moment he just stood there, holding her against his chest in the darkness. She was sure he must be able to hear her ragged breathing, the fierce pounding of her heart. "Claude, please, the door," she again begged, nodding toward the open portal, where the moonlight spilled in.

"Jasmine . . ." he whispered, his voice curiously thick.

"Yes, Claude?"

"Perhaps . . ."

All at once, Claude's entire body stiffened. He planted a chaste, almost brotherly kiss on Jasmine's forehead. Then, in a hollow tone, he whispered, "Close your eyes, my darling, and I'll carry you to paradise."

Jasmine was still concerned about the door, but she closed her eyes as her new husband had bidden. Claude strode across the room with her tightly in his arms. Suddenly, she felt the night air whipping about her thin gown.

Jasmine gasped with surprise and opened her eyes. They again stood alone on the open deck, near the railing. Stunned and confused, she glanced up at Claude. For a blinding moment, she stared into his eyes and saw only unfeeling blackness there. Then she went hurtling through space, screaming, and landed with a crash in the hopelessly wide river below.

She bobbed to the surface, her lungs bursting, her mouth full of brackish-tasting slime as she frantically struggled to tread water. "Claude!" she screamed out hysterically, spitting out the dirty water. "Claude!"

Her first thought was that there must be some terrible mistake—that this must have been an awful, bizarre accident. Any second now, Claude would dive in to rescue her! But then Jasmine spotted him on the boiler deck of the riverboat, his white-clad back turned to her as he quickly strode away. The riverboat chugged off downstream, billowing white smoke into the dark heavens.

Sweet Jesus, this was no accident! Claude Boudreau had *meant* to throw her in the river! But why?

It became difficult for Jasmine even to think as the wake of the steamer swirled around her, threatening to tow her under again. The wave swept her toward the eastern bank, and she screamed as she was suddenly stabbed in the side by something with jagged tentacles. Terrified, she thrashed at the attacking apparition, and it took several frightening moments for her to realize that it was only a dead tree she had gotten herself tangled up in. She quit fighting the lifeless skeleton and instead simply clung to a slippery branch for support, gasping for breath as the tepid water stung her scratched and battered body.

*Why had Claude Boudreau done this to her?* Oh, God! Had she been betrayed again?

Moments later, Jasmine spotted the running lights of a river packet, which was rounding the bend upstream from her. Her first thought as she spotted this new, unexpected vessel was that she would be saved. Then she noted that the packet was navigating close to the western bank of the river, doubtless to avoid the dead trees just beyond center, where Jasmine was marooned. She realized grimly that if she stayed where she was, she might never be spotted.

Perhaps that would be a blessing.

*Oh, God, what am I to do?* she asked herself frantically.

Jasmine tried to weigh her options as she twisted about to eye the shoreline nearest to her. The eastern bank was definitely closer, but it had to be at least a thousand feet away. She didn't swim well enough to make it that far.

Yet she knew she must make a move if she were to survive. Otherwise, the packet would soon pass her by, and God only knew when another boat might come. She could be stuck on this tree until she died from exposure—and Claude would escape. If only she could move just a little farther out into the water, perhaps her cries might be heard by someone on the riverboat as it passed—that is, if the boat or the current didn't tow her under in the process!

Hell. Perhaps she should just stay here and quietly accept her fate.

*No! No!* an inner voice suddenly screamed. If she died, then Claude would never pay for the wrong he'd done her.

Jasmine decided she would climb the tree, then fling herself out toward midriver and take her chances on being rescued by someone on the packet. As she prepared to climb higher onto the tree, she discovered that her nightgown was snared in the tree's sharp lower branches. Disgustedly, she yanked herself free, and heard the fabric on the side of her gown tear. Claude Boudreau would die a slow, agonizing death for subjecting her to this trial, she vowed fiercely.

Jasmine eased her half-clothed form higher on the slippery tree trunk, until she was mostly out of the water. She took a painfully deep breath, then hurled herself into the river. She treaded water as best she could and fought the current, her nightgown tangling about her legs as she waited for the steamboat, which was now rapidly bearing down in her direction.

As the river packet drew closer, Jasmine spotted a tall man on deck, his imposing body outlined by the light from the salon behind him. Even from this distance, Jasmine could hear the bawdy cacophony—raucous laughter, a clinking piano—spewing forth from the riverboat's interior. *A gambling boat*, she thought with disgust.

"Help me!" she called out to the man. "For God's sake, help me!"

That's when the man on deck spotted Jasmine. He stared down at her in amazement as he removed his white hat. And in that frozen moment, when the stranger stared down at

Jasmine, and she back up at him, she knew she would be saved.

## ★ Five ★

With a splash, Jared Hampton landed in the water not far from Jasmine. He bobbed to the surface and, despite his heavy, waterlogged clothing, swam to her side with quick, strong strokes, reaching for her in the darkness. "I've got you, love!" he called out.

Jared hooked an arm around her waist and pulled her toward him. Suddenly, she stiffened and struggled out of his grasp.

Jasmine was suddenly consumed by panic, as she realized that a total stranger had just tried to pull her almost nude body into his intimate embrace! When she'd called out for help seconds earlier, she hadn't really thought things through enough to realize that being rescued would mean . . . this! Suddenly, she almost preferred the idea of drowning.

As Jasmine flailed about to impede her rescuer, Jared caught a glimpse of dark, fear-stricken eyes, of a bare neck, and shoulders encased in a near-transparent nightgown. He knew now that this woman was, indeed, practically naked. No wonder she was so terrified, so reluctant to have a man touch her! Despite her startling state, her reactions were those of a guileless maiden.

For a moment they merely stared at each other as they paddled against the current. Fully cognizant of the treachery of the river, Jared struggled for something to say to reassure the frightened beauty. But before he could completely gather his thoughts, a wicked-sounding hoot drew his attention back to the deck of the *River Witch*. He cursed under his breath, watching half a dozen drunken gamblers spill out onto the deck, their staggering forms outlined by the light from the salon.

"Hey, Hampton, what ya got on your hook down there?" one of the cardsharps called out, while another sneered, "Hey, man, pull 'er in and let's throw *her* down on the table!"

Jasmine gasped, even as Jared mercifully caught sight of his friend, Cactus Jack Malone, sauntering out the open salon doors. "Jack, throw us a line!" Jared barked.

Jack hurried off to grab a rope. Jared again reached for the woman, yet once more she fought his touch.

"No!" she cried, an edge of hysteria in her voice. "You're not taking me up there with those men!"

Again muttering curses, Jared paddled away from the girl to grab the line Jack was tossing out to him. Once he had the rope securely in hand, he swam back toward her.

"Come here!" he commanded, and when she fiercely shook her head, even as the current tugged her farther downstream, he added, "Don't be a fool! You'll drown!"

Still, she resisted his command, and he pursued her with powerful strokes, at last grabbing her about the midsection with his free arm. She struggled against him, until he uttered hoarsely, "Stop it! Please, miss—we could both drown!"

At last the girl quit fighting, and Jared tried not to think of the lush, near-naked woman he now held in his arms— the rounded breasts and smooth belly pressed against him, the long legs paddling next to his.

"Quick, take hold of this rope and don't let go," he directed hoarsely. "I must get out of my coat and get it around you before Jack pulls us out."

"There," he muttered finally. Jasmine felt a waterlogged coat slip onto her shoulders.

With the man's help, Jasmine managed to slide her arms into the wet, heavy coat. He wrapped the jacket securely about her waist, belted the rope about her middle, and tied it. "I'm going to have Jack pull you out. Ready?"

Jasmine glanced wildly at the river packet, where the drunken gamblers still stood ogling her, weaving and snickering to one another. "No—you must come, too!"

He shook his head firmly. "The two of us would be too heavy. We might break the rope, and then where would you be? Don't worry—I'll come along right after you. Set to go, now?"

In the darkness, Jasmine nodded, her lower lip trembling. Her rescuer called out, "Jack, pull her in!"

Jasmine felt herself being tugged through the strong currents toward the riverboat. She spit out water, her heart pounding frantically as she watched two of the gamblers stagger forward to help Jack pull her out. Then, three sets of hands grabbed her and hauled her over the railing, onto the deck. The man named Jack touched her with respect, clutching her hands in his to steady her when she landed on her feet, then carefully untying the rope at her waist. But the gamblers handled her brazenly. Even when she was standing safely on deck, they continued to fondle her, their insolent fingers probing the flesh of her waist and thighs through the wet jacket.

"Let her go," Jack now ordered the other two, in a voice holding such deadly calm it even made Jasmine shiver. They grumbled obscenities, but retreated at once.

The night breeze swirled about her, and Jasmine again shuddered, sweeping hair from her eyes as she watched the cardsharps stagger off. Although the night was warm, she found it was much cooler here on deck than it had been in the water. She turned to face the man named Jack. He was tall and lanky, and his coal-black hair and dark eyes reminded her strongly of Claude Boudreau. She fought down a rising hysteria, mentally reminding herself that this man *wasn't* Boudreau. In fact, the man's high cheekbones and hooked nose suggested he might be part Indian. Now, he told her in a hoarse yet gentle tone, "Get behind me, lady, while I pull Hampton out."

Jasmine retreated behind the tall stranger as he threw out the line to pull in her rescuer. Meanwhile, the gamblers on deck had ceased their caterwauling, but were still gaping at Jasmine crudely, their jaundiced, roving eyes making her miserable consciously of the fact that her rescuer's coat covered her body only to mid-thigh. Below the coat, her thin, wet nightgown clung transparently to her legs and hid little from the men's voracious eyes. She stiffened her spine and held the dripping coat tightly about her, determined not to betray her fear.

Jasmine was torn from her harried thoughts as Jack pulled her rescuer onto the deck. The man landed on his feet, coughing and sputtering as he shook water from his clothing. Jasmine studied him in the scant light. He was tall and well-proportioned. His white shirt and dark trousers were dripping copiously onto the wooden planks. He quickly approached her side. "Are you all right?"

"Yes," she replied breathlessly. "Thank you, sir. You—you saved my life."

"My pleasure," came his gallant reply.

Jasmine nodded to the man, wishing she could better make out his features in the sallow light spilling out from the salon. Then she was again distracted as the six gamblers began moving in closer. Jasmine clutched the coat tighter to her shivering body and glanced about furtively, even as one of the motley crew addressed the man who now stood protectively by her side.

"Hey, Hampton, you gonna share this little fishie you just pulled in?"

Fear jabbed Jasmine in the stomach like a sharp knife. Yet her rescuer calmly placed an arm about her shoulders and told the man who had spoken, "Back off, Cravens. Can't you see that this lady has suffered an unfortunate accident?"

"All I kin see, Hampton," scoffed another, "is what yer holdin' right there ain't no lady. That little piece fell offen' one of them floating brothels, ain't no doubt!"

The gamblers howled uproariously and moved closer, leering at Jasmine and undressing her with glittering dark eyes. Jasmine's heart hammered with fear. She felt the arm about her shoulders stiffen, and the man named Hampton told the group tensely, "If you gentlemen have a chivalrous drop of blood in your bodies, you'll dispense immediately back to the salon."

"But, Hampton, we ain't no gentlemen!" one crusty character jeered.

"Then, do it because I'll call out the first man here who dares touch her!" Hampton roared back.

Hampton's words slowed their advance.

"You heard what the boss said," Cactus Jack informed the throng coolly, aiming a deadly looking revolver in their direction. "Get back to your game, boys."

The disgruntled looking crew began to retreat, grumbling. The man at Jasmine's side breathed a heavy sigh, released her, and turned to face Jack. "Thanks for backing me up, friend," he said.

"No problem, boss."

Hampton nodded toward the salon. "You'd best go back in there and give the boys free drinks. Tell Grady to keep that piano thumping, too. I'll take care of the lady here."

"Sure, boss."

Jack sauntered off, and Jasmine found herself alone with the man named Hampton. He turned to her and she reflexively backed off a step. "Look, it's all right, miss. You're safe now."

Jasmine swallowed convulsively, but didn't comment.

"You'd best come with me," he added.

She backed away another step. "Where are you taking me?"

"To my stateroom."

Jasmine was horrified. "Oh, no—I couldn't!"

Hampton drew closer and firmly took Jasmine by the shoulders. "Look," he told her patiently, "I don't know how you landed in your—er—predicament tonight, but please bear in mind that the danger is far from over." He nodded toward the salon. "I don't trust those men. What they saw of you tonight was enough to incite a riot in far more noble types. I'm taking you to my stateroom to find you some decent, dry clothing, and because it's the only place on this packet where I'm sure you'll be safe. So, what's it going to be? Do you want to take your chances with the scum, or come with me to the upper deck?"

Jasmine shivered. All at once, what she wanted to do was to break down and sob. Tonight had been a nightmare from which there seemed to be no awakening.

"Well?"

Jasmine gathered her fortitude and said, "I'll come with you."

Hampton retrieved his hat and boots from the deck, then led Jasmine toward some stairs to the left of the salon doors. Glancing inside as they passed the open portal, Jasmine spotted the six gamblers gathered at a round table cluttered with whiskey bottles and glasses. The men were smoking cheroots and playing cards. Off to the left, a grinning black man sat at the piano, playing a bawdy-sounding tune. In the far corner of the room Jack stood, coolly overseeing the activities.

Hampton took Jasmine's arm and escorted her up the stairs. Halfway up, they met a portly, white-haired man in black suit and matching cap.

"Is everything all right, Mr. Hampton?" the man asked, glancing from Hampton to Jasmine. Even in the darkness, Jasmine could see the shock and embarrassment registering in the older man's eyes as he viewed her.

"Yes, everything's fine, Captain Ward," Hampton replied. Nodding toward Jasmine, he added, "We had to stop to rescue this lady, who fell off another vessel tonight. You may now proceed ahead full."

"Aye, sir," the captain replied. Tipping his cap toward Jasmine, he added awkwardly, "Evenin', ma'am," and hurried back up the stairs toward the wheelhouse.

Hampton led Jasmine up to the boiler deck, and down an open, railed corridor past a line of doors. He stopped by the last door, opened it, and gestured for her to enter before him. As the boat's whistle blew, Jasmine stepped forward and entered the stateroom.

It was plain and small, but neat and pleasant. A narrow bunk occupied one wall, while an armoire and desk flanked it. A lit oil lamp atop the desk cast a homey glow about the setting. The far corner of the room was occupied by a surprisingly elegant dressing screen, its silk cover decorated with brilliant peacocks, vivid flowers, and elegant bamboo.

As the steamboat lurched forward, Jasmine braced a hand against the wall and pivoted to watch her rescuer enter the room. He tossed his hat on the desk, set down his boots, then straightened. She struggled not to gasp, for the man named Hampton was a glorious vision! Damp, tawny-brown curls framed his beautifully shaped head, and she found herself boldly studying deep-set blue eyes. Their diamondlike clarity seemed to shine through to his very soul. His eyes were fringed by long brown lashes and topped by handsomely curved brows. His nose was classic and straight, the line of his jaw firm and strong; his wide, sensuous mouth held a slight quirk of humor.

Her rescuer's body was equally magnificent, she noted, especially with the wet shirt clinging to his broad, muscled chest, the dark trousers delineating his slim hips and long legs. Spotting his bare feet and the puddle of water surrounding them, Jasmine tore her gaze away, feeling embarrassed to be staring so boldly at a part of a man's anatomy—especially a naked part! She dared to glance up at him and found him smiling back at her, his expression quizzical. "You're all wet," she said at last.

He laughed, a deep, hearty sound that somehow helped ease the awkwardness. "So are you."

As Jared Hampton returned Jasmine's perusal, he mused to himself that she was even more beautiful than he had first thought, with her tall, lushly proportioned body, her perfect oval face, and large green eyes that were warm and compelling enough to melt snow.

When she automatically backed away at his stare, he held up a hand and coaxed, "There, don't go shy on me. I mean you no harm." He moved a step closer and bowed briefly from the waist—a gesture that came across as rather inane under the circumstances. "Jared Hampton at your service, ma'am. And you're . . ."

"Jasmine!" she blurted, still not quite sure what to think of this stranger. As he stood politely waiting for her to finish, she decided she never again wanted to hear Claude Boudreau's name. At last she said, "I'm Jasmine Dubroc."

Hampton grinned. "Well then, Miss Dubroc, don't you think it's about time for us to get you out of that coat?"

Jasmine smothered a gasp, her eyes widening as she clutched the coat more tightly about her. But her host seemed oblivious as he turned to the bunk and picked up a man's black-velvet dressing gown. "Here, put this on," he directed with a kindly smile, extending the garment toward her. "That is, unless you'd prefer to spend the rest of the evening dripping on my stateroom floor."

"Oh," Jasmine said, staring at the puddle surrounding her own feet. "Oh, of course not." She grabbed the gown, then glanced about the room. "But, where—"

"Behind the screen."

Jasmine dashed behind the screen and quickly removed the waterlogged coat and her torn gown. She spotted a stack of clean towels on a small stool in the corner and grabbed one, wincing as she rubbed down her scraped and bruised body. She gritted her teeth and fought tears as she studied the angry welts and bright scratches crisscrossing her pearly flesh. Damn Claude Boudreau for doing this to her! She could so easily have died!

But she knew she couldn't think of that now or she'd fall apart. Resolutely, she towel-dried her hair and donned the velvet dressing gown, securing it with the belt and smiling ruefully as she noted that the folds of velvet were dragging the floor. Seconds later, she self-consciously emerged from behind the screen. Although she was covered from neck to foot, she couldn't be more conscious of the fact that she wore absolutely nothing beneath the velvet robe, and that she was alone with a man she knew nothing about.

"Feeling better?" her host inquired. He surveyed her with approval as he handed her a man's hairbrush.

"Yes, thank you," she replied stiffly.

"If you'll excuse me, then . . . ?"

Grabbing a stack of clothing he'd laid out on the bunk, Jared now disappeared behind the screen. Gratefully, Jasmine sat down on the bed and brushed her hair. It had been good of Jared Hampton to risk his life to rescue her tonight, she reflected. He'd definitely kept a cool head when she'd panicked!

"Ah, it feels good to be dry." Jared now emerged from behind the screen, wearing fresh clothing—a white shirt, buff-colored trousers, and brown boots. Combing a hand through his thick, damp hair, he moved to Jasmine's side and casually sat down next to her on the bunk. Alarmed, she started to bolt away, but he touched her arm gently and said, "Please, don't get up. Don't you trust me?"

Slowly, she shook her head.

"Well, at least that's honest." He grinned, releasing her arm. "Please believe me, miss, I've no reason to harm you. I'm the one who pulled you out of the river tonight. Remember?"

She nodded solemnly.

"I'd just like for us to talk for a moment. Why don't you go on brushing your hair?"

Cautiously, she complied.

For a moment, he watched her draw the brush through her golden strands. "Good," he said, in a tone he might use with a high-strung child. "Now—could you kindly tell me how you ended up in the river tonight? Did you fall off another packet—or what?"

Jasmine stopped brushing her hair in midstroke and stared at her host. Hampton looked very appealing with his ruffled hair and the line of golden stubble she now noted along his manly, square jaw. The concerned expression in his blue eyes touched her deeply, and suddenly, tears stung. How could she tell this man of the utter shame and degradation she had suffered tonight?

As Jasmine floundered for words, Jared studied her carefully, his gaze growing dark as it swept her neck. He reached out for her and she drew back. "Please, don't flinch," he said. As she obeyed him, watching him warily, he touched a thin red line along the lovely curve of her throat. She shuddered as he said with a scowl, "There's a nasty scratch all the way down your neck. I must put salve on it."

The man's kindness was rapidly becoming Jasmine's undoing. "I—I ran into a tree in the water," she admitted in a hoarse tone.

"Jesus," he uttered under his breath, shaking his head. "How you managed to survive . . ." He stared at her with a mixture of concern and determination glittering in his eyes. "Now tell me—how did you end up in the river?"

Jasmine tried to speak, fighting the welling hurt and rage inside her. "I . . . I . . ." Then, to her horror, she burst into tears.

## ★ Six ★

"Oh, God!" Jasmine sobbed. "He—he threw me in the river and I—thought I was dead—d-drowned—and he—he just walked away and all I saw was his back! Just his damned back and the riverboat moving away . . ."

Jared Hampton stared flabbergasted at Jasmine as she sobbed and spoke disjointedly of her experience earlier that night. She was crying as if someone had ripped the very heart out of her. No wonder she was so devastated, he thought, for it was now obvious that what had happened to her tonight was no accident. Fury welled in him.

"There, there," he said, his mouth set in a grim line as he patted her hand and let her hysterics run their course.

When she quieted a bit, he went to his desk, picked up a crystal decanter, and poured her a generous snifter of brandy. He returned to her side and sat down, his jaw tight, betraying the anger and turmoil within. Yet his voice was gentle as he placed the glass in her hand and said, "Here, Miss Dubroc. Please drink this."

Even though Jasmine was unaccustomed to sipping spirits, she dutifully took the snifter from Hampton and downed a gulp. She fought not to choke—the brandy burned going down, yet she welcomed its invasive warmth, hoping the liquor would help soothe her overtaxed nerves.

Jared solemnly watched Jasmine take several more sips. Then, as she wiped a tear with the sleeve of his dressing gown, he reached into his trousers pocket, extracted a clean handkerchief, and handed it to her. "Please, dry your eyes, Miss Dubroc."

Jasmine turned to stare at the stranger sitting next to her. Jared Hampton looked genuinely concerned—protective, even—with his rigidly set jaw and the fierce light gleaming in his blue eyes. Yet there was also a deep, almost haunting tenderness in the bright gaze that rested on her face. "You know, I must thank you again for pulling me out of the river tonight," she murmured, taking another sip of the brandy. "Had you not come along . . ."

"Don't even think of that," he advised. "What I want to know now is how you ended up in the river in the first place. You must admit that you have a way of piquing a man's curiosity," he finished with a kindly smile.

Jasmine nodded and took another sip. "I suppose I would have to go back to the beginning . . ."

"Please do."

"But, it's so humiliating!" she burst out.

Jared placed his strong, steady hand over Jasmine's trembling fingers. "Miss Dubroc, you must know that all the shame of tonight's incident belongs squarely on the head of the craven who threw you in the water."

Jasmine wiped her tears, then took another sip of brandy. She was feeling a bit light-headed now, but she welcomed the giddiness. "I met him only a week past," she finally began.

"The man who threw you in the river?"

She nodded, taking another sip. "His name is Claude Boudreau—anyway, that's what he said it was."

Jared was frowning fiercely. "You're sure the name was Boudreau?"

She was instantly alert. "Yes. Why? Do you know him?"

He shrugged, almost too casually. "Boudreau's a common enough name, I suppose. Tell me, where did you meet this blackguard?"

"In Natchez—that's where I live."

"You don't say?" he put in, smiling. "I'm from Natchez, too."

"Yes, I rather figured you were. I've heard of your family."

His grin broadened. "Strange that we've not met before."

Jasmine did not find it strange at all, since she and this man obviously ran in different social circles. Yet that was not really a subject she cared to pursue at present. She sighed, swirling the remaining brandy in her snifter as she went on. "Anyway, I met Mr. Boudreau quite recently, shortly after my father passed away."

Jared gazed at her compassionately. "My sincere condolences."

"Thank you. He had a bad heart." Jasmine paused, feeling extremely foolish. "Look, I'm sure you don't want to hear all of this—"

"Oh, but I do. Pray continue, Miss Dubroc."

"Very well." She bit her lip, then forged on. She told him about her father's sudden death, the shock she had received at the reading of his will. Jared raised an eyebrow in amazement when she told him that the money had passed to Flossie La Fleume. Then she told of her unexpected encounter with Claude Boudreau on the bluff when the horse had bolted.

"Anyway, within a few days, Mr. Boudreau gained my confidence and convinced me that—that we should marry," Jasmine said.

Jared appeared stunned by the entire account. "You married this scoundrel?"

Miserably, Jasmine nodded. "Yes. This afternoon."

He glanced down at her hands. "You're not wearing a wedding ring."

She stared down at her left hand. "I suppose it must have come off in the water tonight."

Jared was shaking his head. "Then, did you . . . ? I mean, did he . . . ?" Jared's voice trailed off and he glanced at Jasmine meaningfully.

"Oh, no!" she exclaimed, her face flaming. "We didn't have time to . . . I mean, after the wedding, we left on the *Mississippi Belle* for his plantation. Claude threw me in the river before . . . It appears he didn't even want . . ." She paused, stifling a hysterical giggle. It all sounded so insane!

"Well, thank God for that!" Jared was now saying vehemently. At Jasmine's astonished glance, he quickly added, "I don't mean thank God he threw you in the river, but thank God he didn't—er . . ."

"Subject me to a fate worse than death?" Jasmine finished wryly, surprising herself with the bold question. She took a gulp of brandy and grimaced, realizing that she was now soundly feeling its effects. "Frankly, I think the river came close on that account."

Jared nodded, then a deep scowl furrowed his handsome brow. "But if this Boudreau person didn't—er—compromise your virtue, then what in thunder . . . ?" He paused to clear his throat, then smiled stiffly at Jasmine and continued, "Pardon me if I sound indelicate, Miss Dubroc, but when I rescued you from the river tonight, you were wearing a torn nightgown."

"Oh, that!" Jasmine interjected, blushing. "It was the tree I told you about, Mr. Hampton. My nightgown got tangled up in its branches."

"I understand," he gritted. "That bastard!" His eyes narrowed as he continued, "But what's still baffling me is *why* that blackguard threw you in the river. What possible motive could he have had?"

Jasmine laughed bitterly, then gulped down the remainder of her brandy. "I think it may have to do with my money."

"Your money?" Jared asked perplexedly. "I thought you just said your father left everything to—er—Flossie La Fleume."

"Oh, I'm s-sorry," she replied in a slightly slurred voice. "I forgot to explain. Flossie La Fleume was accidentally killed in a barroom brawl before she claimed my father's money, so it went to me. Oh, damn!" she finished, snapping her fingers.

He tensed. "What is it?"

"Well, I was thinking about that while I was in the river tonight. You see, I signed some papers at the bank today, right after Claude and I were married. He told me my account in Natchez would have to be transferred to Louisiana, so I just . . ." She bit her lip, cursing under her breath. "I didn't even read the stupid document before I signed it.'' She looked at Jared with her heart in her eyes. ''It was my money he wanted all along, wasn't it?''

''I fear so.''

''But how could he have known the inheritance would fall to me—I mean, after Miss La Fleume . . . ?''

''He knew—somehow,'' Jared said. He began to pace. ''So that's why he threw you in the river! The miscreant! No gentleman would ever do that to a lady!''

Despite herself, Jasmine fought a smile. ''Well, Claude was certainly no gentleman. But—why do you call me a lady? I mean, after—''

He drew himself up with dignity. ''No southern gentleman ever fails to recognize a lady.''

Jasmine's smile won. Hampton, again pacing, asked, ''You say this reprobate threw you off the *Mississippi Belle*?''

''Yes.''

Hampton snapped his fingers and grinned, a light of fierce determination in his blue eyes. ''Then, we'll chase her.''

''Oh, no, I couldn't ask you to—''

He held up a hand, his expression resolute. ''Of course we'll chase the *Belle*. She can't be that far ahead of us. And I know the captain—Charles Rutledge—quite well. He's a fine gent, and I'm sure he'll pull to for us.'' Nodding to himself with satisfaction, he added, ''Besides, don't you understand? Your honor's at stake here.''

Jasmine felt moved. ''Well, that's really quite chivalrous of you, sir, but perhaps we should notify the authorities, instead. I fear Mr. Boudreau is quite a dangerous man— and I couldn't possibly ask you to deal with him in my behalf.''

Surprisingly, Hampton laughed, and Jasmine felt warmed by the gleam of determination in his eyes, the confidence of his smile. ''Let me assure you that your erstwhile bridegroom has no idea what true peril is. But he's about to find out.'' He strode to the armoire, pulled out a frock coat, and donned it. ''If you'll excuse me, I'll notify the captain to steam ahead full.''

''But—are you sure that won't be a problem?''

"Not at all. You see, I own this packet." At the portal, he paused. "Don't worry, I'll come right back. And don't you go off anywhere."

With a grin, he was gone.

Jasmine used her interval alone to try to gather her thoughts. The brandy had dulled her senses somewhat, but there was still a dull ache in her chest—a hurt she feared might never go away.

She began to pace on her unsteady feet, shaking her head as if she expected the physical motion to clear the confusion. There was something so unreal about tonight. She knew that Claude Boudreau had tried to murder her an hour earlier, but somehow that knowledge refused to sink completely into her brain. It was as if her troubled mind had absorbed all the pain that it possibly could during the past weeks, and she was now fighting true awareness of what had happened as a matter of self-preservation.

She thought about Jared Hampton. He was most assuredly a strange and wonderful man. He seemed to want nothing but to help her. Her instincts urged her to trust him, and this confused her, as well. After all, the men she had known heretofore had brought her only harm!

She remembered how Jared had courageously jumped into the river to save her, how he'd refused to allow her to panic, how he'd held her near-naked form in his strong arms. Mercy! Who could have blamed him if he'd thought the worst of her, and had acted accordingly!

Yet Jared Hampton had acted like a consummate gentleman. He was even going to try to capture Claude Boudreau, and that astonished her most of all! He seemed noble, compelling, handsome—and she had to admit that, despite her instinctive fears, she found he roused her senses.

The door to the cabin now opened and Hampton reappeared. "We're underway," he announced proudly. "Never fear—we'll catch this scoundrel and I'll deal with him posthaste."

Jasmine watched her rescuer stride over to his desk. He

opened a drawer and pulled out a finely tooled Colt pistol. "What's that gun for?"

He shrugged, offering her an easy grin. "It's quite possible I may have to shoot this villain. You don't think he'll take kindly to our tracking him down, now, do you?"

Jasmine was horrified. She quickly moved to his side. "Oh, no, Mr. Hampton! I can't ask you to endanger your life on my behalf. You're doing far too much for me!"

"Nonsense," he promptly denied. "No gentleman worth his salt would do less for a lady under the circumstances." He tucked the revolver into his waist. "Well, I'd best go down to the deck, then, and watch for the *Belle.*"

He was heading for the door when Jasmine hurried after him, grabbing his arm. Braving a smile, she said, "Please, Mr. Hampton, let me come with you to the deck. Don't leave me here alone!"

He shook his head. "This could be quite dangerous. And besides—" he grinned as he studied her in the dressing gown "—you can't come down on deck looking like that!"

Jasmine blushed, glancing down at the dressing gown and realizing that he had a point. "Please—can't you find me something to wear? And as for danger—what could be worse than being thrown into the middle of the river?"

He glanced at Jasmine, nodding sympathetically. "Very well. I'll go see what I can find for you. Wait right here."

Again, he departed. He returned moments later with a pair of dungarees, a jersey shirt, boots that looked several sizes too large, and a small black cap. "It's a deck-hand's garb— the smallest I could find," he explained apologetically, handing her the garments. "I hope these will suffice."

"Oh, they'll be fine," Jasmine returned graciously.

Hampton frowned. "It might be good if you pin up your hair. No sense attracting undue attention from the gamblers while you're on deck." He went back to his desk, opened a drawer, then seconds later returned, placing a dozen hairpins in her hand. "Here."

"An odd item for a gentleman to have in his stateroom," Jasmine remarked.

He only chuckled. "Actually, these didn't belong to a lady," he admitted rather sheepishly. "But they do now."

Jasmine was shaking her head. "It still mystifies me that you could call me a lady—I mean, after finding me—"

"There's something about a lady that goes much further than skin deep," he said. This time, there was not a trace of humor in his voice.

Jasmine found the look Hampton gave her was so frank and oddly stirring that she couldn't risk a response, and she quickly retreated behind the screen to dress.

Moments later, Jasmine and Jared were downstairs at the helm of the boat, standing next to the railing and scanning the waters ahead as the *Witch* plowed through the wide river in the velvet quiet of the night. It was an evening that Jasmine ordinarily would have found quite beautiful. The full moon cast a shimmering glow on the waters ahead and silvered the trees at shoreside; the sounds of cicadas and night birds drifted toward them on the musky sweetness of the night air. Yet the sounds of bawdy laughter spilling out from the salon behind them, and the tinny clink of the piano, reminded Jasmine of where they were and what they were about this night.

Peering tensely into the waters ahead in search of the *Belle*, Jasmine was not aware that Jared, at her side, was quietly observing her. Nor was she aware that he was thinking of how very drawn he felt toward her.

Irresistibly, his gaze strayed up and down her body. The night wind surged, and, awestruck, he watched the dungarees ripple against the contours of her long, shapely legs, even as the clinging shirt outlined her firm, high breasts. That same titillating breeze swept her enticing scent across him. Gossamer strands of her hair, silvered by the moonlight, strayed loose from the small cap on her head, trailing down the shapely column of her throat, as if to dare a man to tug off that cap, pull loose the pins, and let the heavy silk of her hair fall into his hands!

These thoughts captivated Jared.

He knew he must say something to her—make some small

move in her direction. He drew a step closer and said in an unsteady voice, "Jasmine . . ."

She turned to him, looking somewhat wary. "Yes?"

He smiled. "Do you mind if I call you Jasmine?"

To his delight, she returned his smile. "Under the circumstances, I suppose we could dispense with formalities."

"Then you'll call me Jared?"

"I'd be honored to," she replied softly.

They fell into silence for a moment, then Jared sighed. Removing his hat, he drew a hand through his hair and said, "Jasmine, there's something I still don't understand."

"Yes?"

Passionately, he asked, "How could he have done that to you? My God! You're so beautiful, and—"

Her bitter laugh cut him short. Turning to stare moodily ahead, she said tersely, "You're wrong, Mr. Hampton. I'm not the least bit beautiful."

Jared stared at her, flabbergasted by her denial. He took her by the shoulders and gently but firmly turned her toward him. "But you are, Jasmine! Tell me, what did that bastard do to your mind? Why, if you belonged to me, I'd never—"

"Never what?" she asked, frightened yet fascinated by the intense light in Jared's gaze as he stared down at her.

Studying her expression, Jared could easily read her mixed feelings, and he could also see the fear tensing her lovely features. Releasing her shoulders, he reached out to brush a strand of hair from her eyes, smiling down at her tenderly. He didn't answer her question, but after a moment he murmured, in a voice laced with steel, "I'm going to kill him, you know."

Jared's fierce words left Jasmine looking up at him in mingled awe and surprise. He edged closer to her—so close that she could feel his warm breath on her face. His dark visage blocked out the moon as he murmured, "Jasmine—"

Then they both were distracted as the whistle blew. They turned, spotting the running lights of the *Mississippi Belle* up ahead.

# ★ Seven ★

The two vessels paused along the shoreline under an overhang of tall, shimmering trees.

"I'll get Jack to help me lower a rowboat," Jared told Jasmine grimly as he stared ahead at the *Belle*.

She watched him touch the hilt of the pistol at his waist, just inside his frock coat. Jared's expression was determined, dark, his eyes menacing beneath the wide brim of his hat, every muscle in his body taut and ready for action. Observing him, Jasmine again felt touched that this stranger had so gallantly taken up her cause. "Let me come with you," she begged.

"Absolutely not!" came his prompt reply.

Jasmine was biting her lip in frustration, when a voice from behind them inquired with annoyance, "Hey, Hampton, what's going on? Why are we stoppin' again?"

They turned as the half-dozen gamblers again ambled out onto the deck. The men were grumbling to each other, and looked cantankerous. In the darkness, they took no particular note of Jasmine in her deckhand's clothing—something she observed with relief. Nevertheless, hoping to goad Jared into taking her with him to the *Belle*, she edged closer to her rescuer and whispered, "Are you going to leave me with those men?"

"Jack'll keep an eye on them."

"Them and me, too?" she asked.

He smiled reluctantly. "I see your point. Very well, Jasmine—you may come along. Jack!" he called, gesturing impatiently toward his friend. "Come help me lower the yawl.'' To the gamblers, he added, ''Just a brief stop, gentlemen. Please continue with your cards.''

Shrugging and mumbling to each other, they retreated to the salon. Jack and Jared lowered the rowboat into the water, then Jared assisted Jasmine down into the yawl and joined her there. He took the oars and rowed them toward the larger vessel.

Alone with Jared in the quiet of the river, Jasmine stared at the stately *Belle* ahead of them with a mixture of fear and determination. To disguise her nervousness, she asked Jared a question she'd been wondering about for the last hour. ''I don't mean to pry, but would you mind telling me what you're doing out here on the Mississippi, anyway—complete with a boatload of gamblers?''

He chuckled. ''I'm sure all of this seems quite odd to you, but actually, it's only business.''

''Business?''

''I own a packet line,'' Jared explained as he rowed. ''The *Witch* is often taken out for private gambling parties. Jack and I come along to make sure our customers don't tear the vessel—or each other—apart.''

Jasmine glanced back toward the *Witch*. ''You mean those men back there are customers?''

''Indeed, yes.''

''They don't strike me as types who would have much money,'' she put in ruefully.

''Appearances can be deceiving,'' Jared said.

''Don't I know it,'' Jasmine muttered.

They now came alongside the *Belle*, and Jared said firmly, ''Look, Jasmine, I must insist you stay in the yawl while I—''

''Absolutely not!'' she cut in. ''I won't be denied my right to confront that—cad!''

''Don't you understand that this could be dangerous?''

There was no further time to argue, since they were now at midship of the other vessel. A deckhand reached out to grasp the line Jared extended, then pulled the rowboat alongside and assisted the two visitors on board.

Jared and Jasmine were met by the steamer's indignant-looking captain—a tall, angular man Jasmine recognized from earlier that evening.

"What is the meaning of this intrusion, sir?" he demanded of Jared. Then the captain paused, pushed back the visor of his cap and stepped closer to squint at Jared through his horn-rimmed glasses. "Why, you're Jared Hampton, aren't you?" The man extended his hand. "Pardon my rudeness, Mr. Hampton. I didn't recognize you."

"That's quite all right, Captain Rutledge," Jared replied, shaking the other man's hand. "You must forgive this intrusion, but, you see, the lady and I have something of a problem—"

"Lady?" the captain asked, glancing confusedly at Jasmine in her deckhand's clothing. He squinted at her for a long moment, then a new spark of recognition flashed in his eyes. He nodded to her and muttered abashedly, "Evenin', ma'am. Weren't you a passenger on this boat earlier?"

Jasmine glanced at Jared, and noted that he looked rather at a loss. After an uncomfortable pause, Jared tossed Rutledge a meaningful glance, then cleared his throat and said to Jasmine, "My dear, would you excuse us for a moment?"

"Certainly," she politely replied.

Jared and Captain Rutledge walked off together and disappeared around the main stairway, leaving Jasmine with the young hand, who was standing nearby, next to a long row of wooden barrels. The boy blushed as he studied her in her man's clothing, and she smiled back at him lamely as she adjusted the uncomfortable little cap on her head. Lord, she wished Jared would hurry! Claude might still be on board!

Several tense moments later, Jared returned to Jasmine's side, his step slow and his shoulders strangely slumped. "Let's go upstairs and gather your things."

"What about Claude?" she asked.

Observing the deckhand watching the two of them intently, Jared took Jasmine's arm and led her toward the stairway. "Do you remember which room you occupied?"

"Yes, of course I do, but—"

"The captain remembers Claude Boudreau quite clearly," Jared told her. He paused for a moment, then said with a heavy sigh, "Look, Jasmine, I'm sorry, but it appears that an hour ago, Boudreau bid the captain stop at a landing ten miles upstream from here. He disembarked there, with all his luggage."

Jasmine stopped in her tracks. "He *what*? Why didn't we see him, then—see something—as we came downstream?"

Jared looked miserable. "The captain says another man was waiting for Boudreau there—with two horses. No telling where they are by now."

"Oh, my God! Was the captain sure it was Claude?"

"He was positive. Rutledge says he well remembers both of you. He found it odd that a man would leave his bride alone on their wedding night."

"I'll just bet he did! Did Claude offer the captain any explanation for his sudden departure?"

"He said that he had business to conduct in the vicinity, and that he would be rejoining the steamboat—and his bride—later on, downstream."

"And the captain didn't find this story peculiar?" Jasmine inquired in a shrill, indignant tone.

Jared stepped closer to her, gesturing his frustration. "Of course he did, Jasmine! But what was he to do? String the man up for acting like a fool on his wedding night?"

"I see your point," she muttered, her eyes narrowed and her jaw tight.

"Rutledge had no idea what Boudreau had actually done to you," Jared went on through gritted teeth. "Unfortunately, no one saw you being thrown into the river. Anyway, Rutledge told me to offer you his sincere apologies. He gave me his solemn promise as a gentleman that he'll not breathe a word to anyone concerning this matter, and he said to tell you that if only he had known—"

"Yes, yes," Jasmine interrupted wearily. Her pain-filled eyes met Jared's, and she asked ironically, "Claude thought of everything, didn't he?"

"Not quite," Jared gritted back, but before Jasmine could wonder what that ominous comment meant, he added, "Come along, my dear. Let's gather your things."

"Unless he's already stolen them," she said cynically.

"I doubt that," he replied. "Come on—we'll collect your belongings, then go back to the *Witch*. We'll turn about and steam for Natchez immediately, of course."

"But . . ." Jasmine bit her lip, then looked up at Jared. "You've already done far too much for me."

He smiled then, and reached out to take her hand. "My dear, you don't understand. I've only just begun."

In the stateroom on the upper deck of the *Belle*, no trace of Claude Boudreau remained; however, as Jared had predicted, Jasmine's own belongings were untouched. She packed her things, then departed with Jared. She felt as if a log were wedged in her throat, as the import and finality of what Boudreau had done to her began to sink in.

Back on the *Witch*, Jared told the captain to head back for Natchez, then they returned to the stateroom. Jared placed Jasmine's portmanteau on the floor near his bunk, hung his hat on a wall peg, then poured her another brandy. "It may take us half the night to get back to Natchez, since we'll be battling the current all the way. As soon as I get you settled, I'll go downstairs and bunk in the aftercabin."

"Oh, no—I can't cast you out of your stateroom," Jasmine protested, pulling off her uncomfortable little cap and tossing it on the bunk.

He smiled at her over his shoulder. "Would you prefer spending the night with the deckhands and cardsharps?"

She sighed. "I see your point."

"Here, I think you need this," he said, turning and extending the snifter toward her.

She waved him off, and her hoarse voice betrayed her emotion. "I don't think drowning my sorrows is the answer, Mr. Hampton."

Frowning, Jared put the glass down and placed a reassuring hand on her arm. "Jasmine, we're steaming for Natchez even now. You'll feel better once you're home."

Her laugh was mirthless, as she moved away from his touch. "Home! As if there's anything left for me there."

"I'll be there for you, Jasmine," he said.

She did not seem to hear his sincere, soulful remark, as a

horrified expression suddenly lit her face. "Natchez!" she exclaimed, whirling to face Jared. "I bet Claude's on his way back there right now, to clean out my bank account! I must warn Mr. Elroy!"

Jared groaned. "Jasmine, I hate to have to tell you this—but I'd be willing to bet my cotton plantation in Vidalia that Boudreau cleaned out your account before he ever left Natchez with you today."

"Oh, my God!" Jasmine cried, realizations splintering her brain. "You're right, Jared! Claude left me alone for a time today following the wedding, and he must have—I mean, I had signed . . ."

She burst into tears again, and Jared embraced her. She didn't resist him. After a moment, he led her to the bunk, then went to retrieve the brandy snifter from the desk. "Here, you must have this," he said, forcing the drink into her hand as he sat down beside her.

Staring down at the amber liquor through her tears, Jasmine couldn't contain a hysterical giggle. All at once, she felt terribly foolish for breaking down in front of Jared a second time this night. "I'm sorry, Mr. Hampton."

"It's Jared," he corrected firmly. "And don't be."

"Jared." She sniffed, took a sip, then grimaced. "I'm not usually inclined to hysterics, I assure you."

"You have cause."

She looked up at him. "Do you think so?"

"Indeed, I do." Jared watched Jasmine stare up at him, and the expression in her tear-filled green eyes was so vulnerable, it twisted his heart.

She glanced at him expectantly. "Do you think . . .?" Then she bit her lip and glanced away. "Oh, never mind."

"What?"

"Well—I was just wondering—do you think there's any chance of finding Claude now?"

"Oh, we'll find him all right," Jared informed her with a grimly determined smile. "But first, my dear, we must get you safely back to Natchez. You can leave the matter of finding Mr. Boudreau to me."

"Oh, no, I wouldn't dream—"

"Think nothing of it."

"But I couldn't possibly let you—"

"Finished with your drink, dear?" he interrupted smoothly. As she watched in confusion, he poured her another generous glassful. "Here, drink up."

Jasmine shook her head. "Oh, no, I couldn't possibly. I'm already feeling giddy, and—"

"Good," he said firmly, placing the snifter in her hand. "I want you to drink until it all quits hurting."

"But it will probably hurt even more tomorrow," she lamented as she accepted the drink. "Especially my head, I would think."

Jared chuckled as he turned back to the desk to pour himself a generous portion of the brew. "Here, I'll join you. Surely you would not be so rude as to refuse to enjoy a libation with your host?"

He held up his glass. "Let's have a toast. To us. To beginnings, Jasmine."

While confused by his ardent words, Jasmine dutifully clinked her glass against his and took a hearty sip.

Afterward, she grew silent. Observing her, Jared asked gently, "What are you thinking?"

"I was thinking of when I met him," she said unsteadily.

"You mean, Boudreau?"

She nodded, then downed the rest of the brandy. "It's all so ironic. Like I told you earlier, I was almost killed that day. My horse spooked and drew the buggy wildly out onto the bluff, then Claude came along and rescued me."

Jared was scowling. "Sounds to me like Boudreau might have been responsible for your horse bolting in the first place."

Jasmine raised an eyebrow at him. "But, how? I certainly never saw Claude before he appeared out on the bluff."

Jared shrugged. "He might have placed a burr under your horse's harness sometime earlier."

Jasmine's eyes lit with bitter realization and she snapped her fingers angrily. "You know, I think you're right! That means that Claude must have—"

Like a volcano erupting, she sprang to her feet, waving her empty glass drunkenly. "That cad!"

As Jared watched, mesmerized, she began to rave and pace, tearing the pins from her hair as she moved, her heavy golden locks trailing wild and free behind her. "That evil, conniving thief!" She whirled to face Jared. "Twice!" she announced with a furious wave of her hand. "That's twice that villain almost killed me, not to mention my horse! And he told me a snake spooked my horse. Well, he was the confounded snake!"

"I quite agree," Jared concurred.

Wearing an expression of purposeful rage, Jasmine tore over to the desk, grabbed the decanter, and poured the remainder of the brandy into her snifter. Jared watched, appalled, as she downed the entire contents in only a few gulps. He shot to his feet. "Jasmine, you mustn't—"

"Oh, God," she muttered, her face white.

Jared grabbed her firmly about the waist as she began to collapse. She sagged against him like a rag doll, her gaze blank and staring. "Jared, the room is whirling about. Can you make it stop, please?"

"Oh, Lord," he muttered under his breath. "I've really done it now. Aunt Charity will have my hide."

"Aunt Charity?" Jasmine stammered, tottering.

Jared picked her up and carried her to his bunk. Her softness felt heavenly in his embrace, and her flushed, vulnerable expression intensified his guilt for getting her so shamefully intoxicated. Brushing a golden strand of hair from her eyes, he said tenderly, "Jasmine, it's so late. Why don't you just try to forget all this and let yourself sleep?"

"C-can't," she muttered, hiccoughing. "Hurts too bad. What he did to me . . ."

"I know, darling," he whispered, hugging her close to him. "But please try, sweet."

Her lower lip trembled as she shook her head violently and burst out, "I hate all men!" Then, noting his wounded expression, she giggled and added, "Oh. You're a man, aren't you? I'd quite forgotten."

"Jasmine," he said with an indulgent smile, "you're quite drunk."

"I must be to have forgotten you're a man," she said, smil-

ing crookedly. She reached up tentatively and touched the
strong contour of his jaw, staring up into his blue eyes as if
she'd never seen him before.

Jared caught his breath with an effort. Jasmine's trusting
look and sweet touch aroused him more than the most potent
aphrodisiac. He took her hand in his and kissed each lovely,
tapered finger. "Don't hate all men, darling. At least, don't
hate me. Why, you were born to be—"

"Yes?"

"Loved," he said hoarsely. As she stared up at him in awe,
he went on in an emotional tone, "Jasmine—God, woman,
you're so beautiful."

And, even as he moved to kiss her sweet lips, she astonished him by springing up out of his arms!

Jasmine stood tottering before Jared, her features flushed,
her glorious hair falling in thick, curly dishevelment about her
face and shoulders. She shook a fist at him, hot tears in her
eyes. "Why do you keep saying that to me, Jared H-Hamp-
ton? That I'm b-beautiful? It's not true and you know it!"

He was stunned. "Jasmine!"

"Just ask my father!"

"But isn't he dead, dear?"

"Just ask him!" she ranted. "He'll tell you how ugly I
am!" Again she began to pace, half-stumbling over Jared's
long legs.

He stood, grabbing her arm to keep her from falling. "Is
that what your father told you?"

"He didn't have to—I could see it in his eyes—how I
revolted him! And I disgusted Claude, too! I mean, it was
our wedding night—our *wedding* night, Jared! And he didn't
even stay for—he didn't even want—" Her voice broke and
she stood before him with shoulders heaving.

"Jasmine, don't do this to yourself!" Jared pleaded,
watching hot tears stream down the beautiful girl's face. God,
he thought furiously, to have his hands on that bastard Claude
Boudreau at this moment! "Please, dear, you must stop this.
It's the brandy—I was wrong ever to give it to you, and now
you're on a crying jag—"

She shrugged off his touch. "I'm not on a crying j-jig!

And don't you dare ever again tell me I'm beautiful! I'm ugly and a miserable excuse for a wife! He didn't even find me d-desirable! That's why he th-threw me in the r-river and—and maybe that's where I belong!''

And, to Jared's horror, Jasmine stumbled off toward the door. He pursued her and caught her arm, pulling her against him violently, his control broken. "Enough! Jasmine, get this through your head! You're beautiful—and ungodly desirable!''

And he crushed her to him, kissing her passionately.

Jasmine's sobs died in her throat as Jared's wonderful mouth claimed hers, and for the first time, she tasted the true depth of a man's desire. His lips were hot and possessive on hers, and he tasted headily of brandy, and something darker, even more intoxicating—a pure, sexual need. He held her so tightly against him, she feared she would swoon. Yet she was wildly aroused by his hard male chest flattening her breasts, and her nipples instinctively hardened in response, tingling, at his nearness. All memory of Claude Boudreau paled in comparison to this man's passion. There was something so different, so exquisitely right about his touch, his taste. Somewhere in the back of her mind, she knew she should be resisting him, but she didn't care.

"Oh, Jasmine!" Jared breathed after a moment, drawing back to stare down at her. "How dare you even think of throwing yourself in the river! You naughty girl!''

"I just felt so hurt—b-betrayed," she stammered.

He caught her to him fiercely. "I know, darling—but I'm going to take care of you now. I'm going to soothe away all that hurt.''

"You—you are?" she asked in wonder, her eyes wide and tear-filled. As he nodded back solemnly, she added, "No one ever said I was beautiful before. I mean, *he* said it—but he was a liar!''

"Oh, Jasmine!" Jared ran his hands through her thick, shiny hair and said, "If he said it, then that's one statement he made that *wasn't* a lie. You are beautiful, my dear, and I shall say it—and say it—until you believe it. You're beautiful, Jasmine. Beautiful.''

Then he claimed her mouth with his once more.

Tears welled in Jasmine's eyes, but this time they were tears of joy as she gave herself over to this dear, passionate man who had become her savior. His telling her that she was beautiful and desirable, his saving her from herself and comforting her, had touched her deeply. Already tonight, one man had tried to kill her. Now this man refused to let her die—and his protectiveness, coupled with his desire for her, had a devastating effect on her senses!

Feeling her soften to him, Jared groaned and reached for her breasts, his fingers kneading the firm globes through the cloth of her shirt. Jasmine gasped with joy and need, arching wantonly into his bold touch. The liquor had smashed all her inhibitions, and now even her pain was just a dull, aching memory. She wanted to obliterate it, utterly! She kissed Jared back with reckless passion, opening her mouth wide to him and stroking his hot tongue with her own . . .

Yet after a moment, he paused, pulling away from her. "Jasmine, no. We must stop this. You're a lady."

Yet Jasmine wasn't thinking straight. She only knew she would die here and now without Jared's wonderful strength. She wanted to lose herself in him, to forget all her problems and savor the power and magic of his embrace. "Yes, I'm a lady. But tonight you've made me feel like a woman for the first time in my life. Please don't spurn me, Jared. I need your comfort."

"But you don't seem to understand," he said in an agonized voice she was beyond hearing. "I think I'm in love . . ."

Jared swept Jasmine up into his arms and carried her to his bunk. He laid her down, his hands impatiently drawing up her shirt. When he uncovered the lovely mounds of her breasts, he moaned and said, "My God, you're glorious!" She gasped in ecstasy as his mouth closed hungrily on a rosy nipple. As he sucked and nipped the tender bud, she squirmed deliciously beneath him, sharp pangs of arousal radiating down her body, to the warm center of her, that secret place that hungered for his filling heat. She brazenly tangled her fingers in his hair, drawing his head closer to her, deepening the provocative pressure of his mouth.

After a moment, he whispered raggedly, "Darling, I want you so much. But are you sure?"

When she didn't immediately reply, he drew back and looked down into her eyes. "Oh, yes, Jared," she murmured, her face hot and flushed, her eyes dilated with passion as she unabashedly reached for him. "Yes . . ."

Then her arms fell back, her expression went curiously blank, and, a split second later, her eyes closed.

"Christ!" Jared Hampton groaned.

Steadying himself with a deep breath, he pulled away from her and covered her with a sheet. He sat on the edge of the bunk and shook his head to clear his senses. Thank God the girl had fallen asleep just now, he thought to himself. For she was not the only one feeling the effects of the brandy at the moment!

Jared knew that Jasmine's charms would be difficult to resist under any circumstances—yet just now, the liquor had nearly smashed all that remained of his good judgment. A few more seconds with her in his arms, and his hands would have been inside those well-fitting trousers she wore. *He* would have been inside her—quite deeply inside her.

In the morning, he would have hated himself as much as he hated Claude Boudreau at this moment! And the girl might never have trusted him again, either.

Jared turned to stare at Jasmine as she slept—her rosy cheeks, the heavy lashes resting against her lovely face. She was so beautiful, and to hear her say she wasn't had twisted his heart. What the poor girl had suffered—first, from her father, then from the swindler who'd thrown her in the river. Again, outrage rose in him regarding what the despicable Claude Boudreau had done to her. The man would pay—in spades. He'd see to that.

For Boudreau and his kind owed Jared Hampton in a way Jasmine never need know about. He'd settle the score, and then, Jasmine would be his!

Somehow, he'd known, from the moment he'd spotted her

in the river, that he would have to have her. He'd sensed it when he'd first watched her so courageously battling the currents, and he'd known it—to his soul!—when he held her in his arms just now. She was such a strong, vibrant woman—and yet she was so sweet, so vulnerable and trusting. Never again would that precious trust be violated!

He reached out to caress Jasmine's soft cheek. She stirred slightly, turning toward his touch like a flower reaching for the sun, and her movement again exposed the long scratch zigzagging down one side of her lovely throat. He scowled, tracing the angry red line with his fingertip and remembering his earlier promise to rub ointment on her abrasions. Unsteadily, he walked to the desk and fetched the jar of salve from a drawer. He returned to the bunk, sat down, and pulled the sheet off her. His lips caressed each welt before his fingers applied the soothing balm. With each tender stroke he administered, he envisioned a more agonizing death for Claude Boudreau. Strange, he thought as he worked, how the rescuer had so quickly become the prisoner of her heart.

# ★ Eight ★

Jasmine awakened the next morning with a splitting headache and a mind filled with confusion. She gasped with embarrassment as she noted that her shirt was hiked up, exposing her breasts. She yanked it down and pulled the sheet up to her neck, squinting about the cabin in the wan light filtering in through the porthole.

She spotted Jared Hampton sitting at the desk across from her, and remembered everything—or what she *hoped* was everything. ''Oh, my God!'' she exclaimed.

''Good morning, Jasmine,'' he replied, his wide smile

revealing even, white teeth. Watching her again struggle to sit up, he added, "Ready for some breakfast, my dear?"

Her efforts to draw herself upright, and Jared's mention of food, made Jasmine's insides quake with nausea. She clamped a hand over her mouth and muttered, "Please, would you leave me alone for a moment?"

He stood, eyeing her pale countenance with concern. "Jasmine, are you unwell?"

"You've quite a penchant for understatement, Mr. Hampton," she managed to choke out, between the waves of physical illness that remorselessly slammed her stomach. "*Please*, go," she added desperately, her eyes darting toward the door. "Just for a moment."

"Very well," he conceded, scowling. "But do be careful when you get up, Jasmine. We're no longer moving, but I suspect you'll be unsteady on your feet this morning, as you drank quite a lot of brandy last night."

"Please!"

With commendable haste, he departed the room.

Jasmine drew her knees up to her chest and sat with her exploding head resting on her folded arms. She could feel the boat groan and heave at its moorings, even as her insides screamed their own violent protest. The nausea was vividly intense, especially as last night's events replayed themselves in slow motion through her teeming mind.

Her husband had tried to kill her! she recalled. Then Jared Hampton had rescued her, and before the evening was out, she had gotten drunk, had spilled out her deepest feelings to Jared and had thrown herself at him!

Oh, God! She couldn't remember how far they had gone!

After an interminable moment, Jasmine's malaise at last subsided. Breathing a sigh of relief, she climbed out of the bunk, finding that she was indeed quite dizzy and unsteady on her feet. She staggered over to the porthole and peered out. The light hurt her eyes. Finally, as her vision cleared, she noted that the *Witch* was docked at the landing in the port of Natchez-Under-the-Hill. A line of ramshackle warehouses on stilts zigzagged up the contour of the river to the north of her, beneath the red soil of the bluff. Flanking the buildings along the landing was a long parade of vessels. At dockside, stevedores were already bustling about, loading barrels, sacks, and livestock. The air was thick with the sound of freight clanking into place, pigs and chickens squawking or squealing, men cursing. Even as Jasmine watched the scene, Old Saratoga, the cannon up on the bluff, blasted out, lancing Jasmine's ears with its announcement of another arriving steamboat.

Feeling as if her very skull were coming unglued, Jasmine turned from the cacophony of sight and sound. At least she was home, she thought. She probably had no money left, but she had the cottage and Ephraim to return to. She would simply have to pick up the threads of her life and get on with it.

There was no mirror in the small room, so Jasmine completed her toilette as best she could, washing her face and brushing her hair. She noted that the scratches she'd received from the tree in the river last night no longer burned her skin, and she felt the oily residue of an ointment on her neck. Obviously, Jared had applied a salve to her scraped skin after she'd passed out last night. That was quite kind of him, she thought; yet she blushed as she imagined where else his hands must have been.

She was pulling a faded brown frock from her portmanteau when a knock came at the door. "Yes?"

"Jasmine, may I come in now?" Jared called out to her.

"Yes," she replied, nervously laying the dress down on the bunk and brushing wrinkles from her shirt and dungarees as she turned to face the door.

Jared Hampton stepped back into the room, carrying a steaming tin cup of coffee. Jasmine's eyes swept over him. He was still wearing his shirt and trousers from last night, and now, he had a heavy line of whiskers on his face. His eyes were even more beautiful in daylight—a clear, radiant blue.

Just being in Jared's provocative presence again, Jasmine felt her knees trembling. A feverish heat streaked through her as she again recalled their intimacies last night.

Jared was studying her, too, as he stepped forward. He frowned momentarily as he spotted the faded dress laid out on the bunk, but his eyes lit as they came to rest on her freshly brushed, honey-colored hair, and her lovely, if wan and anxious, face. "Here, Jasmine, I've brought you some coffee," he said, holding out the cup. "You'll feel better once you drink it."

Jasmine took the warm cup from Jared, restraining a gasp as his warm hand brushed hers. She found the smell of the dark brew tantalizing. "Thanks, Jared," she told him, glancing up at him shyly as she took a sip.

"Sorry about the tin cup," he returned with a sheepish smile, "but that's all I could find in the galley. I'm afraid the *Witch* is not known for its elegant appointments."

Jasmine laughed ruefully, remembering the seedy-looking cardsharps on board last night. "Don't apologize—the coffee's excellent." Clearing her throat, she added, "Are the gamblers still on board?"

"Oh, no," Jared replied. "Jack and I kicked them all off when we docked—about three this morning. A good thing, too," he went on, "since we need to be thinking of the best way to get you off this boat and back up the Hill unnoticed."

"Indeed." Jasmine took several sips of coffee to hide her nervousness. She found the warmth of the dark brew soothing. Finally, bracing herself with a deep breath, she ventured, "Jared, about last night . . ."

He smiled at her kindly. "You poor darling. I'll wager you're hoping you dreamed it all—that it was all just some bizarre nightmare. But, alas, darling, I must inform you that all of it truly happened."

Feeling faint, Jasmine put her half-empty cup of coffee down on the desk. "It did?"

"Sorry, darling. Whatever your mind is telling you about last night—horrifying as it may seem, it all truly occurred."

"Oh, no," she whispered, tottering.

"There, there," he soothed, stepping forward. "Don't look so distraught, my dear. It's not the end of the world—at least, you managed to survive it all."

Jasmine was stunned by this arrogant assertion. "Noble words—coming from you!"

He looked flabbergasted. "But Jasmine—I'm not the one who did it to you!"

"Aren't you?" she asked furiously.

For a moment, they merely stared at each other, Jasmine glaring and trembling, Jared looking perplexed. "Wait a minute," he said at last. "What are we talking about here?"

"Last night!"

"What about last night?"

She colored to the roots of her hair. "Oooh, you cad! How dare you pretend you don't know what I'm referring to—"

"But I don't!" Patiently, he went on, "Jasmine, I know you had a lot to drink last night—and justly so. But surely you can't be suffering from the delusion that I'm the one who threw you in the river?"

For a moment, she stared at him in total confusion, then she succumbed to half-crazed laughter. "Oh, no, that's not it at all! I only meant—"

He came forward and took her by the shoulders. "What did you mean, Jasmine?" Now, a devilish grin was pulling at his sensual mouth.

"Oh, never mind," she muttered.

"Jasmine?" When she refused to meet his eye, he hooked his thumb and forefinger beneath her chin, tilting her face upward. "Come on—you must tell me what prompted you to ask me such strange questions just now."

Wretchedly, she admitted, "Well, I was just wondering about . . . us."

He chuckled, and she glowered at him suspiciously. The male fingers at her chin moved to gently stroke the contour of her jaw, and she couldn't restrain a shudder.

"What about us, Jasmine?"

She gestured in helpless frustration. "What we—er, blast it, Jared, what we did last night! Merciful heavens, I just can't remember! I mean, did we . . . ?" When his grin merely widened, she pleaded, "Jared, please tell me!"

He chuckled again. "Jasmine, you can't know how much

I'd like to answer that question to suit my own selfish purposes. But alas, the answer is no, darling. We didn't.''

"Oh, thank God!"

"Thank God? Does the idea of intimacy with me fill you with such revulsion?"

"Oh, no! It's just that it would have been . . . so very improper."

"Indeed," he concurred. With a wicked wink, he added, "But I must say that we did become—so much better acquainted."

"Oh, Lord!" she gasped. "You mean, the things—that I do remember—"

He nodded slowly.

She whirled away from him, mortified at the sudden, provocative memory of his mouth on her breast. "Oh, this is disgraceful! What you must think of me—"

"I think you're wonderful, Jasmine," he said fiercely.

"You—you *what*?" She turned to him, her eyes wide.

"I think you're wonderful," he repeated, advancing on her with a passionate gleam in his eye. "And do you know what's most wonderful about you?"

"What?" she croaked.

He reached out and caught her in his arms, and she reeled as she inhaled a lungful of his intoxicating male scent. "What's most wonderful about you, Jasmine, is that when you woke up this morning, your first thought was of me— of what *we* shared last night—not of him—even though the bastard almost killed you last night!" Grinning at her, he added, "Now that we've spent the night together under such—er—compromising circumstances, I suppose we'll just have to get married, won't we?"

Jasmine broke away, shaking her head. "Married? Have you taken leave of your senses?"

"Not in the least," he assured her.

"Married!" she again exclaimed. "But I'm already married!"

"Don't say that," Jared countered darkly. "Your marriage to that cad was never consummated." Crossing his arms over his chest, he announced, "We'll be wed just as soon as an annulment can be arranged."

Jasmine was flabbergasted. "But why should you want to marry me?"

"Why?" His deep-set eyes held a mesmerizing tenderness as he told her, "I'm in love with you."

Jasmine felt quite touched by Jared's words and the passionate light in his eyes, yet she remained very confused. "You can't love me," she insisted, gesturing her perplexity. "For heaven's sake, Jared—you've just met me."

A muscle in Jared's strong jaw twitched, and his voice was laced with steel as he replied, "I love you. And don't again presume to tell me of my feelings."

"B-but, why? Why would you love me?"

His reply was quick and sure. "Because you're strong and courageous. And because you're all woman—sweet and vulnerable and feminine." He stepped forward, again gripping her shoulders. "Jasmine, I know of no other woman alive who could have come through last night's ordeal with her life, much less her sanity."

She laughed shortly. "Whether or not I'm sane is subject to debate."

He smiled. "Say what you will, but I'm not relenting. I love you and you're going to be my wife."

"Jared," she pleaded, "don't you think it's possible that you're mistaking sympathy with my plight for—"

"Jasmine, the last thing I feel for you is pity. And after last night, that ought to be obvious to you, as well. Now, get packed and let's get off this boat. We'll never manage to be wed if we stand here arguing."

Jasmine backed away from him, shaking her head. "I'm sorry, Jared—but this is just crazy! You know nothing about me. Now you're going to marry me?"

"Precisely," he concurred with a proud grin.

Jasmine collapsed on the bunk, too astounded to say another word. Jared sat down beside her and clutched her hand in his. "I'm going to take you back to Natchez proper and install you with my Aunt Charity. Like I said, we'll be wed just as soon as the annulment is secured." Squeezing her hand, he added, "Now, tell me—how many people in Natchez know that you married Boudreau?"

Distracted by his question, Jasmine found her voice. "Well—actually, only a few," she told him slowly, brushing a strand of hair from her eyes. "There's the priest who wed us, the nuns at the orphanage, Mr. Elroy at the bank, and the lawyer, Mr. Gates. That's about it. Truth to tell, Claude bade everyone keep the wedding secret for a time, since I was in mourning for my father. He said he wanted to prevent any unpleasant gossip from circulating before we left town."

Jared laughed ironically. "No doubt, that was part of his plot. He probably didn't want any of the local gossips pointing out that they'd never heard of this fellow you were marrying, or his family."

"You know, I think you're right," Jasmine concurred with a frown.

"No matter. Boudreau's strategy shall be our advantage. Once we're back in Natchez, I want you to tell no one that you married Boudreau."

"But—"

"Tell no one, Jasmine," he reiterated. "As far as you're concerned, you're Miss Dubroc, my fiancée. Pretend Claude Boudreau never existed." In a voice holding such deadly calm that it made Jasmine shiver, he added, "Boudreau's a dead man, anyway. I'll see to that."

"My God, Jared!" Jasmine gasped, studying his grimly resolute expression with fear and foreboding. "You mean you're actually planning to—"

"I'm going to kill him," he informed her calmly.

"But, how can you possibly hope to get away with it, even if you could find him?"

"I'll find him, all right."

Jasmine balled her hands on her hips. "Wait a minute, Jared! I must put my foot down. If anyone has a score to settle with Claude Boudreau, it's me, not you. Claude is not your problem—"

"You don't seem to understand, Jasmine," he cut in fiercely. "Everything about you is my concern now. You're in my hands entirely, my darling."

As Jasmine tried to protest, he laid a finger against her poised mouth. "Just leave everything to me, love. You know, as I watched you sleep last night—you're charming when you sleep, by the way—I conjured up a thousand ways to kill Boudreau. But enough about him. I'd prefer to talk about us."

Slowly Jared slid a hand under Jasmine's hair, his wonderful fingers kneading away the tension in her neck muscles. "Tell me, darling—have you ever seen Jasmine in bloom?"

Jared pressed his warm lips down on hers. Jasmine was too shocked, then too transported, to even think of fighting him. Jared's kiss had a special tenderness about it. His mouth thoroughly gentled and tasted her, even as she savored the heat of his lips on hers, the rough, masculine pressure of his bearded cheek against her face. Shamelessly aroused, she moaned and curled her arms about his neck, melting against his muscled strength and kissing him back. She knew she was behaving like a wanton, reckless creature. Yet when Jared touched her this way, she seemed to lack a will of her own. It felt so good to have him hold her so close, as if she were truly cherished. It made her want to believe everything he told her was true.

And he was so dear, she kept thinking. So very dear. . . .

He smiled, tracing a finger across her passion-tender mouth. "You know, there's a special glow on your face when I kiss you, and I want to see it all over you." He glanced dismissively at the threadbare frock laid out nearby on the bunk, and his voice was tight as he added, "I can't believe your father hoarded away all his money and let you wear such rags! I'm going to dress you in the finest silks and satins—the brightest, most vibrant colors. I'm going to watch you bloom like the beautiful flower you are." Clutching her tightly to him, he added, "And I'm going to teach you to trust again, my darling."

Jasmine was deeply moved by Jared's words, and her senses swam with his arousing masculinity. Yet she managed to protest breathlessly, "Jared, this is happening so fast—"

Surprisingly, he chuckled, kissing her quickly and possessively. "If you think this is fast, my love, prepare to watch your head spin in coming weeks." He nudged her to her feet, then stood himself. "Now, no more nonsense, woman. Pack your belongings and I'll take you to Aunt Charity's."

"But—but won't your aunt mind?"

He waved her off with a laugh. "Aunt Charity will love having someone to redeem."

"*Redeem?*" Jasmine repeated indignantly, glowering at him.

Chuckling, Jared again caught her in his embrace. "Jasmine, darling, accept the fact that you are beyond redemption. I rescued you from the river, and now you're mine!"

# ★ Nine ★

"Jared, this is insane!"

"Jasmine, it's the only way!"

They were now leaving the stable in Natchez-Under-the-Hill in Jared's barouche. The stylish open buggy, drawn by a dappled gray horse, swept past a long line of cotton commission warehouses on Water Street. Moments earlier, the two had disembarked from the *River Witch* without incident, and Jasmine's portmanteau was now safely tucked in the boot of the buggy. Jared had insisted she wear her deckhand garb during the journey to his aunt's house. Jasmine felt absurd in the shirt and dungarees, and boots that were several sizes too large for her feet. Her hair was once again pinned up beneath the jaunty little cap.

"Jared—I feel ridiculous," she told him, gripping the seat as they clattered along the muddy, potholed street in the morning coolness. "What if someone I know should see me?"

"That's the entire purpose of a disguise, Jasmine—no one will ever recognize you." Jared's words were firm as he worked the reins.

"Besides," he continued sternly, "think of the scandal it would cause if word got around town that you'd been spotted Under-the-Hill."

Jasmine rolled her eyes heavenward. "But, Jared, I came down here with Claude only last evening."

"That was different. You were here to board a perfectly respectable steamboat at the landing. Now you've returned, the very next morning, on a gambling packet—not to mention, in a different man's company." After a meaningful pause, Jared continued, "Even though we both quite well understand your delicate circumstances, my dear, suffice it to say that the general Natchez population might not take quite as liberal a view—"

"Say no more—I see your point," Jasmine cut in with a rueful smile. "You do think of everything, don't you, Jared?"

"I do," he agreed with a chuckle. Winking at her, he added, "Besides, I'm beginning to think I like you in those trousers, Jasmine." His blue gaze swept over her body with heart-stopping thoroughness. "It does stir my blood, the way those dungarees show off your legs."

Jasmine blushed, and was about to protest, but Jared stymied her. "Hush, now, else someone shall hear you. Your voice is anything but male, my dear."

Glowering silently, Jasmine studied Natchez-Under-the-Hill as they plodded along. The small community was a collection of ramshackle frame structures, ranging from shipping offices to barber shops to brothels. The image projected was a curious mixture of industry, debauchery, squalor, and stench—wagons and carts lumbered by laden with bags, barrels, produce, and livestock, while nearby, garbage rotted in the dirt streets, teeming with ever-present black flies, even on this unseasonably mild morning. Though it was only ten o'clock, the sound of tinny pianos and raucous laughter spilled out from almost every other doorway. On the sagging boardwalks, merchants, boatmen, hawkers, slaves, and even a few Indians mingled freely, all matter-of-factly going about their business.

Under-the-Hill was quite a colorful community, Jasmine

knew. Already she had seen more than one woman of questionable repute strolling the boardwalks in tawdry satin and feathered hat, usually with a male slave following close on her heels. The painted ladies reminded Jasmine of the unfortunate Flossie La Fleume, and as Jared turned them onto Silver Street, she spotted the weather-beaten facade of the Scarlet Slipper, and her stomach did a funny little lurch. A balding barkeep, wearing a dusty apron and a gartered white shirt, stood outside the saloon, calmly sweeping the walk. Jasmine mused ironically that the establishment's drab exterior, as well as the barkeep's bored demeanor, gave no hint that a mere ten days earlier, a woman had been killed at this seedy establishment.

They were almost past the saloon when the man with the broom glanced up. Surprisingly, he grinned and called out to Jared, "Morning, Mr. Hampton."

"Morning, Stan," Jared returned cheerfully as he worked the reins.

Jasmine stared at Jared, incredulous, as they started up the incline of Silver Street toward Natchez proper. She found she couldn't read his eyes, shaded beneath the wide brim of his hat. "You know that man back there?"

He shrugged. "My shipping office is in Under-the-Hill. I've stepped into the Scarlet Slipper for a drink on occasion."

"But there are prostitutes there!" Jasmine sputtered. At Jared's blandly quizzical glance, she added, "I mean, that's where Flossie La Fleume worked—and was killed. Mr. Gates told me." She bit her lip. "Tell me—did you know Miss La Fleume?"

Jared was silent for a moment, then said, "Dear, don't concern yourself with that now. You know it upsets you."

He snapped the reins and clucked to the horse, prodding the animal up the steep incline, while Jasmine glowered to herself, disappointed by his evasive reply. It was unsettling to think that her rescuer had been a regular customer at the Scarlet Slipper. Yet she doubted pursuing the matter with Jared now would net any answers.

Gripping the edge of the seat for support, Jasmine glanced up the cinnamon-brown hill toward Clifton, a splendid red-brick mansion perched out near the edge of the bluff. As they crested the hill and moved through a densely wooded area, Jasmine found she felt relieved to be home. Soon, they emerged from the trees and moved down the Old Spanish Esplanade past the plaza, where streets jutted off at right angles into the main business district beyond. The city's architecture was an intriguing hodgepodge—stuccoed Spanish-style buildings mixed in with structures of traditional, Creole, or French design.

Clearing his throat, Jared now said, "Don't fret, Jasmine. Soon, I'll have you at my aunt's house, and all this unpleasantness will be behind you."

"But Jared, whatever will your aunt think when she sees me so attired?" Jasmine asked.

He chuckled. "Oh, Aunt Charity will take it all in stride, I'm sure. Now, quit worrying. Why not start thinking about our wedding, instead? I think you'll be quite stunning in white satin and seed pearls—don't you agree, darling?"

Jasmine could only shake her head at Jared's audacity. Ever since he'd told her, an hour earlier, that he intended to marry her, she'd assumed he was experiencing a temporary lapse in his sensibilities. Whatever his reason, she felt sure he'd recover his sanity soon and denounce his folly.

Still, she thought wistfully, it was a lovely fantasy—the idea of being married to such a masterful man as Jared Hampton. It would be like a fairy tale come true.

Yet the last thing she needed was to rush headlong into another romantic entanglement!

They now proceeded through the busy central business district of town, and finally turned onto Woodville Road, a narrow dirt lane lined by tall oaks and curving past magnificent estate homes. The looming mansions were breathtaking, and the air was thick with the mingled aromas of honeysuckle, roses, camellias, and wisteria. Jasmine felt awed as Jared turned into the long arc of a driveway, at the center of which stood a towering, pink-brick home with white, fluted columns. "That's where your aunt lives?" she asked in a stunned voice.

"Indeed, yes."

Jasmine swallowed hard, noting that the circular drive was lined with handsome black carriages. On the shady lawn off to one side, half a dozen black men in livery—obviously, the drivers of the carriages—were laughing as they pitched quoits. "Your aunt seems to have company," Jasmine remarked to Jared nervously.

"Ah, yes, it's Tuesday morning," he replied calmly. "My aunt will be holding Bible study."

Jasmine was horrified. "Bible study! Oh, Jared! You can't take me into that house looking like this! You must take me back to my cottage on Pearl Street!"

"Out of the question—you're staying with my aunt."

"Jared, please, I'd be perfectly safe at—"

"Would you?" he countered. "What if Boudreau should come back? How safe would you be then?"

"But, why should Claude return?" Jasmine demanded with an exasperated gesture, feeling close to panic as they approached the stately mansion. "If what we both suspect is true, Claude has already absconded with everything I have!"

"Still, we'll take no chances," came Jared's adamant reply.

Jasmine was sighing in perplexity, her heart hammering and her palms sweating, as Jared stopped the barouche before the magnificent home. At once, a grizzled black man in butler's garb opened the massive oaken door and came down the steps, his gait surprisingly lithe. "Mornin', Mr. Jared," the old man called out, his wrinkled face split by a wide grin. Spotting Jasmine next to Jared in the barouche, the slave politely added, "Mornin', young mass'r."

Jasmine nodded stiffly at the slave, hoping he wasn't looking at her too closely, as Jared said matter-of-factly, "Daniel, would you please call the stable lad to tend to the buggy and bring in this gentleman's bag, while I take my guest inside?"

"Yessir, Mr. Jared," Daniel said, adding in a lower, confidential tone, "Miss Charity, she gots them 'piscopal ladies in the parlor."

"I'm aware, Daniel," Jared replied with a chuckle.

He alighted from the buggy and was heading for Jasmine's side, when she remembered her disguise and quickly hopped down herself, not wanting to destroy the charade by having Jared assist her out of the buggy. As Daniel went off to fetch the stable lad, Jasmine hissed to Jared, "I'm not going in that house with you, Jared, and that's final!"

"And why not, sweetheart?" he questioned patiently.

"Because those women will see me, and—"

"And they'll think you're a business associate of mine."

"A business associate? Jared, for heaven's sake, why would you come calling at your aunt's house with a deckhand from one of your packets? Besides," she continued, beseeching him with wildly desperate eyes, "some of the Episcopal women regularly donate clothing to the orphanage. I'll be recognized!"

"In that garb?" he countered, with a short, disbelieving laugh, straightening his lapels with maddening self-possession.

"Jared, no!"

Even as she protested, he was tugging her up the steps. "Darling, don't make a scene."

"Jared, please—if you must take me in there, at least take me around to the back."

"That won't work, Jasmine. There's only one stairway in the house, so we'll have to go through the central hallway anyway."

"Oh, Lord!"

Jasmine was still arguing with Jared as he opened the front door and dragged her into the opulent central hallway. She was digging her heels into the Oriental runner, and Jared was yanking her toward the curving stairway, when a childlike, feminine voice called out, "Why, Jared—whatever are you doing?"

Jared and Jasmine turned toward the parlor. Half a dozen sets of curious eyes were watching them through the double archway. The women, all gowned in elegant silk, sat with Bibles in their laps. Jasmine recognized two of the gray-haired dowagers at once.

"Oh my God," she muttered.

And for the first time in her life, she fainted.

Jared caught her in the nick of time, and glanced down at

her worriedly. Luckily, she had pinned the cap to her hair, so it remained in place, keeping her disguise intact.

Gasping their shock, the six churchwomen came rushing out into the foyer, in a collective rustle of silk and petticoats. The shortest of the matrons, a silver-haired woman wearing a mauve-colored frock, said, "Jared, who is this poor lad, and what ails him?"

"Oh, hello, Aunt Charity—ladies," Jared replied charmingly. Glancing down at Jasmine, he informed his aunt, "Sh—*he's* one of my hands from the *Witch*, Aunt. He took ill suddenly this morning. I've brought him home for you to nurse." As several of the dowagers sucked in their breath in fear, Jared added smilingly, "Don't worry, ladies, there's no sign of malaria or yellow jack." He scowled. "Not as far as I can determine, at any rate."

At this, the horrified ladies hastily grabbed their reticules, Bibles, and bonnets, and fled the house, muttering excuses about errands forgotten or chores left undone.

Within less than a minute, Jared, his aunt, and Jasmine were alone. "Jared, what is the meaning of this?" the little woman asked Jared irately. Before he could reply, she waved him off and said, "Oh, never mind, you can tell me directly. First, we must take this poor sick person up to bed."

Charity led the way to the second floor, into an elegant room done in shades of warm yellow. Jared laid Jasmine down on the rosewood bed, then announced proudly, "Aunt, meet my fiancée."

Charity's hands flew to her face. "My Kingdom, Jared!" she gasped, stepping forward and peering at the unconscious lad. "This is most irregular."

Jared laughed as he turned to pull off Jasmine's boots, then carefully removed the cap from her head. He was pulling the pins from her hair and spreading her golden locks out on the pillow when Charity stepped closer and exclaimed, "Why, Jared! He's a woman!"

"Of course, Aunt!" her nephew returned with a laugh. "Surely you don't think I'd be engaged to anything but a woman?" Grinning widely, he asked, "Isn't she beautiful?"

Charity nodded as she scrutinized the girl's lovely, pale

face, her wheat-colored hair, which radiated in shiny waves on the pillow. "Ah, yes, she's quite lovely, son. But, where did she come from?"

"From the river," Jared explained. "Her husband threw her in last night. I pulled her out, and now I'm going to marry her."

"Oh, Jared!" Charity stepped closer to her nephew, stretching upward on tiptoe to place a trembling hand on his brow. "Have you taken a fever?"

Jared removed his aunt's hand and squeezed it reassuringly in his. "Not at all. I'm fine, Aunt. Never better, in fact." He wrapped an arm about his aunt's frail shoulders. "Now, come on downstairs, and I'll tell you all about her."

"Is she all right?" Charity sputtered, glancing back at Jasmine.

Jared waved his aunt off. "She's fine—a real pillar of strength, that one. Why, you should have seen her fighting the river last night! Actually, she's just a trifle indisposed at the moment—too much brandy last night, you see." As Charity threw a hand to her mouth, he added, "And I think she felt a certain aversion to coming calling on you dressed as a man."

"Well, there I can't blame her!" Charity put in stoutly. "You always had a wicked streak, Jared."

He nodded. "That's true." Then, more solemnly, he added, "But no more, Aunt. I've found what I'm looking for."

"Jared, do you mean—"

"I love her, Aunt." He glanced at Jasmine devotedly, and his voice cracked with emotion as he went on, "I know it sounds crazy, coming this suddenly, but when I saw her struggling in the river last night, I just knew it. I knew I'd found my life."

"Oh, Jared!" Tears now welled in Charity's fine hazel eyes as she hugged her nephew. "If those are your feelings, then I'm happy for you, of course. But you must admit that this is all rather singular. I mean, finding your future bride in the river, her already a married woman—"

"That's not her fault in the least, Aunt Charity," Jared

said. "You'll understand that after I explain things to you. Now, come along. Let's go downstairs and let the poor girl sleep it off while I tell you all about her."

The two quietly left the room and headed down the stairway. "You're going to have such fun with her, Aunt Charity," Jared told his aunt cheerfully. "You can call the seamstress—Miss Laveau, isn't it?—and have the dear girl royally outfitted. Won't you be in your glory?"

"Oh, yes, that would be fun," Charity replied in a wistful tone. Accepting her nephew's assistance as they stepped down into the hallway, she added, "There's been so much sadness in this house for so long, hasn't there, love?"

"God, yes," came Jared's hoarse reply.

"What's the girl's name?"

"Jasmine," he murmured proudly.

"Well, that's a lovely name, son."

"Indeed." Inside the large parlor, Jared glanced at the silver tea service on the carved rosewood table and grinned. "Ah, wonderful. In their haste to depart, it seems the ladies have left us oceans of tea, as well as all those delectable little rice cakes Dulcie makes. You know how I love Dulcie's *calas*."

"I do. But something is really troubling me, Jared," Charity went on, as the two sat down in matching French armchairs flanking the tea table. "If this girl is already someone else's wife, won't it be a crime for you to marry her? It seems to me that when Henry was alive, he mentioned something about that being a rather naughty practice. I believe it's called bigamy."

"Oh, that!" Jared waved his aunt off, stuffing a tea cake in his mouth as he leaned back in his chair and crossed his long legs. "I'm going to kill Jasmine's husband. That will obliterate the bigamy problem rather nicely, don't you think?"

"Jared! Surely you jest!"

"Not in the least. What else would you have me do to a scoundrel who threw her in the river and left her to drown?"

Charity became extremely agitated. Her small cheeks were bright and her pale eyelashes fluttered rapidly. "Well, Jared,

I'm not at all sure what the protocol is in such a situation—''

"The protocol is premeditated murder, Aunt," Jared replied, flashing her a ready smile. As Charity gasped in wide-eyed horror, he continued, "Now, don't work yourself into a dither, dear heart." He poured his aunt a cup of tea and handed it to her.

The two shared their repast in silence for a moment, then Charity, feeling somewhat calmer, said, "Very well, now, Jared. Tell me all about this rather startling young lady that you found—er—in the river. Is she from a Natchez family? You haven't even told me who her people are, you know."

"Oh, sorry, Aunt. The name is Dubroc. Her father was Pierre Dubroc, the silversmith. It seems he died recently—"

Jared paused in mid-sentence at his aunt's sharp intake of breath. Her complexion suddenly paled to the color of parchment. "What is, it, Aunt? Do you feel ill?"

Charity was slowly shaking her head. "It's just that—I knew the man."

Jared's frown deepened as he said, "Well, I'll be deuced." Eyeing his aunt cautiously, he continued, "Perhaps before I tell you about Jasmine, you'd better explain to me what you already know."

"Certainly, Jared."

As Charity explained all she knew about Jasmine and her father, Jared listened intently. Then he told his aunt some of the things he knew about Jasmine, choosing his every word with the greatest care.

An hour later, Jared boarded his buggy and headed back for town. He needed to visit Mr. Elroy at Natchez Bank and Trust. He was sure he would discover, as he and Jasmine had surmised earlier, that Boudreau had already cleaned out her account.

His thoughts drifted back to his conversation with Aunt Charity moments earlier. He'd been quite shocked to learn that his aunt had known Jasmine's father, Pierre Dubroc— that the two had visited together on several occasions. Once Charity had made her revelations, Jared had in turn told his aunt all he dared about Jasmine's background—how Claude Boudreau had married her only to get her money; how the swindler had thrown the girl in the river before the marriage was consummated, leaving her to drown; how he had rescued her.

He had wisely left out of his account the entire matter of Flossie La Fleume—knowing that without that one critical link, his aunt would never be able to put together the entire, horrifying picture.

Once Jared had outlined Jasmine's plight, he'd found that his aunt's sympathies had been entirely with the girl. The old woman had agreed with him that an annulment should at once be sought in Jasmine's behalf. "You bad boy, Jared," Aunt Charity had scolded. "Here, you led me to believe you would be obliged to kill this swindler man in order to marry the girl."

"Oh, but I *am* going to kill the cad, Aunt," Jared had replied. "Make no mistake about that. It's a matter of honor now."

"Oh, Jared!" Aunt Charity had thrown up her hands. "Surely you're not going to put us through this honor business again—not after what happened with Melissa!"

"Honor isn't a business, Aunt," Jared had responded sternly. "It's a way of life. I'm killing Boudreau, and that's my final word on the subject."

Now, Jared's thoughts drifted back to Jasmine—beautiful Jasmine, who lay safely abed at his aunt's house. He knew he would find no peace until the girl was his—the memory of her soft curves nestled in his arms, her heavenly, sweet lips on his, was exquisite torture. Last night, her pain had touched him deeply. He was humbly grateful now that she had passed out when she had, since he realized taking her last night would surely have only served to shatter the fragile rapport he had built with her. He knew he must keep his passions under rein until she came to trust him completely —until they could be legally wed.

Thank God Boudreau hadn't violated her! he thought fiercely. Such a desecration of her lovely body might have left emotional scars that would never quite heal. As things had turned out, Jasmine would be his alone to teach of love. He would erase the rest of her ordeal from her mind in time.

As Jared spoke with Mr. Elroy downtown at the bank, Jasmine was beginning to stir back at Charity's house. She sat up and rubbed her eyes, noticing that she was lying in a magnificent rosewood bed. She observed that the room itself was breathtakingly lovely, as well. Across from her on the edge of a Persian carpet stood a rococo highboy, while a matching dresser occupied the space nearby. A mahogany armoire and delicate ladies' dressing table, both carved with fans and scrollwork, completed the room's furnishings.

"Feeling better now, dear?"

Jasmine jumped, twisting her head about to view a previously unnoticed bay window which jutted out on one side behind the bed. There, in a beam of sunlight, sat Jared's Aunt Charity. "Oh, gracious," the little woman said apologetically, slowly getting to her feet. "I didn't mean to startle you, my dear."

Jasmine rubbed a still-aching head as the little woman drew closer. She braved a smile at Charity. "Please, don't apologize. If my memory serves me correctly, you're the one who has cause to feel startled, after your nephew dragged me into your house dressed like a man—in the midst of your Bible study, no less."

Charity smiled back at the girl. "Ah, yes, that was wicked of Jared, now, wasn't it? But from what my nephew later told me, the disguise *was* necessary, my dear."

Jasmine felt the color drain from her face. "Did Jared tell you . . . everything?"

"Now, dear, don't fret yourself," Charity scolded. "Why, you're turning the shade of an oyster even now." The little woman edged over to the night table flanking the bed and picked up a rattan tray covered with a linen cloth. "Here, dear, have some soup. It should still be good and hot. Dulcie brought it up only moments before you awakened."

"Thank you," Jasmine said as Charity deposited the tray

across her lap. She found that the idea of nourishment, especially soup, did sound good at the moment. Perhaps the broth would help soothe the pounding of her head and the gnawing of her stomach.

As Jasmine uncovered the tray, Charity pulled up her chair and sat down next to the bed. Jasmine found that Charity appeared small and frail. Clear hazel eyes peered out of the wrinkled, heart-shaped little face, and tight silver curls framed the old woman's sweet countenance, trailing back to a bun at the nape of her neck. Charity was dressed in a becoming mauve silk frock with a pleated front and two dozen tiny, cloth-covered buttons on the bodice. Her wrinkled little fingers were graced by an abundance of stunning rings—sapphires, diamonds, rubies, and topaz. All in all, Charity Hampton radiated an image of peace, gentility, and kindness, Jasmine decided.

"Something wrong, dear?" Charity now asked her.

"Oh, not at all," Jasmine said quickly, embarrassed to have been caught staring at the little old woman. She quickly took up her spoon and began to eat the rich soup. "This is excellent," she told Charity sincerely, feeling better as the broth descended into her stomach.

"Ah, yes, Dulcie makes wonderful chicken soup," Charity replied. "And Jared loves her rice cakes so. After you—er —decided to take a little nap this morning, my nephew finished off a dozen of Dulcie's *calas* downstairs."

"Um—where is Jared now?" Jasmine asked cautiously.

"I believe he had business at one of the banks downtown," came Charity's reply. "But he warned me to have you up and dressed by afternoon. He said the two of you have several errands to run in town."

"I see." Jasmine took a deep breath, then blurted, "Miss Charity, did Jared tell you . . . I mean, about what happened to me last night?"

"Indeed he did, and I think it's utterly despicable what that blackguard did to you, my dear. I agree with Jared that our only recourse is to seek an immediate annulment in your behalf, so that you and my nephew may wed."

Jasmine's spoon clattered onto the tray. "But, Miss Charity. You mean you approve of your nephew's desire to marry me—a virtual stranger?"

"You're evidently not a stranger to Jared," Charity replied. Before Jasmine could wonder what that comment meant, the old woman went on, "My dear, I've seen the look in Jared's eyes when he talks about you, and that's all I need to see. There's no doubt in my mind that you're the one for my nephew."

Jasmine was shaking her head. "That's quite fine of you, Miss Charity, but it still amazes me that you and Jared would be so accepting of me, under the—er—rather shocking circumstances, that is."

"And why shouldn't we accept you, dear? You're a lovely and charming young woman, and obviously very much a lady."

Jasmine couldn't contain a wry laugh. "That's just what Jared said, right after he found me in the river." She eyed Charity cautiously. "Still, don't you think your nephew is being a bit—rash?"

Charity didn't reply for a long moment, and when at last she spoke, there was a faraway look in her hazel eyes. "Jasmine, my dear, suffice it to say that when I was a young woman like you, my father talked me into making a major decision based on the mind and not the heart. I've regretted that decision to this very day, and I'm determined not to let my nephew repeat the same mistake." Before Jasmine could comment, Charity stood in a rustle of her silk skirts. "Through with your soup, dear?"

"Yes. It was good."

The old woman took the tray. "Shall I send up some more?"

"Oh, no, that was plenty."

"Then I'll leave you to dress, dear." Charity nodded toward the east corner of the room. "Your portmanteau is over there, next to the dressing table. Shall I send up one of the maids to help you unpack and assist you with your toilette?"

"Oh, no, please, I'll be fine. As for my unpacking—that won't be necessary. I'll be returning to my own home later today.'' Offering Charity a lame smile, Jasmine continued, ''I wouldn't dream of imposing on your hospitality further —especially not after I embarrassed you so in front of your guests this morning.''

''Embarrassed me? Nonsense!'' came Charity's stout reply. ''Actually, I can't recall when I've had so much fun. As for your leaving—not a chance, my dear. If Jared hadn't insisted you stay, I certainly would have.'' Charity paused a moment, then went on carefully, ''My nephew told me that you recently lost your father. I'm so sorry, dear.''

''Thank you.''

Charity was silent again, recalling her earlier conversation with Jared, when they'd decided it would be best that she didn't tell Jasmine what she knew about Pierre Dubroc—not yet. Tossing the girl a warm, reassuring smile, she said, ''Jasmine, my dear, I want you to consider Jared and me your family hereafter. Now, do be a good girl and get dressed, else my nephew shall be in a temper with both of us upon his return.''

Charity departed the room, leaving Jasmine no further opportunity to argue. She smiled to herself ruefully. Miss Charity might be quite small and ladylike, but in her way, she had a will of iron, just like her nephew did.

Jasmine thought of Jared as she dressed. It was beginning to dawn on her that he had really meant what he'd said when he'd announced his intention to marry her. If his proposal had been a mere whim, it stood to reason that he would have had second thoughts by now—and he certainly wouldn't have gone so far as to announce his plans to his aunt!

Remembering how Charity had blithely accepted her as Jared's intended, Jasmine had to shake her head. Out of the three of them, she seemed to be the only one who found Jared's sudden desire to wed her the least bit strange!

He did appeal to her, of course, she acknowledged. He was gallant and kind—not to mention attractive! He'd had every opportunity to take advantage of her vulnerability last night, but he hadn't. That spoke well of him.

Yet at the same time, Jasmine didn't know quite what to think of this strange, enchanting man who had pulled her from the river and had appointed himself her savior. He seemed almost too good to be true, and while she disliked herself for doubting him, she had to wonder if he didn't have some ulterior motive in so suddenly and dramatically taking over her life. Was it truly love at first sight, as he'd insisted, or was he planning somehow to use her, just as every other man in her life had?

A few minutes later a young black girl knocked at the door and entered the room. "I be Sarah, Miss Jasmine," the girl said, twisting her fingers together nervously. "Miss Charity, she say I be your maid."

"Oh, I see," Jasmine said, smiling at the girl, who had a sweet face and appeared to be no more than fifteen. "Well, it's good to meet you, Sarah. But actually, I don't need a maid—"

"Miss Charity, she say so," the girl said simply. Sarah walked over to the ornate bed and began straightening the coverlet. "Mr. Jared, he be waitin' for you downstairs in the parlor, missy."

Jasmine smiled to herself. It seemed everyone in this house—from the servants on—had taken charge of her life. "Thanks, Sarah."

Jasmine left the room and went down the breathtaking semi-spiral staircase with its gleaming mahogany banister. Thank goodness her dizziness and nausea had passed now, she thought, swearing that she would never again touch a drop of alcohol.

Jasmine did feel rather apprehensive about what Jared might tell her about his trip to the bank. There was no doubt in her mind that he had visited Mr. Elroy.

Approaching the front parlor, she spotted him before he saw her, and stood just inside the archway for a long moment, studying him. He stood with his back to her, in a far bay window, his head turned toward the sunlight filtering through the Belgian lace panels. Her heart hammered at his stirring presence, and it struck her anew how very handsome he was.

He pivoted slightly now, and she feasted her eyes on his chiseled, classical profile, the sculpted lines of his face. Yet as soon as she saw his mouth, set in hard, tense lines, she knew that the news he brought her was bad.

She cleared her throat. "Jared?"

At once he turned, smiling at her, his blue eyes sparkling, any hint of anxiety gone from his face. "Darling!"

He hurried forward and embraced her, and, before she could react, claimed her mouth in a passionate kiss. His lips were warm on hers and his muscled nearness was dizzying. Afterward, as she stared up at him breathlessly, still clinging to his strength, he chuckled and said, "If you aren't a sight for sore eyes. You know, you gave us quite a scare earlier, when you swooned in the hallway. Who would think that a girl not awed by the mighty Mississippi River would faint dead away at the sight of six Natchez dowagers?"

Jasmine had to laugh at Jared's ironic humor. "I guess last night when I was in the river, I had only myself to worry about. This morning, there was your aunt—"

"Who is absolutely delighted to have you here, so I'll hear no more nonsense, Jasmine." He moved back slightly, his gaze quickly flicking over her. "Feeling better now, love?"

"Oh, yes, I'm fine."

"Good. We've several visits to make this afternoon."

Jasmine bit her lip. "Did you go to see Mr. Elroy while I was sleeping?"

He sighed heavily. "Yes, dear."

"The news was bad, wasn't it?"

"I'm afraid so."

"Blast!" Jasmine muttered, pulling away from his touch. She walked over to the window, her back to him, not wanting him to view the turbulent emotion on her face. "What did he say?"

"Shortly after you signed the papers yesterday, Claude Boudreau returned—alone—and cleaned out your account."

Jasmine whirled on him. "And Mr. Elroy didn't find that—strange?"

Jared glanced at her lamely. "Jasmine, he had no choice. You signed over your entire inheritance to Boudreau."

Now trembling with helpless anger, Jasmine turned back toward the window and stared at the lawn outside, bitter tears burning her eyes. "What did you tell Mr. Elroy—I mean, about what happened to me on the river?"

She heard Jared sigh behind her. "Actually, I thought it would be best to tell him as little as possible. I simply said that you had changed your mind about Boudreau, and that he'll later be returning the money to you. I also asked Mr. Elroy's discretion, and he gave me his word as a gentleman that he'll keep this matter private."

After a moment, Jasmine felt Jared's hands on her shoulders. "Don't worry. I'll see to it that what Boudreau did to you never gets around the Natchez community. I want you to forget him, darling. As for the money, I'm planning to replace it—"

She turned violently, and wrenched herself away from his touch. "No, Jared. I'd never allow that. Besides, it's not so much the money as the principle involved!"

"I know, dear."

Jasmine bit her lip, then burst out, "I'm going after him —that's what I'll do! I'll find Claude, and then I'll—"

"Over my dead body, you will!" Jared cut in fiercely, advancing on her. His eyes were wild with anxiety as he continued harshly, "Jasmine, you wouldn't even know where to begin."

"Then—then I'll figure something out," she insisted, tilting her chin as she stared up at him.

Jared noted the fierce pride clenching Jasmine's lovely features. Yet the slight trembling of her jaw, the tears glistening on her eyelashes, betrayed her raw anguish and stark vulnerability, and he realized how perilously close she was to breaking down. He moved even closer and placed a hand on her shoulder. "Look, my dear, something does need to be righted here," he told her, more gently. "But I insist that you leave that to me—and to my friend Jack."

"Oh, Jared." Studying his warm, caring face, Jasmine was filled with warring emotions—rage toward Claude, tenderness toward Jared, regret, and an urge to retreat, to nurse her wounds, now that the finality of her situation had been made so brutally clear. "Look, I don't want you or Jack to feel obliged to fight my battles for me," she informed him in a tight voice, helplessly clenching her fists. "You've done far too much for me already. Please—just take me home."

Jared pulled her into his arms and ran his hand through her hair. His voice vibrated with emotion as he said, "You don't seem to understand, my darling. You already are home."

His tender kiss smothered her protest.

# ★ Ten ★

Jasmine and Jared stopped at the lawyer's office on Franklin Street first. With Jared providing moral support, Jasmine explained what Claude Boudreau had done to her. Gates conveyed his sympathies, then said he would at once seek a legal annulment of the marriage in Jasmine's behalf, from a sympathetic judge he knew in the Adams County Circuit Court. "Since this is so clearly a case of a marriage secured through fraud, I'm sure Judge Henley will grant our petition promptly and in chambers," Gates said.

Jared explained the need for secrecy regarding Jasmine's personal tragedy, and the attorney agreed to handle the matter with all discretion.

"Well, my dear, it seems to me that things are proceeding splendidly," Jared told Jasmine as they drove away in his barouche. "Your attorney expects your petition for annulment to be granted within a fortnight, which means that we can marry soon thereafter."

Though Jasmine's heart fluttered at Jared's new mention of marriage, she remained determined to proceed with caution where he was concerned. She also knew that she would not be free to marry Jared—or anyone—within a fortnight. Loosening the silk tie on her black bonnet, as the afternoon had grown characteristically humid and sticky, she told him calmly, "Jared, you don't seem to understand. I can't remarry until I'm granted a Catholic dissolution, as well. Until then, I'll still be married to Claude in the eyes of the church."

Jared scowled slightly. "My dear, I didn't realize the church annulment was that important to you."

"It is," she said.

He nodded, then grinned with his usual self-possession. "Then, let's go to St. Mary's right now."

"Thanks, Jared," she said, smiling back rather stiffly. "You've been so very kind and helpful."

On the way to the cathedral, Jasmine told Jared about her special relationship with Maggie, and asked if they might stop at the orphanage after they spoke with Father Grignon. He graciously consented.

Soon, they arrived at St. Mary's Cathedral on Union Street. In the parish office, Jasmine introduced Jared to Father Grignon, telling the priest that her companion was a concerned friend. She then explained the events that had transpired since she had married Claude Boudreau yesterday. The portly, middle-aged man expressed his dismay, and assured her that she had perfect grounds to seek dissolution of her marriage to Boudreau.

"In the eyes of the church, your marriage is ratified, but not consummated," the priest explained. "And there is also quite clearly a deficiency of consent on Mr. Boudreau's part—considering his reprehensible behavior following the mass. We'll simply present your evidence to a tribunal of the Natchez diocese, then your petition will be forwarded on to Rome. Do you have witnesses to confirm your testimony?" he asked.

Jasmine glanced at Jared, and he quickly told the priest, "I'll testify in Jasmine's behalf. And I'm sure that Captain Rutledge of the *Mississippi Belle* will be glad to confirm her story."

The priest nodded. "Fine, then. I'll speak with Bishop Chanche, and we'll set up an appointment to record your testimony. We'll send the petition on to Rome as soon as possible, but the process could take months." The priest adjusted his steel-rimmed glasses and continued, "Even though your separate legal dissolution will doubtless be granted much sooner, you must realize that in the eyes of the church, your marriage to Mr. Boudreau is considered valid until proven invalid."

"I realize that, Father," Jasmine confirmed.

Meanwhile, Jared was scowling. "Father Grignon, Jasmine has already explained to me that this could be quite a protracted process. However, we'd sincerely appreciate it if you could expedite her petition, since we can't wait to be—"

"Father Grignon," Jasmine cut in quickly, horrified at the obvious direction of Jared's remarks, "I know you're a busy man, and Mr. Hampton and I do need to be leaving. We want to stop by the orphanage and check on Mag—well, the children."

The priest smiled. "Ah, yes, the orphanage. Will you be returning to your duties there, Jasmine?"

Jared answered for her. "From now on, Jasmine's main duty will be to be my—"

"Actually, I may not return to full-time teaching quite yet," Jasmine interrupted again, throwing Jared a beseeching look. "I have been through quite an ordeal, Father Grignon—first, losing my father, then this."

The priest nodded sympathetically. "I quite understand. You'll need some time to put your life back in order. But, please remember that you're always needed at the orphanage. And the children miss you already."

"I miss them," Jasmine returned, a quiver of emotion in her voice as she again thought of Maggie.

Jared asked for Father Grignon's promise of discretion regarding all they had discussed, and the priest solemnly gave his word. As Jared and Jasmine were preparing to leave, the priest asked her, "Have you thought about what you'll tell the sisters? After all, they were witnesses at the mass yesterday."

"Oh, heavens," Jasmine muttered, glancing at Jared. "You know, that totally slipped my mind."

"May I offer a suggestion?" Father Grignon went on.

"Please do, Father," Jasmine said.

"As your friend Mr. Hampton has pointed out, this is a matter calling for all discretion. So why not simply say that after the mass yesterday, you discovered that your bridegroom had lied to you—that he wasn't a good Catholic, after all—and that you're seeking your annulment on those grounds?" The priest smiled wryly. "No sense tempting the good sisters to indulge in worldly gossip. And—you could tell them this without actually lying."

Jasmine smiled, nodding. "Thank you—we'll do just that."

Jasmine and Jared left the parish office. As they drove toward the orphanage a few blocks away, Jared asked, "Why didn't you let me tell Father Grignon that we're planning to be wed?"

"Oh, Jared!" she said. "Don't you think the poor man has suffered enough shocks for one afternoon? Here, I asked him to marry me to one man only yesterday. Imagine his bewilderment if today, I'd also told him—"

Jared reached across the seat to touch Jasmine's arm, and his eyes locked hard with hers. "Don't you want to marry me?"

She wanted to be honest with Jared, but hated to say anything that might hurt him. She drew a long, steadying breath. "Jared, I do feel very drawn toward you, but things are simply proceeding too fast. I rushed into one marriage, and look where it got me! Perhaps it's just as well that the church annulment will take several months. That way, we'll both have time to think things through."

"There's nothing for me to think about!" Jared returned darkly, snapping the reins and guiding the horse around a corner. "As for you, my dear—I've felt the way you respond to me. And I simply can't believe you're not feeling at least some of the things that I'm feeling—"

"Oh, I am!" she cried, blushing profusely at his frankly impassioned words, yet still determined to address her doubts. "It's just that—"

"It's Boudreau, isn't it?" he demanded. "You just can't trust me after what he did to you."

"Jared, can you blame me for being cautious?" she asked, with a supplicating gesture. "Heavens, I've only known you for one day." Placing her hand on his sleeve, she reasoned, "Please, Jared, I do—well, I do like you so much! And I would hope that in time things might proceed between us just as you wish. But, please, it's just too soon for us to be making any plans or announcements."

"Perhaps so," he conceded. Yet he still looked unconvinced. "Are you concerned because I'm not Catholic?"

"Well . . ." she admitted slowly, "if I did marry again, it would have to be in the church."

"Then there's no problem. I'll simply take instruction in the Catholic faith before we're wed."

"But, is that what you want, Jared?"

His reply was quick and adamant. "I want you, my darling, and everything you represent." He pulled the buggy to a halt before the tree-shaded orphanage. Hopping down, he approached her side of the conveyance and took her hand. "Now, come along. Let's go see your charges inside."

Accepting his assistance out of the buggy, Jasmine ventured, "Jared, perhaps it would be best if I did go back to work. I can't bear the thought of being dependent on you and your aunt, and I'll have legal fees to pay, as well."

"Jasmine, quit spouting nonsense," he cut in firmly. "What's mine is yours, so I'll hear no more about your needing to earn an income. Besides, you're going to be a very busy girl these next few months—planning our wedding. Afterward, you're going to be even busier being my wife and taking care of our babies." He nodded toward the orphanage. "If you want to help out here one or two days a week, fine. But from now on, your main occupation is going to be *me*, dear girl."

Though Jared's mention of marriage and babies again touched a responsive chord in Jasmine, she was beginning to resent his refusal to take her misgivings into account. She may as well have been doing her arguing with a tree just now, for all he'd really listened to her! "And I have nothing to say about any of this?"

He pulled her close to him, his eyes bright and fervent above hers. "The only words I want to hear from you, dear heart, are 'I love you, Jared.' "

Jasmine couldn't help but soften at that. She sighed. "But what if I can't say that I love you?"

He smiled tenderly, but there was a glint of steely determination in his eyes as he stroked her face. "Ah, then it's time for *me* to be the teacher."

In the office of St. Mary's Orphan Asylum, Jasmine and Jared told the nuns what Father Grignon had suggested. Both Sister Philomena and Sister Scholastica were appalled.

The orphanage directress, Mother Martha, promised Jasmine that she and the other sisters would keep Jasmine's unfortunate marriage a secret while the dissolution was being sought. When Mother Martha asked Jasmine if she would soon be coming back to teach, the girl promised that she would return at least part-time in the near future.

Jasmine asked Mother Martha if she might show Jared around the orphanage, and the nun graciously consented. Jared was chuckling to himself as he and Jasmine left the orphanage office. "The good sisters were so horrified that they witnessed the sacrilege of your wedding to Boudreau, I'm sure they'll never breathe a word of this story to anyone," he told Jasmine.

She showed Jared around the old building. It was a two-story house that had been converted into an orphanage and school. Several small classrooms, the orphanage office, and a dining hall occupied the bottom floor, while sleeping quarters for the girls and the sisters filled the upstairs. The halls rang with the sounds of young voices—chanting the alphabet, reading aloud, or reciting arithmetic.

As Jasmine and Jared went through the hallways and some of the rooms, he carefully scrutinized the building, noting the peeling wallpaper, the threadbare furniture, the sagging boards on the stairway. Upstairs, as he and Jasmine stood in one of the dormitory-style bedrooms, staring at rows of plain iron beds, he remarked, "This establishment is clean, but in some disrepair, I note."

Jasmine nodded. "Money is always a problem for the orphanage. We do the best we can."

"I'm sure you do." Jared smiled. "Tell me, Jasmine, how did you end up a teacher here? I mean—I've noticed that you're not a nun, my dear."

She blushed. "Oh, have you?" Self-consciously, she went over to one of the beds and smoothed down the coverlet, then leaned over to pick up a rag doll from the floor nearby and lovingly propped it on the pillow. Straightening, she told Jared, "Well, actually, a few years back, I finished up my education here in Natchez at Marcilly Academy, a girl's school established under the sponsorship of the Catholic church. Then, when the Sisters of Charity got ready to open this orphanage, they were shorthanded, so Bishop Chanche suggested that they hire me to help out. You see, my father had just suffered his first heart attack, and the church knew that I needed to line up some sort of employment in order to support him."

"I see," he murmured thoughtfully. "That was very considerate of your bishop." He glanced again at the seemingly endless row of beds. "And how do so many children end up here?"

"Oh, they come here for a variety of reasons," she explained. "A number of the girls were orphaned last year, during that dreadful cholera epidemic we had here in Natchez—and yellow fever has broken up many families over the years, as well. Some of our charges lost their parents in fires or riverboat accidents, some were simply abandoned, and we have a few girls whose mothers were prostitutes and gave them up as infants to St. Mary's."

Jared had been listening intently, his brow furrowed. "How many girls are here in all?"

"Oh—about sixty-five."

"Are you able to find homes for them?"

"For some of them," Jasmine replied. "Actually, we've been most successful in finding homes for the girls who are trained in cooking and sewing. But, frankly, a number of the children have been difficult to place."

He nodded grimly. "Something needs to be done about

this," he said, with an expansive gesture toward their austere surroundings.

Jasmine smiled, feeling quite warmed by Jared's interest in the building and in the children's plight.

They were heading downstairs just as afternoon classes were being released. Jared chuckled as a troupe of girls rushed up to greet Jasmine, asking her a dozen questions about where she'd been. The girls appeared basically healthy, happy and well-fed, Jared noted, but wore clothing that was frayed and ill-sized. Jasmine was saved from answering too many of the forthright questions as Sister Philomena and Sister Scholastica came along, graciously greeting Jasmine and Jared, then shooing the girls out the back door for afternoon recess.

One blond little girl lingered behind, rushing into Jasmine's arms as soon as the others had departed. "Miss Jasmine, you're back so soon!" Maggie cried, clinging to Jasmine's waist. The blue-eyed child glanced at Jared for a moment, then looked back up at her teacher. "Where's the man you were going to marry, Miss Jasmine?"

"I—um— Maggie, I decided not to marry after all," Jasmine replied, her voice breaking with emotion as she held the child she had come to love so much. She hated telling Maggie a lie, but felt the child was much better off not knowing of Claude Boudreau's perfidy.

"Good—I'm glad," Maggie replied, surprising Jasmine. As the two girls drew apart, the child took her teacher's hand and added gravely, "I didn't like that Frenchman."

Jasmine couldn't suppress a short laugh. "You didn't?"

Maggie shook her head. "He had black eyes. I don't trust black eyes." She stared up at Jared with a child's frank curiosity, and he grinned back down at her. "I like him. His eyes are blue, like mine. Are you going to marry him now, Miss Jasmine?"

At this, Jared laughed delightedly and Jasmine blushed to the roots of her hair.

Jared stepped closer to the child, his eyes sparkling. Crouching near the little girl, he said, "You must be Maggie."

"Yes, sir," the child replied, staring back at Jared solemnly.

"I'm Mr. Hampton, a friend of Miss Jasmine's." Winking at Maggie, Jared continued, "Tell me, miss, can you keep a secret?"

Maggie smiled, revealing delightful dimples. "Yes, sir, I'm right fine at secrets."

"Splendid. Well, the secret is that Miss Jasmine and I *are* going to be married. Only we can't tell anyone just yet."

"Jared!" Jasmine scolded, staring at him aghast.

Yet his pleading glance cajoled her into silence, even as Maggie cried to both adults, "Oh, that's so very fine!" Then the child's exuberant expression faded and she bit her lip. Turning to Jasmine, she asked plaintively, "But, will I still get to come live with you, Miss Jasmine—in a few months, like you promised?"

Jasmine stared at Jared, her feelings stark in her eyes. He stood, grinning, and placed a gentle hand on the child's head. "Of course you may come live with us, my dear," he told Maggie. "But don't you think it would be more fun to go home with Miss Jasmine today?"

"Do you mean it?" Maggie cried to Jared, her face bright with joy.

Even as Jasmine tried to question Jared, he held up a hand in warning. "Of course I mean it," he told the child, still holding Jasmine at bay with his eyes. "Tell you what—why don't you two girls visit while I go speak with Mother Martha?" To Maggie, he added, "Miss Jasmine is staying at my aunt's house right now. Aunt Charity has a huge pink house with dozens of rooms. I know she'd adore having you come there to live, too, Maggie."

"Oh, may I, sir?" Maggie exclaimed.

At this, Jasmine had to say something. Over Maggie's head, she whispered tensely, "Jared, I'm really touched by your suggestion. But, I insist that we must not impose on your aunt—"

"Nonsense, Aunt Charity will be beside herself with joy, so don't give it another thought," Jared said with a dismissive gesture, already striding off toward the orphanage office, leaving Jasmine to shake her head at his behavior.

He returned in less than ten minutes, telling the girls that Mother Martha would be delighted to turn Maggie over to Jasmine's custody for the time being. Maggie was ecstatic, and laughed gaily with her new guardian as they went upstairs to pack her things. While Jasmine still feared they would be imposing on Jared's aunt by bringing Maggie to Magnolia Bend, she couldn't contain her own excitement in knowing that she and the child would be together. Perhaps she could have a word with Charity in private, then she and Maggie could slip away.

Moments later, the two girls were leaving the orphanage with Jared when they ran into the mother superior in the central hallway. Beaming, the nun extended her hand to Jared and said graciously, "Mr. Hampton, I must thank you again for your most generous contribution to the orphanage."

"My pleasure," Jared said, shaking the nun's hand.

The nun nodded to Jasmine. "My dear, we'll look forward to seeing you again soon."

Jasmine smiled stiffly as she left with Jared and Maggie. She felt unsettled that Jared had felt obliged to make a donation to the orphanage, and she hoped he hadn't used the money to help persuade Mother Martha to release Maggie to her custody. She was dying to ask Jared about it, but didn't want to risk upsetting Maggie.

On the way back to Charity Hampton's house, Jasmine asked Jared to stop by her cottage on Pearl Street, so she could check on Ephraim. "Do you want to bring him with us to Magnolia Bend?" Jared asked.

It was on the tip of Jasmine's tongue to ask Jared just how many people he was planning to invite to live at his aunt's house without first consulting the poor woman, but then she remembered Maggie's presence and thought better of the idea. Flashing Jared a wooden smile, she left Maggie to visit with him in the buggy and went inside.

The cottage was deserted, but she found Ephraim out back tending their small summer garden. The slave was so shocked to see her that he dropped his hoe. Since Ephraim had not actually been around yesterday when she had married Claude, Jasmine decided it would be best to tell him much the same story she'd told Maggie—that at the last minute, she had simply changed her mind about marrying Claude Boudreau. She mentioned to Ephraim that she and Claude had argued over her decision yesterday, and that afterward, she'd decided to stay with a friend for the time being—Miss Charity Hampton.

Ephraim seemed to take Jasmine's story in stride, and as she left, she told him to get in touch with her at Magnolia Bend if he needed anything.

Heading back to Jared's buggy, Jasmine glanced wistfully at her vine-covered bungalow, breathing deeply of the familiar smell of earth baking in the sun, mixed with the scent of nectar hanging in the heavy summer air. The house held bitter memories, it was true; yet the old walls also represented a safety she hadn't known since she had ventured forth in the world twenty-four hours ago. Seeing the cottage reinforced her feeling that it might be best if she didn't stay with Jared's aunt at Magnolia Bend, but she knew she'd have to take this up with Jared or Charity when Maggie wasn't present. Jared had dangled Magnolia Bend before Maggie like a delicious toy, and the child had grabbed his bait.

Maggie bounced up and down with excitement as Jared turned the barouche onto the driveway of Magnolia Bend. The child's blue eyes were alight with wonder as she surveyed the enormous, verdant grounds, as well as the stately manor house itself. Tugging on Jasmine's sleeve, she asked, "Are we going to stay in that mansion, Miss Jasmine?"

"For the moment, darling," Jasmine replied.

"For as long as you want," Jared added firmly.

As Jared halted his conveyance at the center of the shady drive and helped the two girls alight, Jasmine tossed him a reproachful look, which he ignored.

Inside the house, they found Charity Hampton in the front parlor. "Good afternoon, Aunt," Jared announced cheerfully, tugging Maggie into the elegant room. "I've brought home another surprise." Proudly, he announced, "This is Maggie, from St. Mary's Orphanage. Aunt, how would you like for Maggie to stay here with you and Jasmine?"

Charity Hampton was staring mesmerized at the small blond child, while Maggie glanced at the dowager shyly, her little fingers self-consciously twisting a bit of the faded fabric of her skirt. "Well, hello there, Maggie," Charity said, in a strangely emotional voice. Glancing at Jared, she blinked rapidly and added, "Why, Jared, she's . . . lovely."

"Indeed," he concurred. "Maggie and Jasmine became friends while Jasmine was teaching at the orphanage, so it wouldn't do to separate the two of them now, don't you agree?"

"Oh, I do!" Charity replied.

"Miss Charity," Jasmine put in, "I really think Jared's putting you at a disadvantage here—"

"Nonsense!" Charity said, getting to her feet. "This house has been empty and lonely far too long." She crossed the room, still staring reverently at the child. At Maggie's side, Charity paused, reaching out to touch the fine, white-blond hair on the child's head. Then her trembling hand fell back to her side, and her childlike voice cracked as she said, "Welcome, my darling. You're simply enchanting. In fact, you so remind me of—"

And, to Jasmine's amazement, Miss Charity became choked with tears and abruptly fled the room.

Watching Charity dash out of the parlor, Jasmine and Maggie exchanged startled, confused glances. Jared, not taken aback in the least, clapped his hands and remarked, "Splendid! Didn't I tell you, ladies? My aunt's ecstatic!"

"But, Jared!" Jasmine exclaimed, turning to him in horror. In a low voice, she said, "Your aunt was crying—she ran from the room!"

"Oh, that!" He waved her off. "All women cry when they're happy. Isn't that right, Maggie?" he added, winking at the child.

"I'm not sure, sir," Maggie said, biting her lip and staring at the floral-patterned carpet.

Jasmine glanced at Jared over the child's head. "Jared, could we please talk?" she asked in a whisper.

He nodded, then grinned down at Maggie. "You know what, Maggie? About this time every afternoon, my aunt's cook, Dulcie, takes the most delectable rice cakes out of the oven. How would you like to sample some?''

Maggie brightened. ''Oh, yes, sir, I do want to!'' she cried, clapping her hands.

''Say no more, my pet.'' Jared grabbed Maggie's hand and led her from the room, calling over his shoulder to Jasmine, ''I'll be right back, dear.''

Jasmine paced while Jared was gone, still feeling bewildered by Miss Charity's bizarre behavior moments earlier, and by Jared's blithe dismissal of his aunt's hysterics. She had a feeling that there was much going on in this household that she wasn't being told about.

''You wished to have a word with me, Jasmine?''

Jasmine turned to see Jared standing in the archway, smiling at her. He looked so handsome with the afternoon sun sparkling in his eyes and glinting off his wavy brown hair, that she almost weakened. Then she sternly reminded herself that she must address the problem at hand.

''Jared, don't you think you should check on your aunt?'' He shrugged. ''She's fine.''

''But, Jared, she left the room weeping.'' As he started to reply, she help up a finger and said, ''And if you tell me that she's happy again, I'll throw something at you!''

''Will you?'' He crossed his arms over his chest, a slow grin spreading across his face. ''Then, I won't tell you she's happy.''

''You're exasperating, Jared Hampton, do you know that?'' she asked. ''You're smooth and slick as glass. You simply go about doing precisely as you please, regardless of what I may say, and—and there's no getting to you!''

''Indeed?'' He chuckled as he approached her steadily, a meaningful gleam in his eyes that set her pulses racing. ''And this from the girl who has slain my very heart!''

He reached for her and she dodged him. ''None of that, you!'' she scolded in a trembling tone. ''I don't want—''

''Don't you, love?'' With a purposeful maneuver, he blocked her retreat and caught her to him smartly, laughter dancing in his eyes as she squirmed against him.

''No!'' she cried, pushing against his chest, growing angrier by the moment that he was so successfully distracting her from her purpose. Fearing defeat was imminent, she took the offensive. "Jared, why did you give Mother Martha money for the orphanage? Were you trying to buy Maggie for me?"

He released her so suddenly that she tottered on her feet. "Buy Maggie for you?" he repeated angrily. "Don't be absurd, Jasmine. I simply wished to make a contribution to the orphanage. As for Maggie—I explained to the good sister that we would be legally adopting her as soon as we are wed."

"Jared, you didn't!" Jasmine gasped, so stunned she actually took a step backward.

"I most certainly did."

"After you agreed not to announce your intention to marry me!"

"I never agreed, Jasmine," he pointed out.

"You acknowledged my point!"

"I had to explain to the sister that our intentions toward Maggie are quite serious—that we're not merely toying with the child's affections, and that we're prepared to provide her with a good home."

"*We*? Jared, are you actually telling me you're already certain you want to adopt Maggie?"

"Of course," he replied with maddening self-possession. "Haven't I told you that I want whatever you want, my darling?"

Jasmine was shaking her head in disbelief. "Jared, is this the way you do everything? You only met me last night, and now you want to marry me. Then, the instant you lay eyes on Maggie, you want to adopt her, as well?"

"I'm not a man to belabor a decision, Jasmine."

"I'll say you're not!"

"Dear heart," he murmured silkily, drawing closer to her with that familiar, debilitating sparkle in his eyes, "tell me why you're so angry."

She gestured helplessly. "It's just that you seem to have taken over my entire life."

He grinned. "That makes it pretty simple for you, my pet. All you have to do is to love me—and Maggie."

Jasmine was touched by Jared's words, but still determined to hang on to her independence until she could figure out this baffling man. "Jared, Maggie and I aren't staying here," she announced firmly, tilting her chin defiantly toward him as she spoke. "Once she's finished in the kitchen, we're going back to my house on Pearl Street."

"And break my aunt's heart?" he demanded.

"Jared, from the way Miss Charity acted just now, her heart's already broken! I think the poor woman has suffered enough from my presence, and it's high time for Maggie and me to leave!"

Jared and Jasmine were staring at each other in tense confrontation when young Maggie abruptly danced into the room, her small face lit with a smile and her blond locks bobbing behind her. "Miss Jasmine, Dulcie told me I'm to serve the cakes!" the child cried, holding up a small rattan tray covered with a lace doily and filled with rice cakes.

"Why that's wonderful, darling," Jasmine said.

"Now, you two must sit down over there or you shan't be served," Maggie said importantly, pointing toward the two armchairs flanking the tea table.

Laughing, Jared and Jasmine did as the child directed, dutifully munching on the little cakes Maggie doled out. "The kitchen was such fun!" Maggie told the two excitedly. "Dulcie's going to teach me to cook, and Minnie's going to teach me how to make real cloth on a loom!"

"That's wonderful, darling," Jasmine said.

"Can we stay here forever, Miss Jasmine?" Maggie asked her teacher, the expression on her angelic little face so wistful that it twisted Jasmine's heart.

Before Jasmine could answer, Jared repeated firmly, "As long as you want, Maggie," and Jasmine hadn't the heart to contradict him.

Moments later, Charity joined them, looking her usual, serene self. Spotting the rice cakes, the dowager rang for one of the maids to bring tea. "I must tell you again, Maggie, how very welcome you are here," Charity told the child as she settled herself on the silk damask settee, smoothing her skirts about her. Looking at Jasmine, the old woman smiled ruefully and added, "Forgive me for leaving the room so abruptly, my dear. My joy quite overcame me."

"Please don't apologize—I quite understand," Jasmine replied graciously, even though she didn't understand at all.

The maid brought in tea, and, in the moments that followed, Jared and his aunt became better acquainted with Maggie. "Aunt, isn't it about time for your annual summer soiree?" Jared remarked after a moment.

"Indeed, it is," Charity concurred happily.

"Just think—at your gathering, we'll be able to introduce these two girls to all our friends."

"Why, of course!" Charity said.

Jasmine started to open her mouth to protest, then thought better of the idea as Jared excitedly asked Maggie, "Do you like parties, my pet?"

"Oh, yes—I love parties!" the child cried. "Won't that be fun, Miss Jasmine?" she asked her teacher.

"Of course, dear," Jasmine replied, smiling through gritted teeth, as she again found herself incapable of bursting Maggie's bubble of elation.

"You know, Jared, I must have Miss Laveau start immediately on gowns for our guests to wear at our soiree," Charity remarked as she stirred her tea.

There, Jasmine felt compelled to object. "Miss Charity, please, you mustn't. This is simply too much—"

"It's strictly my pleasure, dear," Charity cut in firmly. Before Jasmine could argue further, she went on brightly to Jared, "I'll start on the guest list first thing tomorrow." Charity clapped her hands, her expression rapt. "Oh, we shall have such fun in this house again, shan't we, loves?"

"Oh, yes, Miss Charity!" Maggie cried.

On the sidelines, Jasmine silently groaned her frustration.

# ★ Eleven ★

After tea, Jared excused himself, saying he had additional business to attend to, and that he would return to his aunt's house later that evening for supper.

Once Jared had departed, Charity took Jasmine and Maggie on a tour of Magnolia Bend. Maggie in particular was enchanted by the beautiful home.

What fascinated Maggie the most was Miss Charity's grand piano in the front parlor—a handsome instrument of mahogany, with cabriole legs and a swivel stool topped with pale yellow velvet. When Miss Charity played a minuet for Maggie on the instrument and promised to give her music lessons, she was enraptured.

Upstairs, Charity took Jasmine and Maggie through six large, airy bedrooms, which were arranged on either side of a long corridor. Charity informed the child that she would occupy the room adjoining Jasmine's on the east side of the house. Maggie was dazzled by the lovely lavender room that was to be hers. "Oh, Miss Jasmine, it's so beautiful—I feel like a princess!" she said, staring captivated at the canopied bed. Watching Maggie's exuberance, Jasmine had to smile. She watched the child rush over to open a window. "Why, Miss Jasmine, just look at the garden below! The honeysuckle's climbing almost to my nose, and I can smell the roses even from here!"

In due course, Charity introduced Jasmine and Maggie to those lush formal gardens downstairs—the path curved between beds filled with blooming roses and spectacular annuals of every color and variety. The aroma of nectar was intoxicating. Maggie was particularly charmed by a huge blooming magnolia tree that towered above them in glossy splendor at the center of the formal area. But then the child's heart was stolen away entirely as she spotted an intricately carved white gazebo on a grassy knoll in the distance. Next to the charming pavilion was a small pond, complete with ducks and water lilies. Maggie raced off toward it with a cry of delight, her skirts and hair flying behind her. Laughing, Charity and Jasmine settled themselves on a stone bench nearby.

Jasmine grew silent as she sat with Charity. As much as she hated the thought of spoiling Maggie's fun, she realized that here, at last, was her opportunity to address her feelings with her hostess and to try to slip away from Magnolia Bend. At last, she blurted out, "Miss Charity, I think Maggie and I should leave."

Charity turned to Jasmine with features aghast.

"I think I should take Maggie back to my cottage on Pearl Street," Jasmine said firmly.

"Why?" Charity asked, looking dismayed. "You know that having you and Maggie here is sheer heaven for me."

Jasmine bit her lip, feeling miserably torn. "It's Jared," she muttered at last.

"Yes, dear?" Charity questioned.

Jasmine began to pace. "Miss Charity, your nephew has truly acted like a prince toward me, rescuing me and bringing me here. But—there's just so much I don't know about him. I just can't commit to marrying him less than a day after— well, after what happened to me on the river. I'm just not ready—" she gestured expansively "—to accept all of this. But Jared just keeps saying he's in love with me, and insisting that we shall wed."

Charity was silent for a long moment, frowning. At last, she said, "Please, Jasmine, do sit down." When Jasmine complied, she continued, "First of all, dear, I'm glad you've shared your feelings with me. When Jared told me earlier today that the two of you were planning to wed, I assumed that you were of a similar mind. At any rate, I can certainly understand that you might have misgivings about marrying my nephew right off, considering what that blackguard did to you. And Jared . . . well, I do love the boy dearly. But, having raised him to adulthood, I'm quite aware of his passionate nature. He can be rather pushy at times, can't he?''

"Oh, yes,'' Jasmine agreed with a rueful laugh.

"Tell me—what makes you think that just because you and Maggie are staying here, you must immediately consent to marrying my nephew?''

Jasmine stammered, "Well, I thought—''

Charity placed a warm hand over Jasmine's. "My dear, I do understand your dilemma. In my heart, I know that you and Jared are perfect for each other, but if you need more time before making a formal commitment, then Jared should accept your wishes like a gentleman. I think that, between the two of us, we can prevail upon him to be more patient. But, please,'' Charity continued earnestly, "you and Maggie simply must stay here. You're both in need of a protector, especially with that Boudreau scoundrel loose in the area, and I've had more fun today than I've had in years. I just don't think I could abide it if the two of you left.''

The quiver of emotion in Charity's voice left no doubt in Jasmine's mind about her sincerity, and her warning about Claude made Jasmine think twice about leaving Magnolia Bend. Of course, logic would seem to dictate that Claude Boudreau wouldn't return to Natchez—but then, what had been logical in Jasmine's life of late? Claude *did* know where she lived, she recalled with a shudder, and he *had* tried to kill her. Now, even the remotest possibility that he might reappear and threaten her—or even Maggie—was enough to tip the scales for Jasmine in Charity's favor.

"You're certain our staying with you is no imposition?'' she asked her hostess, glancing wistfully at Maggie, who was now dancing about the weeping willow tree. "Maggie does love it here. And I agree that it might be wise for us to stay with you—at least, for the time being. I doubt Claude will be coming back around, but still . . .''

"Why take chances?'' Charity finished wisely. "Then, it's settled,'' she continued happily, squeezing Jasmine's hand before she released it. "And if Jared should balk at your needing more time to get your feelings in order, my dear, you just let me know and I'll have a word with him."

Jasmine smiled warmly at her hostess. "You're too kind, Miss Charity."

The two lapsed into silence for a moment. Jasmine felt relieved to have gained Charity's support in her quandary with Jared. She was also quite curious about an earlier remark the woman had made. After a moment, she ventured, "Miss Charity, a few minutes ago you said that you had raised Jared. Would you mind explaining that to me? I mean, you're the only relative Jared has mentioned having here in Natchez, and I was rather curious about his family background. The Hampton family is of English origin, is it not?"

"Oh, yes," Charity replied. "Coming to America to live was actually the idea of my husband, Henry. When he decided that we should sell all our lands and emigrate, his brother, George, had a notion to come along as well—bringing with him his wife, Elizabeth, and Jared, who was a mere lad of five at the time. In due course, we all settled here. We bought cotton plantations across the river in Vidalia, and later built homes here on the Hill, as well. Henry and George went into law practice together in Natchez, and George also started his shipping business Under-the-Hill." With a sigh, Charity added, "I lost Henry five years ago. After being robustly healthy all his life, he just collapsed one day. The doctor said it was his heart."

"I'm so sorry," Jasmine said sincerely. "But—what of Jared's parents? Are they still living here in Natchez?"

Charity's expression abruptly became guarded. "I'm afraid Jared lost both his parents nine years after we came here. The tragedy occurred just days before his fourteenth birthday."

"How terrible! What happened?"

For a moment, Charity said nothing, but Jasmine observed an exquisite struggle of emotion on her heart-shaped face. Finally, Charity offered Jasmine a gesture of contrition and said, "My dear, I'm sorry. I'm afraid that's one of the things you're going to have to take up with Jared. Anyway, following the—tragedy—I brought the boy here to live with me. Once he grew to adulthood, he moved back to his family home, Hampton Hall.''

"I see," Jasmine murmured. Yet she remained very confused about what sort of "tragedy" might have robbed Jared of his parents so suddenly—and, more important, why this event was such a secret, at least from Charity's perspective. This new twist served only to increase Jasmine's determination to refuse a commitment to Jared until she knew him much better.

While Charity and Jasmine were talking, Jared had returned to Hampton Hall, which was also on Woodville Road, a quarter mile east of Magnolia Bend. In the parlor, Jared found Cactus Jack Malone waiting for him, as the two had earlier planned. The black-haired, hawk-nosed man looked restless in the genteel surroundings, and was pacing the carpet in his well-worn boots.

"Afternoon, Jack," Jared called, tossing his hat down on an ebony-inlaid desk.

Jack paused to turn and nod at his employer. "Afternoon, boss."

"Well?" Jared inquired as he folded himself into a leather wing chair next to the desk.

The former scout seated himself gingerly across from Jared, as if he feared his coarse shirt and trousers and dusty leather vest might mar the Chippendale chair Jared had indicated for him. Though many of the furnishings at Hampton Hall were beginning to show wear, and the general effect was one of elegance fraying about the edges, Jack was quite unused to even such fading luxury. He had been raised by his father, an obstreperous Irishman who had run a stand for travelers along the Natchez Trace. His mother, a Choctaw squaw, had died at his birth. Soon after Jack had grown to manhood, his father had been killed in a drunken brawl at the crude tavern. Jack had closed the stand, leaving it to the encroachment of the swamp, and had journeyed off to Texas to seek his fortune. In 1837, he'd joined up with the Texas Rangers as a scout, helping the lawmen fight back fierce Comanche warriors who were attacking frontier communities in the newly formed Republic. Eight years later, when Jack returned to Natchez, he'd already earned a reputation as an intrepid scout, as well as the nickname "Cactus Jack." Jack had become Jared Hampton's trusted employee soon after he returned to the City of the Bluffs.

"I did what you asked, boss," Jack said. "I questioned everyone I could Under-the-Hill about that Boudreau fellow—including all the riverboat pilots in port."

"And?"

Jack shook his head, his thin lips stretched in a grim line beneath the dark slash of his mustache. "Nothin', boss. No one's heard tell of that rascal. It's like Boudreau vanished or somethin'. He could be anywheres by now, I'm thinkin'— New Orleans, or up to St. Louie."

Jared nodded, stroking his jaw, his brow furrowed in thought. After a moment he stood and extracted his wallet from the breast pocket of his coat. Crossing over to Jack, he stuffed several large bills in the other man's hand. "You'll find him for me, won't you, Jack?"

Jack also stood, looking ill at ease as he stared at the money in his hand. "Hey, boss, you don't got to pay me for this— not after all you done for me."

Jared waved him off. "Don't be absurd. I wouldn't dream of not paying you. Besides, you'll have travel expenses. And the information you'll be seeking could easily cost money." Jared smiled cynically. "You won't always be dealing with the most reputable sources."

Jack nodded, pocketing the money. "I'll do whatever it takes, boss, to find that slimy weasel."

"I know you will, Jack, and that's why you're the only man for the job, as far as I'm concerned. I'd track Boudreau myself, but then there would be no one here to protect Miss Jasmine." Jared's jaw was tightly clenched and his fists were balled at his sides as he added fiercely, "I'd die if that snake came slithering back here, trying to do her harm, and I wasn't around."

"You're right, there, boss," Jack concurred solemnly. "The girl needs to be watched and protected, in case that varmint resurfaces."

Jared shook his friend's hand. "Thanks for making that possible for me, Jack."

Jack nodded as he clapped on his hat. "My pleasure."

As Jared's friend started out of the room, Jared called out, "Oh, Jack."

"Yes, boss?"

"Don't kill him," Jared said coolly. "I want that pleasure for myself."

"I wouldn't deny it to you, boss," Jack said with a wry grin. "But if that skunk gives me any grief—"

"Beat him within an inch of his life. But, mind you, only within an inch."

"Understood, boss," came Jack's smooth reply as he turned and strode out of the room.

## ★ Twelve ★

That evening, Jared appeared at Charity's house as promised, to share supper with his aunt, Jasmine, and Maggie. Throughout the meal, Jared and Charity discussed the forthcoming soiree, at which they would introduce Jasmine and Maggie to their friends in the Natchez community. The two decided on a date six weeks hence, to allow plenty of time for preparation.

Jasmine wanted to protest this extravagance, but she knew she had little valid reason to object, since this was an annual affair Charity would be holding regardless, and for her to try to change her hostess's plans would be unpardonably rude. What really bothered Jasmine was the fact that she and Maggie were evidently being assigned the roles of guests of honor.

Yet she dared make no comment in front of the child, who hung on every word Jared and Charity said, her lovely young eyes rapt as she in turn asked a dozen excited questions about the planned occasion.

After the meal, Jasmine put Maggie to bed, then joined Jared and his aunt in the front parlor. Jared stood when she entered the room and strode quickly to her side. "Well, my dear, I expect I'd best be getting on home," he told her. "But I'll come fetch you tomorrow to take you to see Hampton Hall." With a wink, he added, "You'll doubtless want to do some redecorating before we're wed."

That comment made Jasmine see red, and she knew she could no longer postpone her much-needed confrontation with Jared. She could not let him go on blithely running her life this way!

Jasmine managed to stay in control as she said stiffly to her hostess, "Miss Charity, if you'll excuse us, I believe Jared and I need to have a word in the library."

"Of course, dear," Charity replied, and a meaningful glance flitted between the two women.

Jared looked rather bemused as he dutifully crossed over to the library with Jasmine. "Well, dear, what is it?" he asked her once they were alone.

She closed the door and turned to face him squarely. In a trembling voice, she said, "Jared, I've just about lost my patience with you."

He looked totally at a loss. "Indeed? Why?"

"I'm not going to marry you!" she cried.

He looked stunned. "Not ever?"

"Well—not today! I mean, I'm not going to promise I'll marry you today!" She drew a long breath and gestured her exasperation. "Jared, I really appreciate everything you've done for me, but I hardly even know you! I made the mistake of marrying one man I didn't know well enough, and I'm not going to do it again!"

Jared's eyes were wild with disbelief. "You think I'm like him?"

"No, no, of course I don't think you're like him! But,

how can I even know what I want after what happened to me? I refuse to be swept up into another—whirlpool!''

Jared frowned murderously. ''You think I'm sweeping you into a whirlpool? I thought I'd rescued you from one.''

''Of course you did, but—''

''What is it you're saying, Jasmine?''

He looked angry and confused, and she could well understand his feelings. Yet she was determined not to be pressured into making what could be another mistake. In a low but steady voice she informed him, ''Jared, I'm saying that either you back off and give me some breathing room, or . . . I'm through with you.''

He stared at her incredulously. ''You can't mean that.''

As he started toward her, she held up a trembling hand and said, ''Jared, by the saints, if you try to strong-arm me again, I shall scream!''

He paused in his tracks, his mouth falling open. ''You're serious!''

''Indeed I am!''

He cursed under his breath. Then he began to pace, scowling darkly. ''I see,'' he muttered at last. He turned to her and said passionately, ''I really had no idea that my presence was such a trial for you, Jasmine.''

''It's not, Jared. It's just that—''

''You don't want to see me anymore. Isn't that precisely what you're saying?''

''No! No—not precisely!'' she cried miserably, feeling guilty that she had to hurt him this way. ''I do think we should get to know each other better, Jared. But I can't be with you every minute of every day—I'm not ready for that. For now, could we just be friends? After what happened to me, I do need a friend, Jared, but not another fiancé. Not yet.''

He glowered at her for a long moment. ''Actually, Jasmine, being your friend is really the last thing on my mind.''

Jasmine felt warm color rising in her cheeks, and her voice shook as she replied, ''You'll have to accept my wishes, Jared, or I swear, I'll—''

"Yes, dear, you've made your terms quite clear," he cut in bitterly.

A grim silence fell between them, and the tension was thick as they stared at each other. Finally, Jared drew a long breath and said, "Very well, then, dear. I suppose you won't want to help my housekeeper redecorate Hampton Hall after all, now, will you? Marie was so excited when I told her you were coming. She's been after me for ages to do something about the general decline of my quarters."

Jasmine felt an acute stab of guilt at his words. She realized that Jared was turning the knife a bit, but it was working. "Jared, if your housekeeper needs help with your house, I'd be delighted to assist her—but only as your friend. You've been kind to me, and I would like to repay you."

"You don't owe me anything!" he gritted out.

"Nevertheless, I'd feel better if I could do something for you. After all, you have done so much for me. Perhaps I could spend some time with your housekeeper while you're at work. You do work, don't you?"

The taut line of his mouth softened just slightly. "Yes, I do work." He stepped forward and added, "So, I guess there's nothing else for us to say, is there?"

She bit her lip. "No, I guess not."

"In that case, may a friend kiss you good night?"

Before Jasmine could reply, Jared planted a chaste kiss on her forehead and walked out of the room.

Jasmine went upstairs to dress for bed. She still felt quite torn, but relieved that she'd finally made a stand with Jared. She knew she'd hurt him by declaring her independence, but in fairness to herself, he'd really given her no choice. If he truly loved her, as he claimed he did, then he'd simply have to be willing to wait for her. And if he changed his mind about her as quickly as he'd sworn his undying love in the first place, then they were just never meant to be. She was already very fond of Jared, and she hated the thought of losing him entirely, but only time would tell whether they were truly right for each other.

While Jasmine was getting ready for bed, Jared was with Charity in the parlor, venting his frustration. She watched him pace the wool carpet, his expression grim. "You say you and Jasmine had an argument?"

"It's over, Aunt," he announced with a dramatic gesture.

"Over? What happened?"

"Jasmine doesn't love me," he declared.

Charity frowned skeptically at her nephew's words. "Jared, do sit down. It makes a body dizzy just to watch you dashing about." When he complied, she went on calmly, "It can't be as bad as all of that. Tell me what Jasmine said to you."

Once he had finished, Charity nodded wisely. "Actually, I can't blame her for taking such a stand."

"You can't blame her?" he cried through gritted teeth. "Women! Now my own aunt is joining in this—conspiracy!"

"Jared, how else can you expect her to react after what that scoundrel Claude Boudreau did to her?"

Jared leaned forward intently. "Aunt, I know Jasmine has been hurt quite badly, but I love her. I want to cherish her and protect her for the rest of her life. I'd die if I lost her—"

"You're going to lose her for sure if you keep trying to corner her this way," Charity interrupted firmly. When Jared didn't reply, she pressed on. "Jasmine expressed her feelings to me this afternoon. If you don't quit pursuing her so aggressively, she's going to pack herself and Maggie up and leave Magnolia Bend. Then, where would we be? She and Maggie would be off on their own, without a protector, and they'd be out of our lives entirely."

Jared was silent, his eyes narrowed in thought.

"Jared, you're a fine boy, and I've always admired your passionate, idealistic nature," Charity continued. "But you've never had a whit of patience. Now, I raised you to be a gentleman, and a gentleman must honor a lady's wishes in these matters, so quit smothering the girl. As a woman, I have an intuition about these things, and I promise you that if you back off as Jasmine wishes, she'll come around in time."

Jared stood and walked over to the window, his back to Charity. "What can I say, Aunt? It seems the two of you have me boxed in."

At this, Charity had to smile. She was glad Jared couldn't see her expression. Jasmine had won that first small victory, it was true, yet Charity knew the war was far from over. Jared had set his cap on Jasmine, and she knew it would take quite a woman to keep her strong-willed nephew at bay for long!

# ★ Thirteen ★

Jasmine didn't see Jared for several days, and while she missed him more than she would have thought, she also enjoyed having some breathing room.

She spent her time with Maggie, working at the orphanage, and helping Charity plan her soiree. At least once a day, Charity mentioned how delighted she was to have Jasmine and Maggie at Magnolia Bend, and Jasmine did very much enjoy Charity's company. Maggie was also in heaven in her new surroundings, enjoying her studies with Jasmine in the mornings, followed by piano lessons with Charity, and cooking and sewing lessons with the black women in the afternoons. Only once again did Jasmine dare bring up to Charity the fact that she felt she and Maggie might be imposing. When she expressed her misgivings, Charity stoutly declared that Jasmine was breaking her heart with these "constant threats of departure," and thereafter, Jasmine dared not say another word. Charity never pressured Jasmine about Jared, and this greatly endeared her to Jasmine. Actually, she felt relieved that she and Maggie weren't off on their own, considering that Claude Boudreau was still at large.

Charity's dressmaker, Miss Laveau, was a frequent visitor at Magnolia Bend during these days. Despite Jasmine's protests to Charity, the matron insisted that both Jasmine and Maggie be measured for elaborate new wardrobes. The skilled seamstress promised Charity that at least some of the new frocks for the girls would be ready within a few days.

About five days after his argument with Jasmine, Jared finally made another appearance at Magnolia Bend, early one afternoon. He was visiting with Maggie and Charity in the parlor when Jasmine came down to say hello, and she found that the sight of him, sitting in a wing chair with Maggie laughing in his lap, made her heart flutter with longing.

"Miss Jasmine, Uncle Jared is here!" Maggie cried, springing up.

Jasmine smiled ruefully at Maggie's words; Jared was certainly wasting no time ingratiating himself with the child!

After Jasmine and Jared exchanged an awkward greeting, he told her, "If you're still interested in helping Marie redecorate Hampton Hall, I can take you down there now."

"Of course, Jared. As I told you before, I'd be happy to assist your housekeeper," Jasmine replied stiffly.

The two departed for Hampton Hall in Jared's barouche. The atmosphere was strained between them as the horse plodded along in the afternoon heat, although Jared did compliment Jasmine on her new pale-yellow frock, one of the first dresses Miss Laveau had finished for her. Other than that, they did not speak, and Jasmine realized that Jared might well act coolly toward her for some time, following her ultimatum several nights ago in the library. She disliked being the cause of such friction between them, but the alternative —letting Jared take control of her life—was simply out of the question at this point.

Like Magnolia Bend, Hampton Hall was set back on spacious grounds surrounded by huge oaks dripping with Spanish moss. Jasmine found that Jared's home presented an even more impressive facade than did Charity's. Hampton Hall resembled a Greek temple—tall, looming, square and white, with stately columns across the front and a wide gallery spanning all four sides. Neat black shutters flanked all the windows, and the heavily carved front door was crowned by an exquisite cut-glass fanlight.

No sooner had Jared pulled up to the house than a black lad in livery hurried forward to take away the horse and buggy. "Oh, Jared—your house is lovely," Jasmine breathed sincerely, her lungs filling with the scent of summer grass and blooming wisteria as he escorted her up the wide front steps to the gray-blue gallery.

"Hampton Hall is in good repair," he replied, "but the inside could use a woman's touch, as you'll see."

Inside, Jasmine discovered what Jared meant. The arrangement of the downstairs rooms was similar to that of Miss Charity's house—twin parlors flanking one side of a wide central hallway, with a library, office, and dining room on the other side. Yet the furnishings and draperies were shabby in comparison to the rich and stylish appointments back at Magnolia Bend.

Jared and Jasmine had just completed their tour of the downstairs rooms when a handsome, dark-haired woman in a straight-lined black dress, completed by a white apron and a lace-trimmed housecap, came in the back door, a bouquet of freshly cut flowers in her hands. "Ah, hello, Marie," Jared called to her. He turned to Jasmine. "My dear, meet my housekeeper, Marie Bernard." To Marie, he added, "Marie, this is the friend I told you about, Miss Jasmine Dubroc."

Marie Bernard set her flowers down on a nearby pier table and stepped forward with a smile. The housekeeper did appear a bit startled when Jasmine in turn graciously extended her hand. "Miss Dubroc," she murmured with a nod as she accepted the handshake.

Jasmine immediately liked Marie, whose name and slight accent confirmed that she was of French origin. As the housekeeper served Jared and Jasmine tea and cranberry nut bread in the front parlor, Jasmine studied the woman and estimated that Marie must be in her late twenties. She had a lovely long face with dark, dramatic eyes, an aristocratic nose, wide mouth, and strong chin.

After a moment, Jared remarked to the housekeeper, "Marie, Miss Dubroc has graciously consented to direct the redecoration of Hampton Hall. May I count on your cooperation and assistance?"

To Jasmine's pleasure, Marie turned to flash her a warm smile. Then she answered Jared, "Why, of course, sir. I'll look forward to helping Miss Dubroc any way I can."

Watching the Frenchwoman leave the room with the tea tray, Jasmine had to smile at Jared. "Jared, your housekeeper is quite a jewel. But really, did you have to tell her that I'll be in charge of the redecoration? I'd be delighted just to help her."

"Don't be absurd. I want you to oversee this project. And I know Marie will be happy to follow your lead. She's been wanting us to refurbish the house for years."

Jasmine was shaking her head. "I'm still stunned that she has received me so graciously. I mean, she's been running this household for some time, hasn't she? I'd think any woman would be bound to resent another woman intruding on her territory that way."

"Not Marie," Jared replied firmly. "She's a devout Catholic, and kind beyond words. It's a miracle, too, considering her background." At Jasmine's quizzical glance, he explained, "Five years ago, Marie and her family started out for Natchez from Tennessee, along the Natchez Trace. They were waylaid by robbers, and Marie's husband and three children were killed. Marie was—well, after the robbers finished with her, they left her for dead."

"How terrible!" Jasmine gasped. Like most citizens of Natchez, she had heard tales of atrocities committed against travelers on the Natchez Trace. The Trace had been particularly dangerous during the early part of the century, when savage Indians and bloodthirsty villains such as the Harpes brothers and Sam Mason had terrorized innocent sojourners along the route from Nashville to Natchez. Even now, the Trace was far from safe. Its hundreds of miles of trail, twisting through boggy swamp and dense forest, provided countless hideouts for scoundrels of every type.

"My friend Cactus Jack found Marie and brought her her

to Natchez," Jared was now explaining. "He later tried to track the villains who had harmed her, but no luck. Aunt Charity nursed her for months. Marie was quite withdrawn at first, but gradually, she came back to life, and eventually she became my housekeeper."

"It's a wonder that she kept her sanity at all," Jasmine remarked. "Her faith was doubtless her salvation."

"I quite agree." Jared glanced about the room. "Well, my dear, I'm sure you'll find your work's cut out for you here. I want you to redo everything, just as you would have it."

There was a hidden resolve in Jared's words that gave Jasmine pause. Tossing him an admonishing glance, she said, "Jared, as I told you before, I want to help you with this project as a gesture of friendship. But I swear, if you try to take advantage of the situation—"

"You've made your point, Jasmine," he replied with a stiff smile. "And I do appreciate your help."

Jasmine found the light in Jared's eyes hard to read, and she had no idea what he was thinking. She did feel relieved that he wasn't pushing them into another power struggle. She glanced about the room, noting again the frayed chairs, threadbare rugs, and faded draperies. She found it odd that Jared had allowed his furnishings to fall into such a state of disrepair. She knew the neglect wasn't due to a lack of funds. She recalled her conversation with Charity days earlier concerning Jared's parents. Here was an opportunity to find out more about him, she realized. Glancing at him quizzically, she ventured, "Tell me, Jared, who decorated these rooms originally? Was it your mother?"

Abruptly, a mask closed over Jared's countenance. "Yes."

Though she noted the tension in his reply and his features, Jasmine was determined to pursue the matter. She leaned forward in her chair. "Jared, your aunt told me a few days ago that you lost both your parents when you were fourteen. I'm so sorry."

"It happens," came his wooden reply.

"But how?" she asked.

Abruptly, Jared walked over to the window, his broad back to her. His voice was strangely cold and alien as he replied,

"My dear, that you must never again ask me. I'd advise you to leave my past alone and begin thinking about our future together."

Before Jasmine could reply, Jared strode back across the room and tugged on a pull cord that hung from the ceiling. Jasmine heard the distant sound of a bell clanging as Jared informed her more gently, "I'm ringing for Marie to show you the upstairs. It wouldn't do for me to take you on a tour of my sleeping quarters here, my dear." The devilish sparkle had returned to Jared's eyes, and his wink informed her that he'd far from given up his plans to win her over as he added, "At least, not yet."

## ★ Fourteen ★

During the next weeks, Jasmine continued with her new routine at Charity's, and she saw Jared once or twice a week. Along with Captain Rutledge of the *Mississippi Belle*, she and Jared attended a matrimonial tribunal of the Natchez diocese of the Catholic church, giving all necessary testimony so that Jasmine's petition for dissolution of her marriage to Claude Boudreau could be forwarded to Rome. About this same time, Jasmine's petition for legal annulment of her marriage to Claude was granted in a chambers procedure conducted by Judge Henley. All parties who had sworn their secrecy about Jasmine's disastrous marriage—her priest, her lawyer, and Captain Rutledge—continued to keep honorably silent, and there was no unpleasant gossip in the community.

During these days, Jasmine often recalled the afternoon Jared had taken her to see Hampton Hall, and his cold refusal to tell her anything about the deaths of his parents. That experience reinforced her feeling that she'd made the right choice in taking a stand with him. He was a wonder-

ful man, it was true; yet in so many ways, she still didn't
know him.

Jared continued to obey Jasmine's ground rules, not pushing her for an acceptance of his suit. But he did start coming
by on Sundays to take her and Maggie to mass. Jasmine also
knew, from some comments Father Grignon had made, that
Jared was beginning to take instruction in the Catholic
faith—proof that he hadn't given up where she was concerned! While Jasmine was well aware of Jared's true motives
in changing his faith, she found she couldn't be so petty as
to refuse to attend mass with him, or to question his sudden
passion for Catholicism.

Though Jasmine and Jared weren't together that much—
and they were almost never together alone—an attraction
continued to build. When she was with him, she could feel
the tension radiating between them, and sometimes she would
catch him looking at her in an almost haunted way. Neither
of them crossed the invisible dividing line she had laid between them, yet sometimes she felt that in holding him off
this way, she was merely intensifying the poignance of her
feelings for him—certainly, she was exacerbating her own
guilt. Yet she stuck by her decision.

Magnolia Bend continued to be Jasmine's new home and
haven. She was becoming very fond of Charity, and by now,
she was truly beginning to believe that Jared's aunt cherished
having her and Maggie there. Jasmine did love her new life
at the mansion. She found that the anger she had felt toward
her father and Claude Boudreau was beginning to fade in the
light of her new existence. She did try her best to repay
Charity for her kindnesses by entertaining guests who occasionally dropped by while Charity was resting, by helping
to supervise the large staff, and by continuing to assist the
dowager with her plans for the forthcoming soiree.

She also spent a number of hours each week at Hampton
Hall, working with Marie Bernard. She was becoming good
friends with Jared's housekeeper, and she was also grateful
that she was able to repay Jared for some of his kindnesses
toward her. Jasmine and Marie had inventoried all the rooms
at Hampton Hall, and had given Jared lists of needed fabrics

and other supplies. Often, as the two women discussed their plans, they had tea in a small anteroom which served as the housekeeper's office. On one such afternoon, Jasmine decided to see if she could learn more about Jared's past from Marie.

"Marie, I understand you've worked for Mr. Hampton for almost five years now," she remarked to her friend that early September afternoon.

"That is correct, Miss Jasmine," came Marie's reply as the dark-haired woman sipped her tea.

Jasmine hesitated a moment, remembering the things Jared had told her about Marie, then added, "Mr. Hampton told me of the tragic circumstances of your arrival here in Natchez, and I just wanted to tell you how very sorry I am."

Marie lowered her eyes. "Thank you, miss."

Jasmine was tempted to offer additional words of comfort to Marie, yet feared this might open an old wound for her. She decided to proceed with her own subject. "There is something you could help me with, if you would."

"How can I be of service, miss?"

"Well—it's Mr. Hampton. He's been a wonderful friend to me, and he's undoubtedly one of the finest men I've ever met, but he refuses to tell me anything of his family—except that he lost both of his parents when he was fourteen."

"That's true," Marie said carefully.

"But—how did they die?" Jasmine asked.

Marie was silent. A slight frown marred her lovely features as she watched Jasmine closely. At last she said, "I know only of the gossip, miss. And that I don't repeat."

"But, Marie!" Jasmine exclaimed, her green eyes entreating the French woman. "I really feel I need to know more about Jared. I want to understand—"

Marie held up a hand and shook her head. "I'm sorry, Miss Jasmine. There's nothing I can tell you."

Before Jasmine could again protest, a knock came at the door behind them. Marie stood, opened the door, and in strode Cactus Jack Malone, looking trail-worn and weary.

Jack smiled when he saw the Frenchwoman, and removed his dusty hat. "Afternoon, Miss Marie." Spotting Jasmine sitting at the table, he nodded and added awkwardly, "Afternoon, ma'am."

Jasmine murmured a greeting to Jack, then Marie said, "It's good to see you again, Mr. Malone. How may I help you?"

"Is the boss around?"

"No, Mr. Malone," Marie replied, a becoming flush lighting her cheeks. "Mr. Hampton is at his office."

"Figured that's where he'd be," Jack said, then added quickly, "But I just come in off the Trace, and thought mebbe I'd check anyhow—"

Abruptly, Jack stopped speaking, and Marie lowered her eyes. Grimacing as he shifted his hat from hand to hand, he told her contritely, "Hey, Miss Marie, I'm sorry. There I go running off at the mouth, talkin' about the Trace, without giving a thought to what your feelings must be—"

"Mr. Malone, please, it's all right," Marie quickly put in, looking up at him and smiling bravely. "I'll not have you questioning your every word in my presence."

"When I think of what them snake-bellies done to you and your kin—" Jack went on to Marie through gritted teeth, his weathered fingers clenching the rim of his hat, "—why, I could still tear 'um apart with my bare hands."

Marie stepped forward and placed her hand on Jack's sleeve. "Mr. Malone, that was five years ago. We must leave the judging to God."

"If you say so, ma'am," Jack grumbled. But his tight jaw and the vengeful fire sparkling in his dark eyes testified that he remained unconvinced.

"May I offer you some refreshment, Mr. Malone?" Marie went on.

"Thank you, ma'am, but I 'spect I'd best get on down Under-the-Hill and see the boss." Clapping on his hat, Jack nodded to Jasmine. "Ma'am."

As Jack turned and left, Jasmine watched Marie return to her seat. A becoming flush still highlighted the housekeeper's lovely face, confirming for Jasmine what she had already suspected—the housekeeper was attracted to the tall, soft-spoken man who, years before, had rescued her on the

Natchez Trace. And, from the way Jack had looked at Marie just now—from his vehement, protective words—the attraction was mutual.

Jasmine wondered what was keeping the two from seeking their happiness together. She suspected that this wasn't a matter she should pursue with Marie at the moment, but she did feel compelled to comment on another subject. While Jasmine had never told Marie of her father's or Claude Boudreau's perfidy, she did find the Frenchwoman's charity toward the villains who had victimized her and her family on the Trace downright astonishing. "Marie, I think it's so remarkable that you've been able to—well, to put your past behind you," Jasmine told her friend tactfully.

"Oh, I was very bitter at first, after what happened," Marie admitted to Jasmine freely. "But I found my bitterness was hurting me, instead of those who had harmed me. I found no harmony in my heart until I made my peace with my God and buried the past, once and for all."

Jasmine long pondered the wisdom of her friend's words. She realized that while her own hurt had receded, she still felt far from *that* forgiving toward the two men who had harmed her! Oh, no! She was far from willing, just yet, to leave the judging to God.

Jack's visit had brought memories of that betrayal back to mind in another way, as well, since Jasmine now remembered that Jared had once told her that Jack Malone would be helping him track down Claude Boudreau. Was that why Jack had been out on the Trace these past weeks? Had he had any luck? She must be sure to ask Jared.

While Jasmine and Marie were still talking, Cactus Jack was dismounting his horse on Middle Street, in the ramshackle community of Natchez-Under-the-Hill. He tethered his roan gelding to the hitching post, nodded stiffly at a passing whore who was giving him the eye, then entered an office upon whose front window was elaborately etched the words, "Hampton Packet Lines."

"Boss in, Pete?" Jack asked the young, harried-looking clerk, who was busy sifting through bills of lading.

The lad nodded as he removed his horn-rimmed glasses and began cleaning them with his handkerchief. "In his office."

Jack entered the inner office without knocking. Inside, Jared, in gold satin vest and shirtsleeves, was at his desk scrutinizing a freight contract. Spotting Jack, he laid aside the document and stood. "Well, hello, stranger."

Jack grinned as he shook Jared's hand. "Hello, boss." As the two men sat down across from each other, Jack added, "Miss Marie said you'd be here."

A slow grin spread across Jared's face. "Ah, so you've been by the house already. Was it to find me—or to get an eyeful of my pretty housekeeper?"

Jack didn't comment, but a grudging smile tugged at his mouth as he withdrew a cheroot from the pocket of his vest.

"Any luck, Jack?" Jared asked at last.

Jack shook his head as he lit his smoke. "Out on the Trace, I heard tell from one a' them traveling portrait painters that a feller fittin' Boudreau's description was spotted up around Jackson. I went on up there, but no luck. No one there seen the snake."

Jared sighed, shifting in his swivel chair. "So, what are you going to do now, Jack?"

"Head south through the swamp country."

Jared nodded. "Good for you."

"I ain't givin' it up, boss," Jack went on vehemently. "I remember when I found poor little Marie. I never could track down them sidewinders that done that to her on the Trace and killed off all her kin. This time I'm seeing it through to the end." Jack smiled. "You know, she looked mighty fetchin', boss—that Miss Jasmine of yours."

"Was Miss Jasmine at my house?"

"Yes, sir, sittin' right there with Marie, both a' them pretty as summer flowers."

"I can't wait to marry her, Jack," Jared said, sitting back in his chair and crossing his hands behind his neck. "And it would help considerably if you could locate this Boudreau fellow, so we could dispatch him to the devil with due haste. You see, while the legal annulment to Jasmine's marriage has already been granted, it may be months before the church annulment comes through from Rome. So, even though Boudreau is not around, he's effectively putting a crimp in my romance with Miss Jasmine.''

Jack nodded grimly. ''Don't worry, boss. That rascal's days are numbered.''

The next day, Jasmine had an opportunity to question Jared about his search for Claude. She now worked at the orphanage several afternoons a week, while Maggie napped or had special lessons with Charity or the black women. Ephraim came by faithfully on each appointed day to escort her in the buggy to her duties.

That afternoon, just as Jasmine was finishing up a reading circle with some of the older girls, she was called to the orphanage office by Mother Martha. There, she found the directress practically drooling over a colorful collection of fabric bolts—ginghams, dimities, muslins, and wools—which were laid out across her desk. Nearby stood Jared. He smiled when Jasmine stepped into the room.

''Oh, Jasmine!'' Mother Martha cried. ''Look what treasures Mr. Hampton has brought for the girls!''

''They're lovely, Jared,'' Jasmine told him sincerely as she inhaled the crisp scent of the fabrics and fingered a bolt of sturdy wool.

Jared shrugged. ''I had to order quite a few fabrics from New Orleans for the renovation of Hampton Hall. And I thought—why not get something for the girls, as well?''

''You're so generous, Mr. Hampton,'' Mother Martha declared, beaming.

''Indeed,'' Jasmine echoed.

''Jasmine,'' Mother Martha continued, ''why not show Mr. Hampton around the orphanage again, so he may see that his recent donation is being put to good use?''

''Of course, I'd be happy to,'' Jasmine said.

Jared voiced his approval when he saw that the funds he had donated had already been used for new paint and wallpaper in several of the rooms. As they walked about, he also doled out peppermint sticks and sassafras candy to the little girls, who glowed with happiness at receiving the treats and fatherly attention. Jasmine felt quite touched.

Afterward, Jasmine walked Jared out to his barouche. "It was so kind of you to bring the fabrics, Jared," she said as they went down the path together. She wasn't altogether shocked to hear a small catch in her voice.

"My pleasure, dear," he said stiffly.

They now stood awkwardly beneath a tree near Jared's buggy, exchanging a look of quiet longing as a whisper of a breeze stirred the heavy, nectar-soaked air. While Jasmine still felt she was right in holding Jared off, keeping him at a distance this way also provided its own potent brand of frustration, she realized—especially when he endeared himself to her, as he had today.

Finally, he caught a ragged breath and said, "Jasmine . . ."

Knowing he was about to address the continuing impasse of their relationship, she quickly blurted out, "Jared, there's something I must ask you about."

He frowned. "Indeed?"

Jasmine caught a deep breath. "Has Jack been searching for Claude?"

Jared hesitated a moment, then finally admitted, "Yes, dear, he has."

"Has he had any luck?"

"Not so far." Jared gave her a resolute glance. "But if anyone can find him, Jack can. I'd go myself, but then I'd have to leave you here, unprotected."

"I wouldn't want you to go," Jasmine said quickly. "Sometimes, I even think—"

"What, dear?"

Jasmine was silent for a moment, recalling Marie's comments about her own past—words that had left Jasmine enmeshed in thought ever since. At last, she said to Jared, "Sometimes I think it would be better if we left the matter of Claude alone. I mean, Jack—or you—could get hurt."

"We can't let fear keep us from seeking justice."

Jasmine exhaled a long breath. "I suppose you have a point there. It's all just—well, so confusing, I guess."

"Aren't you still angry at Boudreau for what he did to you?" he asked.

"Oh, yes, I am," she admitted readily. "But these past weeks have helped me. And I realize that I should have been more cautious, too. I acted hastily in marrying Claude. I let him bedazzle me."

Jared's laugh was short and bitter. "Jasmine, you had just lost your father, for heaven's sake. Boudreau took advantage of your vulnerability."

"That's true. But I still must accept some of the responsibility—and be more careful next time."

At this, Jared scowled. "Damn it, Jasmine, when are you going to realize that I'm not Claude Boudreau?"

Miserably, she said, "I know you're not him. It's just that—"

He gripped her by the shoulders. "And when are you going to end this torture and give me your consent? I've been very patient these past weeks."

She bit her lip and lowered her eyes, and, with a muttered curse, he released her. He had been patient, in his way, she realized. In fact, she felt somewhat surprised that he'd waited this long to press her again. Looking up at him at last, bravely facing the anguish in his eyes, she said, "Jared, I know you've been patient. And I still hope that in time, things will work out between us. But I just don't know you well enough as yet. For instance, there's the matter of your parents. . . ."

He said nothing, glowering.

She forced herself to press on. "I just can't promise myself to a man who is in some ways still a stranger to me." In a trembling tone, she added, "You see, when I met Claude, I didn't even know what love was, and this time . . ."

"You're still convinced I'll hurt you like he did, aren't you?" he asked bitterly.

Not waiting for her reply, he strode off to his barouche. She hurried back to the orphanage, her path clouded by her tears.

# ★ Fifteen ★

During the next couple of weeks, Jared again backed off. Jasmine felt bad that they'd argued, yet feared that if she conveyed her growing feelings to him, he'd again press her for a commitment she still wasn't ready to give.

Jasmine was somewhat distracted from her difficulties with Jared as Charity's annual late-summer soiree approached. Engraved invitations were dispatched, and Magnolia Bend became a beehive of activity. Never had Jasmine seen a household in such motion! Every room in the large house was cleaned from top to bottom—rugs were shaken and new matting laid, upholstery and drapes brushed, fireplaces swept, furniture polished to a high sheen, lamps and chandeliers cleaned. Two black women seemed to become permanent fixtures in the dining room, polishing every piece of silver the Hamptons owned. Every mirror and window in Magnolia Bend gleamed.

Upstairs, all three available bedrooms were aired and cleaned for possible overnight guests. Out back in the kitchen, activities never seemed to cease, as every piece of linen the household owned was washed, ironed, and mended, if necessary. Later, as the big day grew closer, the cooking and baking began, to make ready all the succulent dishes planned for the elaborate buffet. Anyone venturing outside in the mid-September warmth caught the mingled aromas of a dozen delicacies being baked in the kitchen's huge stone ovens.

Charity planned the menus and directed the slaves with a firm but loving hand, while Jasmine and Maggie pitched in to help wherever they could. Jasmine removed and dusted every book in the library, while Maggie, at Charity's request, went from room to room, carefully cleaning all the knick-knacks and gewgaws gracing the ornate rosewood tables. Jasmine had to cross herself when she saw Maggie handling Staffordshire figurines or Meissen porcelain, yet the child's touch was sure and careful, and there were no accidents. Charity, noting Jasmine's anxiety about the child, said simply, "Don't fret yourself, my dear. How is Maggie to learn, if we don't trust her to do things?" Jasmine had to agree.

Miss Laveau was a frequent visitor to the house during these days, as she worked on Maggie's and Jasmine's new wardrobes. By the week of the planned party, the armoires of both girls were bursting at the seams.

Maggie was in heaven, and it warmed Jasmine's heart to watch the child greet each new day with exuberance and confidence. "We're just like Cinderella, Miss Jasmine," the child remarked to her guardian one day. "And Uncle Jared is the prince."

Jasmine had to smile at this analogy. Jared was in many ways a princely character, and he and Maggie had certainly grown crazy about each other.

Jasmine found she did feel quite like Cinderella on the day of the party itself. All was in readiness in the house by midday, except for last-minute cooking and the serving, which would be completed by the servants. Thus Charity, Jasmine, and Maggie were able to rest in the afternoon and then dress in leisurely fashion, each attended by her maid.

Despite their unhurried pace that day, Jasmine was nervous. She knew that several distinguished guests would be present that evening, including Senator and Mrs. Jefferson Davis and Governor and Mrs. John Quitman. She hoped that she would be well-received into the upper echelon of Natchez society.

Her confidence increased as she dressed for the occasion. Sarah did an exquisite job on her hair. She parted it in the middle and pulled it into a bun at the back, with corkscrew curls trailing down the nape of her neck. Then Sarah helped Jasmine don her corset, petticoats, and formal dress, which was breathtakingly lovely. The frock was fashioned of em-

erald-green satin, full-skirted, with a ruffled hem and a scal-
loped lace overskirt parted in the center. The bodice was
tight, the neckline fashionably low, the sleeves puffed and
trimmed with delicate lace. Fully dressed, Jasmine could not
believe the vision that stared back at her from her mirror—
her green eyes had never looked quite so vivid, her wheat-
colored hair gleamed in the light of the lamp, and her willowy
torso and firm breasts were set off to perfection by the lovely
lines of the gown. She felt truly beautiful for the first time
in her life!

Sarah stood by her side, preening happily. "Miz Jasmine,
you is goin' ter be the belle of the ball tonight!"

"Thanks, Sarah," Jasmine replied, unable to restrain a
smile of pure joy.

A knock came at the door, and after Jasmine called out,
"Come in," she was amazed to watch Jared and Maggie step
into the room, hand in hand, both elegantly dressed for the
party. Her first thought was of the impropriety of the situation.
"Jared, what are you doing here?" she asked, blushing.

Jared's blue eyes swept over Jasmine with astonishment
and reverence. "My God, you're enchanting!" he said, his
eyes devouring her in the gorgeous frock. She blushed and
he grinned, handing her a velvet-covered case. "I've brought
you a present, my dear. And don't fret yourself about the
propriety of my being here. Maggie and Sarah will serve as
chaperones, won't you, girls?"

Both girls giggled, as Maggie rushed forward to Jasmine's
side, holding out her right hand. "Miss Jasmine, you're so
very pretty! And look what Uncle Jared gave me!"

Jasmine knelt by the child, studying a ring on Maggie's
right hand—an exquisite cluster of small opals set on a thin
gold band. "Oh, Jared, how sweet of you," she cried, looking up at him and smiling tremulously.

"Doesn't Maggie look wonderful?"

"She does, indeed," Jasmine said, standing. The child
wore a mouth-watering party dress of pale blue taffeta, which
exactly matched her lovely little eyes. The frock was tied at
the waist with a deep-blue velvet sash. Maggie's outfit was
completed by embroidered pantalets, which extended below

the mid-calf-length skirt, along with dainty blue satin slippers tied with ribbons at the ankles. A matching bow graced her hair, which was pulled back to show off her precious oval face; large, sausage shaped curls trailed down the child's neck and back. Jasmine mused that Maggie's maid, Hattie, had done a splendid job of dressing her.

Jared stepped closer to Jasmine. "Now it's time for your present, my dear," he said, again extending the black velvet case. His vibrant blue gaze flicked over her again. "Lord, but I can't take my eyes off you!"

Jasmine again blushed at Jared's compliment as he stepped even closer. He looked so handsome and masterful in his stylish black wool cutaway coat and matching trousers, his elegant attire completed by a black satin waistcoat and pleated linen shirt with white lace jabot. The thick waves of his light-brown hair gleamed in the lamplight and his blue eyes sparkled with devotion as he stared at her. His smile alone was enough to melt her heart, to make her rashly want to stretch upward and kiss that handsome, chiseled mouth of his. There had been such distance between them for so long, she thought achingly, and tonight, she just wanted them to be happy and enjoy this occasion together. Yet as she stared down at the box in his strong, tanned hands, she felt compelled to protest. "Jared, please, a gift is not necessary. You've done too much for me already."

"Nonsense, Jasmine," Jared said firmly, forcing the box into her hands.

When Maggie clapped her hands and cried delightedly, "Miss Jasmine, open your present, please!" Jasmine knew further protest was futile.

Yet when she opened the elegant, satin-lined box, her first gasped words were, "Oh, no, Jared, I can't!" For staring back at her were two of the most exquisite emeralds she had ever seen in her life!

Both were square-cut. The light dazzled off their myriad, perfect facets. The larger one was one hung from a resplendent gold-filigree chain, while the smaller was set on a heavy gold band.

Jared chuckled as he observed Jasmine's awed reaction to

the spectacular jewels. "Oh, yes, you can," he scolded back. "These belonged to my mother," he went on, almost too casually. "And they were meant for the woman I marry."

"Jared!" she cried, looking up at him beseechingly. "In that case, it's quite impossible that I accept them."

"Then, wear them just for tonight," he reasoned, entreating her with his blue eyes. "They do match your dress perfectly, don't they, dear?"

Jasmine was biting her lip, wavering, when Maggie began to jump up and down. "Oh, yes, Miss Jasmine, do wear them! Please do!"

Jasmine found she couldn't fight both of them. "All right, I'll wear them—but only for tonight."

He grinned as he slipped the ring on her finger and fastened the chain around her neck.

"Oh, Miss Jasmine, you look like a princess!" Maggie cried.

"I feel like one, dear," Jasmine replied, the emotion of the moment making her voice hoarse.

"Well, ladies, shall we go downstairs, then?" Jared asked, proudly extending an arm to each girl.

They left the room together. Maggie, full of excitement, bounded down the stairway ahead of the couple. Jasmine found Maggie's exuberance contagious. She did feel proud to be walking down the stairs on Jared's arm. Looking at him, so strong and handsome beside her, it seemed to her at that moment that no problem would be too difficult for them to surmount.

At the staircase landing, Jared paused to draw Jasmine into his arms for their first kiss in many weeks. His lips pressed against hers fleetingly but warmly, and she didn't resist him. "I know you're not ready to hear everything I feel, my love," he told her with a catch in his voice as his gleaming gaze again raked over her. "But, Lord, I must tell you how incredibly beautiful you are. Those emeralds can't begin to compare with your eyes, my darling."

"You do make me feel beautiful, Jared," she managed to whisper back tremulously.

The two were staring at each other, trancelike, when Miss

Charity's fretful voice drifted up to them. "Jared, Jasmine! Please come on down here before our guests arrive, and make sure I haven't forgotten anything."

They dutifully continued down the stairs, joining Maggie and Charity in the large central hallway. Despite Charity's obvious case of nerves, she looked quite regal tonight in a straight-lined dress of gold silk. Around her neck was a stunning necklace of fire-bright topaz. "Miss Charity, you look so pretty," Jasmine exclaimed.

"And you look wonderful, my dear," Charity returned with a warm smile. "Now, all of you, have a good look around and make sure everything is ready."

The foursome toured the downstairs rooms together. The house had never looked lovelier, Jasmine noted. Cut flowers in silver bowls and crystal vases were placed around the rooms. The fragrance of roses, camellias, and gardenias filled the air. In the double parlors, the furniture had been lined up along the walls and the rugs removed to provide plenty of space for dancing. In the front parlor, collections of Strauss and Chopin waltzes were laid out on the piano, as well as on two nearby music stands. A pianist and two violinists had been engaged from the Philharmonic Club to provide dancing music.

In the dining room, two formally dressed male servants stood ready to serve at the lavish buffet, which included almost every tempting dish imaginable, from imported caviar and snails bourguignonne, to pickled herring and Virginia ham. A large sterling silver punch bowl dominated the sideboard, its base encircled by huge, fragrant magnolia blossoms.

"Oh, Miss Charity, everything looks exquisite—and delectable!" Jasmine said. "Don't you agree, Jared?"

"You've outdone yourself, Aunt," he said proudly.

At that point, Maggie gave her own endorsement, by adding, "May I have a cookie, Miss Charity?"

The three adults laughed, as Miss Charity told Maggie, "Of course, darling. But don't you fill up on sweets tonight, or you'll take sick and miss all the fun. I had Dulcie fry up some chicken drumsticks just for you." As Maggie danced off toward the sideboard, Charity asked, "Are you sure I haven't neglected to do anything, loves?"

Even as the two hastened to set her at her ease, there came a knock at the front door. "Oh, dear!" Charity exclaimed. "Our guests are already arriving."

"I'll greet them," Jared put in quickly. With a wink, he added, "Jasmine, will you kindly reassure my aunt that she hasn't forgotten anything?"

As Jared left the room, Charity turned to Jasmine. "Forgive my case of nerves, dear. If only I were twenty years younger. But, alas, when one reaches my age—"

"Miss Charity, you're doing splendidly—much better than I could under the circumstances," Jasmine hastened to tell her, stepping closer to squeeze her hand. "Everything looks so very lovely—and you've gone to so much trouble. . . ."

"Oh, it's nothing," Charity replied with typical modesty. Then, as voices drifted into the room from the hallway, Charity squared her small shoulders and added, "Well, my dear, shall we go greet our guests?"

The two women strolled out into the central hallway, where Jasmine spotted an older couple with a young woman who was obviously their daughter. The beautiful girl was hanging onto Jared's arm as if she owned him.

The girl's hair was a shiny ebony, falling in a riot of curls about her face and shoulders. Her features were perfect—her mouth full and red, her cheeks pink, her eyes dark and mysterious. Her gown—white and full-skirted, with a tight, low bodice interlaced with pale blue ribbons—set off her voluptuous figure to perfection.

The girl turned slightly as Jasmine and Charity entered the hallway. Her gaze flicked over Charity with casual indifference, then came to rest on Jasmine with cool suspicion.

Seeing the girl with Jared, Jasmine was hit by a powerful wave of emotion. She realized that she felt quite suddenly—and quite insanely—jealous, and that it was all she could do not to rush across the hallway and tear that smug young woman away from Jared.

Jared gently disengaged the dark-haired girl's fingers from

his arm. Stepping over next to Jasmine and Charity, he took Jasmine's hand and said proudly to the guests, "Mr. and Mrs. Peavy, Melissa, you of course know my aunt, Mrs. Charity Hampton. Now it's my greatest pleasure to introduce to you my fiancée, Miss Jasmine Dubroc."

# ★ Sixteen ★

There was a moment of tense silence in the hallway. The three Peavys stood staring at Jared, Jasmine, and Charity, almost as if battle lines were being drawn. Jasmine was too flabbergasted to speak—Jared was making their engagement public tonight, knowing full well that she hadn't given her consent!

Yet, wasn't that every bit his style? she asked herself ruefully. She remembered the emeralds, his telling her they were for the woman he married. Obviously, Jared had exhausted his meager patience and had decided to force her hand in public.

It was a skillful maneuver on his part, she had to concede.

Before Jasmine could really analyze her confused thoughts, Mr. and Mrs. Peavy broke the silence, stiffly greeting Charity and Jasmine and voicing polite, restrained congratulations to the newly affianced couple. Yet all the time, their daughter was staring murder at Jasmine!

It did not take Jasmine long to absorb Melissa's scathing gaze—the girl's dark eyes gleamed with malice as they rested on Jasmine, and Melissa's heaving bosom, her flared nostrils, and her petulantly set mouth revealed all too eloquently her animosity toward Jasmine. The hallway seemed to throb with the force of the girl's antagonism. Jasmine realized she was tempted to flash Melissa a smug smile!

"Well, now, may I offer you folks some refreshment?" Charity was asking the Peavys, as if oblivious to the undercurrent of hostility in the hallway.

Yet Jasmine soon realized that Charity was doubtless all too conscious of the palpable tension, for she quickly and graciously maneuvered the three Peavys into the dining room beyond.

As soon as they were alone, Jasmine confronted Jared. Her voice trembled with emotion as she demanded, "Why did you tell the Peavys that I'm your fiancée?"

"It seemed the thing to say at the moment."

"Blast it, Jared, you agreed that we'd wait."

"Jasmine, in the eyes of the law, your marriage to Boudreau is already null and void. I intend to marry you the minute the church annulment comes through from Rome. Bearing that in mind, I don't see how we can wait any longer to make public our intentions."

"But—" Seething with helpless frustration, she cried, "Thanks for asking me! Jared, you promised me you'd back off!"

"Jasmine, I think I've been patient quite long enough."

She planted her hands on her hips. "Indeed? Well, if you persist in telling people that we're betrothed, I'll simply have to set them straight with an announcement of my own tonight."

"And ruin my aunt's party?" he asked with a short, disbelieving laugh. His grin continued to infuriate her. "Now, come here."

"No."

Jared dragged her into his arms, and once again pressed his lips on hers. This was no brotherly kiss, but a thorough and passionate ravishment of her senses which left her dizzy and breathless. As Jasmine clung to him afterward, he chuckled and said, "Do you really not want to marry me, love?" As she would have protested, he laid a finger across her tender mouth and murmured, "Now, don't lie. You know, a moment ago, I watched quite a green-eyed monster emerge when you saw me with Melissa."

Jasmine's cheeks felt scalded now; so he *had* noticed her

jealous expression when she saw him with Melissa! Before she could comment, another knock came at the front door and Jared released her, saying, "Excuse me, dear."

Jasmine reached out and caught his arm. "What's going on between you and Melissa?"

He glanced at her, still looking maddeningly amused. "Why, Jasmine, I believe you are quite jealous." As she tried to stammer a retort, he added firmly, "Darling, there's nothing between me and Melissa. At one time, we were keeping company, but that particular courtship died a natural death a long time ago. Now, if you'll kindly excuse me—"

Jared turned and opened the front door to admit a lavishly dressed elderly couple. Jasmine frowned, dissatisfied by Jared's answers to her questions—especially as she recalled the way Melissa had hung on his arm, and the venomous look the girl had tossed her when Jared had announced that she was his fiancée.

As Jared ushered Mr. and Mrs. David Hunt over to meet her, Jasmine forced herself to smile, and graciously extended her hand to the distinguished couple. Through the corner of her eye, she caught Melissa again staring at her malevolently. The girl had strolled out to the dining room archway, and now stood sipping punch from a silver cup as she coldly observed the scene near the front door.

One thing was for certain, Jasmine reflected grimly. Whatever had occurred between Jared and this dark-haired beauty in the past, the affair was far from dead and buried as far as Melissa Peavy was concerned!

An hour later, Magnolia Bend was teeming with happy guests, and the air was thick with laughter, music, and the mingled aromas of dozens of succulent foods. Jared kept Jasmine by his side every second, introducing her to one and all as his fiancée, and she accepted the congratulations everyone extended with as much grace as possible. Inwardly, she still resented his peremptory announcement of their betrothal. But, as he'd cleverly pointed out in the hallway, she just couldn't bring herself to spoil Charity's party by issuing a surely scandalous denial.

Jasmine also found, much to her astonishment, that she didn't feel nearly as angry toward Jared as she should have, under the circumstances. She realized that she may have precipitated his declaration tonight, for he had indeed noticed the jealousy flashing in her eyes when she had seen him with Melissa. She was coming to feel very possessive toward him, she realized. Could she totally blame him for feeling the same way toward her—for wanting to stake his claim in public? Truth to tell, she'd been a mere heartbeat away from making a very public statement herself, by flying across the hallway and tearing out huge handfuls of Melissa Peavy's hair! Amazing—yet that was precisely how she had felt when she'd seen the girl clinging to him.

Jasmine continued to circulate with Jared, greeting guests. To her immense pleasure, the citizens of Natchez accepted her with grace and eloquence. She struggled to remember the names of all the prominent local citizens she met—the Surgets of Clifton, the Jenkinses of Elgin, the Bislands of Mount Repose, the Elliots of D'evereux. She enjoyed talking with merchant Frederick Stanton about the house he would soon begin building for his family on High Street, as well as his planned trip to Europe to purchase furnishings. She was also pleased to meet Peter Little and his deeply religious wife, Eliza; the elderly couple brought along with them two traveling clergymen who were staying in a guest house the Littles called "The Parsonage." Every well-known citizen from the Natchez region seemed to be in attendance.

A highlight of the evening for Jasmine was meeting Senator and Mrs. Jefferson Davis from Brierfield Plantation near Vicksburg. The Davises, who had married five years earlier here in Natchez, were visiting Mrs. Davis's parents, Mr. and Mrs. William Howell, of the Briers. Jasmine noted that the soft-spoken, graying senator seemed to be at least twenty years older than his beautiful, vivacious wife, Varina. Varina, dressed in a lavender voile gown, congratulated Jasmine warmly on her engagement to Jared. "I know you'll love being married, my dear," the charming brunette confided, her eyes fixed devotedly on her distinguished husband across the room. "My years with Mr. Davis have been wonderful."

Soon thereafter, dashing, white-haired Mississippi governor John A. Quitman arrived with his wife, Eliza. Quitman was an outspoken advocate of slavery, and he soon launched into an animated discussion with Jefferson Davis and several other gentlemen regarding the compromise just passed in Congress admitting California to the Union as a free state, and giving the territories of Utah and New Mexico the right of individual determination where slavery was concerned. Davis and Quitman were both heroes of the Mexican War, at the conclusion of which these territories had been acquired, and both had been violently opposed to Henry Clay's measure. Now, fuming at the passage of the Compromise, both men were arguing that Mississippi should secede from the Union. A southern rights convention had already met in June in Nashville, at the call of Quitman, and would reconvene in November. While both men had had difficulty gathering enough popular support for their views, a few advocates gathered about the two tonight, while other prominent citizens— particularly, millionaires Frank Surget and Stephen Duncan —stepped forward to denounce secession as folly.

Jared soon decided it was time to end the political discussion. Once Jasmine had been introduced to one and all, he grabbed Maggie, who was streaking by, stuffing cookies in her mouth, and called out for everyone's attention.

With Maggie on one side, Jasmine on the other, Jared announced, "Ladies and gentlemen, I call for a toast." Holding up his silver cup and gazing at Jasmine, he said proudly, "To my future bride, Jasmine Dubroc, and to my future daughter, Maggie."

The guests cheered as they toasted with Jared, and afterward, the room erupted in a round of applause and new congratulations. Though Jasmine's cheeks were burning with embarrassment at the unexpected attention, she couldn't help but feel a sense of perverse satisfaction as she again caught the heat of Melissa Peavy's glare from across the room. She realized that Jared's making their plans known to the entire Natchez community did banish some of her doubts regarding the steadfastness of his intentions. That didn't excuse his high-handedess, of course, and she was far from completely convinced that they should indeed marry. Yet she knew she would have to take up these things with him later, in private.

The guests drank, visited, and sampled the buffet, as the music began in the front parlor. In due course, Maggie ran out of energy. She collapsed on a fainting couch in the hallway and fell asleep. Jared carried her upstairs to her maid.

When he returned, he pulled Jasmine into his arms for a dance, and they waltzed in the center of the front parlor, along with several other couples. Having drunk two cupfuls of tea punch generously laced with rum, Jasmine found she was feeling rather euphoric. And she couldn't help but feel intensely relieved that she'd been so well received. It was hard to remain too angry at Jared when she was drifting in his arms this way, surrounded by his warmth, her senses filled with the male scent of him.

After a moment, he asked, "Have you forgiven me for making the announcement, Jasmine?"

Jasmine stared at her left hand on Jared's shoulder, watching the light sparkle off the splendid emerald he had earlier placed on her finger. Ruefully, she asked, "You planned all along to make an announcement tonight, didn't you, Jared?"

He laughed, but his arms trembled slightly as he drew her closer. "Oh, yes, darling. There's no way I'm letting you slip away from me."

His nearness was making her heart hammer wildly, but she managed to protest, "I guess I've been foolish, then, to think you'd honor my wishes."

With his lips close to her ear, he whispered seductively, "Do you truly think you're foolish, my darling?"

Jasmine dared not tell Jared what she was really feeling as he continued to sweep her about the room to the delightful music. They danced together to several more waltzes, and sampled the hearty buffet. As the evening wore on, the tall Jeffersonian windows at the back of the house were raised, and guests began spilling out onto the back veranda for a breath of cool night air. Jasmine and Jared were about to venture outside together, when Captain Tom Leathers, a tall, stocky man Jasmine had been introduced to earlier, joined them near the open back door. Nodding politely toward Jasmine, the bearded man grinned and said to Jared, "May I have a word with you in private, Hampton?"

Jared glanced at Jasmine, and when she hastily said, "Please, Jared, go ahead," the two men excused themselves and moved off toward the library.

Jasmine frowned, wondering what business they had to discuss. But before she could really think about it, Melissa Peavy joined her at the back of the parlor. "Please, Miss Dubroc, I must talk to you," the girl said to Jasmine in an urgent tone.

"Yes?" Jasmine queried sharply, frowning.

Melissa glanced about at the crowded room, then grabbed Jasmine's arm. "Let's go outside where we won't be heard."

Amid Jasmine's protests, Melissa pulled her outside, maneuvering her between the laughing couples on the back veranda to a secluded corner of the dark porch.

Disengaging her arm from Melissa's fingers, Jasmine eyed the girl coolly and demanded, "What did you wish to speak with me about, Miss Peavy?"

Melissa stared at Jasmine for a moment, and Jasmine found her expression hard to read in the deep shadows of the porch. "I must speak to you about Jared," the girl finally admitted, the words laced heavily with bitterness.

"Oh? What about Jared?" Jasmine asked cautiously.

Melissa got straight to the point, her voice a low, cutting hiss. "You may think you know Jared Hampton, Miss Dubroc, but let me assure you that you don't. Jared's a philanderer, pure and simple. He goes through life toying with ladies' affections, then breaking their hearts. I know it's true, for Jared was once engaged to me—and he betrayed my love!"

"No!" Jasmine said sharply. "I don't believe you!"

"Oh, but it's true." As Melissa stepped closer, a narrow beam of light threaded its way through the back window, illuminating the gleam of malicious pleasure in the girl's dark eyes. "Three years ago, Jared was my fiancé. He seduced me, vowing he'd marry me soon, then he broke his word and cast me aside like a broken toy." As Jasmine gasped, Melissa added, "You just wait, it will be the same with you. Just ask yourself this, Miss Dubroc—why should Jared want you, a penniless schoolteacher?''

Jasmine felt color burn her cheeks at Melissa's tactless words. ''But—how did you know—''

Melissa gestured in deprecation. ''Oh, it's all over town that Jared's latest flame is an old maid from a no-account family never received in Natchez society.'' As Jasmine listened in deepening horror, Melissa continued cruelly, ''I know what you're thinking—that everyone here tonight has been polite to your face. Right, Miss Dubroc? But don't delude yourself. No one here would dare insult Jared publicly, since the Hamptons are one of the wealthiest, most powerful families in the region. But make no mistake, my dear— privately, you're the laughingstock of the entire community. Everyone knows what a pathetic fool you are to let Jared toy with your affections this way—''

''Stop it!'' Jasmine cried. ''I'll hear no more—''

''You'll hear plenty more, Miss Dubroc,'' Melissa snapped, closing in ruthlessly and grabbing Jasmine's arm, ''because you know I'm speaking the truth. Just ask yourself this—what do you really know about Jared Hampton?''

''What are you saying?''

Melissa's long fingernails were digging into Jasmine's flesh, painfully so. ''He has a dark side, Miss Dubroc. He disappears on the *River Witch* for days on end, gambling and doing God knows what else. And it's rumored that madness runs in his family. His parents . . . their deaths caused the most ghastly scandal here. And just look what an addlebrain his aunt is—''

''Enough!'' Jasmine cut in furiously, flinging off Melissa's touch. ''I'll not have you say such things about Jared, or Miss Charity, who is the dearest, sanest person I know!''

With those words, Jasmine turned to flee Melissa, but the other girl's cruel laughter followed her back to the parlor. ''You can run away from me, Miss Dubroc,'' the girl called after her, ''but can you hide from the truth?''

Jasmine rushed for the safety of the parlor, blinking away hot tears, as several couples watched in confusion.

* * *

"It's a damned shame about the *Dewey*," Jared was now saying to his friend Tom Leathers, captain of the *Natchez*.

Leathers nodded. "I saw her blow last week when she hit that snag—down near Bacon's Landing, where all the dead trees are. It looked like the world coming to an end when she went up—no survivors, either. I've never seen anything worse, except for the fire in the St. Louis harbor when I was up there last May."

Jared nodded grimly, then said, "Tom, why did you call me aside this way? I know it wasn't to discuss river disasters."

A grin split Leathers's robust face. "Well, no, not exactly." He drew a long drag on his cigar, then said, "Actually, I heard a rumor about you, Hampton."

Jared felt his spine stiffen. "Oh?"

Leathers's grin widened as he blew out smoke and asked, "Is it true that about six weeks ago, you took the *Witch* out for a gambling party, and you later pulled a half-naked lady out of the Mississippi?"

Jared's voice became cold as ice. "Who told you this?"

Leathers shrugged. "I heard it while I was playing cards at the Scarlet Slipper."

Jared stepped closer to Leathers and spoke in a low, deadly earnest tone. "That's the most absurd, insulting rumor I've ever heard in my life, Leathers! Repeat one word of it to anyone and I'll call you out!"

The flabbergasted steamboat captain turned white at Jared's unexpected challenge. Hampton was rumored to be an excellent shot, and Tom Leathers had no desire to tangle with this man, who was, above all, a valued friend. Almost dropping his brandy snifter, Leathers blustered, "Hey, Hampton, I didn't mean anything. I was just having a bit of fun. But I give you my word as a gentleman that I'll not breathe a word of what I heard—"

"Good," Jared cut in briskly, steely anger glinting in his blue eyes as he set down his brandy snifter. "Now, I think it's time for you to leave, Leathers."

At Jared's harsh dictate, Tom Leathers slammed down his own glass and snuffed out his cigar. "Sure, Hampton, whatever you say. But I never thought I'd see the day when my word doesn't mean spit to you."

Leathers turned his back on Jared and strode from the room with dignity. Jared wasn't proud of his actions just now, and he knew he must apologize later. Leathers was a loyal friend, and Jared knew that just as he'd said, threats were not necessary in order to secure his cooperation and silence.

But Jared had panicked when Tom had repeated the rumor about Jasmine. The story proved that there was no way Jared could totally cover up what had happened to the woman he loved on the river that fateful night. True, a wild story circulated by a bunch of gamblers Under-the-Hill would likely be given little credence in Natchez proper. Even if the rumor should navigate up the Hill, the citizens would likely assume that Jared had pulled a drunken floozy from the river, not the woman to whom he'd just announced his engagement.

What worried Jared the most was what Jasmine might think, how she might react, if the rumor became widespread. Knowing how proud and vulnerable she was, he could easily visualize her breaking their engagement, rather than allowing the Hampton family to become tainted by scandal.

"Damn!" he muttered, snuffing out his cigar. How he wished he could strangle Claude Boudreau at this very moment for ever getting them in such a predicament. If only Jasmine were truly his—if only they could marry this night —then he'd never have to worry about losing her!

Jared poured himself another stiff brandy and downed it quickly, a gleam of relentless determination in his blue eyes. One way or another, the girl was going to be his!

He was heading purposefully back into the front parlor in search of Jasmine when Melissa accosted him, grabbing his arm. "Jared, darling," she said, batting her black eyelashes at him, "you haven't danced a single waltz with me tonight. And it's been so very long since we've had a chance to chat."

Jared firmly pried Melissa's fingers from his sleeve. "Melissa, we have nothing to say. And the only woman I'm dancing with tonight is the woman I love—who, I'm afraid, happens not to be you." He smiled nastily. "So, if you'll excuse me?"

He turned his back on her and strode away, still searching for Jasmine. Watching him depart, Melissa trembled with fury.

Jasmine was standing by one of the back parlor doors, still reeling from Melissa's shocking revelations, when Jared joined her. His eyes were bright, his features flushed, and she found herself wondering how much he'd had to drink tonight.

"Jasmine, come with me," he said urgently.

Staring back at Jared, Jasmine didn't know how to react, didn't know what to feel. She wanted to believe in Jared; but, after hearing Melissa's devastating accusations regarding him, she wasn't sure she knew Jared at all, didn't know if she could trust him . . . "I'm growing tired," she said lamely.

He ignored her protest and pulled her outside, past the happy couples on the gallery, through the formal area, and down the dewey grass in the fragrant darkness. "Where are you taking me?" she demanded, hiking her skirts above her ankles to keep them from trailing on the moist ground.

He was grimly silent as he led her past the gazebo to where a small summerhouse stood. The whitewashed octagonal building was used only rarely by overnight guests at the estate. Tonight, it had an abandoned look about it as the moonlight glinted off its many vacant windows.

Jared opened the door with a creak, and pulled Jasmine into the one-room enclosure. When he turned to stare at her, her heart pounded and she caught a sharp lungful of the cool, musty air inside the unused room. "Why did you bring me here?" she asked him, instinctively backing away.

He pursued her, the light from the window etching his handsome features in silver, flashing off his eyes like starlight hitting dark ponds. "Jasmine, I want you to marry me—tonight," he said simply.

She paused, stunned. "Jared, have you lost your mind?"

"Not at all. Run away with me tonight—to Louisiana. We can get a license much more quickly there. Just think, darling—in a few hours we can be man and wife."

Jasmine's heart raced, and every muscle in her body tightened in caution at Jared's words. She knew the last thing she needed to do was to run off with Jared tonight, bedeviled by all these new doubts! How could she be sure Jared even intended to marry her? Was his asking her to run away with him simply a ploy to get her into his bed, to make her his latest conquest, as Melissa had suggested?

"No, Jared, I can't run off with you," she said at last. "We couldn't possibly do anything before the church annuls my marriage to Claude."

He gestured exasperatedly. "But legally, the marriage is already annulled," he again pointed out.

She shook her head. "That's not good enough. It must be annulled by the church, as well, before I can remarry."

He drew a hand threw his hair. "Jasmine, we'll marry again in the church later on—"

"No," she said adamantly, an edge of hysteria in her voice as she again backed away.

He studied her with rising perplexity. "Jasmine, what's wrong with you? Why do you keep backing away from me?"

"N-nothing," she stammered, now fighting tears.

Scowling, he demanded, "Jasmine, an hour ago, you were clinging to me as we danced, and now you look terrified. What has happened since then to make you change so dramatically?"

"Nothing," she repeated, in a voice full of hoarse pleading. "Jared, please, can't we go back?"

"No. Come here, Jasmine." When she again backed away, he snapped, "Damn it, woman! Don't cringe from me!"

In two strides, Jared came to Jasmine's side and pulled her into his arms, smothering her cry of alarm as he crushed his mouth down on hers. He tasted heavily of brandy, and his kiss was desperate in its intensity. His lips bruised her until she at last surrendered with a small cry, opening her mouth to the hot possession of his tongue and curling her arms about his neck.

"Oh, Jasmine—Jasmine," he whispered after a moment, raining her face and throat with gentle kisses. "Darling, you must never pull away from me like that! I couldn't endure it if I lost you. Tell me what disturbed you so tonight—some bit of gossip, perhaps?"

Jasmine stiffened, and Jared drew back slightly, cupping her face in his hands and looking down at her searchingly.

Jasmine blinked at tears. She couldn't face his questions now. Her emotions were too raw, and she was too terrified of learning something that might destroy their future together. In that moment, when faced with the possibility of losing him, she realized that she really did love him! That was why she'd felt so wildly jealous when she'd seen him with Melissa! That was why she hadn't immediately denied his announcement of their engagement! She loved him—brash, irrepressible, and impossible though he was. She had probably loved him for many weeks.

The knowledge filled her, stripped her defenses, left her reeling, vulnerable, as she stared up into his beautiful, haunted eyes. Illogically, she wrapped her arms about his chest and clung to him.

"Darling, please, what is it?" he repeated, his anguished voice twisting like a knife in her heart.

"I'll tell you later, perhaps, Jared," she promised breathlessly, her cheek against his shoulder. "But now—please, just hold me."

"Oh, love!"

Jared's arms tightened about her and he kissed her again —deeply, thoroughly. Feeling her soften to him, he slipped his fingers inside her gown and chemise and caressed her bare nipples. As she shuddered in ecstasy at his provocative touch, he groaned, "God, you're driving me insane, woman! You're ungodly beautiful—so heavenly and soft!"

Jared's fingers moved on Jasmine's breast in a slow, sensuous rhythm, and her breathing quickened at the taut aching of arousal radiating down her body, settling between her thighs with throbbing intensity. She knew she should protest his advances, yet her newly discovered love for him made her powerless to do so. His mouth was again drinking of hers, seducing her, sending her doubts retreating into the shadows. All she could think of was how much she needed and desired him. When he leaned over, firmly pulling aside her gown and chemise and latching his mouth onto her breast, she cried out at the riotous sensations streaking through her. When his tongue flicked over her nipple in ruthless mastery, she jerked in rapture and would have twisted out of his embrace had he not held her so tightly. She felt herself melting all over. Her skin was feverish; her breath came in near-painful gasps. She tangled her fingers in the thick silk of his hair and drew his mouth closer, wanting—needing—to feel the cutting pressure of his teeth on her breast.

At last he straightened and stared down at her passionate face again, his eyes glazed with longing. "Jasmine, I must know you're mine tonight," he said poignantly. "If we can't be married in deed, can't we be man and wife in our hearts from this night on?" He nodded toward a daybed in the corner. "Make love with me—my dearest heart."

Jared's unwitting words about lovemaking broke the spell, reminding Jasmine of everything Melissa had said, making her realize that she had just shamelessly pressed her bare breast into Jared's mouth, that she had squirmed against him like some wanton hussy, that she had almost given him just what Melissa had insisted was all he wanted from a woman, anyway. "No!" she cried, her voice full of hurt, fear, and confusion. "I can't!"

As Jared watched, stunned, Jasmine fled the summerhouse, rushing through the cool night air toward the safety of the looming house beyond.

# ★ Seventeen ★

The next day was Sunday, and though Jasmine was tired, she got up early and got herself and Maggie ready for mass. Jared arrived, punctual as always, to drive the two girls to St. Mary's Cathedral. Jasmine dutifully departed with him and Maggie, but she was tensely silent throughout the outing, refusing to meet Jared's eye. The instant they arrived back at Magnolia Bend, Jasmine muttered an excuse and rushed off upstairs. When Sarah came to her room moments later, telling her Mr. Jared was insisting she come back downstairs, she gathered her fortitude, grabbed the velvet case with the emeralds, and left her room.

Jared looked quite anxious as he watched her descend into the downstairs hallway. He frowned at the box in her hands. "My dear, I was hoping you might consent to go for a drive with me. Don't you think we need to talk?"

Staring up into Jared's bright, worried eyes, Jasmine felt torn, yet she knew she was in no condition to talk with him now. She was still too consumed with turmoil following the events last night. "Jared, I'm sorry, but I'm feeling quite worn out from the party," she told him stiffly. "I think I'll nap this afternoon."

And before he could reply, she thrust the velvet case into his hands and hurried back upstairs. Safely inside her room, Jasmine found she felt bad about dismissing Jared so curtly, but she was tired, and needed time to make some sense of her jumbled emotions. Certainly, she must have her thoughts in order before she even considered confronting Jared with

Melissa Peavy's accusations! After the events of last night, she felt as if she'd been put through an emotional wringer.

A few days later, on Wednesday afternoon, as Jasmine was preparing to leave for the orphanage, Jared dropped by. "It's your day for St. Mary's, isn't it?" he asked her in the central hallway. "I'll take you."

"Oh, no, that won't be necessary," she protested nervously. "Ephraim should be by any minute."

"I saw him waiting outside as I drove up," Jared responded with an easy grin. "I assured him that I would escort you to the orphanage, and I took the liberty of asking him to run some errands for me in town."

Jasmine ground her teeth. She felt wary about going out with Jared, since she was still agonizing over the party and Melissa's charges. "Look, Jared, I'm planning to spend the entire afternoon sewing curtains with Sister Philomena, and I have no idea when we'll be finished. You'll be bored silly."

He shrugged. "I'm taking you, dear. It'll be good to see the children again. And I have some business to discuss with Mother Martha."

Jasmine knew that further protest was useless, under the circumstances, so she left with Jared in his barouche. As they drove along the tree-lined streets in the warmth of the late September afternoon, he cleared his throat and said awkwardly, "Jasmine, about Saturday night . . . I wish to apologize, my dear. I had a bit too much to drink, and I suppose that unleashed some passions in me that ordinarily would have been . . ." He paused to cough. "Well, anyway, my dear, what I'm trying to say is that I was quite overcome by my feelings for you. I hope I didn't scare you off for good —and it won't happen again." Unexpectedly, he grinned. "Leastwise, not until we're married."

Listening to Jared, Jasmine hoped the brim of her sunbonnet was hiding her deep blush. Actually, despite some embarrassment at his forthrightness, she felt touched by his penitence. He sounded so sincere, and had demonstrated to her that he felt far from pleased with his behavior Saturday night. Yet she still had to wonder if more than liquor had spurred his recklessness when he had dragged her out to the summerhouse and passionately tried to bed her.

"Jasmine?" he prodded after a moment, when she didn't respond. Tipping his hat at another couple in a passing buggy, he asked, "Do you accept my apology?"

She glanced at him, and as he turned to wait for her reply, she studied his features. His square jaw was tense, and she found his deep-set blue eyes looked so vulnerably expectant that she had to nod her assent.

He heaved a sigh of relief, then added, "But you haven't quite forgiven me for announcing our betrothal, have you?"

"Jared, you must be aware that your announcement was —well, quite premature. And you also broke your promise to me."

"Dear heart, for that I do again humbly apologize," he replied sincerely. "Do have mercy on a man in love. Besides, do you really think there's any doubt that we'll eventually wed?"

"Not according to you," she said shortly, though her fingers did tremble quite badly on her reticule.

At the orphanage, Jared was attacked by a troupe of laughing little girls, and Jasmine had to smile as she left him in the downstairs hallway dispensing peppermint candy. Going up the creaky stairs, she glanced downward and noted that even the normally stern-faced Mother Martha was grinning from ear to ear as she accepted a stick of candy from Jared.

Mercy, Jasmine thought to herself, rounding the landing, how could she have doubted such a fine man as Jared? He doubtless had more integrity than Melissa Peavy would ever possess in a lifetime. Why had she even considered giving Melissa's obvious, vengeful lies any credence?

Jasmine's guilt mounted during the afternoon, which she spent, as planned, sewing muslin curtains with Sister Philomena. The new panels would replace the moth-eaten rags now hanging in the upstairs dormitory windows. Jasmine knew that Jared's recent, generous gift to the orphanage had paid for the cloth, as well as for numerous other improvements that had been implemented already.

Half an hour later, Jared wandered into the upstairs sewing

room with Mother Martha. The nun was beaming; even her steel-rimmed glasses seemed to shine with new warmth as she smiled. "Jasmine," she began, "Mr. Hampton has the most wonderful idea. He wants to plan a benefit day for the orphanage."

"We came up here to see what you and Sister Philomena think," Jared said, grinning at her.

As Jared and Mother Martha sat down, he added, "I was thinking we might hold the benefit about a month from now, out on the Old Spanish Parade Grounds. The weather should be quite lovely then, don't you think? I thought of hiring Finnegan's Family Circus—the one that was so popular here two years ago."

"Wouldn't a circus be expensive?" Jasmine asked.

He shrugged. "Hiring it will be my contribution, of course. What you ladies will need to do is to organize the women of the church to bring covered dishes, plan booths, sell tickets—"

"Sell tickets?" Jasmine repeated.

"Yes. Mother Martha and I were thinking we'd charge twenty-five dollars a ticket for the circus and noon meal— which is rather steep, I'll grant, but all the money will benefit the orphanage. You women can also set up booths selling everything from baked goods to needlework, and those will garner additional revenue."

"Why, that's a great idea!" Jasmine exclaimed.

"Indeed!" echoed Sister Philomena.

Jared nodded and grinned. "The citizens of Natchez will love this, I know. We'll ask each Natchez family attending to sponsor an orphan for the day." Jared turned to the mother superior. "As I was telling Mother Martha, these girls need to be adopted. This will be the perfect way to get the children acquainted with families in the Natchez community."

"Oh, Jared—that will be so fine!" Jasmine cried. "But, what will we do if we can't line up enough families to sponsor all the girls? It would be unthinkable to leave anyone out."

Again, Jared was ready with a smile and a solution. "Well, there are sixty-five girls here in all, and I see no problem in finding sixty-five families willing to sponsor a child. After all, this will be the event of the social season here in Natchez, and no one will want to be left out. Should there be any children left over once the tickets are sold, I'll sponsor those girls personally, of course.''

At this point, both sisters clapped their hands and expressed their enthusiastic thanks to Jared. Jasmine was too moved to speak. She lowered her eyes, trying to concentrate on her sewing and fight tears. Here, Jared was doing all these wonderful things for the children at the orphanage, and he wasn't even a Catholic—yet! She felt the worst kind of traitor for ever doubting his motives, and in that moment, she realized that she must somehow manage to surmount her own fears and talk with him as soon as possible, about Melissa's accusations.

''Jasmine?''

She looked up to see Jared and the two sisters staring at her expectantly. ''Yes?'' she asked him.

''Do you think the benefit will be a success?''

Jasmine was feeling so choked with emotion, she doubted she could speak. At last she nodded and managed to say hoarsely, ''I think it will be a sensation!'' Then, as her trembling fingers missed a stitch, she stabbed herself in the thumb and muttered, ''Ouch!''

Jared and the nuns chuckled at Jasmine's exclamation, and he stood, crossing the room to take the hand Jasmine had pricked. ''You know, ladies, there's really no excuse for your having to sew endless seams by hand,'' he said, turning to wink at the two nuns. ''I must buy you one of those new-fangled sewing machines my aunt has. What do you think, Jasmine?''

Jasmine looked up at Jared raptly. ''I think you're far too kind.''

''Not at all, my dear.'' He frowned thoughtfully as he studied the tears in her bright-green eyes, and rubbed her wounded thumb with gentle fingers. ''There, dear,'' he said, in the tender tone he often used to soothe small hurts for Maggie or the other girls. ''It's only a scratch. You don't have to cry about it, do you?''

''No,'' Jasmine whispered, looking up at Jared with love in her eyes. ''I don't have to cry at all.''

Late that afternoon, Jared dropped Jasmine back at Charity's house, telling her that he must hurry off to a Masonic lodge meeting and supper.

Jasmine felt disappointed, because now she was most anxious to talk to Jared—to explain why she'd acted withdrawn since the party, and to bring out into the open the things Melissa had said.

She realized that she had felt so vulnerable on the night of the party that she'd let Melissa's charges knock her totally off balance. But now, in retrospect, she found it increasingly difficult to believe that a man as fine as Jared could do the horrible things Melissa had told her. Just as important, Jasmine no longer wanted to have any secrets from Jared, and she dearly hoped that if she made the first move, he would tell her the truth about his past. Though she still hadn't committed herself to Jared outwardly, she knew that inwardly, she was lost—her emerging love for him, steadfast and strong, simply refused to be denied any longer. It was high time to set aside the obstacles in their path and begin looking toward their future together.

While Jasmine realized that the best course of action would be to wait and talk with Jared the next day, she knew she wouldn't be able to sleep until she made her peace with him.

At nine that night, she grabbed a shawl and bonnet, left her room, and tiptoed downstairs. The first floor was unlit, without a servant in sight. Jasmine hurried to the front door, her way guided by the moonlight filtering in through the cut-glass fanlight. Creaking open the door and stepping outside, she breathed a sigh of relief.

The evening that greeted her was clear, dark, and cool. A half-moon and a thousand stars glittered in the black heavens above. Jasmine began to regret her hasty flight the minute she headed down the long, tree-lined driveway. Hearing an owl hoot ominously from his perch overhead, she had a sudden, uncanny feeling that some danger lurked in the moss-draped, silvery recesses of those nearby trees—almost as if unseen human eyes were watching her. She realized that it was foolish for her to venture forth on this dark night, a

woman unescorted and defenseless. While Natchez had settled down somewhat from its earlier frontier days, the city
still harbored a strong unsavory element, especially Under-
the-Hill, and lawlessness was all too common.

Jasmine hurried along Woodville Road, stiffening her spine
and scolding herself for her fears. She was out now and well
on her way to Hampton Hall, so she may as well make the
best of things. She did breathe a deep sigh of relief when she
arrived at Jared's house, and saw that the downstairs rooms
were still heavily lit.

When she knocked on the front door, a surprised Marie
Bernard admitted her. "Why, Miss Jasmine, do come in and
get yourself out of the night air. This is an unexpected surprise."

"Hello, Marie. Sorry to intrude so late," Jasmine said as
she stepped into the central hallway. "Is Mr. Jared home?"

"Why, yes, he just got in. May I take your bonnet and
shawl?"

"Thanks, Marie," Jasmine said, handing her the two
items. "Is he in his study?"

"Yes, miss. Shall I announce you?"

"Please don't bother, Marie—I think I'll surprise him,"
Jasmine said, heading off down the hallway toward Jared's
office. She knocked on his door, and when his deep voice
called out, "Come in," she entered the small, cozy room.

Jared was sitting at his desk, poring over an account book.
The scowl lining his brow as he worked only deepened the
masculine appeal of his chiseled face.

He glanced up, startled, as Jasmine entered the room, then
smiled. "My dear! What a pleasant surprise!"

"Good evening, Jared."

He stood, coming to her side and kissing her warmly.
"Well, this is quite an honor. Tell me—what brings you here
at this hour? And how, pray tell, did you get here? Did
Ephraim fetch you, so late at night? Now, that's what I call
true devotion."

"Actually, I walked from your aunt's house," she admitted.

Jared's blue eyes darkened and he muttered an expletive. "You walked? You mean you came all the way here from Magnolia Bend, in the dark, unescorted?"

"Jared, I was fine."

"Don't you know that the Natchez streets are dangerous at night? Why, only tonight, Tom Leathers mentioned that the volunteer watch has been increased lately due to a rash of robberies near the bluff."

Jasmine bit her lip. She was eminently aware that coming here had been foolhardy, and she still hadn't shaken the feeling that someone had been watching her as she walked. Yet she also refused to be sidetracked from her purpose at the moment. "Look, Jared, I arrived here without a scratch, so please, let's not argue about it. I promise I'll take greater care from now on."

"Very well. Then, tell me, what drove you to come here at this hour, risking life and health in the darkness?"

"I wanted to talk to you."

"About what?"

All at once she felt at a loss. After they sat down on a leather settee next to the snapping fire, she forced a weak smile. "It concerns the party at your aunt's house last Saturday night."

"Ahah! Just as I thought. You *are* still angry that I announced our engagement."

"No, that's not it. I mean, not exactly. Actually, it concerns Melissa."

His expression grew guarded. "What about her?"

As Jasmine explained what Melissa had told her, Jared's countenance darkened. When she finished, he cursed under his breath and stood, crossing the room to stand at the draped window.

When at last he spoke, his first words stunned her. "That damned bitch," he said. Turning to face Jasmine with fire in his eyes, he said, "How dare she try to poison your mind against me that way!" The tension in his face deepened, and his gaze gleamed with hurt as he took a step forward. "And you believed her, Jasmine? Do you really think my aunt and I are mad?"

"No, of course not!" she denied, feeling miserable. "But, Jared, there's still so much I don't know about you—what happened to your parents, your gambling, and . . . what happened between you and Melissa," she finished in a tight voice.

He sighed, nodding grimly. "I'm sorry my dear, but I'm just not ready to tell you about my parents—not yet. As for my gambling—sure, I've gone gambling on the *Witch*, many times. And . . ." He paused, smiling at her rather lamely. "There have been some women—not ladies, mind you, but women." Moving closer to her, he continued fervently, "Jasmine, I'm thirty years old. Surely you can't think I've always lived the life of a monk. There was a big emptiness in my life before I met you, and perhaps at times I tried to fill it in the wrong way." He came to her side, sat down, and took her hand. "But know this, my love. Since I've met you, there has been no one else for me but you. And since that night on the *River Witch*, I've had no desire to go gambling again—nor will I ever do so in the future."

Jasmine felt quite moved by his ardent, sincere words. "And—about Melissa?"

He sighed, drawing a finely shaped hand through the thick silk of his hair. "We were engaged at one point. But you must know that everything else she told you was false. I *never* seduced her."

"Then, why did you break off your engagement with her? I mean, if you are the one who ended things?"

"I was," he said tersely. He struggled visibly for a long moment, then shook his head and said, "Jasmine, I'm sorry, but I can't tell you that without violating my code of conduct as a gentleman."

When she frowned, he added, "All I can do is to reiterate that what happened between Melissa and me wasn't my fault. Aside from that, my dear, you're simply going to have to trust me on this. You have to take some things about me on faith."

Jasmine found that her sense of fairness urged her to agree with him. He *had* made a beginning—a big step for him. "You're right, Jared," she said at last. "After all, you took me on faith, didn't you? I mean, when you saw me in the river that night, you could have thought—well, the most ghastly things about me. Yet you always treated me as a lady.''

"That's because you *are* a lady," he said solemnly, lifting her hand to his mouth and kissing it.

Though she shuddered at the arousing heat of his lips on her flesh, she still found herself needing additional reassurance. "Jared, about your parents," she nudged him. "When are you going to tell me?"

A faraway, painfully sad look gripped his eyes. "The time will come, my dear. I promise you that. Until then—"

"Until then, I will try my best to trust you," she promised.

"Oh, my dearest heart!" he cried, pulling her into his arms. "I love you so much! Lord, how can I live until you're my wife?"

He pressed his mouth hungrily into hers, and, where his words hadn't totally assuaged her doubts, his lips took over. Later, when he walked her home in the moonlight, she could have sworn that her feet never touched the ground.

# ★ Eighteen ★

The next morning, as Jasmine worked with Maggie on her lessons, she found her doubts about Jared returning. It was strange, she mused, how when she was with him, his magic increasingly wove its spell about her, making her uncertainties recede. Yet when they were apart, the same old fears crept back in.

Of course, Jasmine was grateful that Jared had begun to share his past with her; he'd laid a foundation upon which they might build mutual trust. She did so want to believe in him and their love. Yet so much still remained unanswered in her mind.

That afternoon, Charity had invited Jasmine to attend a meeting of the Natchez Anti-Gambling Society, and thus, at one o'clock, Jasmine was in her room dressing. As Jasmine buttoned her stylish frock, she mused that it was ironic that Charity belonged to the Anti-Gambling Society, when her own nephew occasionally indulged in games of chance. Of course, last night Jared had assured her that he was finished with such folly. And Charity had also explained to Jasmine that the main purpose of the Anti-Gambling Society was to keep Natchez free of the pickpockets, gamblers, and other riffraff that occasionally swelled to such numbers that they even took over the streets up on the Hill. In the past, the Anti-Gambling Society's vigilance committee had issued several ultimatums to the unsavory element in town, requiring such types to evacuate Natchez in two days' time, and thereby rendering the city streets safe again.

Jasmine added a couple more pins to secure the bun she'd fashioned. She was about to don her broad-brimmed straw hat with its trim of ribbons and flowers, when a knock came at her door.

"Come in," she called, and Charity Hampton entered the room, looking quite elegant in a tailored gray silk dress with lace-trimmed collar and satin piping on the sleeves and hem. "Oh, dear," Jasmine greeted the dowager, quickly donning her hat. "Am I late?"

Miss Charity waved her off. "Not at all, dear. We don't even have to leave until one-thirty. I came by your room first hoping we might have a few moments to chat."

"Certainly," Jasmine said with a smile. "Won't you have a seat?"

Charity crossed the room to sit down on the chair in the bay window, and Jasmine moved to sit down across from her on the bed. "What's on your mind, Miss Charity?"

The woman eyed Jasmine sympathetically. "First of all, dear, I've been meaning to apologize for my nephew's rather rash conduct Saturday night. I do hope you've forgiven him for so dramatically announcing your betrothal. You can't have known he was planning to do so."

Jasmine laughed dryly. "Indeed, I didn't know. Were you aware of Jared's plans?"

Charity waved Jasmine off. "Heavens, no, my dear, or I would have prevailed upon the boy to see reason. I know he's a headstrong young man, Jasmine, but I assure you that his heart's in the right place." Cautiously, Charity added, "How have the two of you been getting on since then?"

Jasmine sighed. "Oh, in some ways better, but in other ways . . ." She shook her head, her voice trailing off.

Frowning thoughtfully, Charity said, "Actually, my dear, I've been debating for days whether to have this chat with you. You see, at the party Saturday night, I saw Melissa Peavy take you aside. And ever since that moment, I've noticed tension between you and Jared. I take it Melissa told you of their previous engagement?"

"Yes," Jasmine murmured, feeling somewhat surprised that Jared's aunt had been so observant at the party, and that she was also aware of the emotional nuances between her and Jared.

Charity sighed, and as she laced her small fingers together, the light from the window sent showers of brilliance spinning off her many stunning rings. "I can well imagine that Melissa embellished the story of her engagement to my nephew to her own advantage, and I also know that Jared would never divulge to you the true reason he broke off with her. He's such a gentleman. In fact, he'd be furious at me if he knew I was telling you this now, but I feel I must."

Jasmine felt her spine tense. "Tell me what?"

"You see, soon after their engagement was formally announced, Jared caught Melissa in the garden behind her parents' house with a friend of his. I'm afraid Melissa was—er—naked to the waist. Jared called the other gentleman out, there was a duel—"

"Oh, my God! Did Jared kill . . . ?"

Charity shook her head. "The other man was wounded, but survived. He left Natchez in disgrace soon thereafter, and, of course, Jared broke off his engagement with Melissa.''

"I can't blame him," Jasmine said grimly. She blinked rapidly, clenching her jaw to bite back rising fury. "So it was Melissa all along who was responsible for the breakup. And she told me Jared simply abandoned her!"

"I had a notion she would lie," Charity commented ruefully. "Anyway, dear, I felt I had to tell you the truth. When I saw Melissa take you aside, I knew she'd try to drive a wedge between you and Jared."

Jasmine nodded to her friend, her green eyes gleaming with bitterness. "You're right, Miss Charity. That's precisely what she did. And I'm so glad you've told me the truth."

"Do you think there's a chance for you and Jared now?" Charity asked wistfully.

Jasmine smiled as she blushed self-consciously. "Yes, I do," she told her friend at last. "Actually, I'm . . ."

"In love with Jared?"

"You knew!"

"The two of you are meant for each other." Gravely, Charity continued, "And Jasmine, dear—you simply mustn't ever again let anything come between you."

Jasmine felt warmed by Charity's words. Then she bit her lip as another one of Melissa's accusations flitted to mind— this one so humiliating that she hadn't even dared to bring it up with Jared. "Miss Charity, there is one thing . . ."

"Yes, dear?"

"Melissa also said—well, she said that privately, everyone in the Natchez community is laughing at me."

Charity looked stunned. "Why would anyone laugh at you, my dear?"

"Because . . ." Jasmine twisted her fingers together nervously, then blurted out, "Because of my humble background, according to Melissa. She said that everyone in town thinks Jared is marrying beneath his social station."

"Balderdash!" Charity retorted indignantly. "Why, the nerve!" Leaning forward intently, Charity continued, "Jasmine, I'll have you know that Melissa's grandfather came over to this country as an indentured servant!"

Jasmine couldn't contain a short laugh. "Surely, you jest!"

"Not at all. The Peavy family has its roots in poverty, my dear. Why, the girl's father, Edgar, started his career here in Natchez without a farthing. Later, he made his fortune in the lumber business." Charity fixed Jasmine with her sincere, compelling gaze. "You must understand, Jasmine, that it has been this way with a number of our citizens. No one thinks any less of anyone else for it. And no one would dream of laughing at you! Believe me, I would know. Why, all of my friends think you are enchanting."

Jasmine felt greatly reassured by Charity's words. "Thanks. You've made me feel so much better."

"Good. I'm glad we've had this chance to talk. Ready to go, dear?"

Jasmine nodded, picking up her shawl and reticule from the bed. As the two women headed for the door, Jasmine murmured, "Miss Charity, about Jared's parents . . . I mean, their deaths. . . ."

Charity paused, turning to place a lined hand on Jasmine's sleeve. The little woman's brow was deeply furrowed, and there was great sadness in her hazel eyes as she slowly shook her head. "Jared still hasn't told you how he lost George and Elizabeth?"

"No."

Charity sighed heavily, patting Jasmine's arm. "My dear, I'm sorry. But I still feel that this is something Jared must be willing to share with you on his own. I do hope you understand . . . ?"

Jasmine braved a smile. "Of course I do."

But she didn't understand at all.

That evening, as they'd earlier planned, Jared escorted Jasmine and Charity to a performance of the Philharmonic Club. Jasmine was dying to be alone with Jared so she could set things right. She yearned to admit her love and beg his forgiveness for not trusting him. But no opportunity presented itself during the concert. Back at Magnolia Bend, as the three adults shared coffee in the front parlor, a sleepy-eyed Maggie wandered in in her nightgown, with a book tucked under her arm. When the child complained petulantly that she couldn't sleep because no one had read her a bedtime story, Jared apologized profusely, whisked child and book up into his arms, and headed off upstairs. Jasmine smiled to herself as she watched him leave, then realized that Jared would surely leave for his own home soon after he read to Maggie. She knew she dared not go dashing down to his house in the darkness as she had last night—not after he'd scolded her so soundly for her recklessness then. Yet how else would she get a chance to speak with him privately?

Inspiration struck while he was still upstairs. Jasmine hurried to the library, grabbed pen and paper, and wrote Jared a note: "Meet me at the summerhouse. Midnight. Love, Jasmine."

A smile curved her lips as she folded the note carefully and tucked it inside the wide satin sash at the waist of her frock. Moments later, when she stood in the downstairs hallway kissing Jared good night, her hand slipped inside his frock coat and she placed the note in the pocket of his satin vest.

Two hours later, Jasmine hurried for the summerhouse at the back of Miss Charity's property. The night was cool and clear, the air delicately laced with the intoxicating scent of late-blooming flowers. The atmosphere was thick with sound—bullfrogs croaking, cicadas buzzing. Starlight gleamed on the pond up ahead near the gazebo, while above in the dark heavens, a chimney swift made a graceful arc across a pale-yellow moon. Altogether, it was a glorious night, Jasmine mused—and yet, as she went from tree to tree in the darkness, she again got the insidious, creepy feeling that someone was watching her.

At last she reached the small octagonal summerhouse and stepped inside. She closed the heavy panel, leaned against it, and caught her breath. Her feeling of unease continued until her eyes adjusted completely to the darkness and she realized that her sole companions were the musty air, shifting light, and cobwebs.

She stepped farther into the room. Near the window was

the narrow daybed where Jared had bid her lie with him the other night. The moonlight now danced in quicksilver patterns on the old velvet coverlet.

Jared! How she ached to be with him and to tell him what she was feeling. Had he found her note? Would he come? Would he think her unspeakably forward for inviting him here?

Oh, God, let him come before she lost her nerve!

He did.

At first she gasped when the door creaked open behind her. She whirled about, then relief flooded her as she saw that it was him. "Jared," she whispered.

He closed the door. Moonlight glinted off his smile as he crossed the room to her. "Why, Jasmine. I must say that this is—well, rather dramatic."

"You got my note?"

He chuckled. "Indeed I did."

"I had to see you," she said in a rush.

"But, darling, you were with me all night," he teased.

"Alone," she said. "I had to see you alone."

"Alone it is, then," he said huskily. With a sexy grin he added, "Aren't you even going to kiss me hello?"

Jasmine rushed forward into his embrace, kissing him and boldly thrusting her tongue into his warm mouth. Within seconds, he was gently yet firmly pushing her away. "My God, woman!" he said unsteadily. "You shouldn't kiss me that way. Not when we're alone like this."

"Shouldn't I?" she asked.

He took her face in his hands and asked, "Darling, what's on your mind tonight?"

Her eyes shone with exultant tears as she gazed up at him and said, "I love you."

"Oh, Jasmine!" Jared looked overcome with joy. His eyes were passionately dark and glazed above hers. "How I've yearned to hear those words from you!"

"They're true—I love you so much!" she exclaimed, hugging him to her tightly. "And—I'm sorry I ever doubted you."

"Doubted me?" he repeated, backing off slightly, gently

removing her hands from his neck and holding them in his. "About what, darling?"

"About Melissa," she admitted. At his puzzled glance, she explained, "Your aunt told me the truth, about how Melissa was the one who betrayed you."

"I see." Abruptly, he turned and moved off, and she watched his broad back stiffen. "My aunt had no right to tell you that!"

"Jared, please, don't get angry!" Jasmine pleaded. "I know how seriously you take your honor and all that. But your aunt—well, I think she knew that Melissa was coming between us, and that I had to be told the truth."

Jared turned to her, his eyes flashing, and his voice held a surprising edge of bitterness as he asked, "Then you didn't believe me when I told you the broken engagement wasn't my fault?"

Jasmine lowered her eyes and bit her lip. She couldn't bring herself to lie to him about it. "I suppose I didn't—not completely," she said in a small voice.

He laughed shortly. "Tell me then, do you think I'm mad, as well?"

"Oh, no, Jared, not at all!" she cried, devastated by the dark hurt in his eyes. "I'm sorry I gave any of Melissa's accusations the least bit of credence! It's just that—well, after what my father did to me, after what Claude did . . . I guess it's been hard for me to trust you completely."

"Even though I love you?" he asked.

"I love you, too," she whispered.

"Do you?" he asked, in a strangely haunted voice.

Jasmine felt miserable. Everything she said to Jared tonight seemed to be coming out wrong. Instead of making things better between them, she had made things worse by confessing that she hadn't trusted him.

Looking at him and seeing the pain in his eyes, Jasmine knew what she wanted to do—what she had to do—to make him believe that she really did trust him and love him. Her heart was pounding as she walked across the room to him and touched his arm. "Jared, I'm ready to make love with you," she said simply.

He backed off, looking stunned as the moonlight played off his features. "Jasmine, do you know what you're saying?"

She nodded. "I'm saying I love you and I want to make love with you. Oh, Jared!" She stepped forward and embraced him with trembling arms. He felt stiff and unyielding, yet she forced herself to continue. "Saturday night, you asked me to commit to you completely. You asked me to become your wife in my heart from that moment on. I was scared, so I refused—"

"Jasmine!" He grasped her shoulders, holding her back slightly. "Darling, you were right to refuse. I had too much to drink that night, and I asked too much of you."

"But, you didn't!" she insisted. "I'm glad now—about Saturday night, because I've been forced to confront my own feelings. You didn't ask too much of a woman who should have believed in you and your love all along."

"But, Jasmine—the annulment, your faith—"

"You mean more to me than any of that." In a shaky voice, she continued, "It was scary to trust you, Jared, after everything that happened to me. And I'll admit I wasn't ready to Saturday night." She looked up at him with her heart in her eyes. "But I am now."

"Jasmine." His voice broke as he hugged her to his chest and ran his hand through the wispy curls framing her face. She could hear his heart pounding fiercely as he whispered, "Oh, Jasmine. You don't know how I've needed you! You don't know how tempted I am now, at this very moment—"

"Then, make love with me."

"Oh, God. We shouldn't, Jasmine."

"I think we should. Please, don't make me beg."

"Beg," he repeated with a low, ironic laugh.

To her confusion, he slipped out of her arms. Then her feeling of disappointment became relief as she watched him walk over and draw the heavy drapes beyond the daybed. "Jasmine, are you truly sure?" came his anguished question.

She nodded. She *was* sure, she realized. She wanted to be his, to commit herself to him totally—to join herself with him and leave no room for turning back. Breathlessly, she told him, "Until we can be married in the church, we'll be married in our hearts."

"Oh, love!"

Jared returned to Jasmine's side and caught her to him fiercely, his arms tight yet strangely trembling as he held her. His kisses were hard and demanding, and soon his hands eagerly sought her breasts. Even though the two dozen tiny mother-of-pearl buttons on the bodice of her dress drove him to distraction, he patiently undid each, whispering endearments in her mouth between ardent kisses. At last her bodice was freed, and Jared's fingers slipped inside her chemise to caress her bare breast.

"Oh, Jared!" She gasped at the wonderful sensation, feeling her nipple harden almost painfully against his fingertips, as her body convulsed with the delicious shivers of arousal his nearness brought.

"From this moment on, you're mine!" he said passionately.

"I think I was yours from the moment you spotted me in the river," she whispered back.

"I've loved you from that moment," he said, in a voice so full of poignant feeling that she began to weep. "Darling, don't cry," he added tenderly, drawing her closer.

She looked up at him, unashamed of her joyous tears. "It's just that you're—so wonderful, Jared. You've been so good to me, every step of the way. You've believed in me every minute. And I've resisted you so. Can you forgive me?"

"There's nothing to forgive." He pulled back slightly and grinned. "Besides, your coyness has added interest to the game."

"Oh?" Now she was smiling, too. "Then, will it lose its challenge after tonight?"

"You'll always be a challenge to me," he laughed.

And with those words, he swept her up into his arms, carried her across the room, and set her down next to the daybed. A slat of moonlight slipped through the center opening of the drapes beyond, and he undressed her in the silvery beam of light, caressing her body with his hands and eyes.

She shuddered with desire as her garments hit the floor one by one, feeling no shame as his desire-darkened gaze raked over her. His fingertips were exquisite torture on her heated flesh as he removed her chemise, petticoats, then her pantalets, stockings, and shoes, his merest touch seeming to brand her with his fire.

"You're so beautiful, love. So very beautiful," he whispered, letting down her hair and kissing the silken tresses.

Once she was naked, she reclined on the daybed and watched him undress, smiling as he impatiently ripped at studs and cravat, then watching the moonlight spill over his muscular chest, his flat stomach, and lower. When she saw his desire, so large and hard, she felt a corresponding twinge of near-painful arousal deep in her womanhood. So this was what a man looked like—*her* man. Again, she felt no embarrassment as she stared up at him, no fear as she lay before him, naked and hungry for his touch. She felt only love and desire—both so deep they welled in her heart like tears.

At last he joined her on the narrow bed, covering her soft body with his hard, muscular length. His naked flesh, so warm and male, felt heavenly against her softness. She could feel her nipples tingling as they touched the coarse hair on his chest, and the hardness of his male shaft against her lower belly was driving her insane. She could feel that vast maleness grow even larger, throbbing and hot against her feverish skin, and she wondered how it would feel when his marvelous heat penetrated inside her. The very thought made her mouth go dry.

"I love you," he whispered as he kissed her.

"I love you too—so much!" she cried.

Jared plied her mouth with his until her lips felt tender and bruised, then trailed kisses down her sensitive throat. He moved lower, caressing her breasts with his hands and sucking the tender nipples with his mouth. She writhed beneath him, floating in a sea of rapturous sensation, panting at the achingly acute arousal radiating from her swollen breasts downward to her loins. She whispered encouragements in his ear and ran her hands through his silky hair. When her hands stroked the firm muscles of his shoulders and back, then moved caressingly down his chest and belly, he groaned an agonized response, his fingers moving boldly to the mound where her legs were joined. She caught a painfully sharp breath and bucked against him in ecstasy.

"You want me," he said proudly, his fingers slipping between her thighs, driving her crazy as he felt her wet eagerness, the distended small bud of her passion.

"Oh, yes, I want you!" she cried.

Jared realized he should take more time to ready her—explore her thoroughly with his fingers and perhaps his mouth. Yet he was close to losing control now. His desire was so hard and distended it would surely explode soon. And he realized that this first time, he wanted to touch her only with the essence of him, to jolt them both to their souls with the impact of this first joining, their love. "Darling, I don't think I can wait—"

"Then, don't," she whispered.

Needing no additional encouragement, he parted her soft thighs and gathered her close to him. When he pushed hard against her virginal membrane, she winced and he said hoarsely, "Damn, I'm hurting you."

"It's all right, Jared," she whispered back. "I want you so. I want us to be close this way. . . ."

"God," he groaned, hearing the pain in her words, yet going crazy at the unrestrained welcome that filled her voice, her deeply dilated eyes.

She arched slightly against him, struggling hard to accept him, even as her tight flesh resisted. Her loving eagerness, her passionately innocent movements, made him lose his control, and he couldn't even hear his own ragged breathing over the mad pounding of his heart. She was his, he realized—totally his. She had never belonged to another and she never would. There was no more potent aphrodisiac than knowing that he was her first love, her last—that she would open herself to him this way and to no other, ever! The very thought made him grow iron-hard against her, and it was the most pleasurable agony he'd ever known. "God, love, what you're giving me tonight—"

"What you're giving *me*," she whispered, drawing his lips down to hers. "Please, Jared. Oh, please."

She was begging him! It was so sweet, he wanted to cry. He went spiraling over the edge then and became lost in her hot readiness, her scent, the very womanhood of her. His manhood pierced the fragile membrane, and he whispered a hoarse apology as his lips smothered her cry of pain. He could feel the tension in her slim body as he began to invade her tight recesses, yet he was now so hungry for her that he was powerless to control the urge to join himself with her as deeply as he could. She was hot and willing and untried, and he was out of control, desperate to drink thoroughly of her secrets. He drew her closer and drove deeper, feeling her flesh accept him, and the taut pressure and heat of her around him was so exquisite he thought he would die.

Beneath Jared, Jasmine too was drowning in the wonderful joy and pain. The first moments seemed brutal; she felt her tender tissues stinging and splitting as Jared penetrated her. The tip of him felt so huge and swollen that she could have sworn he would never fit himself inside her. Yet he did, impaling her with his driving heat, filling her until she thought she would burst, until she gasped and wanted to pull away, but knew she'd be lost if she did. The sensation was unbearable and wonderful, at the same time. She felt totally possessed, completely his. . . .

"God, you're heaven!" he groaned.

He began to move inside her, at first gently, then with fierce urgency. The soreness faded somewhat, yet the pressure was still intense as he withdrew and probed deeper each time. She felt herself throbbing, burning, then softening to his demanding possession, accepting him. He felt so good, so right . . . everywhere on her flesh. She could feel his mouth melting into hers, could feel her nipples contracting beneath his hands. . . . She could feel him deep and hard and unyielding inside her, shooting a shaft of liquid fire straight to the core of her with each hard thrust. It was paradise—this total intimacy, this melding. It was so wildly stirring that her face burned and she could barely catch her breath. She wanted something more, but didn't know what it was, or how to reach for it.

Then he helped her. When she began to moan, tossing her head from side to side, his hands slipped boldly beneath her. "Meet me," he demanded, and when she arched upward, he held her fast, his fingers digging into her soft bottom. His eyes locked with hers and he drove home with such depth and power that she cried out. They hung there at a climax so gripping, Jasmine could feel her back arching, her entire body clenching about his. She sobbed and kissed him desperately as he shuddered into her, bathing her with his seed. Then he collapsed on top of her, and utter contentment swept over them both.

"Are you all right?" he asked hoarsely moments later.

"Yes, fine," she said breathlessly, yet she couldn't restrain a small wince as he withdrew from her tender flesh.

He left her for a moment, and when he returned, she felt the softness of a handkerchief between her thighs. "Jared—"

"Lie still. I fear I've made you bleed, love."

"Isn't that as it should be—I mean, the first time?" she asked shyly.

"Yes, my darling," he said, leaning over to kiss her. "Still, perhaps I was a bit too passionate."

"I don't think so." With a reckless smile, she added, "I was passionate, too."

She heard his husky chuckle. "Oh, yes, my love. You were passionate, too."

Once he was through ministering to her, he kissed her again, quite tenderly. Then he sighed and said, "Much as I'd like to keep you here with me all night, Jasmine, I think you'd best get dressed now. I must get you back to the house before you're missed."

Though she knew Jared's words made sense, Jasmine felt hurt that he wanted them to leave so soon after their encounter. "Jared, I . . . ." She paused, realizing that she wanted to ask him if he'd been disappointed—if the passion she'd revealed had made him think less of her.

He stood and picked up his trousers. "I love you, Jasmine," he said. "But we must get you back now."

"I love you, too, Jared," she whispered, standing and turning away to hide her confused features as she reached for her clothes.

## ★ Nineteen ★

The next morning, Jasmine awakened as pale amber rays drifted in through the lace-curtained window. She felt a twinge of soreness as she stretched in bed. Memories rushed in of how she had given herself to Jared in the summerhouse the previous night. At first, she smiled as she recalled the exquisite moments of passion they had shared; then, a frown crept across her lips as doubts assailed her.

She didn't regret making love with Jared; she had felt that nothing less than a total commitment on her part could convince him of how deeply she loved him and trusted him. Yet after he'd taken her virginity on the narrow bed in the summerhouse, he'd reacted so strangely—almost abruptly. He'd made her hurry and get dressed, then he'd taken her back to the main house, kissing her quickly at the back door and insisting that she go inside.

He'd acted almost like a stranger toward her. Again she wondered if she'd disappointed him.

Jasmine didn't have too much time to consider her doubts, since she had a very busy day planned. After she attended to Maggie's lessons, she and Miss Charity would be visiting several prominent local families, lining up sponsors for the girls from the orphanage for the daylong benefit Jared had planned with the sisters from St. Mary's. Time was of the essence, too—less than four weeks remained until the day the New Orleans circus was booked. Many of the Catholic churchwomen were already busy either selling tickets or making handmade items to sell in the booths, and scores of others had promised to donate food for the luncheon or booths, as well.

During that day and several that followed, Jasmine saw Jared mostly when other people were around. They attended a horse race and a supper party. The rest of Jasmine's time was spent organizing the orphanage benefit, or tutoring Maggie, or working with Marie Bernard on the redecoration of Jared's home. The renovations of Hampton Hall were coming along well. The needed fabrics had arrived from New Orleans, and several slaves were busy reupholstering furniture or making new drapes, while local craftsmen had been hired to make necessary repairs to the plaster and wood, and to paint and hang new wallpaper.

One afternoon, Jared shocked Jasmine by telling her that they would be spending the entire next day together. "I'm taking you to Vidalia, my dear, to show you my cotton plantation." When Jasmine protested that she had several important activities planned for that day, he told her with a calm smile, "Cancel them."

The next morning, they headed for Natchez-Under-the-Hill in Jared's barouche. As they drove down the cool, shady streets, Jasmine noted that the leaves were just beginning to turn. The crisp smell of the fall greenery was enticing.

Although they didn't talk at first, Jasmine felt quite comfortable with Jared today. The fact that he had invited her to see his plantation seemed to reaffirm his commitment to her. As always when she was with him, she found her doubts receding, though neither of them had broached the delicate subject of their intimacies in the summerhouse.

As Jared turned the horse down the tricky grade of Silver Street, Jasmine peered down at the ramshackle community of Natchez-Under-the-Hill and couldn't restrain a giggle. When Jared glanced at her quizzically, she said, "I was just remembering the last time we were here. I'm glad you're not forcing me to wear pants this time."

He laughed, but his voice was serious as he said, "The

circumstances were vastly different that other morning. You were leaving a gambling packet after spending the entire night out on the river, and secrecy was necessary. Today, however, you're simply boarding a ferry with your fiancé, all fine and proper.''

Jasmine nodded, feeling warmed that Jared had referred to himself as her fiancé, a verbal confirmation that he still thought of her as the woman he would marry. Again recalling that first morning after they met, she murmured, ''My life has certainly changed since then.''

''For the better, I hope?'' he teased.

''Oh, yes. Definitely for the better.''

In due course, they arrived at the noisy, bustling landing, and were loaded, buggy and all, onto a flatboat. They remained inside the barouche as the ferry was oared across the river toward the timbered lowlands on the other side. Jasmine enjoyed the trip. The morning air was full of bracing coolness, of the scent of wet earth and the duskier smell of the river.

When the ferry docked, Jared paid the ferryman as he strode by to extend the ramp. Seconds later, he clucked to the horse and they went rattling down the plank, bouncing onto the crude brown road.

Working the reins, Jared smiled at Jasmine and said, ''Welcome to Louisiana, my dear.''

Bypassing the small village of Vidalia, they veered off down a rutted dirt road and headed north through the wooded countryside, more or less parallel to the river. Towering trees stretched over the roadway, forming a canopy to shade their path. Jasmine enjoyed watching the light sift through the dense green arc of sycamore and oak above them, raining light showers down onto the conveyance as they moved.

Moments later, they entered a large, cleared area and Jasmine viewed for the first time Jared's plantation home beyond. The large frame house stood on a rise, with huge gnarled oaks flanking either side of it. While it was much plainer than the elegant townhomes which characterized Natchez proper across the river, the manor house was nonetheless built on what Jasmine considered a grand scale. It was almost totally symmetrical, a pleasure to the eye.

Though the columns were slender and square, they seemed to stretch on forever, in wraparound, railed verandas that graced both stories. The tall, plentiful windows were flanked by neat dark-green shutters, and identical entry doors, carved from cypress and surrounded by elegant sidelights, graced the center of each story. Matching, curved stairways stretched from the ground to the raised first story, like two arms curved outward in welcome. "Oh, Jared, the house is lovely!" Jasmine exclaimed.

He nodded, but his smile was stiff, displaying none of Jasmine's enthusiasm. Moments later, as he pulled the buggy to a halt before the looming house, a brown-haired man in a black suit quickly emerged from a smaller, one-story cottage sitting beneath a large pecan tree off to the west. "Good morning, Mr. Hampton," the hatless man called out, looking rather flustered as he strode briskly toward the conveyance.

"Good morning, Mertson," Jared replied, as the thin gentleman, who looked to be in his early twenties, drew closer to them.

"Have you come to go over the accounts this morning, sir?" Mertson asked, shifting from foot to foot as he stood before the conveyance, glancing curiously from Jared to Jasmine. She noted that the man had thin but handsome features, and dark, expressive eyes that hinted of some inner sadness. "I'm afraid there's some disorder in the office this morning," the overseer continued to Jared rather sheepishly. "Had I known you were coming, sir—"

"Don't concern yourself with that, Mertson, I'm not here on business today," Jared said, alighting from the buggy and extending his hand to assist Jasmine down. Smiling at her as he helped her to the ground, he told her, "My dear, this is my overseer, Mr. Mertson." To the overseer, he added, "Mertson, meet Miss Jasmine Dubroc, my fiancée. We've come this morning so that Miss Dubroc may see the plantation."

Mertson grinned in surprised pleasure. "Well, this is quite an honor, ma'am," he said, nodding to Jasmine, who smiled back her own greeting. "Congratulations to you both, sir," Mertson added to Jared.

"Thanks, Mertson," he replied.

"Well, sir, if you're not needing me, then . . ." the overseer said, clearing his throat.

"No, not at all," Jared assured him.

Mertson nodded and left the couple.

Jared scowled thoughtfully as he watched Mertson retreat to his cottage. "Andrew Mertson is a fine overseer," he told Jasmine. "The finest I've ever had for this property. But I'm afraid I'm going to lose him soon."

"Oh?" she asked.

"Andrew is originally from New Hampshire," Jared explained, "and after his family moved down here four years ago, he never forgot his childhood sweetheart back in Portsmouth. He's corresponded with the young lady all this time, and I'm sure she wants to marry him. However, poor Mertson's been unable to convince her to come down here to live. I think the unfortunate chap is about ready to give up and move back east so that they can at last wed."

"What a shame," Jasmine said, glancing about at the serene, tree-graced grounds. "It looks like they could have a good life here."

"Yes, I suppose they could," Jared agreed, his voice strangely tight. He cleared his throat and smiled at her. "Well, my dear, would you like to ride about the estate?"

"What about the house?" she asked.

He shrugged. "It's not much to see."

"Oh, Jared, please! I really do want to see it."

"Very well, then."

Together they climbed the staircase to the gray-blue porch, then Jared opened the varnished door and bid Jasmine enter before him. Inside, two enormous rooms—a parlor and dining room—stretched on either side of a long central corridor. In the parlor on the left, two female slaves curtsied a brief greeting to the newcomers, then continued with their dusting.

Jared smiled back at the black women and acknowledged them by name, a display of deference that Jasmine found quite touching. Yet he seemed strangely impatient as he escorted her through the rooms. She found the decor here was much plainer than was Jared's home in Natchez—the planked walls and ceilings were painted white, the floors were of varnished cypress, and there were few rugs in evidence. The furnishings were simple and sometimes bordered on crude— horsehair settees, slat-back chairs and rockers, squarish-looking cupboards and tables that had obviously been made by slaves.

Jasmine got an eerie feeling as they toured the downstairs. Despite the servants in attendance, and the airy whiteness of the walls, there was a strange, almost haunted feeling to this house—a dark air of tragedy that somehow seemed to permeate the very woodwork. Much as she chided herself for her superstitions, she couldn't shake off the disquieting sensation.

"Who built this house?" Jasmine asked Jared as they climbed the plain railed staircase to the upper floor.

"My parents had it constructed soon after we emigrated here from England," he explained. "My family lived on this plantation our first few years in this country. Then my father bought his first steamboat to transport our cotton to market, and soon thereafter, he became so involved in the river trade and in his law practice in Natchez that we built Hampton Hall on the bluff and moved across the river. My mother was quite pleased at the time, since she liked the Natchez social whirl, and wanted to be closer to Aunt Charity."

"I see," Jasmine murmured. Jared's tone had been rather gruff and rushed as he spoke, and it was clear that he disliked talking about his parents. But at least he was sharing a bit of his past with her, if unwillingly. "Do you remember those days very well?"

"Actually, I try my best to forget them," came his terse reply. "I was only five years old when we emigrated."

Jasmine frowned, realizing that it was useless to try to prod Jared further now. She would have to be content with making slow progress where the secrets of his past were concerned.

Upstairs, Jared led her down a long hallway past several plain but spacious bedrooms, and they paused before each open portal so Jasmine could glance inside. The fifth room they passed intrigued Jasmine because of its lovely walnut bed. "That was my room," Jared explained briefly. "After we're married, that's where you and I shall sleep when we come over here—if we come over here."

"Oh, I hope we will sometime," she murmured back with a smile, again feeling warmed that he'd mentioned their wedding plans. And the thought of sharing a marriage bed with Jared was doubly thrilling to her senses!

Jared was leading Jasmine back toward the stairs, when she glanced over her shoulder and said, "Wait! There's a room back at the end of the hallway that we haven't seen yet—the one with the closed door."

Jared tugged her firmly away, toward the stairs. "I really don't want to see that room," he said, in a surprisingly curt tone. "And furthermore, I don't like this damned house. Shall we go?"

Jasmine was so shocked and hurt by Jared's shortness with her, she found herself blinking back tears as they went down the stairs together. Why was he suddenly so angry? she asked herself. And why had he brought her here anyway, if he hated the sight of this house and it brought out this strange darkness in him? Her unfailingly solicitous suitor of past weeks was gone; Jared seemed an impassive stranger as he tugged her down the stairs. Even his usually warm blue eyes were clouded over with turmoil as he firmly escorted her out the front door.

Moments later, they were back in Jared's barouche, following the narrow road past the manor house and slave quarters toward the cotton fields beyond. Jasmine noted that Jared still looked unapproachable—his jaw was tight and his eyes were fixed on the roadway as he uttered commands to the horse. Something about seeing the house had really upset him, she realized. Or was it her?

Jasmine tried to cover her hurt and confusion by studying the landscape through which they were traversing. Just before the road veered off into the fields, they passed the cotton gin—a large, two-story structure busily attended by slaves, who were unloading just-picked cotton from wagons at the front, and carrying baskets of lint over to the press at the back. In the center of the structure, draft horses plodded about in a circle, turning the enormous, loudly squeaking wheel which powered the gin mechanism above.

Jasmine glanced from the gin to the vast sea of white beyond, where dozens of field hands in straw hats were stuffing the fruit of the cotton plants into burlap sacks. "I see it's harvest time," she remarked to Jared.

"Yes. Just beginning."

Jasmine sighed to herself and glanced back at the fields. Jared continued to say little, but occasionally nodded to the field hands as they continued along the narrow path curving between endless rows of cotton. Then they entered another wooded area, and before long Jasmine noted off to the west an enclosure fenced with wrought iron and shaded by several enormous, still-blooming crepe myrtles. Inside stood several tombstones.

"Look, Jared, a cemetery," she said. "May we stop?"

"No," he said harshly. Then, more gently, he added, "Jasmine, my parents are buried there." As she started to question him further, he warned, "Please, don't ask."

Jared turned away to cluck to the horse, and Jasmine bit her lip until she tasted blood. She was feeling more frustrated and hurt by the moment. Jared had insisted she come with him to Vidalia today, yet now it couldn't be more obvious that he didn't want her here. She felt terribly confused, and couldn't even read his expression beneath the low brim of his hat. She didn't know whether to cry or to beat him over the head. She knew he was quite sensitive regarding the subject of his parents, but that didn't excuse his riding roughshod over her feelings. He was in such a peculiar mood. Why had he brought her along?

She found out soon enough, as he turned the barouche off the road onto a weedy, twisted path. They bounced along the potholed trail, winding through the trees for a hundred yards or so, then emerging into a clearing. Before them stood a neat brick cabin, with a pitched cedar roof that extended down over the wide front gallery. Flagstone chimneys on either side of the structure lent the cottage a homey appeal. Surrounding by the thick woods, the cabin seemed set off in its own private world.

Jared stopped the buggy. Turning to Jasmine, he smiled at her for the first time since they had left Natchez earlier that morning. "This is why I brought you here, my dear," he said, as if reading her mind. "To see this."

"This is your cottage?" she asked.

He nodded as he alighted from the buggy. "Actually, it's a hunting lodge I had built a few years ago." He extended his hand to her. "It's where I stay when I come over here."

She took Jared's hand and let him assist her to the ground. "Then it's where I'll want to stay, too, when we come over here."

He grinned. "Is it?"

"Of course." He fetched a pail of water from the cistern and brought it over for the horse. She tried to maintain a cheerful facade as he took her arm and led her toward the cabin steps. While she'd felt encouraged by his smile a moment earlier, she still wasn't sure what to expect from him today.

Together they entered the one-room structure. The inside was pleasantly large, with an open, beamed ceiling and rough puncheon floor. There was a table in the center of the room, and a settee and two rocking chairs gathered about one stone fireplace. Cast-iron cooking pots and utensils were lined up along the matching hearth across the room, and there were guns on the rack above. In the corner beyond the cooking area was an iron bed, covered with a colorful quilt. Gauzy white curtains graced the windows, letting in filtered light. The mood of the cabin was of coziness and warmth.

"Why, it's charming!" Jasmine exclaimed.

"Very few people know of this cabin," Jared replied as he removed his coat and hat, tossing them down on a chair. "It's where I come when I want to be alone."

"Is it?" she asked with great interest, doffing her straw hat and placing it next to Jared's on the chair. She wandered over to the heavy table, fingering the rough wood as she glanced about and tried to picture Jared here alone. "Then I feel all the more special because you've shared it with me," she said with a smile.

"That's not all I'm going to share with you," he said in a husky voice, approaching her.

He caught her to him fiercely, almost violently. His breath was hot on her ear as he whispered, "God, woman, I can't wait to get your clothes off."

"I beg your pardon?" she gasped and backed away, startled by the boldness of his remark.

He pursued her, the peculiar heat still glowing in his eyes. He pulled her to him roughly. "I said, I can't wait to get your clothes off. I want to make love to you, Jasmine, and this time I want to see you. All of you."

Still confused by his audacious words, Jasmine squirmed against him. "Jared, why are you angry at me?"

To her amazement, he laughed. Even as she backed away again, he steadily stalked her, still grinning, glints of wry humor at last reaching his eyes. "Angry, indeed! Impatient, perhaps. Half out of my mind with wanting you, perhaps. But, angry?" He backed her against the table, his hands gripping her shoulders, his blue eyes smoldering down into hers. "I'd advise you to start undressing, Jasmine, or else I'll be compelled to start ripping, and doubtless will fetch you home looking quite a disgrace later on."

"But, Jared, I thought—"

"Turn around," he ordered.

She complied, and felt his impatient fingers undoing the buttons at the back of her dress.

"What did you think, my darling?"

"That . . . oh, God!"

Jared had pulled down the bodice of her dress, untied her chemise, and was latching his mouth hungrily onto one of her breasts. "I thought that you—that I had disappointed you the other night," she gasped, struggling to breathe as hot needles of arousal streaked down her body.

"Disappointed me?" he finished incredulously, his arms clenching about her, his teeth nipping at her breast, driving her insane. "You were sheer heaven, my love!"

"But—you acted so strange, afterward."

"I felt that perhaps we should have waited until we were

wed—that you might have regrets, or that I may have hurt you, frightened you—''

"No—no," she denied.

"No?" he repeated with a chuckle.

Then she lost all track of rational thought as Jared pulled her clothing down even farther, exposing her midsection. He pulled her close and plunged his tongue into her navel. She caught a painfully sharp breath at the wondrous sensation, then bucked against him ecstatically as his hands slipped inside her pantalets and boldly caressed her bare bottom. His fingers kneaded her soft flesh, binding her against him as his tongue moved in a hot, seductive circle at her front. Jasmine tangled her fingers in Jared's thick hair, feeling so weak with desire, she was surprised her legs supported her.

Jared was now planting hot kisses on her lower belly, his lips moving inexorably lower as he spoke in a tortured tone. "I told myself I wouldn't do this again, and I went through hell for four days, but it was no good. God help you, girl, even if you hated it, I'd have you again now!"

"I don't hate it," she cried, in a voice raw with her own need as his mouth closed on the silky mound between her legs. "I love it, every second—just as I love you!"

"Oh, Jasmine—my dearest heart." Abruptly he stood, pulling her to him and kissing her so hard and deep she thought she would faint. His tongue engaged hers, demanding surrender and gaining it in full measure. She clung to him, trembling, as he became her only reality in a world whirling crazily about her.

"Oh, God, love, I can't wait," he said, the words laced with his pained desperation.

With a fierce, almost animal groan, Jared lifted her onto the edge of the tabletop. He pulled her clothing aside, and within seconds, thrust himself fully into her waiting warmth. She moaned at the wondrous, throbbing pressure of him sheathed inside her; the friction was exquisitely intense. Every inch of her was stretched tautly to receive the hard proof of his love.

"Oh, God, woman, you feel so wonderful," he whispered, surging deeply.

Jared wrapped Jasmine's long legs about his waist and plunged into her with breathtaking need. She moaned incoherently, and as he increased his tumultuous pace, her mouth went so dry she could barely swallow. She felt herself slipping away into a new realm of bliss, where the pleasure was so intense it bordered on pain. When she at last gave herself over to the moment and to him, the convulsion of rapture ripping through her was so powerful, her eyes flew open and she cried out his name. He whispered a soothing endearment even as he gave her the full measure of ecstasy she sought so desperately.

When her breathing at last subsided, when her madly racing heart calmed a bit, Jasmine glanced up to see Jared smiling down at her. "My love," he whispered, leaning over to kiss her, his warm lips trembling on hers. "My love. . . ."

After a moment, he drew back slightly, his eyes raking over her body with loving thoroughness. "You should see yourself. There's a blush all over your face, going all the way down your body, to where we're joined." He grinned. "Is your backside sore?"

She felt her blush deepening. "Well, this table does leave something to be desired."

He chuckled. "I wanted you so badly, I couldn't even get you to the bed. What you do to me, woman!"

"What you do to me!"

"Did I thoroughly scandalize you?" he asked, suddenly serious.

"You can scandalize me that way any time," she quipped back. Watching a slow grin spread across his handsome face, she added with feigned petulance, "I must say, though, that you were rather irritable—before."

"Indeed I was. But I think you've managed to clip my horns, woman. Forgive me?" he added tenderly, running his hand through her thick, wavy hair.

Again, she set her features in a mock pout. "For your surliness, yes. For the rest—there's nothing to forgive."

"That's my girl."

Slowly he withdrew from her flesh. As he helped her off the table, she muttered, "Ouch!"

"What is it, darling?"

"Oh, it's nothing!" she said, her face burning as she slid to her feet.

"Jasmine? Damn it, have I hurt you?"

"No, you didn't, not at all. It's just that—" She paused, thoroughly mortified. "I'm afraid you got a couple of splinters in my—um—"

He chuckled. "Then it will be my pleasure to remove them."

She was horror-stricken. "Oh, no you won't!"

"Oh, yes I will."

He led her firmly to the bed.

During the next three hours, Jasmine discovered anew what love was, what passion meant. Jared was insatiable as he made love to her on the sun-drenched feather bed, with the colorful quilt and the sheets folded at its foot. He spent long moments exploring her body—first with his eyes, then with his hands and his mouth. He aroused her to a fever pitch of excitement, while maintaining perfect control himself. Then he drew her beneath him and possessed her, all the time looking down into her eyes and watching her every reaction. He rocked her with long, slow strokes, and when she beat on his chest and begged for release, he only smiled, showing no mercy. When she hooked her elbow around his neck and scorched his lips with her own wild need, his control broke and he drove home with a sweet violence that left her limp and totally satiated in his arms. Later, he drew her on top of him, twisted her breasts in his hands, and let her set the pace. She watched his responses this time, loving the way his eyes darkened, his moans as her hands roved over him intimately. When they reached release together, tenderly this time, he smiled up at her and whispered, "I love you," and she whispered back the same.

They talked. Jared told her all about his travels to Europe, and how he was planning to take her and Maggie there next year. She confessed that ever since she'd read Thomas Shelton's translation of *Don Quixote*, she had secretly hungered to see Spain, and he assured her that her hunger would soon be assuaged. When she remarked that he somewhat reminded her of Cervantes' whimsical hero, in that he often went charging into situations without thought, he scowled in mock outrage and tickled her until she screamed for mercy. He soon decided that making love with her again would be much sweeter revenge.

His vengeance became her victory.

Afterward, Jasmine cuddled with Jared, glorying in their nearness and feeling grateful that their lovemaking, their sharing, had somehow quenched the turmoil in him. She had a nagging fear that Jared's terseness with her earlier had to do with much more than his mere impatience to be with her. There was still the dark mystery regarding his parents, which one day would have to be addressed. But she pushed her uncertainties aside, deciding that they could deal with those problems another day. For now, she wouldn't let anything spoil this rapturous afternoon—she wanted only to bask with Jared in the glow of their newfound closeness and reaffirmed love.

And she did. When they left the cabin together that afternoon, they both knew that they had crossed a boundary together and entered into a new dimension of intimacy.

As they drove back to the ferry, Jared asked, "What about the annulment, Jasmine? Any word?"

"Well, Father Grignon said it will be granted in perhaps another month or so."

"Good," Jared replied. "We need to start planning our wedding, my dear." She glanced at him quickly, and he added, "Darling, we must set a date, and the sooner the better. Otherwise, I fear you may be walking up the aisle with your belly quite swollen with my child." He pulled the horse to a halt and turned to her, grinning. "Not that I'd mind that, but you might be a trifle embarrassed."

"I wouldn't be," she said, her heart in her eyes. "I'd be proud to carry your child, Jared."

He reached out to stroke her cheek. "Would you be?"

"Oh, yes! So proud!"

"And to hell with what everyone else thought?"

"Yes! To hell with them!"

He laughed with wonder. "Oh, my dearest heart. We're laughing now, but in truth, I fear you could well be carrying my child." He leaned closer to her, and his eyes were glazed as he whispered, "I'm not going to stop, Jasmine. I can't. Not now."

"I can't either," she whispered back.

"Meet me at the summerhouse at midnight?"

"Oh, yes, my love!"

# ★ Twenty ★

Jasmine felt as if she were walking on air when Jared took her home late that afternoon. He kissed her good-bye on the front gallery of Charity's house as the cool breeze swirled about them, tugging at their clothing and flooding their senses with the aroma of late-blooming honeysuckle. He had to attend a meeting of the Planters Association at a downtown hotel that evening, and after he left, Jasmine wondered how she could live until midnight, when they would once again meet out at the summerhouse.

When she arrived at her bedroom upstairs, she spotted a familiar velvet box sitting on her dressing table. She hurried over and opened it, and the two fabulous emeralds again winked at her from the satin-lined interior. The gesture was just like Jared, she thought lovingly. She smiled as she slipped his ring back on her finger.

That evening as Jasmine sat in her room, laboriously embroidering linen napkins that would be sold at the upcoming orphanage benefit, she relived her every second with Jared earlier that day at his hunting lodge—the moments of intense passion, the interludes of tenderness and tears. She remembered the erotic sensation of his hands, his mouth on her flesh, how wondrous it felt to be touched by him, even when he'd gently plucked the splinters from her bottom and had kissed the small welts the rough tabletop had brought.

That night, and during the nights that followed, the summerhouse became their haven—their private world of unbridled passion. Jasmine slipped out of the house each night at midnight, and hours later, she raced the dawn back, her face flushed, her hair tangled from passion and the early morning breezes, her body tender and bruised by the long hours she'd spent with Jared on the daybed. Dawn was generally breaking by the time she tumbled into bed in her own room, and, in a cruelly short time, Maggie invariably came bounding in to awaken her. By midmorning, Jasmine was yawning over her lessons with the child, and she soon fell into the habit of napping with her in the afternoons. At suppertime, Jared would generally reappear to share the evening meal with Jasmine, Charity, and Maggie. Then, at midnight, she'd rush out to meet him once more.

Sometimes, Jasmine felt a stab of guilt that she was carrying on her passionate love affair with Jared, knowing that she was still married to Claude as far as the Catholic church was concerned. Yet, as Jared had pointed out, her marriage to the swindler Boudreau had never been a true marriage in that it had not been consummated, and it had already been annulled in the eyes of the law, so Jasmine refused to think of what she and Jared were doing as wrong. They were married in their hearts, and soon enough they would be married in deed; for her, for them both, this was enough. Each day, Jasmine found herself falling more deeply in love with Jared, and each day, her bitterness about both her father and Claude Boudreau receded farther into the back of her mind.

Jasmine was quite busy during this period, helping prepare for the orphanage benefit Jared was sponsoring, attending the numerous social activities that she, Jared, and Charity had been invited to now that the Natchez fall season was in full swing, and preparing for her own wedding. At Jared's insistence, they'd finally set a date for the wedding—December 5, two months hence. Charity had ordered invitations from the printer, and was proceeding with the wedding plans, even though Jasmine feared that perhaps the annulment might not come through in time for her and Jared to marry in the church. However, neither Jared nor Father Grignon seemed to share Jasmine's anxieties there. The priest informed Jasmine that he had already received an acknowledgment of her petition from the pontifical tribunal in Rome, and that he now expected the dissolution to be granted within a month to six weeks.

Jasmine and Jared now spent time together with Maggie each day, and a sense of family was building among the three of them. Jared often took the girls for drives along the bluff at sunset, and the three would watch, awestruck, as the sun seemed to sink into the Louisiana lowlands beyond them. Jared had also explained to Maggie that once he and Jasmine were wed, a formal deed of adoption would be approved by the Natchez Orphans Court. Maggie was ecstatic at the news that she, Jasmine, and Jared would be together always. Jared had also taken Maggie down to Hampton Hall, and the child had chosen the room she wanted for her own.

The redecorating of Jared's house was almost complete now; the rooms of Hampton Hall were resplendent with the rose, green, and gold color scheme Jasmine had selected. As the work progressed, Jasmine deepened her friendship with Marie Bernard. At Jasmine's insistence, the two women were now on a first-name basis. While Jasmine had never confided in Marie about her father and Claude Boudreau, the two of them shared an interest in the decorating, and Marie had also become quite involved in the upcoming orphanage benefit. Together, she and Jasmine were embroidering stacks and stacks of linen dresser scarves, napkins, and small tablecloths, all to be sold at the booths.

Cactus Jack Malone was back in town now, after what had seemed a long absence, and a couple of times while Jasmine was working at Jared's house with Marie, the soft-spoken man stopped by, ostensibly looking for Jared. Jasmine was not fooled, however; she realized that Jack really came by hoping to steal a few moments with the pretty housekeeper. While the two continued to exchange yearning, secretive glances whenever they were together, Jasmine found, to her dismay, that they were making no progress in their relationship. Jack, in particular, seemed almost unbearably reserved around Marie, as if he feared she were some delicate bird that might fly away if he made the slightest move in her direction.

One afternoon, as they sat in Marie's small office, embroidering daisies on dresser scarves, Jasmine ventured, "What do you think of Mr. Malone?"

Marie smiled, looking up from her work. "Why, I think he's a fine man."

"I think he likes you," Jasmine said, setting aside her own handwork.

Marie actually blushed, and avoided Jasmine's eye as she replied, "Oh, no, Jasmine. Mr. Malone is polite, but I'm sure he has no interest in . . ."

"Indeed?" Jasmine asked, raising an eyebrow. "Then why, pray tell, does Mr. Malone stop by here every chance he gets?"

Marie bit her lip and blinked rapidly. "Why, he's looking for Mr. Jared, of course."

"Marie! You know good and well that Jared is almost always at his office during the day—and Jack knows it better than either of us."

Marie was silent for a moment. "I just don't think he's interested in me," she said at last, in a strained, tight voice.

"And why shouldn't he be?"

Marie glanced up at Jasmine, the turmoil obvious in her dark eyes and tense features. "Perhaps he feels . . . well, I would think it would be only natural that Mr. Malone would feel I was somewhat . . . tainted."

"Marie!" Jasmine scolded.

"Jasmine . . ." The Frenchwoman gestured helplessly, then went on in a hoarse tone, "Jack's the one who found me and my family, who saw . . . everything those men did to me."

"Then he well knows that absolutely nothing that happened was your fault!" Jasmine returned stoutly. "And he's watched over you ever since, hasn't he, Marie?"

She frowned thoughtfully but did not answer.

Jasmine mulled over her conversation with Marie as the two women finished their embroidery. Even though Marie

seemed to have laid aside her bitterness about the outrage
dealt her on the Natchez Trace, the pain was still there, lurking
in the back of her mind, ready to spill over to the surface.
Old wounds were hard to heal, it seemed. Jasmine knew this
well herself.

That evening, Jared escorted Jasmine and Charity out to
supper. Back at Magnolia Bend, when he kissed Jasmine
good night, he winked at her, whispering a reminder in her
ear about their nightly rendezvous.

But right after he left a hard rain began, and the downpour
continued for hours. Jasmine knew that Jared would not expect her to venture outside in it, and eventually she went on
to bed. Yet she lay tossing and turning all night, missing
Jared, listening to the crack of thunder and the hard drone of
the rain, and wishing she could be in his arms.

The next morning dawned clear, and Jasmine decided she'd
do something she'd never done before—she'd go visit Jared
at his office Under-the-Hill. She missed him and didn't know
if she could wait till tonight to see him. Doubtless he'd lecture
her soundly for venturing into the seamy part of town where
he worked, but being with him would be well worth the
inevitable scolding. She was particularly anxious to have a
word with Jared about Jack Malone and Marie Bernard. Jasmine was sure that the two would get together with the proper
nudge, and she intended to see that it was provided. She and
Jared were so happy together that she wanted Jack and Marie
to find the same bliss.

An hour later, Ephraim was nervously driving her through
town; his dark eyes darted about anxiously as they approached
Silver Street. Yet the ride down into the teeming waterfront
community was uneventful, aside from an occasional seedy-
looking character directing a whistle or lewd remark at Jasmine. She ignored the scattered taunts and ribald invitations,
keeping her expression icily detached, her gaze firmly fixed
on the roadway ahead as Ephraim drove the horse at a brisk
trot. Even in the fall coolness, fat black flies buzzed at
Sugar's back as they turned onto the rutted expanse of

Middle Street, passing a sagging, weather-beaten brothel, a loudly bustling lumber mill, and a paradoxically neat, well-patronized barber shop. The air was laced with a strange mixture of rotting garbage, newly cut timber, and the oozing mud which forever sluiced off the buggy wheels as they bounced along.

When they at last reached Jared's office, Ephraim breathed a sigh of relief and reined in the horse. He helped Jasmine alight from the buggy, then stood guard by the conveyance while his mistress went inside.

Jasmine lifted the hem of her serge skirt and stepped gingerly across the muddy boardwalk, approaching the office. The bell on the back of the door jangled as she walked crisply inside. In the front cubicle, a young clerk who sat at a desk cluttered with documents glanced up at her. "Yes, miss?" he inquired, standing and self-consciously adjusting his glasses as Jasmine walked in.

"You must be Peter Fenton, Mr. Hampton's clerk," Jasmine said with a bright smile. "Mr. Hampton has spoken of you several times. I'm Jasmine Dubroc, Mr. Hampton's fiancée."

The young man blushed. "Pleased to make your acquaintance, ma'am."

She smiled. "Is he in?"

The clerk looked even more flustered; his gaze darted toward the door to the inner office. Clearing his throat, he sputtered, "Er—yes'um, Mr. Hampton is in. But I'm afraid he's quite busy at the moment—"

"That's quite all right," Jasmine assured the young man with a wave of her gloved hand. "I'm sure Mr. Hampton won't mind in the least if I go in." She turned and approached the door to Jared's office.

"Miss Dubroc, please, don't—" the young man called after her.

But it was too late. After knocking perfunctorily, Jasmine swung open the door to the inner office and discovered why the young clerk had acted so agitated.

Jared was calmly stuffing several bills into a prostitute's

hand. Jasmine's eyes grew enormous. She froze at the portal, surveying the shocking scene inside Jared's office. The love of her life stood grinning at his desk as he handed money to the painted woman, and she in turn flirtatiously smiled back at him as she accepted the bills. The woman was most definitely a creature of the streets, Jasmine noted with distaste. The odor of her cheap perfume was overpowering even from across the room, and the flashiness of her gold satin gown, the tawdriness of her feathered hat, seemed to scream out her identity. The woman's cheeks were heavily rouged, her heavy lips were painted bright red, and though she was blonde, she reminded Jasmine strongly of Flossie La Fleume.

Jasmine absorbed all of these distressing details in a mere instant. Then Jared and the strange woman simultaneously noticed her presence, and whirled to stare at her. "Why, Jasmine!" Jared exclaimed with obvious shock. "My dear, whatever are you doing in this part of town?"

"Whatever, indeed?" Jasmine bristled, closing the door as she stepped into the room. She noted with some satisfaction that the painted lady looked quite flustered as she stuffed the bills Jared had given her into a small sequined reticule and extracted a wrinkled handkerchief to cover her nervous sniffs.

Jared hurried to Jasmine's side. "It's good to see you, my dear," he said in a calm voice, even though his blue eyes were admonishing her. He took her arm and led her toward the other woman. "Jasmine, meet a friend of mine—Savannah Sue Stallings. Sue, this is my fiancée, Miss Dubroc."

While Jasmine managed to nod stiffly to the other woman, Savannah Sue lowered her handkerchief and took a cautious step forward. "Howdy do, ma'am," she said to Jasmine. The woman was on the plump side, Jasmine noted. Her face was well-rounded, her bare neck and shoulders fleshy, and her voluptuous breasts threatened to spill out of her low-cut gown. "I don't mean to be causing no trouble, ma'am, but Mr. Jared here, he been helping me out with my ma. You see, Ma's stuck back in Georgia and she got the consumption somethin' fierce, and Mr. Jared here—well, he's been kind enough to give me a loan on account of Ma's doctor bills."

Sue paused, eyeing Jasmine anxiously. The hand holding

her handkerchief was trembling slightly. "That's quite fine of Mr. Jared," Jasmine said at last, in a frosty tone.

Sue sighed in obvious relief. "Yes'um. Well'um, I'll just be mosey'n on, then." She nodded to Jared. "Thanks again, Mr. Hampton. And Ma, in her last letter, she said to tell you, God love you, sir!"

"Thanks, Sue," Jared said, grinning, as the woman hurried from the room. He turned, taking Jasmine's hand and fixing her with a stern scowl. "My dear, I'm afraid you've been very naughty."

"I've been naughty!" Jasmine bristled, throwing off his touch.

Ignoring Jasmine's retort, Jared scolded her with his index finger. "You know I've warned you repeatedly that you must never venture forth unescorted in this part of town."

"No wonder! I might have spoiled your fun, obviously."

His scowl deepened. "Whatever are you referring to, Jasmine?"

Jasmine was tempted to stamp her foot. "That woman. What was she doing here?"

Jared shrugged. "I thought she explained her presence here quite well."

Jasmine's mouth fell open. "Jared! Since when have you kept company with street women?"

He chuckled. "I do believe you're jealous, Jasmine."

"I do believe you're right!"

Jared drew closer and placed his hands on Jasmine's rigid shoulders. "Jasmine, Sue is simply someone I help out on occasion. As she explained, her mother is ailing back in Georgia. I have—well, I inherited a great deal of wealth, my dear, and when I can, I do try to help out those less fortunate than I. So, giving Sue a few dollars is really no different from contributing to the Ladies' Beneficent Society, or to the orphanage, or—"

"To me?" Jasmine demanded.

He laughed shortly. "What's that supposed to mean?"

She began to pace, saying haughtily, "Well, perhaps I'm just another one of your worthy causes, Jared. You have so many."

"But, Jasmine—you're the only worthy cause I've promised to marry."

Though Jared's words were laced with wry humor, Jasmine was not appeased. She stared at the squalid alleyway behind Jared's office and demanded, "Where did you meet her?"

"As I told you, I occasionally stop in for a drink at the Scarlet Slipper—"

"She whirled on him. No more!"

He laughed. "I beg your pardon, Jasmine?"

Jasmine's hands were on her hips, the fists balled, and her chin was tilted stubbornly. "I said, no more. You're not stopping by the Scarlet Slipper anymore."

Jared's grin widened, and amusement danced in his eyes. "Are you telling me what to do now?"

"Yes!"

"Jasmine, I do believe you're throwing a temper tantrum," he remarked with a chuckle.

"Oh—you cad!" she said, seething, as scandalous possibilities ran rampant in her mind. "Tell me, Jared—where were you the other night when you said you had a meeting? Were you with Sue then?"

"Jasmine!" He shook his head in disbelief. "Do you really think that, after all we've shared at the summerhouse, I'd have anything left for another woman?"

Jasmine blushed, knowing Jared had spoken the truth. Yet still, her wounded pride forced her to hedge. "Well . . ."

"Jasmine, come here."

"No!"

In two strides, he was at her side, pulling her close and looking down at her with a combination of indulgent amusement and righteous anger. Further argument was forestalled by his passionate lips—first roughly silencing her, then drinking of her sweetness, then soothing, seducing. . . . Within seconds, Jasmine found herself sitting in Jared's lap on his leather settee, moaning shamelessly as she clung to him and kissed him back. "Do you still think it's Sue I want?" he asked huskily after a long moment.

"No," she admitted.

He sighed. "Still angry at me?"

"Not if you promise never again to visit the Silver Slipper."

He chuckled and hugged her close. "Very well, my passionate, possessive creature. You have my word as a gentleman." More seriously, he went on, "But, Jasmine, if Sue comes back needing more money for her mother, I'm planning to give it to her."

"Fair enough," Jasmine conceded. "May I be present?"

"Oh, my dearest heart!" Jared exclaimed. "Don't you know I'd have you by my side every second if I could?" He kissed the tip of her nose, then added vehemently, "God, I missed you so last night! That confounded rain!"

"I missed you, too." She grinned at him. "And I also confounded the rain—numerous times."

He laughed as he swooped down for another kiss. A long moment later, he remarked, "You know, I never asked you why you came down here."

"Oh, yes." Reluctantly, Jasmine slid out of Jared's lap, settling herself next to him and smoothing her skirts about her. "It concerns Cactus Jack—and Marie."

"Oh?"

"I think—well, I think the two of them are in love, but I'm afraid nothing's going to come of it unless Jack makes a move."

Jared smiled. "I see. You're very observant, Jasmine."

She laughed. "Well, one would have to be blind not to see the looks the two of them secretly exchange. I know Marie would be very receptive, if only Jack would make a move in her direction."

Jared stroked his jaw and nodded. "Perhaps I'll have a word with Jack, then." There was much emotion in his eyes as he looked at her and added, "Wouldn't it be wonderful if they could find what we have?"

"Oh, yes, wonderful!"

Jared stood and helped Jasmine to her feet. "Well, my pet, since you've been foolish enough to venture down into this hellhole, it behooves me to see you safely home."

"Oh, no," Jasmine said. "That won't be necessary. Ephraim is waiting for me outside."

"Then, I'll escort you to your conveyance."

She smiled and took his arm. But as they started to leave the room, she paused. "Jared?"

"Yes?"

She bit her lip, then said, "I noticed that Cactus Jack was gone for some time before he stopped in at your house the other day. Have you had him searching again—for Claude?"

"Yes," Jared replied grimly.

"Still no luck? I mean, I'm assuming you would have told me, if—"

"Yes, my dear, I would have told you." Jared shook his head regretfully. "As you've already surmised, we've still made no progress. And unfortunately, Jack's going to have to stick around here for the time being. Harvest season is my busiest time of year, and his assistance is always invaluable, both with my packet line here and with my plantation over in Vidalia." Jared fixed Jasmine with a direct, determined look and squeezed her hand. "But don't worry, my dear. Jack and I are both keeping our eyes and ears open. And, in six weeks or so, he'll again be venturing forth to search for Boudreau. We'll find that scoundrel, and then I'll deal with him appropriately."

Seeing the murderous light in Jared's eyes as he spoke of hunting down Claude, Jasmine was almost afraid he *would* find her erstwhile husband. And at that moment, she realized as never before how very much Jared meant to her—much more, even, than seeking her own revenge. . . .

## ★ Twenty-one ★

Late October was soon upon them. The carnival to benefit the orphanage took place on the last Saturday of that briskly cool month. The weather was clear and beautiful out on the bluff at the Old Spanish Parade Grounds where the event was to be held. Jared, Jasmine, and Maggie drove out early that morning to help with the preparations. Charity would be joining them later, bringing along her contribution to the day—large quantities of freshly baked goods from the Magnolia Bend kitchen.

Jasmine was excited as Jared parked his barouche on the outskirts of the parade grounds, beneath a huge, red-gold sycamore just beginning to shed its leaves. Watching him hop down, Jasmine smiled and thought of how dashing he looked in his black wool suit and elegant silk top hat. As he helped the two girls alight, he grinned and remarked, "My, don't you two look enchanting today!"

Jasmine smiled at the compliment, inhaling a deep breath of bracing fall air as her slippers contacted the spongy ground. She and Maggie wore coordinating dresses, both fashioned of rose-colored silk.

Jared was still grinning proudly as he strode to the boot of his buggy and extracted a muslin bag filled with the handwork Jasmine and Marie had laboriously completed and were donating to the event. The threesome then approached the large clearing.

The parade grounds were already a beehive of activity. At the front, two roustabouts from one of Jared's packets were crouched on the ground, hammering away on a large wooden archway. Wrapped with colorful bunting, the arch would later be raised as the official gateway to the day's events.

Walking past the roustabouts, they entered the enormous, grassy area of the bluff where the citizens of Natchez walked on fine evenings. To the north of the clearing, beneath sheltering oaks, stretched several lines of wooden tables and benches, brought out from the Catholic church a day earlier. Churchwomen were now draping the tables with oilcloth, in preparation for the noon meal. Beyond the eating area, another group of tables delineated the booth area. Men and women were spreading colorful cloths and laying upon them the items to be sold—everything from homemade preserves, fruit, and cake to knitted shawls, crocheted baby booties, glassware, and dishes, even a set of cups and saucers hand-painted by John James Audubon, which a generous family had donated.

At the southern edge of the clearing were parked the brightly painted wagons of Finnegan's Family Circus. The members of the troupe were now eating breakfast by open fires, and the aromas of ham, bacon, and coffee filled the air.

But what seized Jasmine and Maggie's attention was the huge, colorful, red-and-white-striped balloon at the edge of the bluff. Its underinflated body was encased in hemp netting, and its bottom appendix was attached to a hose that twisted off through several elaborate boxes to the side. Hearing a hoarse, wheezing sound, Jasmine surmised that the apparatus was slowly being filled with some sort of gas from the huge boxes. Two men in shirts and dungarees were monitoring the process closely, watching the balloon and checking various connectors.

Jasmine turned to Jared. "Is it a hot-air balloon?"

He shook his head. "No, hydrogen. Those boxes you see yonder are gas generators." To Maggie, he added, "Best to stay well back, honey. Hydrogen can be dangerous."

"Where did it come from?" Jasmine asked him.

"It's with the circus," he replied. "Mr. Finnegan's brother-in-law, Thaddeus McCoy, launches the balloon in every town the circus visits. They'll be taking her up later today."

"Can I go up? Oh, Uncle Jared, please!" Maggie cried, clapping her hands and jumping up and down, her skirts and curls bobbing.

Jared grinned at the child and pinched her pink cheek, but made no comment. Handing the sack of handwork to Jasmine, he said, "Well, my dear, I'd best go speak with Mr. Finnegan to make sure everything is ready."

Jasmine smiled as she watched Jared stride off to the area where the circus people were. Taking Maggie's small hand and squeezing it affectionately, Jasmine said, "Come on, honey. Sister Scholastica promised me she'd sell these items at the orphanage booth, so let's go find her and see if we can help."

In the hours that followed, the parade grounds teemed with noise and activity as the booths and the circus performance area were prepared. Rows and rows of covered dishes and enormous jugs of tea were set out on the buffet table for the noon meal. Once all was ready, Jared grabbed Jasmine and Maggie, and the three stood at the front gate taking tickets and greeting people. As had been planned, the families brought along the orphans they were sponsoring for the day. Jasmine was thrilled to see her students happily integrated among the esteemed Natchez citizenry. The benefit had totally transcended church lines, Jasmine noted with pride, and practically every prominent family in the community had become a patron of the event in one way or another.

By midday, the event was well underway. The entire area was bustling with people and full of laughter. The attendees were enthralled by the jugglers, clowns, equestriennes, and acrobats. The entertainment was continuous, and when the families were not watching members of the troupe perform, they were busy buying at the booths. With the activities in full swing, Maggie soon broke away from Jasmine and Jared at the ticket area, and flitted about the parade grounds like a happy, free spirit, spending much time sampling the delicacies at Charity's bakery booth.

The most pleasant surprise of the day came for Jasmine when Cactus Jack Malone showed up with Marie Bernard. "Jared—look!" Jasmine cried to her fiancé, nudging Jared in the side as she watched Jack help Marie out of a small black buggy in the parking area beyond them.

At her side, Jared chuckled. "Looks like Jack heeded my advice."

"You spoke with him about Marie?"

"Yes."

"Oh, Jared, I could just hug you!"

He turned to her, grinning and lifting an eyebrow. "Well?"

"Not in public," she whispered demurely, and he chuckled.

Jasmine eagerly watched Jack and Marie draw closer. Both were elegantly dressed, walking arm in arm in the bright sunshine. They looked very happy together.

When the couple arrived at the gate, Jack shook hands with Jared before handing his employer their tickets. "Have we missed all the good grub, boss?" he asked, grinning as he stroked his thin mustache.

"Not at all," Jared assured him. "In fact, the serving line will not open for another half hour. Marie, you look just lovely," he added to his housekeeper.

"Thank you, sir," she replied, smiling, her dark brown eyes aglow and a flush of happiness highlighting her cheeks.

"I adore that lavender dress, Marie," Jasmine added sincerely. "The color is perfect for you."

"As the rose is for you, Jasmine," Marie replied.

"Let's be sure to talk later on!" Jasmine called to Marie as she and Jack went through the gate.

Later, after all the tickets had been taken, Jasmine and Jared did join Jack and Marie for the noon meal at the eating area under the trees. The four laughed as they sat in the cool, dappled shadows and sampled the hearty fare: ham, fried chicken, soda biscuits, beans, corn on the cob, potato salad, pickled vegetables, fruits, and every dessert imaginable. Maggie was still busy stuffing herself with cookies at Charity's booth, although Jasmine had stopped by earlier and had insisted the child eat a ham sandwich.

The talk at the long table was lively. Toward the end of the meal, Frederick Stanton, looking quite lordly in a white suit and matching panama hat, stopped by the table and clapped Jared on the shoulder. "A splendid day, Hampton, and a complete success!" the ruddy-complected German told his friend.

"Thank you, Frederick," Jared said, standing and turning to shake the other man's hand.

"I must say that the balloon is a touch of pure genius," Stanton added.

Jared grinned. "Looks like it's almost completely inflated now, too. Care to have a closer look and meet its owner, Thaddeus McCoy?"

"I'd be honored," Stanton replied.

Jared glanced back at the table. "Join us, Jack?"

"Sure, boss." Nodding to the ladies, Jack put down his napkin and stood.

"Jared, please be careful!" Jasmine called out, but her fiancé merely waved her off as he strode toward the balloon with the two other men.

Jasmine turned back to the table to see Marie smiling at her. She was grateful to have this private moment with her friend. "Join me for a walk, Marie?" she asked.

"Certainly, Jasmine."

The two women excused themselves and went strolling through the trees on the outskirts of the large clearing, following a leaf-strewn path that circled the parade grounds. As soon as they were out of earshot, Jasmine exclaimed, "Marie, you don't know how delighted I am to see you and Jack together!"

Marie blushed and smiled. "Thank you, miss."

"What happened?" Jasmine asked.

"Well, about a week ago, Jack came to see me," Marie explained. "And he told me what was in his heart."

"Yes?" The two had paused beneath a tree.

Marie took a deep breath, then confided, "It seems that Mr. Malone has wanted to court me for some time, but he was afraid . . . well, he thought that after what happened to me, I'd never again want a man to touch me."

"Oh, Marie! What did you tell him?"

Marie smiled serenely. "I told him he was wrong."

"I'm so glad!" Jasmine exclaimed. "You mean, all those years, the two of you could have been together, except for this misunderstanding?"

"Perhaps the years were needed for healing," Marie said wisely.

Jasmine nodded. "You may be right."

A thoughtful silence settled between them. Then, in the clearing beyond, the crowd cheered as a lovely young woman in colorful costume raised herself to a standing position on the back of a prancing white horse. Gesturing toward the equestrian display, Marie said, "It was wonderful of Mr. Jared to do all this."

"I know. I'm sure this day has cost him thousands," Jasmine replied.

Marie nodded. "Mr. Hampton is the most generous man I've ever known."

Jasmine mulled over Marie's words for a moment. "Marie, there is one thing."

"Yes?"

In a low, confidential tone, Jasmine said, "Last week, I went to Mr. Jared's shipping office Under-the-Hill, and when I walked in, I found him giving money to a prostitute."

To Jasmine's amazement, Marie only smiled ruefully. "I'm not surprised."

"You're not?" Jasmine asked, raising an eyebrow.

"Mr. Jared is a soft touch. Those girls from the Scarlet Slipper are always taking advantage of him—giving him some sob story or other in order to get a handout."

"Those girls?" Jasmine inquired in a rising voice. "You mean, there's been more than one of them?"

Marie sighed. "Unfortunately, yes. There are two or three who have come by the house on occasion—usually at night, when they're unlikely to be spotted."

"Oh, good Lord!" Jasmine gasped.

Marie placed a reassuring hand on Jasmine's sleeve. "Jasmine, you must know that Mr. Jared would never betray you with one of those women. When they do come by, they never stay for more than a minute or two. Mr. Jared usually gives them some money in the front hallway, and then they're off. That's all they want—really."

"But still—to think of them coming to Jared's home!"

Marie nodded sympathetically. "I know. The thought is rather distasteful. But, Jasmine, I really believe that if one is to love a man, one must accept his quirks and faults." With a musing smile, she went on, "I know, for instance, that I must accept Mr. Malone's shortcomings."

"Oh? What faults does Cactus Jack have?"

"You might call it wanderlust," Marie responded frankly. "As you may have noticed, Jack frequently travels for Mr. Jared. And he's told me it's not just his job. He likes going on the road—being out in the countryside, close to nature.

He's also told me that he must soon venture forth on a mission for Mr. Jared, and he says he can't marry me until that quest is completed. He says this will give me a chance to decide whether I like his being gone for long stretches.''

"I see." Jasmine felt a stab of guilt that she had never confided in Marie regarding Claude Boudreau, and the reason Jack Malone had been searching for him. "Did Jack tell you what this mission is about?''

"No, miss.''

Jasmine bit her lip, then asked, "Do you think you'll learn to accept Jack's being gone a lot?''

"Why, Jasmine,'' Marie said with a serene smile, "I already have. I would not want him any other way.''

During the next hour, Jasmine stood in for Miss Charity at the bakery booth, to give the widow a well-deserved rest. She did her best to appear cheerful as she stood in the cool shade of a pecan tree, selling cookies and slices of cake and pie to the line of people endlessly trooping by. Yet inwardly, Jasmine remained enmeshed in turmoil following her conversation with Marie.

It had been a shock for her to learn that Jared was helping to support more than one prostitute from Under-the-Hill—and he hadn't even bothered to tell her! At first, Jasmine had felt angry, then hurt, and now she was seesawing between the two, trying to get her feelings into perspective.

From what Marie had said, Jared was not romantically involved with any of these street creatures. But the whole business made Jasmine wildly jealous, nevertheless. After all, these were women of very loose moral fiber, and even though she knew Jared would never intentionally betray her, she didn't trust them.

"Miss Jasmine, we have a present!''

Soon after Charity had returned to the bakery booth, Maggie, followed closely by Jared, came bounding up with two long, slender items clutched in her small hand. "Here, Miss Jasmine!'' the child said proudly, thrusting one of the objects toward her.

Jasmine took the present, which turned out to be a lovely silk fan with ivory sticks. Opening it, she gasped in pleasure. On opposite ends of the silk panel were painted two colorful balloons, each enclosed in a circle of gold fleur-de-lis; between the balloons was a third circle, picturing a couple embracing. The entire effect was exquisite!

"They're from Uncle Jared," Maggie was saying jubilantly. "Mine's just like yours, except it has a little girl in the center of the fan."

"Oh, Jared, they're lovely!" Jasmine exclaimed, glancing over Maggie's head at him.

"Indeed!" Charity echoed from Jasmine's side.

Jared stepped forward, grinning, and this time he extended a small brass box to Charity. "I wouldn't want you to think I'd forgotten you, Aunt."

"Oh, Jared!" Charity exclaimed, taking her treat. "Look, Jasmine, it's a brass cachepot with a picture of a balloon ascension painted on top!" To Jared, she added, "Jared, where did you get these lovely things?"

"Special-ordered from England," Jared explained. "I wasn't sure they would get here in time for the benefit, but Mr. Patterson brought them out to me today." Glancing from Charity and Maggie to Jasmine, he said with a catch in his voice, "I want the three women I love to long remember this day."

"Oh, we shall, Jared," Charity returned fervently. "Thanks. You always were such a thoughtful boy."

"Thanks, Jared," Jasmine added, smiling at him, her green eyes glowing with the love she felt for him. "You've made today special for all of us in so many ways."

Jared smiled back at her lovingly, then turned to Charity. "May I steal Jasmine away now?"

"Certainly. I'm quite refreshed after that delectable meal, and most everything has already sold here, anyway. You two go enjoy yourselves!"

Jared took both girls by the hand and led them away from the booth. "Well," he told them, "it's just about time for the balloon ascension."

Jasmine nodded as she glanced at the balloon towering at

the edge of the bluff. The envelope was now fully inflated, straining at its ties as two men in dungarees and work shirts attached a large wicker basket. "Where shall we stand to watch it go up?"

"How about from two thousand feet in the air?"

"I beg your pardon?" Jasmine asked.

Jared grinned proudly. "We're going up in it—you, me, and Maggie. Thaddeus McCoy invited us."

"Whooppee!" Maggie cried, clapping her small hands in glee, even as Jasmine simultaneously protested, "Oh, no, Jared, we can't!"

Jared, unperturbed, was pulling them both toward the edge of the bluff. "But," Jasmine sputtered, "I thought you said hydrogen was dangerous!"

"Not if it's properly used," Jared assured her. "You're not afraid to go up, are you, Jasmine?" he added, winking at her solemnly.

"Well, no, but—"

They had now reached the balloon, and Jared nodded toward one of the men attaching the basket. "Jasmine, this is Thaddeus McCoy. Thaddeus, meet my fiancée, Miss Dubroc. And this irrepressible little creature is Maggie."

"Afternoon, ma'am—little miss," McCoy said, dusting off his rope-burned hands as he turned to smile at the girls. Jasmine noted that McCoy was very capable-looking. "It'll be a pleasure to have you and the wee lass aboard today," he added to Jasmine.

"But—is it safe?" she asked him.

"Aye, ma'am," McCoy returned solemnly. "Actually, this hydrogen balloon is much safer than the hot-air variety, since there's no fire under the envelope to set the thing ablaze." He turned back to the balloon and asked his assistant, "All secure, Sid?"

"Yes, sir," the wiry young man replied as he double-checked the knots mooring the basket to the envelope.

"Well, folks, ready to board?"

McCoy hopped in first, using a crate as a mounting block. Then he and Jared helped the girls climb into the large wicker basket, and Jared boarded last. In the meantime, a crowd had gathered on the trampled grass near the balloon, and were excitedly exchanging comments as they waited for the ascension. "We'll probably bring her down south of here," McCoy was telling Jared, "since the wind's coming off the north today. There's plenty of farmland down there, so we should have no trouble finding a field for our landing."

"My friend Jack Malone is going to follow us," Jared interjected.

"Good. My assistant will be tracking us, as well."

Charity now appeared at the head of the crowd, waving a handkerchief at Jared. "Don't tell me you and the girls are going up in that contraption?"

He dismissed her anxieties with a casual shrug. "The balloon's quite safe, Aunt Charity. Care to come along?"

"Oh, no—I shouldn't dream of it," Charity sputtered, her hand fluttering to her breast. "Just take care, will you?"

Jared nodded to his aunt, and McCoy motioned to his assistant, who came forward to help him detach the sandbags used for ballast. Seconds later they lifted off, amid the cheers of the crowd.

Jasmine, hanging on to Maggie with one hand and the basket with the other, felt her stomach fluttering wildly as they soared upward, leaving the earth behind. Jasmine and Maggie gaped downward in wonder—at the parade grounds where the crowd stood cheering, at the lush green curtain of trees along the bluff's rim, at the silvery wide river below, and at the community of Natchez-Under-the-Hill sprawling along its edge.

Soon, the balloon sailed high up into the heavens, buoyed along on air currents, the deliciously cool breezes whipping about them and rattling the hemp netting that encased the envelope. Glancing downward again, Jasmine found that the people below her now appeared tiny as ants, and a barge drifting down the gleaming Mississippi looked as flimsy as a toy boat. Feeling the delicious, cold fingers of the wind stroking her face, she glanced upward at billowing clouds that seemed close enough to touch, and floated by in fluffy visions. Never in her life had she felt or seen anything quite so awesome or stirring—it was as if they were actually drifting through heaven. Even the normally irrepressible Maggie appeared reverent as she gazed about, her small hands gripping the edge of the basket, her blue eyes huge and luminous.

Jasmine glanced at Jared over the child's head, and when she saw the love gleaming in his blue eyes as he gazed back at her, her heart welled with adoration. At the moment, she knew how truly special she was to him. "Thank you, Jared," she whispered, with tears of joy in her eyes. "If I live to be a hundred, I'll never forget this day."

He smiled back, then turned slightly to address McCoy. "If you don't mind, Thaddeus, I've never kissed my fiancée in a balloon before."

"By all means, sir!" McCoy rejoined with a hearty chuckle.

Jared leaned across Maggie to tenderly place his lips on Jasmine's, and at that moment, feeling the warmth of his mouth on hers, she seemed to spiral upward another thousand feet! Her eyes brimmed with tears and she ached with the love she felt for him.

Then Maggie interjected petulantly, "I've never been kissed in a balloon either, Uncle Jared!" He laughed and leaned over to plant a loving kiss on the child's cool, soft cheek.

In due course, they had to return to earth. When they drifted over a wide, just-harvested cornfield, McCoy pulled the rope to the valve at the top of the balloon. The gas began its escape, and they started their slow descent.

Everything went perfectly until the balloon hovered about fifty feet above the stubbly field. Suddenly, shots rang out from the trees to the south of the clearing where they were landing.

There were four in all—distant, but quite discernible. As soon as the first report came, Jared yanked Maggie and Jasmine to the floor of the basket with him. "Stay down!" he ordered them. Within seconds, the shooting stopped. Jared called up to McCoy, "You all right, Thaddeus?"

"Aye, sir," came McCoy's terse reply. "Hold on, folks, and stay down!"

McCoy pulled the rip-panel rope, and the balloon made a

swift and bumpy landing. In the cramped bottom of the basket, Jasmine held on to Maggie, shielding the child with her body as all three of them were bounced and jolted about.

At last, mercifully, the basket quit moving. "I think we're safe now, folks," said Thaddeus McCoy.

Jared stood and glanced about cautiously, then helped the girls to their feet. "You two all right?" As the girls nodded back shakily, he glanced up at the rapidly deflating envelope and said, "Let's get out of this thing before the balloon collapses on top of us."

McCoy and Jared quickly hopped down, then helped the girls climb out of the basket and pulled them to the eastern side of the balloon, to block visibility from the forested area from which the shots had come. The four stood numbly watching the envelope sag onto the top of the basket. As Jasmine comforted Maggie, Jared turned to McCoy. "Do you suppose it was a hunter who fired the shots?"

McCoy was shaking his head grimly. "No—not unless he had a hankering for roast balloon." McCoy pointed to the envelope, and Jared, scanning the material, whistled as he observed two bullet holes in the balloon's varnished fabric.

"Well, I'll be damned," he said.

As Jared spoke, a barouche emerged from the woods to the north of them and the foursome ventured outward slightly, watching tensely as Jack Malone approached in Jared's buggy. The gray horse harnessed to the barouche galloped toward them at a reckless pace. About ten yards away, Malone reined in the gelding, then sprang out of the buggy and hurried toward them. Jack's features were taut and white as he asked Jared, "You folks all right?"

"We're unharmed, Jack," Jared replied.

"Well, thank God. I heard the shots, boss, but by the time I got here, whoever done it was gone. Was they aiming at you?"

Jared gestured toward the limp envelope. "Either that, or they like to use hydrogen balloons for target practice."

"Tarnation!" Jack muttered, stepping closer to the balloon and scowling at the bullet holes Jared and McCoy had already observed. "Why, that blame contraption could have exploded with all of you hangin' under it."

"No, sir," McCoy contradicted, stepping forward to face Jack. "A bullet alone wouldn't generate enough heat to detonate the hydrogen."

"Thank God for small blessings," Jared said ironically. With a haunted look in his eyes, he turned to study the girls. Jasmine smiled back at him bravely, while Maggie was still clinging to her guardian, her little face pale and drawn. "You all right, honey?" Jared asked the child. When she nodded back shakily, he went over to her and gently lifted her into his arms, hugging her trembling little body close to him. "Everything's going to be all right, now, Maggie."

After a moment, Jared nodded to Jack. "Will you take Maggie to the buggy?"

"Sure, boss."

Jack took the child and walked off. Jared turned to Jasmine and took her hand. "Are you all right, my dear?"

She nodded, even though she was still trembling, and her stomach was churning violently. As soon as Maggie was safely out of earshot, she said to Jared, "God, that was so scary! We all could have been killed."

He shook his head grimly and placed his arm about her waist. "My dear, I'm afraid that if whoever did it had wanted to kill us, we'd be dead by now."

Jared's words sent a chill down Jasmine's spine. "What do you mean?"

Jared glanced up at her, his gaze anguished. "I mean that someone was toying with us, sadistically." His arm tightened about her waist as he called out to McCoy, "Need a ride back, Thaddeus?"

"No, sir," the showman replied. He was over by the balloon, gathering up the fabric. "Thanks, anyhow, but Sid should be coming along any moment with the wagon, to fetch me and the balloon on back. If you pass him, you might give him a steer in the right direction, though."

"Will do," Jared promised, leading Jasmine off toward the barouche.

Jasmine was silent as she and Jared climbed into the crowded buggy with the others. Jasmine sat down between the two men, settling Maggie in her lap. She watched Jared take the reins, his expression grim, while Jack, on her other side, tensely surveyed their surroundings, his hand on the butt of the pistol in his lap. She sighed as the buggy lumbered forward. The day, which had started out so beautifully, had ended on a dire, disastrous note.

*Someone was toying with us. Sadistically*, Jared had said.

Jasmine knew of only one man who was capable of such cruelty. And the very possibility made her blood run cold.

# ★ Twenty-two ★

During the next few days, no trace was found of the person or persons who had fired at Thaddeus McCoy's balloon. Jared reported the incident to the local sheriff, who promised to investigate the matter, but who also assured Jared that the episode was doubtless the ill-conceived prank of a group of drunken hunters.

Jared was not satisfied by that explanation, and, in the days that followed, he became extremely protective of Jasmine and Maggie, not letting the two girls venture out of Magnolia Bend without an escort. Jared told Jasmine privately that he suspected Claude Boudreau might be behind the frightening incident. Cactus Jack searched the town for the swindler, but he found no trace of him.

During this period, Jared also put a stop to his midnight meetings with Jasmine at the summerhouse—something that caused her great frustration. Though Jasmine begged and pleaded, Jared insisted that, for the time being, they must not meet at night. Jared explained that even if he met her on the

back gallery of Magnolia Bend and walked her to the summerhouse, there were simply too many trees between the main
house and the small cottage at the back of Charity's
property—the passageway would be perfect for an ambush,
particularly at night. Jasmine realized that his reasoning made
sense, especially as she recalled her feeling that she was being
watched at night. Nevertheless, she sorely missed her more
intimate times with Jared.

The high point of this period for Jasmine came four days
after the carnival, when she spent an afternoon working at
the orphanage. Ephraim dropped her off that day, since Jared
was in Vidalia for the afternoon, conducting business at his
plantation.

As soon as Jasmine stepped in the door to St. Mary's, she
learned from Mother Martha the exciting news that the benefit
day had netted more than ten thousand dollars! She also
learned that since Saturday, six families had approached the
mother superior wanting to adopt girls. Jasmine was still
reeling from this exciting news when a delivery man came
to drop off the new Elias Howe sewing machine that Jared
had bought for the orphanage.

Jasmine and the sisters had great fun setting up the elaborate machine. They tested out some seams on the new contraption, while several of the orphan girls gathered about,
watching raptly and listening to the hum of the shuttle. When
Jasmine left, she promised the sisters she would stop in town
later and pick up additional threads, patterns, and needles.
The sisters asked her to give Jared their heartfelt thanks.

Outside the orphanage, Jasmine found Ephraim patiently
waiting for her in the buggy, wearing his familiar straw hat.
As she grasped the gnarled hand he extended to help her
board, he grimaced in pain. She noticed how stiff his hands
were as he valiantly snapped the reins, and how tense his
wrinkled features were as he struggled to hide his discomfort
from his mistress.

"Ephraim, your rheumatism's ailing you again, isn't it?"
Jasmine asked.

"I make out, missy," the old slave replied.

Jasmine gave him a scolding look. "Look, Ephraim, I have some shopping to do in town, but first I'm dropping you off back at the house so you can rest."

"Oh, no, Miz Jasmine!" Ephraim protested. "Mr. Jared, he tell me not to lets you go nowheres by yo'self."

"Ephraim, I'm simply going to run a few errands in broad daylight. Nothing will happen to me."

Jasmine finally convinced the old man that she would be fine alone. She dropped him off at the cottage on Pearl Street, then drove the buggy back to the central business district. On Main Street, she parked her buggy, then walked down the boardwalk toward Patterson and Wiswall's Merchandising Emporium. The November afternoon was agreeably cool, and Jasmine found that her lightweight woolen dress was perfect for the weather. She smiled a greeting to several passing shoppers she knew. Then, crossing the alleyway flanking the Rice Hotel, she was suddenly and brutally grabbed from behind.

Before she could even react, she was dragged into the shadows of the filthy alleyway. A ruthless arm crushed her waist, while a hard hand, smelling of tobacco and tasting of dirt, was clamped savagely over her mouth. She tried to struggle away, but then froze as something hard and cold probed her spine. She heard the ominous click of a pistol being cocked.

"There's a gun in your back, bitch," came a hoarse male voice. "Do exactly what I say, or I'm blowing your guts all over the ground with the rest of the garbage."

Jasmine was terrified. Her heart was beating so hard she feared it would burst in her chest. And speaking was impossible with the cruel hand smothering her mouth.

"All right, woman," the voice went on, "I'm going to let go of your mouth now. But make no mistake. This gun will still be square in your back, and if you scream, you're dead. Understood?"

Jasmine nodded convulsively.

Her mouth was released and she caught a ragged lungful of fetid air. The odor of refuse and soured food in the narrow lane was overpowering, even in the coolness. She tried to turn toward her captor, but the man forestalled her by prodding her back with the gun and hissing, "Don't you dare, bitch. Eyes straight ahead. Now, walk to the back entrance to the hotel."

"Please," Jasmine pleaded, holding out her reticule, "if it's money you want—"

A low, bitter laugh cut her words short. "I don't want your measly coins. Now, do as I say or I'm cutting you in two!"

Jasmine knew further protest was futile. Prodded by her captor's gun, she walked unsteadily through the garbage-strewn alleyway toward the back service lane. Her heart hammered more fiercely with each step, and every breath stabbed her lungs. Reaching the back passageway, she followed the man's guttural order, and they entered the back of the hotel through an open doorway nearby.

To Jasmine's dismay, they passed not a single soul as they proceeded into the dark cavern of the hotel and walked up the sagging back stairs of the dusty, untidy building, entering the upper hallway.

"Here," the gunman said gruffly, shoving her toward a doorway.

Jasmine creaked open the door and stepped into a seedy-looking hotel room. Beyond her, a thin mattress covered with a filthy scrap of sheet sagged on an iron bed, while nearby, a cracked bowl and pitcher sat on a scratched, bare bureau. The room's solitary window was covered by a torn, yellowed cloth shade, and the wooden floor was heavily scarred. Jasmine swallowed convulsively as she watched a scrawny gray rat skitter out from beneath the bed and scurry under the bureau. She knew that the Rice had once been a fine hotel, but it was rumored that the establishment had gone to seed ever since Anton Rice, a purported libertine, had taken over for his father. Everything Jasmine had seen so far confirmed the gossip.

Hearing the door shut behind her, she whirled to face her captor. "Sir, I demand to know the meaning of—"

"Good afternoon, Jasmine."

"Oh, my God!" she gasped, staring at the man. Her heart

pounded frantically and her mind whirled as she recognized her kidnapper. He looked different, wearing a full beard. For a moment, she prayed her mind was playing tricks on her.

But as he removed his hat and stepped closer, still pointing the gun at her middle, no doubt remained in Jasmine's terrified mind. She would know those malignant black eyes anywhere!

She was staring squarely at the hated Claude Boudreau!

"What's wrong, Jasmine?" he now asked, mocking her with his dark eyes. "Cat got your tongue?"

She lunged at him then, but he backhanded her brutally with his left hand, sending her sprawling to her knees. Jasmine gasped for her breath, her bonnet askew, her jaw throbbing as she stared up at him with bright hatred.

"You're quite a nervy little bitch for a woman facing a man with a gun," he told her coolly. Pointing the revolver squarely at her chest, he added, "Dare to touch me again, *dear wife*, and you can bet I won't be fending you off with my hand."

"Don't call me your wife, you stinking lowlife!" she hissed back at him, her bosom heaving.

He shook his head ruefully. "Unless I've taken leave of my senses, it seems that we did marry on that fateful day three months past." With a frighteningly calm smile, he added, "You know, something told me I should have put a bullet through your head that night before I threw you in the Mississippi."

"Why didn't you?" Jasmine asked, hatred gleaming in her green eyes.

He chuckled. "Actually, Jasmine, I never dreamed you'd survive being thrown in the river. Your spirit and resourcefulness astonish me."

"No doubt," she spat at him. Jasmine bit her lip and clenched her fists, hating the sight of him. How could she ever have let this black-hearted charlatan deceive her? And why did the thieving scoundrel have to reappear in her life now—when everything had been going so well for her? Eyeing his lanky form with ill-disguised malice, she asked, "You're the one who tried to kill us last week, aren't you, Claude?"

He grinned. "You mean when you were riding in the balloon with your illustrious fiancé, Mr. Hampton?"

"So it *was* you!"

He made no comment. Gesturing with his gun toward a straight chair not far from where she knelt, he said, "Sit down, Jasmine. You and I are going to have a little talk." When she did not reply but stared murderously at him, he moved closer and pointed the pistol at her forehead. His eyes were black and as remorseless as a bottomless pit. "I said, sit down, bitch."

Jasmine grudgingly got to her feet, wincing as she placed her weight on her bruised knees. She walked over to the straight chair, sat down, and righted her bonnet, rubbing the welt on her neck where the ribbon tie had cut into her flesh. She was dying to stroke her battered jaw, as well, but she refused to give Claude the satisfaction of knowing he had hurt her. She kept a sharp eye on him as he seated himself on the edge of the bed and laid the pistol across his lap. "What happened to your French accent, Claude?" she asked him ungraciously.

He shrugged, but again did not reply.

"Is there anything about you that's real?" she continued bitterly.

He raised an eyebrow. "Jasmine, we're not here to talk about me. We're here to talk about you, my sweet, adulterous wife."

Jasmine gasped and threw a hand over her mouth.

"Oh, yes, my dear," he said with cynical triumph, "I know all about you and your noble Mr. Hampton."

"He saved my life that night on the river—which is more than I can say for you!" she spat.

"Ah-ha! So that's how you managed to escape the ravages of the Mississippi—your Mr. Hampton came along and rescued you?"

Jasmine did not comment.

"So now you're trying to keep our marriage a secret while you seek a quiet annulment and fornicate with your Mr. Hampton on the side?"

Jasmine felt her face flaming at Claude's coarse, contemptible words. So he *had* been watching her and Jared at night, she realized with sick horror. The very thought of Claude spying on them in the darkness—hiding in the bushes like a slimy snake, perhaps even slithering up to a window of the summerhouse to peer inside—made her want to vomit. Nevertheless, she managed to keep her voice cool as she informed him, ''In the eyes of the law, Claude, our so-called marriage is already null and void.''

''Ah, but what about in the eyes of the church, dear Jasmine?'' he mocked. ''As I recall, you're a devout Catholic, and I do know that it can take ages to obtain a church annulment.''

Jasmine was tempted to ask Claude how he knew this, but resisted the impulse. Damn him for being so clever! ''What do you want, Claude?'' she snapped.

He grinned back, displaying the gleaming white teeth of a predator. ''Nothing much—twenty-five-thousand dollars should do it.''

''You're crazy!'' she cried.

''Not in the least, Jasmine.''

''My God!'' She was shaking her head, her features incredulous. ''Your gall amazes me! To think that after all you've done to me, you could ask—And what on earth happened to the money you stole from me, anyway?''

''Not that it's any of your damn business, but it's already been spent.'' Smiling nastily at her outrage, he added, ''Surely you can't expect a man of my appetites to subsist forever on such a paltry sum.''

Jasmine's fury was escalating with every word Claude said. ''Why, you . . . ! You can sit there, calmly asking me for more money, when you've already stolen everything I have? And even if I could raise that kind of money—which I can't—why on earth should I give you another dime?''

''Why?'' A smirk of cruel pleasure spread across his angular face. ''To keep me from exposing you, of course, dear Jasmine.''

''What?'' she cried, bolting to her feet. ''Are you out of your mind? You're the one who committed a crime, Claude!

And make no mistake—I have every intention of turning you in to the sheriff for stealing my money and attempting to murder me!''

At once, all traces of humor left Claude's face, and Jasmine watched his features pale, then grow tense. She observed his discomfiture with great satisfaction, but her triumph was short-lived as he again raised his gun and pointed it at her. "Are those your plans, my dear? That's a bit of bravado you may come to regret."

She stared at him, feeling the color drain from her face as she again looked down the deadly barrel of his pistol.

"Sit down, bitch," Claude said, in a voice so pitilessly cold it made Jasmine fight a shudder.

At once, she complied. "That's better," he said, again laying down his pistol. In a deceptively lazy voice he continued, "So, you would like to turn me in to the authorities, would you, my dear? Well, let me explain some things to you. You have much more to lose here than I do, should you attempt to expose me. You see, it would be your word against mine. If you go to the authorities, I'll simply tell them that after our marriage was consummated that night on the riverboat, you threw yourself into the Mississippi, fearing you had displeased me, and that I've been going mad trying to find you ever since." As she tried to protest, he held up a hand in warning. "And think of the scandal you'll cause if you make this disgraceful affair public! Especially now that you've been publicly proclaimed Jared Hampton's fiancée!" With sadistic relish, Claude concluded, "Besides, if you do expose me, I'll see to it that the annulment you are seeking from the church is never granted."

"You'll what?" Jasmine cried.

"I'll block the annulment. I'll also tell the dear father who married us that our marriage *was* consummated that night before you so recklessly ran off." He smiled malevolently. "Although I suppose you could circumvent me there easily enough, couldn't you, my dear? All you'd have to do is to go see your physician, then furnish proof to the church that your—er—virginal state is still intact."

"You bastard!" Jasmine gasped.

"Indeed," he agreed, his depraved smile not wavering in the least.

By now, Jasmine was nearly blind with rage. Claude had thought of every contingency, it seemed! "Wasn't it enough that you almost killed me—that you took all my money?"

"No," he replied implacably. "I want twenty-five-thousand dollars more, or I'll expose you publicly for the adulteress you are, dear wife."

"Quit calling me your wife!" she snapped.

He chuckled, giving her an open-handed gesture. "In the eyes of the church—"

"Since when have you given a damn about the eyes of the church—or about anything, except your own selfish purposes?"

He continued to grin, but his black eyes held a frightening menace. "Have it your way. Just get me the twenty-five thousand."

"But—that's crazy!" she raved. "You know I don't have any money—you took it all!"

"Get it from Hampton," Claude instructed. "His family has millions. If that popinjay wants you, he'll pay for you." Before she could comment, he eyed her up and down with insulting eyes and added, "And there's something else I want from you, you sneaky little slut. I want you to spread your legs for me."

Jasmine stared at Claude in revolt and disbelief as he went on, "If Hampton desires your services so badly, you must be a pretty good roll. He'll get most of the pie eventually, but not before I've had my slice." Stroking his bearded jaw, he went on, "Actually, I would have stayed to sample your charms that night on the riverboat, but I couldn't risk missing the rendezvous point, where my friend was waiting with horses."

"Why you—you're beneath contempt!" Jasmine hissed. "You had everything planned that night, didn't you, Claude?"

"Yes, everything," he admitted, "except the overpowering lust I felt when I saw you in that thin little night-gown. Too bad there wasn't more time . . .'' With a wicked chuckle, he added, ''But we'll remedy that situation soon enough, won't we, my pet? Here, I thought you were just a dowdy little schoolteacher. But you like lying beneath a man, don't you, my dear? You service Hampton often enough.''

Jasmine again bolted to her feet, only to freeze once more as Boudreau's pistol was raised and leveled at her midsection. ''Sit down.'' As she hastily obeyed, he added, ''Well, dear, will you meet my terms? Twenty-five thousand—and the use of your body for one night.''

Jasmine swallowed the bile rising in her throat and strug-gled to contain her burgeoning rage. As repelled as she felt by Claude's demands, seeing his gun pointed at her once again had made her realize that her main purpose at the moment was to get out of this room alive. If she didn't seize control of herself, she'd doubtless nettle him until he lost his meager patience and shot her. On the other hand, if she pretended to play along with him, she could get away, and then possibly figure a way to turn the tables on him. Taking a steadying breath, she asked, ''And if I do what you ask?''

He shrugged. ''Then I'll quietly leave your life forever, my dear.''

''Would that I could believe that!''

''Believe that if you do not do precisely what I ask, all of Natchez will soon know what a little slut you are. And don't underestimate me there, Jasmine. You already know what an excellent actor I am.''

''May I leave?'' she asked him through savagely gritted teeth.

''Will you meet my terms?'' he countered.

''Yes,'' she hissed, hating herself for appearing to give in to this man she loathed, but knowing that at the moment, feigning weakness might well be her only strength.

''Then you may leave,'' he said, startling her with his acquiescence. ''But remember this, Jasmine. I expect you to comply completely within one week. I'll be in touch within a few days so that we may make the arrangements to—er—consummate our little deal.'' He stood and came to her side, the pistol in hand. Roughly pulling her to her feet, he pressed the cold barrel of the pistol against her breastbone. Grinning at her terrified gasp, he added in a soft tone, "Don't even think of crossing me, bitch. And remember, the money won't be enough. You'll also give me the thorough servicing you owe me from our wedding night.''

As Jasmine stood trembling in helpless terror and revulsion, he pressed the gun harder against her flesh, hurting her, transmitting a terrifying sexual message that was mirrored in his merciless black eyes. With fiendish delight, he whispered, "I'm a mean lover, Jasmine. I assure you that Hampton's lovemaking will pale by comparison when you spread your legs for me. I intend to make you beg and scream for more. And I'll see to it that when you go back to your gentleman stud, there'll be little left.''

At last he retracted the frightful pistol from her flesh. Jasmine recoiled from his odious touch, grabbed her reticule from the floor, then dashed for the door. But even as she grabbed the knob, he stopped her with a voice that chilled her blood. "Don't tell Hampton.''

She whirled to glare at him. *"What?"*

"I said, don't tell Hampton,'' he repeated.

"And just how am I supposed to get the money from him unless I tell him?''

Claude shrugged. "That's your problem. You'll have to use your feminine wiles. Because if you tell Hampton about our meeting, I warn you, it will be my greatest pleasure to kill your honorable fiancé.''

# ★ Twenty-three ★

*A remedy must be found!*

This thought kept running through Jasmine's mind following her meeting with the despicable Claude Boudreau. How she hated him for coming back into her life! Just as everything was falling into place for her and Jared—just as her anger toward Claude was mercifully receding—he had to reappear, bringing all her rage boiling to the surface again. Every time she remembered her encounter with him at his hotel—each time she recalled his cruel taunts and nefarious demands— she was filled with a revulsion bordering on physical illness.

Much as Jasmine longed to turn the tables on him, to somehow seek her own revenge for his perfidy, she found herself in a terrible quandary; for if she refused to do what Claude demanded, his threatened consequences could be disastrous. But she couldn't give in to him and betray her love for Jared.

Jasmine considered going to the local sheriff and turning Claude in, but quickly discarded the idea. As Claude himself had cruelly pointed out, it would be her word against his about what had happened on the riverboat. And if she did go public, Claude would cause a scandal that would never die down. Jasmine was certain that Jared and his aunt would be ruined socially, and she simply could not face being responsible for it.

More than anything else, Jasmine wanted to share her dilemma with Jared, yet she knew that this was impossible, as well. If he should discover that Claude was in town, he'd call the blackguard out. And if Claude were threatened, she wouldn't put it past him to murder Jared. Hadn't Claude made brutally clear to her that he would kill Jared, should she tell her fiancé anything about what was going on? Jasmine very much feared that Jared, with his code of chivalry, was ill-equipped to deal with a man with no conscience or sense of honor.

How she hated withholding this information from her beloved! Jasmine shuddered to think of Jared's reaction if he learned that Claude was back in Natchez and that she had kept this fact secret from him. It seemed that Claude had her boxed in at every turn, and the feeling of helpless rage, of being powerless to control her own life, became exquisite frustration for Jasmine.

During these same days, Jasmine's relationship with Jared became strained. Hating herself for the lie she was living, she avoided him whenever possible, staying busy with other activities. When she was with him, she was tense and uncommunicative. On more than one occasion, Jared remarked that she seemed withdrawn and preoccupied, and asked her what was troubling her. She put him off each time with a lame excuse—saying that she had a headache or that she had slept poorly the night before, which, generally, was the case.

Jasmine knew that she would soon hear from Claude again—that he'd be demanding that she comply with his outlandish terms for keeping his silence. Yet no solution to her dilemma presented itself.

She ate little, slept even less, and became more and more withdrawn. Dark circles began to appear beneath her eyes.

In a cruelly short period of time, Jasmine did hear from Claude Boudreau again. She was in her bedroom at Magnolia Bend, getting ready to leave for an afternoon at the orphanage, when Sarah came by to tell her a black lad with a message was waiting for her downstairs. "He say he got to deliver a letter to you personal," the maid informed Jasmine. "You want to see him, missy?"

Jasmine nodded grimly.

Downstairs, she found a nervous black lad, dressed in

worn, dirty clothing, waiting for her near the front door. "Here, missy," the boy said, his eyes downcast as he extended an envelope to her.

"Thank you." Jasmine took the letter and gave the boy a coin. After he left, she went into the parlor and ripped open the envelope.

The message inside was terse and to the point: "Meet me at sunset. Old Spanish Parade Grounds. C. B."

Jasmine crumpled the letter in her hand, feeling more helpless and desperate than she ever had in her life. She considered not going to the meeting, but realized that the consequences might well be calamitous. Today, Claude would expect his extorted money, or a firm promise of when the money—and her body—would be delivered. The entire situation was nightmarish.

Jasmine stared down at the ring on her left hand—the emerald Jared had given her in honor of their engagement. She did have a few assets that she might be able to sell in order to satisfy Claude—the ring, the matching necklace, her cottage on Pearl Street. Doubtless, she'd have a fine time explaining to Jared where the jewelry had gone, but she had to sell it—she had to try to raise the money. She couldn't, of course, come anywhere close to the twenty-five thousand Claude had demanded—nor would she surrender her body to that bastard!

Would Claude be satisfied with less than his full demand? Jasmine decided she would simply have to go meet with him, much as she hated the idea. She'd have to try to reason with him—grovel, if necessary—somehow convince him to take what she could offer and leave her life forever!

While Jasmine was agonizing over Claude Boudreau's note, Cactus Jack was meeting with Jared in his shipping office Under-the-Hill.

After the men exchanged greetings and sat down, Jared got straight to the point. "Well, Jack, do you have something for me?"

"Could be, boss," the soft-spoken Malone replied, crossing his long legs. "Though we've been busy with the harvest, I've still had my feelers out for Boudreau. And I'll have to say that my hat's off to that rascal. He's been harder to track than a weasel with wings. Every time I get a tip on where he might be hiding out, he's vanished without a trace.''

Jared leaned forward, resting his forearms on his cluttered desk. "But this time you think you may have found him?''

"Maybe, boss.''

"Spill it out, man!'' Jared ordered.

Jack held up a hand in caution. "Now listen here, boss, I ain't swearin' I've found the man for you. It's just that a stranger registered at the Rice Hotel a few days back who fits this feller's description—kinder.''

"Go on.''

"He's registered in the name of Alfred Whitman—a dark feller with a beard. Aside from the beard, he fits the description of Boudreau pretty well.''

"As do a thousand other men,'' Jared put in ruefully, leaning back in his swivel chair. "What makes you think this Whitman is our man?''

"Well—until this afternoon, it was just a hunch on my part, I reckon.''

"What happened then?''

The former scout sighed and slowly shook his head. "Boss, I hate to come between a man and his ladylove . . .''

Jared drew tensely upright again. "What does any of this have to do with Jasmine?''

Jack looked uncomfortable; a muscle twitched in his jaw as he met Jared's eye. "Well, boss, like I said, I had a hunch about this Whitman feller. So, this afternoon, I decided to follow him when he left the hotel. He walked a few blocks, then he grabbed one of them shoeshine boys that hang out along Lawyer's Row—''

"Yes?''

"He gave the lad a coin and stuffed a letter in his hand. Anyhow, I decided to follow the boy, and he went on out to your aunt's house with the letter.''

"My aunt's house?'' Jared echoed in disbelief.

" 'Fraid so, boss. Anyhow, the black lad wasn't inside

but a few minutes, when he come back out minus the note. That's when I collared him."

"Yes?"

Jack emitted another long sigh. "The boy told me a man downtown give him a silver dollar to deliver a note to Miss Dubroc out at Magnolia Bend."

"Damnation! You mean that scoundrel's been in touch with Jasmine?" Jared stood, his face livid, his fists clenched at his sides. "I must go to her at once, find out what Boudreau said, and—"

"Begging your pardon, boss, but I don't think your lady wants you to know she's been contacted."

"What?" Jared's face paled.

Jack shifted uneasily in his chair. "A few minutes after she got the note, Miss Jasmine went on out to the orphanage, like nothin' happened. Now, I hate to say this, boss, but it seems to me that if she'd a' wanted you to know what was going on, she'd a' come straight here to see you."

Jared collapsed into his chair. After a moment, he said without conviction, "Perhaps the man who contacted Jasmine wasn't Boudreau, after all."

Jack shrugged. "Maybe not. But if I were you, boss, I'd keep an eye on that lady of yours."

Jared nodded slowly, a grim light in his blue eyes.

Toward sunset, Jasmine drove her buggy out to the Old Spanish Parade Grounds. A few moments earlier, she'd had quite an argument with Ephraim, trying to convince the old man to let her venture forth alone in the buggy again. She'd finally ended the discussion by simply hopping into the conveyance and driving off. The memory of Ephraim standing on the lawn of the Pearl Street cottage, scowling at her abrupt departure, would not soon leave her. She hated to think how the old man might react if he knew what she was really doing this evening!

Jasmine parked the buggy under a large pecan tree and climbed down, stroking Sugar's flank when the horse whinnied nervously. Noting that there was no other conveyance parked nearby, Jasmine drew her cloak tightly about her and made her way down the spongy, leaf-strewn path. The clearing was quiet and still; Claude was nowhere in sight. The view of the sunset from the bluff was quite spectacular; the sun appeared to hang suspended above the Louisiana lowlands to the west. The barest whisper of a breeze stirred the trees all around. Yet the beauty of the setting was largely lost on Jasmine as she glanced about the deserted area and waited for her adversary to appear.

Jasmine was beginning to think that Claude wasn't planning to show up at all—that he was playing a cruel joke on her—when he stepped out from behind an oak tree to the south of the parade grounds. Jasmine gritted her teeth as she watched him swagger confidently toward her. He was wearing the same brown suit and bowler hat he'd had on when he had abducted her days earlier. As he drew nearer, Jasmine struggled not to betray her trepidation and the nausea his odious presence evoked.

"Sorry not to join you at once, Jasmine," Claude now said in greeting. "I had to make sure you were alone." When she didn't reply, he stepped closer, and the odor of stale tobacco and soured whiskey swept over her as he asked, "Well, Jasmine? Do you have the money yet?"

"I'm not a magician, Claude," she snapped back.

His dark eyes narrowed to dangerous slits. "What do you mean? When will you have it?"

She bit her lip, then blurted, "That's what I came here to talk to you about."

His scowl deepened. "Indeed?"

Jasmine took a deep breath and plunged in before she could lose her nerve. "Claude, I find your demands totally unreasonable. There's no way I can raise the kind of money you want. And furthermore, my going to—to bed with you is totally out of the question. However, if you'll just be patient, I promise you I'll try my best to raise several thousand dollars. You'll have to be satisfied with that, for it's the best I can do."

Claude was clearly enraged now—his features were taut and dark, his nostrils flared. His voice came in a snarl as he stepped forward and grabbed her by the shoulders. "You've been toying with me, haven't you? You lying little slut!"

Boudreau drew back his hand, and Jasmine realized with horror that she was about to be savagely slapped, when a cold male voice called out, "Touch the lady again, Boudreau, and you're a dead man."

Jasmine gasped and Claude released her, then both turned as Jared emerged from the trees on the north side of the clearing, a pistol in his hand. "Back away from the lady, Boudreau!" he barked out.

Claude moved away from Jasmine, and she gratefully ran toward Jared. "Jared, I'm so glad to see you—"

His terse words cut her off. "Get behind me, Jasmine."

Jasmine swallowed hard as she stared at Jared. He looked like a stranger—his features were murderously cold, and his blue eyes were fixed with blood-chilling menace on Claude. "Jared, I can explain—"

"Hush, and get behind me!" he snapped.

Jasmine had no choice but to comply. She dutifully moved behind Jared. "Now, stay put," he gritted to her over his shoulder, not taking his eyes off Claude for an instant as he strode forward.

Jasmine lingered at the edge of the clearing, trembling and wringing her hands, watching Jared approach Claude. In a way, she felt relieved that Jared was here; yet she feared what Claude might do now. She noted that Claude's expression betrayed no emotion. He was wisely not moving, his eyes trained on Jared as the armed man approached.

Jared paused within a few feet of Claude, keeping his pistol pointed at the swindler. "You're Claude Boudreau, I take it?" he inquired coldly.

Claude nodded.

"I thought as much," Jared said with distaste. "I will, of course, be demanding satisfaction for your robbery and attempted murder of my fiancée. But we'll not settle this with the lady present. My seconds will call on you."

Suddenly, Claude laughed. "Are you challenging me to a duel, Hampton?" he asked Jared incredulously.

"I am. Are you accepting my challenge, or are you declining, like the coward you are?"

"Why I accept, of course," Boudreau replied. He glanced meaningfully at Jasmine. "It will be my distinct pleasure to blow you in two, Hampton."

"That remains to be seen," Jared said flatly. "You'll be hearing from my representatives regarding the details," he added, backing away, his gun still trained on Claude. "In the meantime, stay away from the lady, or you'll never make it to the duel alive. And don't think of skipping town, either. I'll have a man watching you day and night until this affair is settled."

"Jared, no!" Jasmine implored in a low, tense voice, hurrying to his side. "You mustn't challenge Claude to a duel! Don't you understand that his word is not worth spit? You must turn him in to the sheriff, right now!"

Jared shook his head grimly, still keeping a keen eye on Claude. "That's not how gentlemen settle things in these parts."

"But—he's no gentleman!" she cried.

Beyond them, Claude laughed at Jasmine's remark. Jared appeared far from amused as he grabbed her arm. "Come along, my dear."

Keeping his gun on Claude and ignoring Jasmine's protests, Jared backed her into the woods, then pulled her down the path and out into the parking area where his barouche now stood next to her buggy. Cactus Jack Malone was leaning against the barouche, smoking a cheroot. "Boudreau's out in the clearing," Jared told him. "Keep your eye on him— every minute. I'm taking Jasmine home." He gestured toward her conveyance. "You can take Jasmine's buggy." Jared hesitated a moment, then added, "If that scum should try to skip town—"

"I know just what to do, boss," Jack said, stamping out his cheroot and striding off toward the clearing.

Jared turned back to Jasmine. "Let's go, my dear."

Jasmine felt miserable as they drove off in Jared's barouche, knowing that he was coldly furious at her. His blue eyes were icily fixed on the road, and his face was an impassive mask as his clenched hands snapped the reins. She was frantically trying to gather her thoughts when he remarked bitterly, "You know, I've been wondering why you've been acting so strange, so withdrawn lately, my dear. Now I know—you've been seeing Claude Boudreau again, haven't you?"

"No, Jared, I haven't been seeing him!" she protested. "That is—other than today, I've seen him only once."

"Indeed?"

"Yes! He grabbed me off the street a few days ago and told me—Jared, he's been trying to blackmail me!"

The line of Jared's mouth grew formidably tight. "Go on."

"He wants twenty-five-thousand dollars." Saying the words, she bit her lip, knowing she dared not tell Jared what *else* Claude was demanding!

"Twenty-five-thousand dollars," Jared repeated ruefully. "Even if you had that kind of money, which you don't, why on earth would you give it to Boudreau?"

"Because he threatened to expose us publicly if I didn't!" Jasmine exclaimed. "Claude said he'd tell everyone, including the priest who married us, that my marriage to him *was* consummated that night on the riverboat, and that afterward, I ran off."

"I see. An interesting bit of fiction."

"Perhaps so—to you and me, Jared. But if Claude spreads his lies, you and your aunt would be ruined socially." In a tight voice, she concluded, "Claude told me I would have to find a way to get the twenty-five thousand from you."

"Then, why didn't you tell me about him?" Jared demanded.

"Because he said he'd kill you if I told you—and now, that's just what he intends to do!" She clutched his arm and continued in a desperate tone, "Jared, I'm really frightened! I think you made a terrible mistake just now. Please don't go through with this duel. Turn Claude in to the authorities. He doesn't play by your rules, and I'm sure he's planning to cheat somehow. He's the type to shoot you in the back as you walk down the street—without giving it a second thought!''

Jared was silent for a long moment, his expression grim, as they turned down Orleans Street and proceeded through town. When at last he spoke, his words were low and harsh. "Jasmine, for Christ's sake, I can take care of myself! It wounds me that you have so little faith in me—and in our love. Claude Boudreau comes back to town, blackmails you, and you don't tell me a damn thing about it? How do you think that makes me feel?"

Her fingers recoiled from his arm. "Jared, I—"

"What has really been going on between us, Jasmine? Has it simply been so much moonlight and wine? Fool that I was, I thought I had found a woman I could love and trust—a woman who loved and trusted me. Yet at the first sign of adversity, you take things into your own hands and shut me out."

"Jared, I did it because I love you!" she cried.

"Love me?" he repeated cynically. "I think you've made it brutally obvious how little you feel for me." When she again tried to protest, he continued fiercely, "I think we've said all that can be said for now, Jasmine. I'm taking you home to Magnolia Bend, then I'm fetching Ephraim to keep watch over you every second. And I swear, you'd better not move an inch until this matter is settled, or I'll keep you locked up until our wedding day."

Jasmine was stunned. "Jared, you mean you still want to marry me, after what you just said—"

"Jasmine, I am a man of honor," he informed her tersely. "My word is my bond. Yes, I'm gravely disappointed in you. But I said I shall marry you, and I shall."

Jasmine reeled under the impact of his words. He was disenchanted with her, yet he would marry her simply on principle? "Well, I won't hold you to your empty promises. Not if—"

"Hush, Jasmine! I said we'll discuss this no more!"

Jasmine bit her lip and blinked back tears as for the first time, she had to ask herself whether Jared's honor meant more to him than she did.

# ★ Twenty-four ★

The next twenty-four hours were sheer torture for Jasmine. Jared dropped her off at Magnolia Bend that evening, and, early the next morning, true to his word, fetched Ephraim to keep an eye on her. After Jared explained that Claude Boudreau was back in town and had been threatening Jasmine, and that it would be best if she didn't venture from the house for the next day or two, the old man parked himself on the front gallery of Magnolia Bend, intent upon keeping a watchful eye on his mistress.

Upstairs, Jasmine paced and worried, following a sleepless night. While she had asked Charity to oversee Maggie's lessons this morning, she dared not share her dilemma with Jared's aunt, for she feared the old woman would have a stroke if she learned that her precious nephew was planning to duel the dastardly Claude Boudreau. And Jasmine remained terrified that Claude would, indeed, kill Jared!

Jasmine also felt wretched about her estrangement from Jared—an alienation she felt responsible for. She had kept silent regarding Claude's presence in town in order to protect Jared; yet, now that he knew the truth, she feared he might never trust her again.

No matter what, she loved Jared, and she must somehow see to it that Claude didn't kill him!

Jasmine knew her first move had to be getting by Ephraim—in fact, she knew she would need his help if she were to save Jared. Perhaps she should tell Ephraim the truth.

She dressed in her light woolen dress, grabbed her reticule, a shawl, a bonnet, and gloves, and went downstairs. As soon as Ephraim saw her coming out on the gallery, he struggled to his feet, brushing wrinkles from his old jacket and trousers. "Miz Jasmine, you ain't going nowheres today. I got my orders from Mr. Hampton, and I ain't gonna let that Mr. Boudreau come 'round here pesterin' you no mo'."

Jasmine struggled not to frown as she walked across the gallery to the sunny spot where Ephraim stood, next to two ladder-back rockers. Ephraim had come to idolize Jared in the past weeks, and she knew the old man was determined to carry out his orders.

"Ephraim, I think we need to talk."

Ephraim's jaw jutted out in a familiar attitude of stubborn resolve. "We talk, missy, but I ain't changing my mind. I promised Mr. Jared that I would pertect you, and I gonna do jes' that."

Jasmine sighed, thinking unkind thoughts about male pride and vanity as she sat down on one of the rockers. Reluctantly, the old man joined her, and Jasmine told Ephraim everything—how Claude had married her, then stolen her money and abandoned her on the river, how even now he was attempting to blackmail her, and how he had accepted Jared's challenge to a duel. The servant listened in stunned silence. "Don't you see, Ephraim," Jasmine finished, "it's Mr. Jared who is in danger now—not me. Even when Claude first accosted me a week ago, it's Mr. Jared he threatened to kill if I crossed him. Now, I'm sure Claude will use every underhanded trick in the book to achieve his ends—and that may well include killing Mr. Jared! Ephraim, please—we've got to stop the duel!"

The old black man had removed his hat and was scratching his woolly silver head. "You in a pickle, missy."

"Well put!" she agreed, with a short, humorless laugh. She reached out to touch his sleeve. "Ephraim, will you help me?"

He still looked far from convinced. His brown eyes narrowed on his mistress. "What you want me to do, missy?"

"Well, we must find out where and when the duel is to be held, so we can put a stop to it. Do you think you could ask around? I know you have plenty of friends in town and Under-the-Hill.''

"If I go askin', missy, then I cain't pertect you," Ephraim pointed out doggedly.

"Ephraim, please!" Jasmine cried, her green eyes beseeching him as she gripped his arm. "You must believe what I'm saying! Mr. Jared is the one in danger of his life now—not me! Do you really want us to stand idly by while he gets killed?"

"No, missy."

"Well, if you and I don't get to work immediately, that could well be the case by sundown. Claude's the type to shoot Mr. Jared in the back—make no mistake about that!"

Ephraim sighed heavily, his hands gripping the rim of his straw hat in his lap. "I don't like none of this, missy, but I'll do what you say. I don't want Mr. Jared shot in the back. I'll go ask around. What you gonna do?"

Jasmine sighed in relief. "Well, first, I think I'll go see the sheriff. Dueling is illegal in Mississippi, you know, and maybe he can prevail upon Jared to call off this madness."

Old Ephraim shook his head. "Mr. Jared, he gonna be right riled when he find out we is doin' this."

"Better that he be angry than dead," Jasmine said grimly.

Jasmine and Ephraim agreed that they should embark separately on their mission, then meet later at the house on Pearl Street, to compare notes. Jasmine borrowed a docile horse for Ephraim from the Magnolia Bend stable, then set forth for town in their buggy. She silently prayed that some news of the duel would surface through the grapevine.

Jasmine headed for the city jail on the town square to speak with the sheriff. She hoped the lawman would intervene and convince Jared to call off the duel, yet she held out little real hope that he would cooperate. Even though duels were illegal in Mississippi, they were all too common, and often tolerated, among the gentry. As far back as Jasmine could remember, there had been several in Natchez each year. Sometimes the frays came as a result of political differences, but she also recalled more than one challenge being issued over a seemingly trivial matter, such as a minor breach in courtesy.

Jasmine prayed she'd be able to stop the duel in time. She was far from panicked at this point, since duels were rarely arranged on the spur of the moment—a rigid code was involved. They were often held at dawn or dusk, which made Jasmine feel confident that she'd have at least until sunset today to intervene. She knew that the details were arranged by trusted seconds. Sometimes the seconds could effect some compromise between the perpetrator of the insult and the wounded party, forestalling actual bloodshed. Jasmine knew a compromise would be impossible in this case, although she did remember a few cases when a duel was called off because the challenged party had reneged. To refuse a challenge usually meant that the man would be ''posted''—publicly labeled a coward in a handbill or newspaper advertisement. Jasmine could only pray that Claude would be cowardly enough to flee town; yet a sixth sense warned her that he'd more likely hang around until he found a way to get what he wanted.

As Jasmine had suspected, she found the local sheriff to be of little help with her problem. The thin-featured, balding man didn't so much as bat an eyelash as Jasmine sat across from him at the city jail and explained what Jared and Claude Boudreau were planning.

''And just where is this alleged duel supposed to take place, Miss Dubroc?'' he asked when she had finished her account, his bland expression bespeaking his lack of interest as he rapped his fingertips on top of his desk.

''I don't know, Sheriff,'' Jasmine replied. ''That's why I've come to you for help.''

The lawman shrugged, pulling a cheroot from the pocket of his leather vest. ''There's not much I can do—not without proof.''

This angered Jasmine, and she sat forward in her chair. ''*Proof?* Shall I bring you Mr. Hampton's corpse?''

The sheriff was quiet for a moment, scowling and chewing on the end of his thin cigar. ''Tell me, just why are Mr. Hampton and this other man at odds?''

"They're . . ." Miserably, Jasmine lowered her eyes. "Actually, Sheriff, it's over me."

He laughed dryly. "I figured as much. And I'm sure the two of them will settle it just fine."

Jasmine glanced up, her eyes widening. "You mean you're planning to do nothing? May I remind you, Sheriff, that dueling is illegal in this state?"

That barb scored. The sheriff tossed down his unlit smoke and leaned toward Jasmine. "Look, miss, I don't need any *female* telling me what the law of the land is hereabouts! Not that it's really any of your business, but I've already got my hands full, keeping the river rats and gamblers from taking over this town and the racetrack. Do you know how many street fights we have Under-the-Hill in just a week's time?" Not giving Jasmine a chance to reply, he shook a finger at her and continued, "Now, gentlemen in these parts settle things among themselves. That's the way it's been ever since I can recall, and that's the way it's staying. Don't none of us menfolk need any *female* telling us how to conduct our business." Even as Jasmine glowered at him, the sheriff grabbed a disorderly stack of papers from his desk and began shuffling through them. "Now, if you'll excuse me, miss, I got important business to attend to here."

At that, Jasmine bolted to her feet, her eyes shooting sparks of ire. "Indeed, Sheriff," she said in a furious hiss. "Excuse me for troubling you with such a trivial matter as my fiancé's life!"

Jasmine left the jail, slamming the heavy door behind her. She was fuming as she drove off in the buggy, wondering what she'd do next. Perhaps she should have leveled more with the lawman, she thought. Perhaps she should have told him everything she knew about Claude Boudreau. Then she shook her head. Sheriff Brady had been determined to stay out of the affair, and telling him of Claude's betrayal on the river would have accomplished nothing—except, possibly, to start a scandal.

Jasmine decided that she would go by the cottage on Pearl Street, mull over her options, and wait for Ephraim. As she turned down the familiar street, a crisp breeze sent a shower of autumn leaves down upon the buggy. Staring ahead at the cottage, Jasmine found a desperately bold plan forming in her mind.

Inside the bungalow, she rushed over to her father's rickety old desk and opened the middle drawer. She heaved an enormous sigh of relief as she saw that the object she sought was still there. Removing her gloves, she carefully picked up her father's small Colt cap-and-ball revolver. She checked the cylinder; it was still fully loaded. She balanced the cold, deadly weapon in her hand for a moment, checking to be sure the hammer was safely set on the notch between the chambers. Then, gingerly, she placed the gun in her reticule. Opening another desk drawer, she pulled out a leather pouch of supplies. It still contained everything she would need—a powder flask, caps, and bullets.

She smiled to herself grimly. As Sheriff Brady had just pointed out, Natchez had never been a completely safe place in which to live. When Jasmine was twelve, she had been frightened by a vagrant who had accosted her outside in the garden while her father and Ephraim had been away. Although the man had only wanted some food, and had left promptly when Jasmine fetched him a loaf of bread and a jar of soup, Pierre Dubroc had later been enraged to hear of the incident. Soon thereafter, he had taught her to use his gun, just in case any trouble arose when he and Ephraim were away. Once a year or so, her father had even let her practice her aim on cracked old mason jars out in the backyard. Jasmine hadn't forgotten how to load or shoot the pistol, nor was she afraid to use it now.

Jasmine grabbed the pouch and her reticule and headed back for town. Distasteful as the idea was, she would go by the Rice Hotel, see Claude Boudreau once more, and prevail upon him to leave town. If he resisted, she would pull the gun on him and show him she meant business. And if he grew violent, she would remorselessly shoot him. Later, she could claim self-defense, but that didn't really matter to her at the moment. What mattered was not letting that conniving bastard kill Jared!

Strengthened by her new resolve and feeling a pitiless calm, Jasmine parked her buggy on Main Street, across from the squalid hotel. As she stepped into the street, a strong hand grabbed her from behind and pulled her back onto the boardwalk. "What do you think you're doing here, Miss Dubroc?" a strained male voice demanded.

Jasmine whirled to find herself facing a glowering Cactus Jack Malone. Damn it, why did *he* have to be here?

"Mr. Malone, you gave me quite a start," she murmured, forcing a smile. "And what are you doing in town today?"

"I'm following Mr. Hampton's orders," Jack replied sternly, still holding Jasmine firmly in tow. "Now, tell me what you're doing out alone like this."

Ignoring his curt order, Jasmine nodded toward the hotel and asked, "You're watching Claude, aren't you?"

"Mebbe. Look, ma'am—you'd best tell me what you're doing out by yourself, or I'm taking you straight to Mr. Hampton."

Jasmine managed to disengage Jack's fingers from her arm. "Oh? Don't you approve of helpless females venturing forth on their own?"

Jack tipped his battered felt hat back on his head, looking somewhat at a loss. "Ma'am, I don't got no quarrel with you. But you know Mr. Hampton don't want you out gallivanting around—not with *him* in town." Jack inclined his head toward the hotel. "So, would you kindly tell me what you're—"

"Oh, very well!" Jasmine snapped. "I came to town to see if the sheriff would intervene and stop the duel."

Jack didn't bat an eyelash, but his dark eyes were keenly fixed on Jasmine. "I see. Did Sheriff Brady help you?"

"No!"

Jack nodded. "I didn't figure Horace would lift a finger there. He doesn't nose in on disputes between men."

"But—what are we to do?" Jasmine cried.

Jack shrugged. "Nothin', ma'am." Fixing her with a formidable look of reproach, he added, "Mark my word, miss. You sure as Sunday ain't going anywhere near the Rice Hotel—not with that Boudreau rascal inside."

"But, how can you expect us to just stand idly by?" she asked Jack, gesturing wildly. As a passing elderly couple glanced at them curiously, Jasmine lowered her voice to an intense whisper and went on, "You know Jared could be killed! Don't you care what happens to him?"

"'Course I do. But this is a matter of honor between gentlemen, ma'am. It ain't our place to butt in."

"You men and your damnable codes of honor!" Jasmine cried. "I'm sick to death of it. All I know is that Jared may soon be dead if I can't find out where and when this duel is to take place." She stepped closer to Jack, desperation in her eyes as she gripped his sleeve. "Jack, you know, don't you? Won't you tell me?"

"You know better than to ask me that, Miss Jasmine," he scolded, frowning back at her. "Now, let's get you in your buggy and out of here. Tell you what—if you promise me you'll head straight home, I won't tell Mr. Jared I seen you."

Despite the grudging promise she eventually made to Cactus Jack, Jasmine knew she would make one more stop before going home—at Hampton Hall. She prayed that Jared wouldn't be there, for another possibility had dawned on her—she would prevail upon Marie Bernard to help her!

Thankfully, he wasn't home, and Jasmine spoke with Marie at length in the housekeeper's small office. Jasmine had decided it was high time for her to really level with her friend, so she told Marie the entire story of Claude Boudreau's perfidy—including how he was blackmailing her and was threatening Jared's life.

*"Mon Dieu!"* Marie gasped when Jasmine finished her account. She reached across the table to place her hand on Jasmine's. "I always sensed that you had encountered some ill fortune in your past, Jasmine, but I had no idea! You mean this man married you, then stole all your father's money and left you to drown?"

Jasmine nodded soberly.

"It seems that we have both suffered tragic pasts," Marie remarked ironically.

"Indeed, we have."

Marie leaned back in her chair and studied the other woman quizzically. "Why have you not told me this before, Jasmine?"

She sighed, a faraway expression in her green eyes. "I'm not sure," she admitted at last. "Perhaps because I wanted to forget it, to put the past behind me."

"A healthy sentiment," Marie agreed.

"Yes—but it seems Claude Boudreau has other ideas," Jasmine muttered, with a gesture of frustration. "Marie, what can we do? We can't let Jared be killed in this duel, and neither Jack nor the sheriff will help me! We must find out where Jared and Claude are planning to meet."

"Then what?" Marie asked, looking perplexed herself.

"Well—then the sheriff will have to act," Jasmine said with bravado.

"Do you really think he will?"

"I don't know!" Jasmine cried. "But we have to try. I'll intervene personally to stop the duel, if necessary."

"Jasmine, you wouldn't! What could you do?"

"Plenty! I won't let Jared be killed!"

Her expression grim, Jasmine picked up her reticule from the floor near her feet and placed it on the small table. She loosened the drawstring, then pulled out her father's pistol and held it barrel-down for Marie to see.

"Jasmine!" Marie gasped, her dark gaze riveted on the gun.

Jasmine's jaw was set defiantly as she stared at her friend. "It's my father's pistol, Marie. He taught me how to use it, and I'm completely prepared to do so now if I must."

Marie's hands flew to her face. "I believe you would. Do you have any idea how insane that is? What if this Boudreau person should become violent and try to—"

"I'll shoot him before he gets within three feet of me."

Marie's hands fell helplessly to the table, and her face turned parchment white. In a tight voice, she said, "But it's wrong to kill, Jasmine."

"Right. It would be entirely wrong for me to let Claude Boudreau kill Jared!" Saying the words through gritted teeth, Jasmine balanced the gun in her hand, pointing it away from the table. She glanced up at her friend. "Marie, is there somewhere behind Hampton Hall where I can practice with this?"

"Jasmine!"

"Marie, I must!" Setting the gun down carefully, Jasmine leaned toward her friend. "I remember how to use the pistol, but it's been years since I've actually fired it."

"Jasmine, no, you mustn't—"

"Marie, I can't practice at Magnolia Bend. Miss Charity would have a stroke if she saw me. And if Claude should threaten me again, don't you want me to be prepared?"

The two women fell into a tense silence. At last, Marie sighed and said, "Very well, Jasmine. There's a small rise at the back of Mr. Hampton's property where you can practice." Frowning at the gun, she added vehemently, "But I still say what you're doing is wrong."

Jasmine replaced the gun in her reticule and set the bag back down on the floor, then faced her friend. "Tell me, Marie, what would you do if you discovered Jack had been threatened in a similar manner?"

Marie again grew silent, her eyes dark with pain, and Jasmine knew her friend was recalling her own helplessness years earlier, when her family had been killed on the Natchez Trace. At last she nodded in resignation. "I see your point, Jasmine. You must be prepared for whatever might happen. But you mustn't do anything rash." She leaned forward and placed her hand on Jasmine's. In a confidential whisper, she said, "Perhaps I can find out something about this duel."

Jasmine's heart raced with wild hope. "Oh, Marie, do you think you can?"

"It's possible." Sternly, the housekeeper went on, "But if I do hear anything, I'll pass it on to you only if you promise me you won't do anything yourself without first consulting me."

"Marie!"

"I must have your word, Jasmine. I want to help Mr. Jared, but I can't have your getting hurt on my conscience, either."

Jasmine sighed, nodding. "Very well, Marie, I promise."

# ★ Twenty-five ★

That afternoon, dark clouds moved in from the south, and rain began to pour. The thunderstorm didn't do much for Jasmine's anxious, depressed state of mind; however, due to the inclement weather, it was unlikely that Jared and Claude would duel any time today. That meant that the two men would likely meet to settle their dispute sometime tomorrow.

That evening, Jared showed up for supper at Magnolia Bend, as was his habit of late, and Jasmine breathed a sigh of relief when she saw him. He greeted her with a chaste kiss on the forehead, and spoke with her little during the evening. Instead, he visited with his aunt during supper, and later read Maggie her customary bedtime story.

Jasmine tried to get in a word alone with Jared when he left, but his cool, firm words cut her off. "Jasmine, we've already been over this. There's nothing you can say to me now that will change a thing."

And, taking his umbrella from the nearby stand, he opened the front door and hurried to his waiting carriage. Jasmine realized that he had not even kissed her good night.

She went to bed and tried to sleep, but her fears were magnified in the darkness—especially with the rain still pelting down so ominously outside. She couldn't escape the terrifying thought that she might never see Jared again. Finally, she gave up on slumber, got up, and lit the lamp. She checked on Maggie in the next room and found that the child was blissfully sleeping through the din. Back in her own room, she paced, and her fears grew with her every step.

She would have to see Jared, she decided at last. Somehow,

she must convince him not to duel Claude tomorrow. But how could she possibly speak with him at this hour? If she went down to Hampton Hall and simply knocked on his door, she was sure Jared would dispatch her straight home, without even listening to her.

No, she would have to surprise him—that was her only hope. Jasmine knew that there was a huge, sturdy oak tree right outside his bedroom window. She could climb the tree, enter his bedroom, and threaten to awaken the entire household if he didn't listen to her.

She wondered if she had taken leave of her senses. To climb into Jared's bedroom window in the middle of the night was sheer insanity! Yet no other possible solution to her dilemma presented itself.

The problem was, how would she climb the oak tree in one of her dresses?

That question had Jasmine stumped for quite a while, until she remembered that she still had the deckhand's outfit that she'd worn home from the *River Witch* that morning, months earlier. It would be no problem climbing the tree if she wore britches. Her hair was already plaited for the night, so it wouldn't get in the way.

Jasmine located the outfit and cap in the back of one of her dresser drawers. She dressed hurriedly in the shirt and dungarees, and tiptoed downstairs, grabbing an umbrella from the stand before she creaked open the front door. Once she was outside, she discovered to her dismay that the cold wind and rain were slanting at her so fiercely, her umbrella was rendered practically useless. She was soaked to the skin within seconds.

Yet she refused to abandon her mission. She hurried down the dark, soggy lawn, then ran down the road in the driving rain and booming thunder, shivering as her slippers sloshed through the mud. At last Hampton Hall stood looming before her, illuminated by a bright flash of lightning. Jasmine hurried to the side of the house, discarding her umbrella beneath the tall oak that stretched upward to Jared's window. Though the bark of the tree was rough, it was also quite wet, allowing Jasmine a tenuous handhold at best. Nevertheless, she gripped a limb, swung a leg upward, and began her climb. Luckily, the denseness of the tree's canopy protected her from much of the wind and rain as she clambered up its trunk.

At last she reached Jared's window. It was closed, but fortunately, not locked. She raised the glass pane, then grasped the ledge, and gingerly eased a leg between two lace panels. No sooner had she gotten one leg into the room when she heard the ominous click of a pistol being cocked, and a hoarse voice ordered, "Stop right there! Who are you?"

Half in and half out of the window, Jasmine leaned forward, squinting into the darkness of the room, recognizing a shadowy figure in a nightshirt beyond her. "Jared—it's me!"

"Oh, my God!" he exclaimed.

She heard Jared put down his pistol. Then he rushed to her side and pulled her dripping body into the room. "Jasmine! What on earth are you doing here? Do you realize I could have shot you?"

"I had to talk to you," she said, her teeth chattering.

"My God—you're soaked to the skin and cold as an icicle!" he said, running his hands up and down her arms. "Stay right there while I light the lamp."

Seconds later, the room was flooded with the yellow glow emanating from an oil lamp. Jared stood next to his bed, eyeing her up in down in the drenched uniform, which clung damply to her body. Setting the lamp down on his night table, he grabbed a quilt from his bed and hurried to her side to wrap it around her. "I can't believe you've ventured forth alone again, at night, no less, after I've told you—"

"Jared, please—I had to talk to you," she repeated breathlessly.

"Very well—you're here now," he said gruffly. "Go sit by the hearth. I'll close the window, then get a fire going. We'll talk—right after I beat you senseless for pulling this foolhardy stunt!"

Jasmine shuddered as she sat down in the rocker next to the fireplace. Jared closed the window, then went to his dresser, opened a drawer, and grabbed a towel. "Here, dry your hair."

"Thanks, Jared." Unplaiting her hair and working the towel through her saturated tresses, she watched him kneel to start the fire, his handsome face clenched in a fierce, worried scowl. As he worked, Jasmine shivered and said, "Jared, I've come to beg you not to duel Claude. I couldn't bear it if something happened to you!"

"Nothing's going to happen to me," he muttered as he lit a match.

"How can you be so sure? Claude has no honor! He'll do anything to win!"

"Don't you think I know that? I'm quite capable of taking care of myself, Jasmine."

"But, Jared—"

"I'll hear no more about it!" he cut in, in a voice so curt it made her shudder with more than the cold. He added a log to the pile of kindling he'd set ablaze, then dusted off his hands and turned to face her. The light from the fire gleamed in his brown hair and glinted off his deep-set eyes as he said firmly, "Now, my dear, let's get you out of those wet things and heat up that frozen little body of yours. I'll have to see if I can borrow some clothes from Marie for you to wear. Then it's home and into bed for you."

Jared stood, pulling Jasmine to her feet. He took the damp quilt from her shoulders, the towel from her hands, and pulled off her jersey shirt, leaving her shapely torso clothed only in her thin, soaked camisole. His eyes darkened as he stared down at the taut peaks of her breasts, outlined through the wet, transparent cloth. He caught a ragged breath. "My God," he said tightly. "You shouldn't have come down here, Jasmine."

"Jared, I'd just die if something happened to you!" she burst out. "Maybe you don't love me, but I love you so much that—that I know I'd die without you!"

"You think I don't love you?" he asked, his gaze half-crazed with mingled passion and disbelief.

"Well, yesterday, you said—"

"Oh, my poor darling!" He drew her shivering body close to his. "My love, yesterday I was angry and frightened for you. I said some things I didn't mean. Of course I love you, silly goose!''

"Then, don't fight Claude!" she cried.

Jared drew back, frowning. "Do you realize what you're saying? You can't ask a man to make a choice like that!"

"I'm asking! You don't have to fight him for me!"

"It's not just you—it's the principle of the thing!"

"To hell with the principle! It's you I care about!"

"Don't you think I know that? Don't you know I'm doing this because I care about you?"

For a moment, they simply glared at each other, both breathing hard, tension stretched between them like a taut wire. Then Jared groaned and said hoarsely, "Damn it, Jasmine! Don't do this to me!"

Jared caught her fiercely to him. His arms trembled about her slim body as he buried his lips in her wet hair. She clung to him, and their nearness ignited a desperate desire in them both. After a moment, his hands slipped boldly inside her camisole, caressing the firm mounds of her breasts. "God, darling, it's been so long since we've been alone like this," he said in a choked voice. "Please, let's not argue tonight. You've scared me witless—but, Lord, I need you so!"

"I don't want to argue either," Jasmine told him with tears in her eyes. "I just want—"

"I know," he said, then smothered the rest of her words with his kiss.

Jasmine kissed him back, drinking in the warm taste of his lips on hers, loving the bold texture and heat of his tongue deep in her mouth. When the kiss ended, both were fighting to breathe, their eyes locked with urgent longing. "Darling, you're still shivering so," he said worriedly, again rubbing her bare arms. "Let's get the rest of these wet things off you."

Jared quickly stripped Jasmine's remaining clothing off her trembling body. Then he stared as if hypnotized at her exquisite naked form, outlined by the golden flicker of the fire—the sleek column of her neck; her firm breasts, with their taut nipples; her flat belly; the golden mound of hair marking the place where her thighs were joined; and her shapely long legs. "My God, you're so beautiful!" he said. Stroking the nape of her neck, he went on in a cracking voice, "Do you know what happens to ladies who climb through gentlemen's bedroom windows in the middle of the night?"

"I hope it happens to me," she said fiercely.

"Just try to get away, love."

Jared pulled her down into his lap in the rocking chair, and clamped his mouth passionately on hers. By now both of them were gasping, ravenous with hunger for each other. Jasmine felt no shame sitting naked in his lap while he was still dressed in his nightshirt, and the bold pressure of his manhood rising up against her bare bottom was wildly titillating. The fire felt so warm, snapping and blazing next to them, and the scent of cedar drugged her senses as she drifted in the haven of his embrace, his kiss. Her arms were comfortably curled about his neck, allowing him free access to her body. He stroked her face, her neck, her breasts, then moved lower. His hand slipped between her thighs, and his thumb stroked the bud of her desire. She gasped as he slipped one finger inside her, then two. For a moment she stiffened, fighting the intensely pleasurable pressure, but his touch merely grew bolder. His kiss ravished her senses until she melted to him and flowed with hot darts of sensation too powerful to control. When he leaned over to suckle her breast, even as he continued the sweet torture with his hand, she felt her entire body convulsing at the unendurable ecstasy. He continued mercilessly until she cried out and clutched him to her, tears streaming from her eyes. Then his mouth tenderly covered hers again.

"We must get you to bed," he murmured against her wet mouth, his hand gently stroking her leg. "You're still covered with gooseflesh."

"I'm not shivering from the cold now, but from—"

"I know," he said, smiling.

She trembled as he carried her to his bed. She felt weak, achy, satiated, yet still unbearably hungry for him—ravenous to feel the fullest consummation of their love. On the bed, he removed his nightshirt, then drew her into his arms again, and her senses soared at the captivating feel of his hard, warm, male flesh covering her softness. Outlined by the fire, he was bronzed and magnificent above her. She adored every chiseled plane of his handsome face, every sinew of his strong body. She watched, mesmerized, as the gilded light danced in his wavy hair, in his beautiful blue eyes. "I love you so much," she whispered achingly.

"You are my heart," he whispered back.

They made love with sweet desperation, clutching each other tightly, whispering endearments. Each suffered with the private torment of knowing that tonight might well be their last time together.

Jared trailed kisses down Jasmine's neck, then suckled fiercely at her breasts again, even as her fingernails dug into the smooth flesh of his back. When his fingers moved once more to where her legs were joined, she bucked and writhed, reaching out to grip his manhood in her hand, feeling it pulse and grow harder. "Jared, please," she begged, sure she was losing her mind. He groaned and parted her thighs, and plunged into her with his hot, fierce need. She moaned her joy and arched to meet him, her tender womanhood stretching to receive him fully. After a moment, he rolled over and drew her on top of him, and her eyes widened with delicious pleasure as he thrust up inside her, huge and deep.

"You're so beautiful," he whispered, clutching her about the waist, rocking her loins into his with each powerful stroke. She threw back her head in abandon and he watched her, enraptured. Her face was beautifully flushed with passion, her hair edged in fire as it curled riotously about her neck and shoulders. The tips of her breast were so tight and red with passion that just the sight of them made his mouth grow dry. He felt the tumultuous beginnings of his climax and gripped her to him tightly, calling her name. She looked down at him and as their gazes locked, he saw reflected in her eyes the same sweet bursting agony that was tearing apart his own senses. She cried out as he drove home, shattering them both, yet joining them forever.

As she collapsed on top of him and pressed her aching

mouth to his, neither dared voice what both were feeling—
that no matter what happened tomorrow, they had this.

"Warm now?" he asked moments later, as they snuggled
together beneath the covers.

She nodded through her tears. "Jared—"

He seemed to sense what she would ask. "The rain has
stopped now," he remarked. "Time to get you dressed and
escort you home, my love."

"But, about tomorrow—"

He grasped her face in his hands and looked down at her
intently. "I'll tell you but one thing, my love. By this time
tomorrow night, it will all be over. Never again will you
have to concern yourself with Claude Boudreau." Smiling,
he added, "We have tickets for the theater for tomorrow
night, remember? I'll call for you at seven-thirty."

"Nothing's changed, has it Jared?" she asked sadly.

He stood, took his dressing gown from the foot of the bed,
and held it open for her. There was great sadness in his own
eyes as he replied, "My dear, questions of honor never
change."

# ★ Twenty-six ★

The next morning dawned foggy and gray, and rain continued to fall. Jasmine tried to keep her mind off her worries
as she worked with Maggie on her lessons. Yet her mind kept
drifting back to the danger Jared faced, and she kept reliving
their bittersweet encounter the previous night—the glory of
their lovemaking, the disheartening fact that nothing had
changed afterward. Again it dismayed Jasmine that Jared
seemed to hold matters of honor above all else—even, it
seemed, above his love for her.

At midmorning, Ephraim dropped by, and Jasmine spoke

with him briefly in the hallway while Maggie had tea with Miss Charity. When Jasmine asked Ephraim if he'd heard anything about the duel, he shook his head sadly. "I'm sorry, missy. Ain't no news in town to speak of." Jasmine thanked him and made him promise to keep trying. She felt despondent for the remainder of the morning, realizing that her only real hope for information was now Marie Bernard.

By early afternoon, the fog was burning off, and the rain was gradually stopping. The belated appearance of the sun made Jasmine grow wild with anxiety. She realized that with the return of clear weather, the duel would surely be held sometime that afternoon, probably at sundown. As the day lengthened, with no news, Jasmine grabbed her bonnet, reticule, and shawl, deciding she would go down to Hampton Hall to see if Marie Bernard had heard anything.

Jasmine was swinging open the front door to leave when she spotted a tall, dark gentleman out on the front gallery, his spare, bowlegged form outlined in a slanted beam of sunshine. "Yes? May I help you, sir?"

The man looked dirty and tired, as if he'd been traveling for a long time. He wore cracked, dusty boots, dark trousers, a leather vest, a dingy white shirt, and a dark twill jacket. Intelligent gray eyes peered out from beneath the brim of a large, western-style hat. The man's face was long and angular, with sharply honed features, a handlebar mustache slashing across his weathered countenance. Beyond him at the hitching post, a tired-looking red horse, obviously a stable nag, stamped the ground and swished its tail.

The man removed his hat and ran a hand through his dark-brown hair. The cool breeze swept the mingled odors of male sweat, leather, and tobacco toward Jasmine.

"Are you Miss Dubroc?" he asked.

"Yes," she replied cautiously. "And who are you, sir?"

The man reached into his breast pocket, extracted a simple silver star, and held it up for Jasmine's perusal. "I'm Doyle Murchison, ma'am. United States Marshal, Southern Territory."

Jasmine stared at the badge. "What can I do for you, Marshal Murchison?"

Murchison replaced the badge in his pocket. "Could we speak privately for a moment?"

Jasmine hesitated. The man was a total stranger to her, yet he looked sincere, his badge had appeared genuine, and she found she instinctively trusted him. Besides, she didn't have the heart to turn away anyone who looked so weary! "Certainly, Marshal," she replied. "Come on inside where we can talk. I'll have someone attend to your horse."

Jasmine led Murchison inside, hung her bonnet, reticule, and shawl on the hall tree, then took his hat and jacket. As soon as she and Murchison were seated in the parlor with cups of coffee, Jasmine got straight to the point. "What can I do for you, Marshal?"

Murchison set his coffee cup down on the table before him. Lacing his long, tanned fingers together, he frowned thoughtfully and said, "Tell me, Miss Dubroc, are you acquainted with a fellow who calls himself Claude Boudreau?"

Jasmine felt all color drain from her face. "How do you know about Claude?"

Murchison's scowl deepened as he leaned back in his chair and crossed his lanky long legs. "Well, ma'am, for nearly a year now, I've been hunting a criminal by the name of Hank Rawlins. He's a slippery skunk—he never stays in one place for more than a few days, and he changes his appearance frequently. He's also used a number of aliases, and I have a hunch his latest one may be Claude Boudreau."

The fact that Claude may have been involved in other crimes did not surprise Jasmine in the least. "I see," she murmured, frowning. "Tell me, just what has this Rawlins character done, Marshal?"

"He's a master criminal, ma'am. Either alone or with others, Rawlins has committed every crime imaginable—murder, rape, robbery, extortion, you name it. He's known to be sadistic, violent, and completely without heart or conscience."

Jasmine felt her skin crawl at Murchison's words. "Sounds rather like Claude Boudreau to me," she couldn't help commenting dryly. "Please, go on."

"Well, ma'am, the federal government got involved in the

search for Rawlins a couple years back, when him and some of his cronies robbed a mail shipment. And, like I said, I have reason to believe he may be the man who recently came into your life and swindled you, as Claude Boudreau.''

Jasmine's mouth fell open. "How did you know that Claude swindled me?"

"Well, ma'am, in the course of my travels, I've questioned a lot of people about Rawlins—most of them from the seamy side of life, I might add. Anyhow, I recently questioned some professional gamblers down New Orleans way. One of the boys told me how he played cards on a riverboat a few weeks back with a fellow calling himself Claude Boudreau. Seems this Boudreau fellow got drunk and bragged to the others about how he'd swindled a schoolteacher in Natchez out of her dead daddy's money. The gambler I questioned had no idea how I could locate this Boudreau person, and since I was heading upriver toward St. Louis anyhow, I decided I'd stop off here in Natchez and see if I couldn't find the lady who got took in by this bamboozler. After I got off the riverboat here, I made some discreet inquiries, and it wasn't too hard to find a schoolteacher who'd recently lost her daddy—not in a town of this size." Murchison paused, studying Jasmine's face, which was contorted in a mixture of curiosity and outrage. "And it seems from your reactions that I am speaking to the right party, ain't I?"

"You are," she said tensely.

"Ma'am, if you don't mind, I'd like to hear in your own words what this Boudreau feller done to you."

Jasmine nodded, sighing heavily. "Of course." Sparing no detail, she told Murchison how Claude Boudreau had married her, stolen her money, and left her to drown in the Mississippi, and how she had lived through the ordeal only because Jared Hampton had come along to rescue her.

When she finished, Murchison whistled, shaking his head. "Sounds like the work of Hank Rawlins to me. Tell me, have you seen this fellow since he run off with your money?"

"Why, yes!" Jasmine exclaimed, leaning forward in her chair, her eyes alight. "In fact, he's in town right now!"

"You don't say?" Murchison asked eagerly.

Jasmine told Murchison how Claude had recently reappeared in Natchez, how he was blackmailing her even now, and how Jared had become involved, too. She explained, "Mr. Hampton—my fiancé—found me with Claude out on the bluff a couple of nights back. I was trying to convince Claude to leave me alone, when Jared . . . Anyway, Mr. Hampton saw the two of us together and challenged Claude to a duel."

"Has this duel taken place?" Murchison asked.

"No—but after what you've told me, I'm more frightened than ever that Claude—or Hank Rawlins, or whoever he is —may kill my fiancé!"

"He's done worse before," Murchison concurred grimly.

"Wait a minute!" Jasmine cried. "Why are we sitting here talking? I know what we must do! You must go arrest Claude—immediately! He's staying at the Rice Hotel, and—"

Murchison shook his head. "Hold it just a minute, ma'am. It's not quite that simple."

"And why not?" Jasmine inquired indignantly.

"Several reasons, ma'am," Murchison replied patiently. "First of all, I've spoken to you today of crimes this Boudreau feller has *allegedly* committed. In reality, it could be very hard to pin any of Hank Rawlins's crimes on the man you know as Claude Boudreau. I don't even have any real proof that Boudreau actually *is* Rawlins—it's just a hunch on my part. And like I already told you, we're dealing with a slippery character here—a man with a dozen different names and disguises, who keeps moving about—"

"But I've just told you where Claude's staying!"

"Right, ma'am. I know you have. Maybe Boudreau's still there, maybe he ain't. But the point is, this ain't the moment for us to go off half-cocked—not before we have solid proof."

"But Claude Boudreau tried to murder me!" Jasmine cut in. "I've told you all about it."

"Ma'am, begging your pardon, but since the two of you were alone that night, that'd be your word against his, wouldn't it?" As she started to protest, he held up a hand.

"Now, we might make the arrest stick, but more'n likely Boudreau would beat the charge. Then he'd be scot-free, plus he'd be tipped off that we're on to him."

"Then what can we do?" Jasmine asked, gesturing her exasperation.

Murchison scratched his stubby chin. "Well, here's one thing, ma'am. If we could just catch Boudreau in the act of dueling with your Mr. Hampton, we might be able to hold him on that. Dueling is illegal in this state, after all. You wouldn't happen to know when and where the duel is going to take place?"

Jasmine shook her head.

"Would Mr. Hampton tell us?"

"No," she said despondently. "I am trying to find out myself, though."

Murchison nodded. "Well, ma'am, I think our best bet then is to lie low on this till the witness can be found up in St. Louis."

"What witness?" Jasmine asked, leaning forward intently.

Murchison grinned, displaying a mouth full of crooked, tobacco-stained teeth. "Sorry, ma'am, I meant to tell you about that. You see, about a year ago, Rawlins operated briefly in the St. Louis area. While he was there, he married the wealthy madam of a whorehouse. Within weeks, he stabbed the woman, robbed her blind, and left her for dead. Yet the woman lived, I hear tell. They say before Rawlins tried to do her in, this floozy witnessed some of his other crimes—like when he gunned down two fellers in cold blood up there during a bank robbery. This woman is also supposed to know the names and whereabouts of other criminals Rawlins was tied in with at the time. Trouble is, no one can locate this doxy. In fact, that's why I'm on my way to St. Louis now—to see if I can find her. I suspect she fears we'll prosecute her, though we really just want her testimony. She's the only one who can link Rawlins to what he done up there. And when she fingers the other gang members Rawlins was hooked up with in St. Louis, I'm betting they'll be only too glad to squeal on him to escape the hangman's noose."

Jasmine had been listening, flabbergasted, to Murchison's

account. "You mean Boudreau—Rawlins—has been married before? To a—a whorehouse madam? And he robbed and attempted to murder his other wife, as well?"

"Yes, ma'am. Rawlins has turned this little trick at least one other time that we know of. That's what led me to suspect this Boudreau feller could be Rawlins in the first place."

"Oh my God!" Jasmine gasped, her fists clenched in her lap. "Then, if Boudreau really is Rawlins, I was never legally wed to him in the first place. On top of everything else, the man is a bigamist!"

"Could be," Murchison concurred dryly.

"Marshal, can't you arrest him now—today?"

Murchison shook his head. "Ma'am, I'm sorry, but I must build a case that will hold water. I have to find the woman in St. Louis and a couple of Rawlins's cronies, at the very least. Right now, what we have is simply too flimsy."

Much as she hated to admit it, Jasmine realized that Murchison's argument made sense. "So you're going on to St. Louis, then?"

"Yes, ma'am. Right after I conclude my business here in Natchez, I'm taking the first steamboat upriver."

"If you don't mind my saying so, Marshal, why did you come see me if you're not prepared to arrest Claude yet? Is there something you need my help with?"

"Well, yes, ma'am. Actually, I'd be much obliged if you could somehow try to delay this Boudreau fellow here in Natchez while I'm gone gathering my evidence. If he comes around again, promise him you'll get him the money he wants, but beg him for more time. Also, I hope I can count on your discretion in this matter. The last thing we want is for Boudreau to find out we're on to him."

Jasmine nodded. "Of course. You can depend on me there, Marshal."

"And be careful," Murchison added, fixing Jasmine with a stern look. "The man is deadlier than a cobra."

"I'm well aware of that," Jasmine said with a humorless laugh. "But what about Mr. Hampton, and the duel? Is there nothing we can do to stop it?"

Murchison was about to reply, when both he and Jasmine heard voices out in the hallway. Within seconds, a very flustered-looking Marie Bernard rushed into the room, wearing a black cloak and bonnet. Both the marshal and Jasmine stood. Marie threw the stranger with the handlebar mustache a curious, confused glance, then addressed Jasmine in an urgent tone. "Jasmine, may I speak with you alone?"

"Do you have news of the duel?" she asked, tensely.

"Well, yes, I do, but . . ." Marie's voice trailed off as she frowned, again glancing at Murchison.

"Marie, this man is a federal marshal," Jasmine hastily explained. "He's hunting for Claude Boudreau, so you can tell him anything you were planning to tell me."

"Very well, Jasmine," Marie replied. Though her brow remained furrowed, she quickly went on, "A few minutes ago, I overheard Mr. Jared talking with Jack in the library. It seems that they came to the house to fetch Mr. Jared's dueling pistols. Anyway, I heard them saying that the duel is to be held at sunset today, on the Vidalia sandbar. It was supposed to have been held yesterday, but they had to postpone it because of the inclement weather."

"Sunset, on the Vidalia sandbar," Jasmine repeated. "Gracious, it's close to the end of the day now!" She turned anxiously to the lawman. "Well, Marshal Murchison?"

He nodded grimly. "It seems I haven't a moment to spare." He smiled briefly at Marie. "Thanks for the information, ma'am. Well, if you two ladies will excuse me, I think I'll go fetch the local sheriff and see if we can't make an arrest."

"Why do you need the local sheriff?" Jasmine asked. "I already tried to get the man to put a stop to the duel, and he refused to lift a finger."

Murchison grinned. "Saying no to a lady is one thing, ma'am. But saying no to a federal marshal tends to be stickier. I'm sure your sheriff will be only too glad to cooperate with me—and I will have to fetch the man along, since it's a state law Boudreau is violating here. I've no authority to arrest him on my own."

"What about Mr. Hampton? Won't he be arrested for dueling, too?"

"Ma'am, I've got no quarrel with your Mr. Hampton— and I'm sure the sheriff will feel the same way. Anyhow, ladies, I'd best be about my business."

"May I come along?" Jasmine asked.

"Absolutely not," came Murchison's firm reply. "This could be treacherous. Just sit tight, Miss Dubroc. I promise you I'll have your Mr. Hampton back to you as soon as possible."

Murchison left, and Jasmine turned to embrace Marie. "Marie, thank you so much. You may have just saved Jared's life!"

An hour later, at sundown, four men were standing on the sandbar on the western side of the Mississippi River, their rowboats moored in the mud at the edge of the fingerlike island.

Jared Hampton and Jack Malone, who was acting as his second, stood on the northern tip of the narrow bar. On the opposite end were Claude Boudreau and Anton Rice, proprietor of the hotel where Boudreau was staying. Rice had agreed to act as second for Claude.

Jared and Claude had removed their coats. As the principals waited, the seconds went to work, measuring and marking the distances, then loading the flintlock pistols.

Once the pistols were loaded by the seconds, Jared and Claude were called to the center of the bar, where each second handed a loaded pistol to his principal. Jack then pulled a coin from his pocket and handed it to a nervous-looking Anton Rice. "Care to make the toss, Mr. Rice?" he asked the shorter man.

Rice, whose bulbous red nose betrayed his addiction to alcohol, nodded and took the coin in his sweaty fingers. He lost the toss. Jared's side, as winner, was designated to give the signal to begin, while Claude, as loser, was allowed to select the direction he wanted to face. The two principals exchanged not a word during these proceedings.

Boudreau elected to face to the south, and Jack directed the two men to turn back-to-back. As Jack called out the numbers, the two men paced off, their boots thudding on the sandy ground. At the count of ten, they turned.

"For Jasmine!" Jared called out, firing at Claude.

Out in the Mississippi, Marshal Murchison and Sheriff Brady were in a rowboat, frantically rowing toward the Vidalia sandbar. With a feeling of helpless frustration, Murchison spied the two men on the bar as they squared off and turned. "Damn—looks like we're too late!" he said.

## ★ Twenty-seven ★

At Magnolia Bend, night had fallen, and although Jasmine remained distraught about Jared, she dutifully joined Maggie and Charity in the dining room for supper, and tried to pretend nothing was amiss. Miss Charity was just remarking to Jasmine that it was odd that Jared hadn't shown up for the meal, when abruptly, he burst into the room.

"Jared!" Jasmine cried, bolting to her feet in her excitement. Her eyes swept over him, and she noted with intense relief that while he looked angry and exhausted, he also appeared unharmed.

"Good evening, Aunt," Jared said to Charity, conspicuously ignoring Jasmine's greeting. "I'll be having a word with Jasmine in private, if you don't mind."

Charity frowned her confusion. "But, Jared, don't you want any supper?"

"If you'll excuse us, Aunt."

Before anyone could say another word, Jared grabbed Jasmine by the arm and yanked her out of the room.

Despite Jared's obvious agitation, Jasmine could not contain her joy as he pulled her into the library down the hallway. "Jared, I'm so glad you're—"

"Shut up!" he hissed, releasing her and shutting the door, then turning to face her, his eyes blazing with fury.

Jasmine was so stunned by Jared's terse order and the raging violence in his eyes that she could only stare at him blankly. The man facing her was an implacable stranger, taut with seething frustration.

"Do you know what you've done?" he demanded, breathing hard as he took an aggressive step toward her. "You couldn't leave it alone, could you, Jasmine? You had to interfere, didn't you?" As she started to protest, he shook a finger at her and added, "Oh, don't try to deny what you did! Murchison told me you bid him stop the duel."

"What happened?" Jasmine asked in a small voice.

"You spit on my honor is what happened! Boudreau got away, Jasmine. As soon as he saw Murchison and the sheriff rowing up, he dived off the sandbar, swam to the Louisiana shoreline, and disappeared into the woods! And I could have had the bastard! We were just reloading for the second round, when that damned marshal—"

"*What?*" Jasmine interrupted, moving toward him. "You mean, there was a first round? You and Claude fired at each other?" Frantically, she eyed him up and down. "My God, Jared. Were you hurt?"

His face livid, Jared snapped, "No, my dear, I wasn't hit, and neither was Boudreau. Both weapons misfired on the first round. Do you have any idea how humiliating that is for a gentleman, Jasmine? To have the weapons misfire, then to have . . ."

Jared paused, his features twisted in a combination of anger and incredulity, for as he had spoken, Jasmine had succumbed to hysterical laughter.

In murderous silence, Jared watched her. At last he inquired, "Do you find me an object of humor now, my dear? Do you find me, perhaps, a pathetic, laughable figure?"

"Oh, no, no!" Jasmine cried, realizing how badly she had injured Jared's pride with her demented mirth. "It's just that I was so afraid that . . . and then both the pistols . . ."

Jared stepped forward and gripped Jasmine by the shoulders. "Why couldn't you let me kill the bastard, Jasmine? Damn you, why did you have to interfere?"

Not waiting for her answer, he released her and turned to leave the room. Jasmine pursued him into the hallway, calling out, "Jared, please! I did what I did because I was afraid that Claude would kill you!"

"Were you? I think you'd better decide which one of us it was that you wanted to save!"

And he left her, slamming the front door behind him.

Jasmine sagged against the closed door, trembling, feeling stung by Jared's parting words. Though she had laughed due to hysterical relief, now Jared thought she had scorned his system of honor. Obviously, he valued it above all else—including his love for her. And she, Jasmine, had doubtless committed the unforgivable in his eyes . . .

She was dabbing at a tear with her hand and turning to head upstairs when Charity rushed into the hallway, her taffeta skirts swishing on the Persian runner. "Jasmine, dear, what is it? Where is Jared? Aren't we going to the theater tonight?"

Jasmine had forgotten all about it, and she was certain that Jared had, as well. She braved a smile at Charity, struggling not to reveal the emotional pain now tearing her apart. "Um—Miss Charity, Jared asked me to beg your forgiveness tonight. He's rather tired this evening, and he decided we should forgo Shakespeare this once. As a matter of fact, I'm feeling rather done in myself, so if you wouldn't mind reading Maggie her story . . ."

Jasmine's voice trailed off, her words choked with tears as she rushed for the stairway. Charity watched her disappear up the steps, a frown of alarm and worry wrinkling her heart-shaped face.

The next morning as Jasmine arose, Sarah handed her an envelope with her breakfast tray. "A gentleman came by early and left this, missy, while you was still sleepin'."

Jasmine thanked Sarah, and once her maid had left the room, opened the letter and read it as she drank her coffee.

The correspondence, from Marshal Murchison, got straight to the point:

> My dear Miss Dubroc,
>
> As I'm sure you've heard by now, I was unable yesterday to apprehend Claude Boudreau, who is now, unfortunately, once again at large. A check of the Rice Hotel has revealed no trace of the man. I do apologize for the fiasco at the sandbar last evening, but at least your Mr. Hampton appears to be safe, for the moment.
>
> I shall depart for St. Louis this morning to seek the evidence we discussed, but expect to be coming back through Natchez within a few weeks. In the interim, if you should hear from Boudreau/Rawlins, please write me care of the Planters Hotel in St. Louis. I suspect that our man may well resurface in your area, and make further attempts to blackmail you.
>
> Last, I implore you to exercise all caution in dealing with this ruffian, should he contact you once more.
>
> Until we meet again—
>
> Your obedient servant,
>
> Doyle Murchison, United States Marshal

Jasmine read the letter twice, then folded it, frowning pensively. She could only pray that Marshal Murchison would find the necessary evidence in St. Louis and return to Natchez before Claude Boudreau managed to kill Jared!

While Jasmine was reading Murchison's letter, the marshal himself was sitting in Jared Hampton's study at Hampton Hall. Though Murchison was due shortly at the Natchez landing to board a steamboat bound for St. Louis, he had decided that he must speak briefly with Hampton before he left town, to apprise the man of the danger that he faced. He was also hoping that Hampton might be willing to help him nab Hank Rawlins.

Jared had received Murchison coolly and had listened po-

litely to the marshal's account of the activities of Hank Rawlins, as well as the marshal's suspicion that Rawlins might
well be Claude Boudreau. When he concluded his remarks,
Jared shrugged. "Actually, Murchison, none of this surprises
me that much. I've known for some time that Claude Boudreau is quite beyond redemption."

"Aye, sir," Murchison concurred. "That's why I'm
here—to warn you not to pursue Boudreau on your own.
You see, you left the sandbar in such a rush yesterday, I got
no opportunity to inform you of the danger you could face."

Jared raised an eyebrow at his guest. "Indeed, Marshal?
How very generous of you to come here and warn me. However, sir, it occurs to me that, had you not interfered last
evening, your little problem would now be solved. Claude
Boudreau—or Hank Rawlins, as you would have it—would
now be dead."

Murchison sat forward in his chair, his gray eyes narrowed
on Jared. "I take it from what you're saying, sir, that it's
still your intention to take the law into your own hands?"

"I'm still determined to kill Boudreau, if that's what you're
asking," Jared said flatly.

The marshal shook his head. "Miss Dubroc warned me
that you wouldn't cooperate."

"Did she, now? Actually, Marshal, I should think you'd
be grateful that I'm planning to kill Boudreau—it makes no
further effort necessary on your part."

"I'm not interested in your vigilante style of justice, Hampton!" Murchison retorted grimly. "Once I gather the needed
evidence, I have every intention of making Boudreau pay for
his crimes—all legal and proper."

"Suit yourself," Jared replied, again shrugging. "However, in the interim, *I* have every intention of settling a matter
of honor between myself and Boudreau. After what he did
to my fiancée, no less than his death at my hands will bring
me satisfaction."

The lawman gestured his exasperation. "Don't be a fool,
Hampton! You don't have any idea what you're up against
with this scoundrel. I implore you to leave this matter to the
proper authorities, before something truly tragic happens."

Jared stood in an obvious gesture of dismissal, his blue eyes immutable. "And I implore you, Marshal Murchison, to save your sympathies for Claude Boudreau. He'll be needing them far more than I will, I assure you."

## ★ Twenty-eight ★

Two weeks passed. While Jasmine and Jared continued to see each other almost every day, the atmosphere remained strained and cool between them.

Early in November, Father Grignon stopped by Magnolia Bend to see Jasmine, and presented the young woman with the decree of dissolution of her marriage to Claude Boudreau, which had just arrived from Rome. After the priest left, Jasmine took the official-looking document upstairs and tucked it in the back of one of her dresser drawers, reflecting ironically that, considering what Marshal Murchison had recently told her, it may never have been necessary for her to seek a Catholic annulment of her marriage to Claude at all, since the marriage may well have been bigamous.

That night, when she had occasion to walk Jared to the front door following supper, she mentioned to him that she had received the document from Father Grignon earlier that day. "I know," Jared informed her. "Father Grignon mentioned the dissolution to me when I went by his office today for my instruction. I'm being confirmed in the church on Sunday," he added.

Jasmine bit her lip. "Jared, you mean you still want to . . . ? Don't you think we should reconsider our—"

"No, I don't, my dear," he interrupted coolly, kissing her on the forehead as he left her.

Jasmine gritted her teeth as she stared at the closed door. Jared's treatment of her had become a frustrating ritual—a chaste kiss on her forehead when he arrived, a chaste kiss on her forehead when he left, and few, if any, words to her in between. He was holding himself back from her, using his anger to construct a cold, hard barrier between them, perhaps because he feared what he might do if he truly gave vent to his raging feelings. Yet Jasmine realized she'd almost prefer bearing the brunt of his anger to watching his icy withdrawal slowly freeze out their love.

It deeply distressed Jasmine that Jared was letting the foiled duel come between them this way. They'd been through so much together, yet before, they'd always managed to stay close and keep communicating. Now, all communication had been shut off—by Jared. Again, Jasmine had to question Jared's love for her. He'd always been so eminently fair with her; he'd never before held a grudge or let a misunderstanding stretch on this way. Now, his withdrawal seemed totally disproportionate to the "crime" she'd committed.

Jasmine also knew that she'd done everything in her power to try to make Jared understand why she'd felt compelled to put a stop to the duel in the first place. It was up to him now to forgive; the next move had to be his.

Jasmine's sole consolation during these painful days was the fact that Claude Boudreau had, by all appearances, vanished from the region again. He'd made no further attempt to contact her, and as far as Jasmine knew, he hadn't contacted Jared, either. Jasmine did stay in touch with Marie Bernard daily, to see if she'd picked up on any progress Jared might be making in the case, but as far as Marie knew, neither Jared nor Jack had had any luck in tracking Claude. Jasmine continued to practice with her pistol behind Hampton Hall when she was sure no one was around. If Claude should resurface, she was going to be prepared!

Ironically, the plans for their wedding proceeded, at Charity's direction. The invitations had been mailed, and acceptances as well as wedding gifts were pouring in daily at Magnolia Bend. The appointed day would arrive in less than a month, and Miss Laveau now stopped by Magnolia Bend almost daily to fit Jasmine, Charity, and Maggie in their respective dresses as bride, matron of honor, and flower girl. More than once, Jasmine thought of going to Charity and calling the wedding off, but she couldn't help but cling to the hope that things might still work out. She realized that Charity must have noticed the distance between her and Jared; however, the old woman made no comment. Jasmine reasoned that Charity's reticence likely stemmed from a fear that acknowledging the estrangement might well forestall their marriage.

Things finally reached a head one clear, cool November afternoon, as Jasmine walked the grounds of Magnolia Bend in her cloak and bonnet, thinking of her unhappy relationship with her beloved. She was strolling along the shoulder-high privet hedge that separated the grounds from Woodville Road, when she spied Jared's barouche coming down the lane toward her from the east. Jasmine's heart leapt as the buggy moved closer—as she spotted Jared at the reins, a huge bouquet of flowers laid out on the seat next to him. Perhaps, at last, he was coming to reconcile with her!

But the buggy continued on down the road, past Magnolia Bend. Jared didn't even glance in her direction, and she noted a faraway, preoccupied expression on his face as he passed her.

Watching the barouche move off toward town, Jasmine was at once consumed with anxiety and jealousy. Where on earth was Jared going? And to whom was he planning to give the flowers?

Heedless of the fact that she was not dressed for riding, Jasmine ran to the stable and bid the lad throw a saddle on the closest available horse. Within minutes, she had mounted a black mare and was galloping the animal down the driveway toward the street.

Luckily, Jared hadn't been in a hurry. She spotted the back of his barouche just before they entered town. He proceeded on through the central business district toward the bluff, then turned north onto Cemetery Road.

To Jasmine's confusion and deepening puzzlement, Jared led her all the way out the tree-shaded road to the Natchez Cemetery, where he parked his barouche beneath a tall, fluttering elm. From a safe distance, she watched him alight from the buggy, the flowers in hand.

She tethered her horse to a large lilac bush, then slowly approached Jared from behind, clutching her woolen cloak tightly to her in the crisp breeze. She watched Jared pause before a recent-looking grave, observed him laying the flowers down before a plain marble headstone. He removed his hat and stared down at the grave. The brisk wind tugged at his coattails, ruffled his hair, and sent dead leaves swirling about him. After a moment he lifted a hand to his eye, and Jasmine could have sworn he was wiping a tear.

He didn't even seem to notice when she came to stand to his right, directly behind him. Then she read the tombstone, and cried out to him in horror, "*Florence La Fleume*?"

If Jared was shocked by Jasmine's presence, he displayed no sign as he turned to face her. "Hello, my dear," he said, in a resigned tone that hinted that he had almost expected her to come. He nodded toward the tombstone. "You know, I was going to tell you all about Florence someday. Perhaps the time has come at last."

Jasmine was stunned by the pain in Jared's eyes. Whatever had Florence La Fleume meant to Jared that he would lay flowers on her grave, and stand above it with tears in his eyes?

She quickly set aside her feelings of shock, anger, and betrayal. It seemed that Jared was, at last, willing to communicate with her, and she wasn't about to do anything to discourage him. "Yes, perhaps the time has come for us to talk," she heard herself replying, in a calm voice that hardly mirrored her feelings.

Jared took her arm and led her to a sun-dappled stone bench beneath a huge magnolia tree. He was silent for a long moment as the wind wheezed about them, playing its low dirge and rustling the leaves of the tree above. At last, he turned to her and said, "First of all, Jasmine, I've been meaning for some time to apologize to you. I've been—well, quite preoccupied lately, and I know I've been acting like a callous bastard."

"I can understand how you might have felt hurt—after I stopped the duel," she replied carefully. "Are you still angry at me?"

He shook his head. "I think I was angrier at myself—because I wasn't able to accomplish what I wanted. You did interfere, my dear, but in my heart, I think I knew from the beginning that you did so out of love for me. It was wrong of me to take out my frustration on you afterward. It was just my wounded male pride, I guess," he finished with a self-deprecating smile.

"I understand," she whispered.

He took her gloved hand in his and squeezed it. "I'm glad."

Gesturing toward the nearby grave, she asked, "Jared, who was this Florence La Fleume? I mean, I know my father knew her. In fact, I met her once myself, at the reading of my father's will. And I know she later died in a barroom brawl. But—how is she connected to you? Why did you put flowers on her grave just now?"

Jared turned to Jasmine, his eyes bright with tears. "Because she was my cousin."

"What?" Jasmine cried, her heart lurching at his words.

A muscle twitched in Jared's strong jaw as he said hoarsely, "Florence La Fleume was actually Florence Hampton, Aunt Charity's daughter."

Jasmine's mouth fell open as she released Jared's hand. "Merciful heavens, Jared! This is simply beyond belief! You must explain!"

He nodded, his eyes narrowed to shutter his pain. "I'm afraid it's quite a long and sordid story."

"Please! I must hear it all!"

"Very well, my dear." He paused for a moment to collect his thoughts, then spoke with his gaze fixed upon an unseen point in space. "You know, there always was something rather strange about my cousin Florence. Even when we both were children, I couldn't help but notice how Florence would play up to men at every social gathering. I think the poor child did so because she was starved for affection—my uncle had ignored her from the day she was born. You see, Uncle

Henry had wanted a son, and Florence was his and Aunt Charity's only child. Anyway, even though my uncle cruelly ignored her, Florence's forward behavior around men used to enrage him. I remember one occasion, when Florence was only eleven, and she sat in the lap of one of our gentleman guests at a social gathering and tweaked his mustache. After the guests had gone home, my uncle slapped her nearly senseless and called her a little slut.'' With a bitter laugh, Jared concluded, "It's no wonder she later became one!''

"How horrible!'' Jasmine exclaimed, feeling intense sympathy for Jared's cousin.

He nodded. "Uncle Henry was a cold-hearted bastard. He was a lot like my own father, in fact. After I went to live with him and Aunt Charity—''

"Wait a minute!'' Jasmine interrupted tensely. "After you went to live with your aunt and uncle . . . ? That would have been when you lost your own parents, wouldn't it, Jared?'' As he nodded, she clutched his hand and said firmly, "Before you go on, you must tell me how your own parents died.''

Jared threw Jasmine an anguished look. "Darling, please. You don't want to hear this. The circumstances were quite appalling, and—''

"Jared, I must know,'' she said, squeezing his hand.

He signed raggedly, and ran his free hand through his wind-ruffled hair. "Very well. As I've told you already, my father and Uncle Henry were a lot alike. Just as Uncle Henry had little respect for Aunt Charity, my father had no respect for my mother. Beyond that, Father was also irrationally jealous. He accused Mother of betraying him with everything in pants here in Natchez. I used to hear them shouting at each other at night, and it was horrible—the screams, the recriminations. Anyway, all my mother ever really wanted was to be a good wife, but eventually, Father's cruelty drove her to seek friendship with a young law clerk my father employed. The inevitable finally occurred, almost as if my father had orchestrated it.'' Jared's jaw was tight, his voice constricted with pain as he added, "Father found my mother in bed with the law clerk, and he . . . shot them both, then killed himself.''

"Oh, my God, Jared!" Jasmine gasped. "How awful! No wonder you didn't want to tell me about it! How old were you when this happened?"

"Fourteen," he said.

Her heart ached for him. Suddenly, she snapped her fingers, her eyes lighting with realization. "It happened in Vidalia, didn't it? At the plantation house?"

"Yes," he said, his voice almost inaudible.

"Oh, darling, no wonder you didn't want to take me through the house there! I could almost feel the tragedy as we walked through those halls! How agonizing it must have been for you! You should have said something to me."

"What should I have said?" he demanded, his eyes full of crazed pain as he turned to face her. " 'My dear, here's the house where my father blew my mother's brains out, then splattered the walls with his own blood.' "

"Oh, Jared! Don't tell me you saw—"

"I found them," he said raggedly.

"Oh, my darling!" she cried, tears spilling down her cheeks as she embraced him. For a long moment, she just held him, both of them trembling with the emotion of the moment. "And you were just fourteen! Was it terrible for you afterward?"

"I survived," he said as she gently released him. "The incident was officially passed off as an unfortunate accident, but there was quite a scandal here locally, as you might well imagine. It was even rumored that madness ran in our family." He laughed bitterly. "The rumors rather pleased me, you know, since I almost preferred the gossip to the truth— that my father was a heartless, sadistic old bastard who had murdered his own wife. Anyway, that was when I came to live with Aunt Charity, Uncle Henry, and with Florence, bless her heart."

Jared said Florence's name with such despair that Jasmine knew there was another Pandora's box remaining to be unlocked. "Did something happen between you and Florence?"

"We became very close, though never in a man-woman sense," Jared confided. "Florence—God rest her soul—was truly my best friend that first year I lived with Uncle Henry and Aunt Charity. Then, tragedy struck for her.''

''What happened?''

''When Florence turned nineteen, she met a young swamp farmer at the county fair. It was love at first sight for both of them, and, within a week, Florence had decided she wanted to marry the lad. I'm sure you can well imagine Uncle Henry's reaction to that!''

''Did she do it anyway?''

He nodded. ''They ran off to Louisiana and were wed by a justice of the peace. Everything was fine for a few months. Then, that first winter, Florence's young husband caught the measles during an epidemic. He later died of pneumonia.''

''Oh, Jared!''

''Florence was devastated, of course. Yet when she came back home, my uncle—the bastard!—threw her out of the house. Afterward, he told all his friends here in Natchez that both his daughter and her husband had died during the measles epidemic.''

''How terrible—to say his own daughter was dead!''

Jared nodded grimly. ''Aunt Charity and I wanted desperately to help Florence, but before anything could really be done for her, she disappeared. Later, I found her Under-the-Hill. By then, she had become a prostitute. She had dyed her hair red, and had taken the name of Flossie La Fleume. Aunt Charity and I did everything in our power to get Florence out of that hellhole, but she steadfastly refused to leave. She said we must pretend Florence was dead, just as Uncle Henry had told everyone. And she said if we didn't keep her secret, she would leave Natchez forever and we'd never see her again.

''Anyway,'' Jared continued in an unsteady voice, ''Aunt Charity and I visited with Florence over the years, and we kept her secret. Even in her death, we kept it. However, while she was living, never did we stop trying to persuade Florence to leave her life Under-the-Hill. But all she would do was visit with my aunt and me occasionally at my shipping office. We did feel a new surge of hope after Uncle Henry died. We were sure that Florence would then have a change of heart. But she never relented. We begged and pleaded, but she always just laughed and assured us that she was beyond salvation. Yet my aunt and I could hear the tears in that laughter.''

"Oh, Jared!" Jasmine cried when he had finished. "That's such a tragic story!"

"I feel so responsible," he said brokenly, his eyes shifting to Florence's grave. "I should have been able to do something to save her."

"Jared, you're not responsible," Jasmine assured him. "You're not the one who set Florence along the path she took. I'm sure you and your aunt were the only good things in her life."

"Oh, I don't know," he said, shaking his head. "Sometimes I do think madness runs in our family."

"No, Jared, it's not madness," Jasmine assured him, thinking of her own life. "Don't you see? Jared, you must know that I understand your cousin now! I understand so much now! You see, there's a third man who was very much like your father and your Uncle Henry—a man who also knew your cousin Florence, bizarre coincidence though it may be.''

"Your father?"

She nodded. "He always made me feel so ashamed of myself, so inferior. And I know that's what your uncle did to your poor cousin. The truth is, parents sometimes visit these things upon their children, even if they don't intend to. That's why I never can quite believe that you love me, Jared,'' she finished with a catch in her voice.

As he tried to interrupt, she held up a hand and continued, "As for your cousin Florence—she simply expressed her feelings of unworthiness in a different manner from me."

"Perhaps so."

Shaking her head, Jasmine continued, "Jared, do you realize how uncanny all of this is? Florence was your cousin, and she knew my father. Our lives were connected all along, yet we never even knew it!"

"Oh, yes, our lives were connected all along," he concurred grimly.

Jasmine frowned, as ideas began to spin through her mind. "Wait a minute, Jared! Florence was your cousin, and my father's friend. Then my father died, and Florence inherited his money. Then Claude Boudreau came along and. . . ." She turned to him wildly, her thoughts fragmented, splintering. "My God, this is too much! It's too confusing! Tell me, is there more?"

He drew a long breath, then met her anguished, confused gaze. "Jasmine, I know I've been angry at you at times for keeping things from me, and now I must beg your forgiveness, too, my darling, for I've also withheld quite a lot from you." As she eyed him with feverish speculation, he nodded. "You're beginning to put it all together, my dear, and I assure you, it's quite an ugly picture. I didn't want to tell you before, because I wanted to spare you further pain."

"Tell me!" she cried, desperately clutching his sleeve.

"So be it. You see, I didn't just happen along in the *River Witch* that night you got thrown into the Mississippi. Jack and I were trailing the *Mississippi Belle* because I very much feared Claude Boudreau may have murdered Florence."

# ★ Twenty-nine ★

"Oh, my God, Jared!" Jasmine cried. "You mean Claude killed your cousin to get my father's money? But that makes no sense! Oh, I know! He did it to get to me! He somehow found out about Florence, and how I was next in line to receive the inheritance. But *how* did he find out? And how did he kill her? Heavens, Jared, this is simply incredible!"

"Quite," he agreed. He stood and helped Jasmine to her

feet. "There's someone else I think should tell you the rest of this story."

"Who?"

"Savannah Sue at the Scarlet Slipper."

"Savannah Sue! Why, she would have known your cousin, too, wouldn't she? Is that why she still comes by to see you?"

"I've known Sue for some time," Jared admitted. "She and Florence were good friends. Please, Jasmine, I think you should hear the rest of this from her lips."

"All right, Jared," she said.

He fetched Jasmine's horse and tethered the animal to the back of his barouche. Then he helped Jasmine board the conveyance. They drove out of the cemetery and proceeded south toward town. Jasmine's mind was still reeling from his revelations. To think that Flossie La Fleume had been Jared's cousin!

In due course, Jared turned the horse down Silver Street and they descended into Natchez-under-the-Hill. "I hate bringing you down here, my dear, but I feel this is absolutely necessary," he remarked, holding the horse in tight rein on the steep incline.

Soon, they turned down a cluttered alleyway, which reeked of garbage even in the coolness. A mangy gray cat skittered by, arching its back and hissing in protest as Jared parked his rig at the back of a looming, ramshackle building. Nodding toward a yawning doorway, Jared said, "This is the back entrance to the Scarlet Slipper."

He helped her out of the barouche, then together they entered the dusty back hallway. As they headed for the stairs, a short, voluptuous woman in a tight, sequined red-satin gown descended the creaky steps. "Hi, Rosie," Jared called up to the black-haired girl. "Seen Sue this afternoon?"

"Good afternoon, Señor Jared." As Rosie stepped off the staircase to join them in the hallway, Jasmine noted that the girl was quite lovely, with her aristocratic Spanish features and dark, flashing eyes. The paint she wore on her face seemed to mar rather than enhance her classic beauty. "Sue's upstairs," the girl informed Jared, smiling at him brazenly, then glancing coolly toward Jasmine. "Third door on the right."

"Thanks, Rosie."

The woman batted her lashes at Jared, then moved off toward the front of the building with a provocative sway of her ample hips. Jasmine dutifully followed Jared up the stairs, silently clenching her teeth. She was sorely tempted to ask him if he knew every prostitute who worked here, yet she knew such a remark would come across as quite petty, considering their more important mission at the moment. She remained very apprehensive and confused.

At the top of the steps, they turned down a narrow corridor, then Jared knocked on the third door. A tired female voice called out, "Who is it?"

"Sue, it's Jared Hampton," he called back. "I'm here with my fiancée, Miss Dubroc. We'd like to talk with you for a moment, if you don't mind."

"Just a minute, honey," a nervously shrill voice called back.

Moments later, a confused-looking Savannah Sue opened the door, wearing slippers and a faded cotton wrapper. Her hair was disheveled and her face appeared plain, almost homely, minus its customary paint. "Well, this is a surprise," she said, self-consciously brushing a tendril of stringy blond hair from her eyes as she glanced from Jared to Jasmine. "Won't you folks come in?"

Sue stepped back, and Jared and Jasmine entered the pitifully plain room. Jasmine glanced about, noting that the old iron bed with its thin mattress was unmade, and the bedding looked yellowed and soiled. The stark afternoon sunshine poured in the window, illuminating the dust that hung everywhere—in the air, on the battered wardrobe and dresser, on the crazed old mirror hanging over the dressing table. The sun was cruel and indiscriminate, flooding Sue's face, outlining the ravages of time, the wrinkles, and the sadness there. Over everything there hung the odor of cheap perfume and a desolation so intense that Jasmine was sure she could also smell it. She felt an acute stab of guilt that she had ever felt jealousy, or harbored unkind thoughts toward the unfortunate creatures who lived in this establishment. These women deserved only her sympathy, she realized.

Jasmine turned toward Jared and they shared an empathetic glance. In that moment, she felt regret that she had ever resented his wanting to help these women. She understood so much as she stared into his anguished blue eyes—his helpless frustration over his cousin's plight, his overwhelming desire to make this private hell a bit more bearable for Sue and the others. . . .

Sue evidently noticed the pity in the eyes of her guests, for she brushed a hand over her wrinkled wrapper and said rather defensively, "I'm sorry the room ain't done up, folks. And I ain't got no refreshments to offer you, neither. But you see, I wasn't expecting no company—"

"Please, Sue, you mustn't apologize," Jared hastened to reassure the woman. "We've intruded on you. If you'll just be so kind as to talk with us for a few minutes, we'll be on our way." He nodded toward Jasmine, then told Sue, "There's something I want you to explain to Miss Dubroc."

The corners of Sue's eyes crinkled with confusion as she glanced from Jared to Jasmine. Slowly she drawled, "Well, then, won't you folks take a seat?"

Since there were no chairs in the room, Jasmine and Jared sat down together on a scarred cedar chest that slumped against one wall, across from the bed. Sue sat down on the bed opposite them, the iron springs groaning as she parked her weight. "Well, Mr. Jared? What do you want me to be tellin' your lady friend?"

"I want you to tell Miss Dubroc about Florence—how she died, and what happened previous to that," Jared said simply.

Sue slanted Jared a quizzical look. "Does your lady friend know about—"

He nodded. "She knows that Florence was my cousin. Please, Sue, just tell her how Florence died and what was on your mind afterward when you came to see me."

Sue glanced at Jasmine and dutifully began. "Well, you see, miss, Flossie was my best friend. From the first day she come to the Scarlet Slipper, there ain't been no secrets between the two of us. Flossie told me all about losing her husband, and about her no-good father that threw her out of the house afterward." Leaning forward with lips pursed indignantly, Sue continued, "I tell you, miss, it always confounded me how that old coot could have such a nice daughter like Flossie—not to mention his nephew, Mr. Jared, here, who was always coming 'round to help us out, even then."

"Go on, Sue," Jared directed. "Tell Miss Dubroc about my cousin's death."

Sue emitted a heavy sigh, shaking her head. "Well'um, that was just terrible. There was a big fight one night here at the Scarlet Slipper. Guns was fired, and the next thing I knew, I looked over and there was poor Flossie laid out on the floor with a bullet through her head. It like to broke my heart!" Choking on her final words, Sue drew a handkerchief from her wrapper pocket and noisily blew her nose.

While she collected herself, Jared explained to Jasmine, "Sue was the one who came and told Aunt Charity and me of Florence's death. We arranged a discreet funeral—Florence would have wanted that, you see—for just Aunt Charity and myself and a few of Florence's friends. Then, afterward—"

"After the funeral, I come back one evening to talk with Mr. Jared," Sue explained to Jasmine, sniffing. "You see, some strange things was happening here at the Scarlet Slipper right before Flossie was gunned down by whoever done it. The more I thought about it, the more peculiar it seemed."

"Yes? What was peculiar?" Jasmine prodded.

"Well'um," Sue went on, "A few days before poor Flossie was kilt, she told me she was coming into some money. It seems like some silversmith she was friends with died and left all his loot to her."

"My father's inheritance!" Jasmine gasped.

Sue glanced, flabbergasted, from Jasmine to Jared. "It was *her* father that Flossie was making time with?"

"Never mind, Sue," Jared said, his voice gruff with embarrassment. "Please, just tell Miss Dubroc what happened."

Sue was shaking her head. "Well, I'll be a horse's beehind! To think that it was this lady's daddy Flossie was servicin' on the sly.'' Catching Jared's reproachful glance, Sue quickly cleared her throat and told Jasmine, ''Pardon my language, ma'am. I don't even know for a fact that Flossie and your daddy were . . . Well, you know what I mean, ma'am.'' As Jared started once again to intervene, Sue hastily went on, ''Anyhow, Miss Dubroc, Flossie told me about this here money she was supposed to be getting. But she wasn't sure she should keep the old man's stash. Seems she'd met his daughter . . .'' Sue paused, snapping her fingers. ''Well, lordy, ma'am, that woulda been you!''

''Yes!'' Jasmine confirmed, her green eyes gleaming with avid interest. ''Please, go on, Sue.''

''Well, ma'am, about this time, right after Flossie told me about the old man leaving her his money, a French feller started stopping in here at the Scarlet Slipper every day.''

''Claude Boudreau!'' Jasmine gasped.

''I don't rightly recall no name, but he was a handsome devil. Them black eyes of his kinda gave a body a shiver, though. Anyhow, in no time a'tall, this Frenchie and Flossie was keeping company. Every day, them two was at the corner table drinkin', with their heads together. Flossie told me she really liked that feller. In fact, seems she told him about the inheritance—about how she wasn't sure she should take the old codger's money.'' Sue clamped a hand over her mouth. ''Oh, pardon me, ma'am.''

''Never mind. Just go on,'' Jasmine urged.

''Well, Flossie told me how Frenchie kept telling her the old man's money was her due. But, still, Flossie told me she didn't want it. 'I ain't no blood kin of that poor old man.' That's just what she told me, ma'am.''

''Bless her heart,'' Jasmine said, shaking her head. ''Then she was killed.''

''Yes, ma'am—killed like a lamb to the slaughter, God rest her soul. You know, there was so much noise and confusion here that night, and afterward for several days, I was plum prostrated with the grief of it—you know, losing my best friend and all. And it wasn't till after poor Flossie was cold in the ground that I got me to ruminating about it all . . .''

"Yes?" Jasmine queried in a rising voice.

"I got me to thinkin' that drat it all if that confounded Frenchman wasn't here the night poor Flossie got scratched!"

Jasmine felt utterly numb. "Of course," she whispered.

"Now, mind you, I'm ain't sayin' old Frenchie started the brawl, then drilled one through Flossie's head," Sue continued, "but I sure 'nough took myself to Mr. Jared's office and told him all about it. Him and me agreed that it looked right peculiar. Yes'um."

"Trouble was," Jared put in to Jasmine, "neither Sue nor I could figure out how this Frenchman might have profited by my cousin's death. He certainly would not have been in line to receive this mysterious inheritance Flossie had told Sue about." Jared glanced at Jasmine. "But now we know differently, don't we, my dear?"

Their eyes locked for an electric moment, as Sue put in, "We do? Mind fillin' me in, then, Mr. Jared?"

Jared turned and smiled kindly at Sue. "Another time, perhaps," he told her. "We've imposed on you long enough." He pulled Jasmine to her feet. "I will tell you this much, however," he added to Sue. "You were absolutely right in your suspicions of the Frenchman. He's a dangerous man, and if you should see him again, run like hell and come straight to me. Do not—I repeat, *do not*—have anything to do with the man. Have I your promise there, Sue?"

"Why a'course, sir," Sue said, getting to her feet. "I ain't got me no intention of cozying up to that black-eyed snake."

Jared nodded to her. "Thanks for everything, Sue."

"Yes, thank you," Jasmine added.

"Any time, Mr. Jared," Sue said, walking her guests to the door. "Just wish I coulda done more. You folks be careful, now."

Jasmine and Jared trooped down the stairs in silence. Once they were seated in Jared's barouche, she shook her head in incredulity. "Mother of God, Jared!" she gasped to him. "It's all so diabolical—so much more evil than I ever could have dreamed! Claude Boudreau killed your cousin because he found out she was planning not to accept my father's inheritance. Then, he came after me—obviously having learned from Florence that I was next in line in the will! It's monstrous! Claude would corrupt the devil himself!"

"Indeed," Jared concurred grimly. "We're damned lucky Boudreau merely threw you in the Mississippi that night, and didn't put a bullet through your head, as well."

"He told me as much himself," Jasmine muttered under her breath. "Wait a minute!" she went on to Jared. "If you were told all of this by Sue, then that night when you followed me and Claude, you already knew—"

"No, I was far from putting the entire picture together then," Jared interrupted. "You see, at the time, things weren't making much more sense to me than they were to Sue. I, too, thought the Frenchman's presence at the saloon the night my cousin was killed was quite suspicious. But, like I told you just now, I could figure no way the man might have profited by my cousin's death. Anyway, after Sue came to see me, I did make discreet inquiries here locally, and learned that a Frenchman meeting the description of the man at the saloon was courting a Natchez lady—you. I was told your family was thought to be quite poor, and actually, I had little time to put things together before I learned that the Frenchman had purchased two steamboat tickets and was taking you off on the *Mississippi Belle*. Since I was determined to pursue the matter, I decided to organize a gambling party that night in the *River Witch*, to see where Boudreau was heading, and to try to learn more about Florence's death from some of the gamblers who had been in the saloon the night she was killed."

"So that's why you came out on the deck of the *River Witch* that night! You were scanning the waters ahead for the *Mississippi Belle*!"

"Yes, I was. Yet even when I spotted you in the water, I didn't connect you with Boudreau, since I had never actually met you before." With a grim laugh, he added, "The last thing I expected to see in the river that night was a half-clothed lady. But after you told me your story, everything became clear."

"Oh, Jared!" Jasmine cried, feeling overwhelmed by the

magnitude, as well as the tragedy and injustice, of the situation. "We've all been victims of Claude Boudreau, it seems—you and your aunt, me, your cousin Florence. . . ." All at once she paused, her face paling, as a central truth at last became apparent to her, and pride forced her to pursue a most painful subject. Turning to Jared, she asked, "Then you've done all of this to avenge your cousin's death?"

At first he looked stunned by her question, then he adamantly replied, "Oh, no, love! I've done it for you, too!"

Yet Jasmine was not ready to hear his words of reassurance, especially as she recalled how Jared had kept this critical information from her for so long. Shaking her head, she said hoarsely, "No wonder you were so angry at me after I stopped the duel between you and Claude! I kept you from wreaking your vengeance on him for what he did to your cousin!"

"Jasmine, no!" Jared said, grabbing her by the shoulders and turning her to meet his intense gaze. "Of course I was angry when you foiled the duel, and afterward I said things —well, you know already that I didn't mean them! Try to understand how frustrated I felt—"

"Because of Florence."

"Because of you! I hated Boudreau for what he did to you that night on the Mississippi! I was furious afterward, and terrified that he might get his hands on you again! After what he had already done to my cousin—do you think I could bear to lose you, as well?"

"I don't know, Jared," she said, staring at her lap so he wouldn't see the hot tears stinging her eyes. "I'm just so confused by all of this. . . ."

"Damn!" he muttered under his breath, glancing around at the squalid alleyway. "Let's get out of here," he added, slapping the reins on the horse's back.

Jared drove them back toward the bluff. After a long moment of silence, he remarked, "Darling, I can't deny that part of what I've done was for Florence. I'm not ashamed of that."

"I don't want you to be ashamed of that! It's just—"

"Jasmine, hear me out," he interrupted. "You must know that everything I've done—*everything*— has been for you, too. I'm sick and tired of the women in my life being victimized by unfeeling bastards. First, my mother, then Florence and Aunt Charity, then you.'' Vehemently, he continued, ''Darling, I swear to you that Claude Boudreau shall yet pay for the despicable thing he did to you that night on the riverboat! It's been on my mind every moment since! And after we spent that long night together—after the intimacies we shared—there was never any doubt in my mind that I would do the honorable thing and marry you.''

Without intending to, Jared had wounded Jasmine with his last words. ''It's all honor with you, isn't it, Jared?'' she asked him brokenly. ''First with your cousin, now with me. You're like some knight in shining armor, always looking for a cause to take up, for someone to save. The prostitutes, the orphans, Florence. Then you found you couldn't save your cousin, and I conveniently came along, all primed for redemption. Well, I release you from your honor where I'm concerned. I don't want you to marry me out of some blind allegiance to your almighty code!''

Jared was shaking his head in disbelief. ''Jasmine, what are you saying?''

''I'm saying it's over!'' she cried.

At the top of the hill, he pulled the buggy off the roadway beneath a pecan tree, and turned to clutch her arm. ''Look, Jasmine, I said some things badly just now. When will you believe that it's truly you I want, above all else?''

''You want your revenge against Claude Boudreau more!''

''Not more than I want your love, Jasmine,'' he whispered achingly.

She lowered her eyes. ''I wish I could believe that.''

''Oh, Jasmine!'' Jared drew her across the seat into his arms. Holding her resisting body tightly to him, he said, ''I knew I shouldn't have told you any of this!''

''I had a right to know.''

''But your finding out has made things so much worse.'' He drew back slightly, lifting her chin and staring down into her anguished, tear-filled eyes. ''Jasmine, do you really think I could feel so little for you? That all of this is just a cause to me?''

"I don't know," she whispered back miserably.

"Jasmine, please. God, don't tell me I'm losing you now? I've really botched up telling you this, haven't I?"

She sighed raggedly, pulling away from his touch and staring down at her gloved hands. "Jared, I just can't be with you right now. I've learned so many shocking things this afternoon and—well, I'm feeling overwhelmed by it all. I must have time to sort things out. Please, will you just take me home?"

"Very well, Jasmine." His blue eyes were dull and defeated as he turned to snap the reins. "But you must promise me one thing—that you won't decide anything about us until we can talk again. Will you give us that much of a chance?"

She nodded slowly, wiping a tear. "Of course I will, Jared."

# ★ Thirty ★

An hour after Jasmine and Jared left the Scarlet Slipper, a tall, dark stranger strode in. It was still afternoon and the saloon was nearly deserted, except for Stan, the barkeep, and Rosie, who sat at a corner table sipping a glass of cheap sherry.

"Barkeep, give me a whiskey," the bearded man growled as he approached the bar.

"Sure, mister," Stan replied. He pulled a bottle down from a glass shelf behind him, then poured a shot of whiskey into a small, grimy glass. As he handed the man his drink, Stan reflected that there was something vaguely familiar about this tall, scowling stranger.

"Leave the bottle," the man snapped as he took the drink and tossed a bill down on the scarred surface of the bar.

"Whatever you say, sir," Stan replied amiably, taking the money.

Privately, Stan didn't like the looks of this customer. Though the man wore a respectable-looking brown suit and a derby hat, there was something decidedly mean about his countenance. *That* was what was so familiar about him! Stan decided. Those black eyes. They reminded him of the eyes of the Frenchman who'd been on the premises months before.

The man also looked primed for a fight, and this made Stan even more uncomfortable. In his eight years as barkeep at the Scarlet Slipper, Stan had been accidentally wounded in many a barroom fight. Once, he'd even been shot in the shoulder by a stray bullet. And only a few months past, poor Flossie La Fleume had lost her life during such a brawl.

No, he didn't like the looks of this man, Stan decided.

If Stan had known what was now going through his customer's head, he would have felt doubly unsettled. For the man sitting at the bar gulping down shot after shot of whiskey was indeed in a foul temper. By all rights, the stranger figured, he should now be hundreds of miles away from this hellhole, with Jared Hampton's money safely tucked in his pockets. Instead, he was now on the run from the law! Damn that little bitch, Jasmine Dubroc! She had played him for a sucker instead of handing him his money outright, as she should have! Then she'd brought Jared Hampton in on it. Hell, the scheming little whore had probably told her lover where they were planning to meet.

Then Hampton had challenged him to a duel. Actually, at first he had relished the thought of killing that pompous millionaire and punishing Jasmine—that is, until the damned federal marshal had appeared and ruined everything! Now, not only did he not have the money which was rightly his, he had been forced to stay on the move, day after day, in order to avoid capture.

He'd make them pay! he vowed silently. He'd give Jasmine and Hampton a scare they'd never forget, then he'd collect —royally!

Oh, yes. Hank Rawlins was not a man to toy with!

And Hank Rawlins was in a mean, mean mood.

"Well, hello, Señor Frenchie."

Rawlins pivoted to watch the Spanish whore park her bottom on the stool next to his. "Who you callin' Frenchie?" he growled.

The Spanish woman batted her long black eyelashes at him. "Begging your pardon, señor, but I thought you looked familiar—like a man who used to come around here a few months ago."

"I've never been in this dump before," he informed her.

"*Lo siento*," the girl replied smoothly. "It is my error then, señor."

Rawlins coldly sized her up. He liked her big breasts, the way they almost spilled out of the low-cut satin dress she wore. And he liked her rounded little bottom—in fact, right now, his hands ached to raise welts on that fat little behind until it wiped the smirk off her painted face. There was a maddening self-assurance about this little Spanish piece, and it made him ache to set her in her place.

Hank Rawlins was a master of such fare.

He pulled a cheroot from his pocket and slowly lit it, praying his hands weren't revealing the sudden tremor of sadistic excitement that coursed through his body. "You free?" he asked the girl casually, forcing himself to grin at her as he tossed his match on the floor and eyed her up and down meaningfully.

"Why sure, honey," she replied. "Whatcha have in mind?"

Rawlins glanced at the balding barkeep, who'd been listening intently to the exchange. The man cleared his throat, then turned away to wash some glasses. "Not here," Rawlins told the girl as he dragged on his cheroot, still smiling lazily. "I like my privacy when I'm with a woman, if you know what I mean."

Rosie smiled back.

Wordlessly, the two stood and left the saloon together, walking down the boardwalk in the cool crispness of the afternoon. Rawlins led the girl past freight offices, a cotton warehouse, and several other saloons, to a ramshackle boardinghouse on Middle Street, two blocks away. The small, two-story house was gray from neglect, with shutters askew and windowpanes missing, and the galleries on both stories were sagging dangerously.

Hank tossed down his smoke and led Rosie inside. As they entered the foul-smelling house and walked down the creaking hallway, Rosie heard a baby's muffled, pitiful cry, then watched several huge cockroaches climb the tattered wallpaper lining the corridor. "Señor, are you sure we should come here?"

Ignoring Rosie's question, Rawlins grabbed her arm and tugged her toward the back of the house.

He led her into a small, squalid room and shut the door behind them. He doffed his hat and frock coat, then unbuckled his belt. His smile was gone now, and he was staring at the Spanish woman with such unfeeling blackness in his eyes that she began to feel genuinely frightened.

"Señor, please," she begged, glancing around at the filthy, unkempt room. "I do not wish to stay here! This place is a sty!"

He laughed, removing his belt. The floorboards groaned ominously beneath his booted feet as he walked toward Rosie, casually doubling the heavy belt in his hand. "Oh, it's a sty, is it? Then it's just the right place to bring a pig."

Rosie gasped, but it was too late. Hank raised the belt and struck her across the side of her head with such brute force that she passed out even before she fell back and hit her head on the iron bedpost.

Hank stared dispassionately at the unconscious Spanish woman sprawled on the floor, watching a thin line of blood trickle down her forehead. Roughly he lifted her and threw her onto the bed, then ripped her dress from bodice to hem and shredded her silk bloomers. He forced her thighs apart, then knelt between them, squeezing her full breasts brutally until he felt his member growing ramrod stiff. Ah, yes, he was in a mean, mean mood, he decided.

Hank used to enjoy taking women this way back when he worked with John Murrell and his cronies fleecing travelers along the Natchez Trace. Murrell had been a master of disguise, and Hank an eager protégé who had learned his lessons well at an early age. *Win the pigeons' trust, then pluck 'em*, Murrell had always told him. After becoming adept at his teacher's methods, Hank had added several sadistic twists of his own. He had raped his first woman when he was but fifteen. When she screamed, it had been his vengeance against the mother who had beaten him senseless, again and again, when he was but a child.

What his father had done to him had been worse.

Hank undid his trousers and wielded his rigid organ above Rosie like a savage knife. Right before he took her, he slapped her pitilessly until she awakened. Then he shoved his fist into her mouth and thrust into her cruelly. He smiled into her terrified eyes, savored the agonized moans bubbling in her throat, and thought of Jasmine. He should have done this to the little bitch that night on the Mississippi—all this and much more! He would yet, he vowed, the thought sending him grinding downward with merciless force.

Right before he climaxed, he yanked his fist from Rosie's mouth. Her screams of pain were like sweet music to his ears.

Two hours later, Rosie limped back into the Scarlet Slipper, her body on fire with pain as she held her shredded clothing about her. The establishment was now full of Saturday-night revelers, yet as soon as the Spanish girl stepped inside the door, Savannah Sue rushed up to her side. "My God, Rosie! What happened to you?"

"Please, Sue—just help me upstairs!" Rosie begged.

In Rosie's room, Sue gently eased her friend's torn clothing from her battered body. "My God, Rosie, who done this to you?" Sue gasped, studying Rosie's flesh, which was a mass of welts, bruises, and cuts.

"The worst of it you can't see!" Rosie gasped convulsively through her tears. "He said he'll make it hurt ten times worse if I ever tell anyone!"

"Jesus!" Sue cried. "Rosie, you must tell me what animal done this to you! I'll get Mr. Jared to fix his wagon!"

"No! No!" Rosie cried, beseeching her friend with wildly fearful eyes. "If you're my friend, you'll never say a word about this to anyone. I'll die for sure if he gets his hands on me again!''

Rosie tottered, and Sue grabbed her friend's arm to keep her from collapsing. "All right, Rosie, just take it easy, hon. For now, let's get these wounds washed and put you in bed.''

"You won't tell anyone?" Rosie asked plaintively.

Sue stared into Rosie's face. Her lovely dark eyes were now agonized, her once beautiful features swollen almost past recognition. "I won't tell no one, honey.''

Sue helped Rosie sit down on her bed, then wet a cloth at the basin and began to wash her wounds. Despite her promise, Sue privately vowed that she'd learn more about this terrible incident.

She'd speak to Stan, the barkeep, about this—that's what she'd do. Tomorrow, when things were quiet.

# ★ Thirty-one ★

During the next couple of days, Jasmine mulled over the astonishing revelations Jared had made to her when she followed him to the cemetery. In a way, she understood him so much better after their talk; she at last comprehended the private hell he had endured for so many years. This made her love him all the more, especially as she realized that Jared had truly risen above the tragedy of his past—that he had not let the cruelties of his father or uncle cripple him or embitter him.

Yet Jasmine also faced so many new doubts. She had always wondered about Jared's "instant" love for her that night he had rescued her on the river, and it had always perplexed her that Jared had accepted her and her story so readily. Now she knew that when he had rescued her, he was already well aware of Claude Boudreau's lack of moral fiber, since he'd already suspected that Claude had murdered his cousin. It was, in fact, Florence's death that had made Jared accept her own story so easily.

Now Jasmine very much feared that Jared had transferred his feelings for Florence—particularly, his thwarted desire to rescue his cousin—onto her. She knew that Jared and Florence had never shared a romantic relationship, yet in a very real way, she suspected that Jared had become attracted to her on the rebound following Florence's death, that Jared had shifted his obsession to redeem his fallen cousin onto the new woman in his life.

One afternoon, Jasmine decided to have a talk with Charity. Though she hated the idea of invading the old woman's privacy, she felt compelled to convey her sympathies about Florence's death.

Jasmine tucked Maggie into bed for her afternoon nap, then went downstairs. She found Charity in the front parlor sitting next to the snapping fire. "Jasmine, dear, come join me for tea," the old woman called out with a smile.

Once she was seated across from Charity with a warm cup of tea in her hands, Jasmine got straight to the point. "Miss Charity, I want to tell you—well, Jared told me that Florence was your daughter."

Surprisingly, the old woman merely nodded. "I'm glad, my dear. I knew that one of these days, Jared would tell you."

"I just wanted to say that I'm sorry! The whole story is just so tragic."

Again, the old woman nodded soberly as she took a sip of tea from her china cup.

"And I wanted to offer you my condolences," Jasmine went on. "I mean, when Jared brought me here to live, I had no idea that you had buried your own daughter mere days before. I do remember that you cried when you first saw Maggie, but that was my only real hint that something might be troubling you. And at the time, you and Jared insisted your tears were of joy."

"They were, my dear," Charity assured Jasmine with a warm smile. "That darling Maggie has been my salvation these past months—as you have been. You know, Maggie so reminds me of my Florence, before she lost all her innocence, all joy in living.'' With a trembling hand, Charity placed her cup and saucer down on the tea table before her. She turned to Jasmine, her eyes filled with resigned sadness. ''This may sound strange to you, but when Florence passed on, it seemed like Jared and I had already done most of our grieving. You see, the Florence we knew had died many years before. That poor child just wasn't the same after she lost her husband, and after Henry—well, rejected her so heartlessly. After that, Florence never really was ours again. I'm sure Jared told you how tirelessly we tried to help her.''

''Oh, yes.''

Charity sighed. ''At any rate, my dear, for years I had known that Florence could easily get killed in that rowdy establishment where she worked. Then . . . well, the inevitable occurred, as you are well aware.''

''Yes,'' Jasmine replied slowly, setting down her own cup and saucer. She frowned to herself, realizing that Jared had not told his aunt that he suspected Claude Boudreau had murdered Florence. That was doubtless for the best, she mused. Far better that the old woman think Florence had been accidentally killed, than for her to find out her only child had been deliberately murdered by the same miscreant who had later robbed Jasmine and thrown her into the river!

Taking a deep breath, Jasmine ventured, ''Jared and Florence were once good friends, weren't they?''

''Oh, yes, my dear. After that poor boy came here to live—well, he'd been through so much already.''

Jasmine nodded. ''I know. Jared told me about his parents. It's a wonder he got through it all with his sanity.'' Realizing what she'd just said, Jasmine shook her head and smiled lamely. ''I'm sorry, Miss Charity. Jared and I have also talked about the rumors—you know, about madness running in the family and all. People can be so cruel.''

''Indeed, they can.''

''Miss Charity, how did Jared react when he lost Florence?''

''Well, naturally, my dear, we were both distraught for

days. But as I told you already, we felt Florence had really been lost to us many years before.''

"Yet Jared still wanted to save her," Jasmine murmured, as if to herself. "He never got to."

Charity was eyeing Jasmine intently now, deep lines radiating outward from the corners of her eyes. "My dear, there is something I've been meaning to ask you."

"Yes?"

"What's wrong between you and Jared? I mean, one would have to be blind not to notice the tension between the two of you these past weeks."

"Oh, I don't know, Miss Charity." Jasmine brushed a wisp of hair from her eyes as she tried to sort through her thoughts. What could she say to Charity to explain things, without causing the old woman more pain? At last she said carefully, "Miss Charity, after my talk with Jared a few days ago, I do feel I understand him better. But it's just that I'm—well, I don't mean to sound ungrateful, but I'm afraid that after Jared lost his cousin, he latched onto me as someone he could save in her stead." To Jasmine's horror, she found tears welling in her eyes as she went on, "I—I love him so, Miss Charity, but I fear he's deluded himself about his feelings for me. I think I may have been—well, simply convenient. I fear that if Jared marries me, he'll come to his senses later on and realize he's made a mistake."

"Oh, Jasmine!" Charity cried. "I had no idea you felt this way." The old woman came to sit by Jasmine on the settee. Taking the girl's hand, she said vehemently, "My dear, you must know that Jared loves you more than life itself. You and Maggie have brought so much joy to our lives! I think the problem you are having must be with yourself, my dear."

Jasmine laughed ruefully as she stared at her lap. "You're very perceptive."

"Well, as I've told you before, one can easily see why a young woman might have some misgivings to overcome, after being thrown into a river by a heartless blackguard who stole all her money. I know it was far from easy for you to give your heart and your trust to another man."

"I think it goes deeper than that," Jasmine admitted. "I think it has to do with what my father did to me, too."

"Yes?"

"Oh, Miss Charity, I'm not sure I should say this. You see, ironic though it is, this also has to do with your daughter Florence."

"Are you referring to the fact that your father left Florence his money?"

"You knew!" Jasmine gasped.

"My dear, I knew your father," Charity said. "And I also knew of his relationship with my daughter."

Jasmine was incredulous. "You did? Then you knew that my father and Florence were . . . ?" Jasmine blushed and glanced away, her voice trailing off as she bit her lip.

"Let me explain something to you, dear," Charity said gently. "You see, Jasmine, odd as this may sound, I know for a fact that your father and my daughter Florence were but good friends. Pierre met my daughter at the Scarlet Slipper during his more active days, and, like Jared and myself, he tried to convince her to give up her life Under-the-Hill. Later, when Pierre was confined, he and Florence became frequent companions during the day, while you were teaching. Eventually, of course, I learned of Florence's visits with your father, and that's when I first went to see Pierre, fearing that he was—er—using my daughter. But when I met with your father, I learned that he, too, had Florence's best interests in mind."

"Why, I had no idea!" Jasmine said. "I never thought my father was capable of such—sensitivity."

"I know he never showed that side of himself to you, dear." Noting Jasmine's bemused expression, Charity continued, "Oh, Pierre talked to me about you a great deal. He said you had been locked in yourself ever since your mother had died, and that he felt great guilt that he had at times taken his frustration out on you by saying unkind things. He didn't know how to reach you, Jasmine. He said it was the greatest failure of his life. He would try to go to you in the spirit of kindness and fatherly love, and instead find himself expressing only his anger. I don't think even he really knew the reasons. However, it was all tragically clear to me, my dear. You see, your father once showed me the miniature of your mother, and told me you were the image of his dear, departed wife. One could easily ascertain that you simply reminded Pierre far too strongly of his own loss. But you must know, my dear, that your father truly loved you and thought quite highly of you.''

"That's what Flossie—I mean, Florence—said, when I met her at the reading of my father's will,'' Jasmine remarked, wanting to believe Charity, but still feeling very torn. "But, like I've already told you, my father left all his money to her!'' Carefully, she added, "Had it not been for your daughter's—er—tragic and untimely death, I never would have even received the money that Claude later stole from me.''

Charity nodded sadly. "There was a reason your father did that, Jasmine. He hoped Florence would use the money to leave her existence Under-the-Hill. He once told me that it was imperative for Florence to know that a man cared enough about her to do this for her. As for you, my dear— your father felt his money would be ill-used by you. He thought it would become your shield against the world. He thought you had sacrificed enough for him and that you should marry and seek your own happiness. Therefore, he left you only the house, so that it might be sold as suitable dowry. Your father and I further agreed that, once he passed on, I would take you under my wing and see that his wishes were carried out.'' Charity smiled, squeezing Jasmine's hand. "You see, even then, my dear, I had you in mind for my Jared.''

Jasmine was shaking her head. Her father had really cared about her, after all? He'd even made plans so she would be provided for after his death? "I can't believe this!'' she cried to Charity. "Why didn't you tell me any of this before?''

"Well, dear, after Pierre's funeral, I wanted to give you a week or two to collect yourself before I came calling. Then, of course, I lost my dear Florence. And before I knew what was happening, Jared appeared, bringing you and Maggie here to live. When my nephew told me what that despicable

Boudreau character had done to you on the Mississippi, I wanted to tell you then and there about my conversations with your father. But Jared warned me to keep my peace for a time. He told me your emotional wounds ran quite deep, and that you needed time to be ready to hear what I had to say.''

Jasmine suddenly had an overpowering desire to be alone, to sort out all these startling revelations. She hugged Charity, tears spilling from her eyes. ''Thank you, Miss Charity. I can't tell you how much your words have meant to me. And, you know, Jared was right—so right!''

Jasmine left the room and went upstairs to her bedroom, tears brimming in her eyes as she lay down on the bed. It was all so ironic! The man she had assumed had hated her all her life had never hated her at all! Her father had really loved her, in his way. He'd even made plans for her for after his death!

Knowing this, Jasmine wept. This time, her tears were not of bitterness or rage, but of release. She could feel a deep wound healing inside her at that moment, and, for the first time since she'd met Jared Hampton, she no longer felt unworthy of his love.

Later, once her tears had passed, she arose, fixed her face, and put on a fresh dress. All she could think of was that she must go to Jared and share her feelings with him, beg his forgiveness for ever doubting him, and make her peace with the man she loved.

She hurried to his house at sunset, but he wasn't there. Marie, who had expected him home by late afternoon, was beginning to grow worried.

Soon night fell. Jasmine paced Jared's parlor. It wasn't like him not to come home on time, and the reasons her mind kept suggesting for his lateness made her frantic with worry.

# ★ Thirty-two ★

Jared had had a stressful, busy day—it was the height of harvest season, and every river packet he owned was in constant use. The day's business had been complicated by the fact that one of Jared's customers, a local planter, had shown up with more than twice the number of cotton bails he had originally contracted with Jared to ship to New Orleans. Although the man had informed his factor down in the Louisiana port city to expect the huge shipment, he'd neglected to mention to Jared that he anticipated an unusually large harvest. Jared had appeased his customer as best he could, by shipping half the cotton and arranging for the remainder to be warehoused nearby until he could arrange for transport. Now he faced the frustrating task of trying to contract the additional shipment out to another packet line, since he was fully booked for the remainder of the season.

Jared started up the rutted incline of Silver Street toward Natchez proper, passing a dray loaded with vegetables. He nodded to the passing man and held his roan stallion in tight rein as the dust flew. Continuing upward, he turned his thoughts to Jasmine. Lord, he could not wait until the two of them were wed! More and more, he feared his marriage to Jasmine might never take place. During the past weeks, their relationship had taken one disastrous turn after another. First, Claude Boudreau had reappeared in their lives, and Jasmine had interfered in the duel. Then, Jasmine had learned about Florence, and now she thought that he was going after Boudreau simply because of what the scoundrel had done to his cousin. Of course he wanted to avenge Florence's

death—and rightly so! Yet his desire to vindicate Jasmine
following Boudreau's perfidy had always remained foremost
in his mind.

Damn the man! Boudreau—or Hank Rawlins, as Marshal
Murchison thought him to be—seemed to be at the root of
most of their difficulties. Yet now Jared suspected that his
problems with Jasmine went even deeper than that—that in
some ways, Boudreau had only served as a catalyst to bring
their differences into focus.

What troubled Jared most of all was that Jasmine couldn't
believe in his love or trust him. Time after time, she had let
other events and people come between them. It was almost
as if she were forever searching for a reason to doubt him.
Somehow, she had to becoming willing to make that leap of
faith—to believe in him and in what they had. Without a
total commitment on both their parts, their future together
could be doomed.

Jared could understand Jasmine's initial doubts about their
relationship, after all she had suffered, but when would she
put her past behind her?

He sighed. He knew he would love Jasmine until the day
he died. But he also recognized that he was selfish enough
to want it all—that something within him would not be at
peace until she returned his love and trust fully and uncon-
ditionally.

Jared crested the bluff into a still, frigid darkness, which
was relieved only by the distant hooting of an owl and the
sporadic splotches of fading light that sifted through the dense
trees on either side of the road. He was squinting at the
obscure path ahead and clucking to his horse when all at
once, two dark figures jumped out at him from the trees, each
grabbing one of his bridle leads. Jared reached for his pistol,
but one of the masked bandits shoved a revolver up into his
face and said, "Don't try it, mister."

Jared froze. The menacing barrel of the pistol was so close
to his nose that he could smell the metal and oil. Slowly he
raised his hands, staring past the barrel at the two nasty-
looking characters who had waylaid him. Though his assail-
ants were shadowy figures in the dusky light, he could tell

that they both had bluntly featured, bearded faces, and wore the clothing of roustabouts—jersey shirts, dungarees, and small caps. In the close quarters, they both reeked of dirt, human excrement, soured liquor, and stale tobacco.

The two looked like they meant business, Jared thought grimly. He knew that robberies were all too common in this region, and he also recognized that he must keep his wits about him if he were to stay alive. "Look, if it's money you want, my wallet is in—"

"Shut up!" the first man hissed. Nodding to the other, he added, "Get his pistol!"

Rough hands reached inside Jared's frock coat, removing the pistol at his waist. "Now, git down!" the first man ordered Jared. "Slowly."

Jared cautiously dismounted his roan stallion. The horse whinnied nervously as one of the men grabbed Jared, turned him, and roughly shoved him against the animal's flank. Jared's hands were tied tightly behind him with a sharp piece of rope. Then he was again turned, a dirty tasting bandanna shoved into his mouth, and another tied about his head to secure the gag.

Prodding Jared toward the woods with his pistol, the first man called back to the other, "Bring his horse. We don't want it going home on its own and settin' folks to frettin'."

The small group started off into the shadowy trees—first Jared, then the bandit with the gun at his back, then the man leading the horse. Once they had trooped to the north about a hundred yards, Jared spotted a wagon ahead of them in a clearing, with a large work horse harnessed to it. As the three entered the small open area, Jared recognized Claude Boudreau hopping down from the wagon seat. Even in the near-darkness, Boudreau's black eyes and evil countenance were readily discernible.

Boudreau approached Jared, a sadistic grin splitting his face, revealing sharp white teeth. "Why, good evening, Hampton," he said.

With that, Boudreau doubled his fists together and viciously slammed Jared in the midsection. The force of the blow knocked the hat from Jared's head and the breath from his body. He doubled over in excruciating pain. Then a new agony assaulted him as Boudreau's hard fists descended brutally on his shoulder blades. Jared tumbled to the ground, paralyzed, still unable to breathe. He feared that at any moment, he might choke on the noxious cloth jammed in his throat, and his entire body felt battered. At last he was able to catch a ragged breath through his nose, a mere split second before Boudreau's boot brutally kicked his already agonized gut.

Above him, he could hear Boudreau chuckling. "Throw him in the wagon, boys."

Jared groaned as he landed on the unyielding surface of the wagon bed. He heard his horse whinny again, as one of the bandits tethered the animal to the wagon gate. Seconds later, he heard the draft horse snorting, then the conveyance lurched forward. Every bone in his body was jolted as they plowed through the uneven terrain at a reckless pace.

Claude Boudreau's cruel voice drifted back to Jared. "If you're afraid to die, Hampton, please don't concern yourself. By the time we get finished with you, you'll be praying for death."

Jared's mind spun as the bandits took him deeper into the woods. He'd realized moments earlier that his hands were tied not with rope but with bailing twine. He knew that the twine used on cotton bails wasn't nearly as strong as most people assumed. A good jerk might snap it—and might also slash his wrists to the bone.

It was a chance he would have to take. His only hope was to get free of his bonds and somehow surprise his captors when they stopped to complete their dirty work. He gritted his teeth, twisted his wrists together, then jerked with all his might. He silently thanked God as he heard a splitting sound. Tears came to his eyes, not just from the pain but from gratitude. Now he had a chance. He couldn't simply die and risk letting these miscreants harm Jasmine!

He twisted his wrists out of their bonds and waited, keeping his hands tightly coiled behind him so as not to alert his captors. By the time Boudreau stopped the wagon under some trees deep in the woods, every muscle in Jared's body was taut and ready. The pain seemed to add to his alertness.

"Get him out, boys," came Boudreau's lazy voice. "And take off his gag. I want to hear that sanctimonious bastard scream for his life."

The wagon creaked and shifted as the two heavy men alighted. Jared watched them stroll around toward the back of the wagon. In the meantime, Boudreau, at the front of the conveyance, was climbing down. Jared waited until the bandits had lowered the gate and were reaching for him, then sat up, slamming the closer of the two in the face with his doubled fists. Blood spurted from the man's nose and he screamed as he fell to the ground. For a split second afterward, the second man appeared too stunned to react, and Jared pressed his advantage. With a quick movement, he slid forward, kicking him brutally in the groin before he landed on his feet. The second bandit doubled over in gurgling agony as Jared yanked the gag from his own mouth.

Suddenly, a bullet whizzed by Jared's head, and he hunkered down, peering around the corner of the wagon. He spotted Boudreau coming toward him, pistol in hand. At the opposite corner of the wagon, Jared could hear his horse screaming in terrible fright and he ached to comfort the animal. But he knew he had to deal with Boudreau first.

As Boudreau cornered the wagon, Jared sprang to his feet, lunging at his adversary in the darkness. He grabbed Boudreau's wrist, tearing the gun out of his hand savagely. Even as Boudreau yelped in pain, Jared knocked him unconscious with a stunning blow to the jaw. He leaned over, picked up Boudreau's pistol, and was preparing to use it on him when the sound of another gunshot split the night air.

The next thing Jared knew, he was on the ground, his vision blurred and blood trickling into his eyes. He knew he'd been hit, and while he felt dizzy and nauseated, he knew it couldn't be too serious, or he'd be dead by now. He gingerly touched his scalp and felt the bloody ridge across the crown of his head. Thank God, he'd only been creased.

Who had fired it? Probably the first bandit, he decided, since he could still hear the one he had hit in the groin groaning and retching off to one side.

Boudreau's pistol was no longer in Jared's hand, nor was it next to him on the ground. He assumed it must have flown out of his hand when the bullet hit him. Rotten luck! He had no time to search for it. Hearing boots plod through the brush toward him, he quickly rolled under the wagon and crawled on his belly toward the other side. He emerged and maneuvered himself in a crouch toward the wagon gate, where he reached up and untied his horse. Then, without mounting the animal, he fled blindly into the woods, leading the horse along by its reins.

In a bordering thicket of trees, Jared paused to mount the roan, feeling weaker and dizzier every second. He squeezed his thighs against the animal's flanks, thanking God that it knew the way home. As the horse galloped wildly through the trees, heading back toward town, Jared hung limply over the saddle, swaying to and fro, drifting in and out of consciousness and clutching the reins in his clenched fists.

He passed out right after he viewed the blurred gaslights lining the town square. His last thought was of Jasmine.

By nine o'clock that evening, Jasmine was frantic with worry. Marie came into the parlor with fresh coffee.

"Jasmine, please sit down," she urged. "You're working yourself into a state. Don't worry—Mr. Jared knows how to take care of himself."

"But this is so unlike him!" Jasmine cried, flinging a hand outward as she paced. "He always comes directly home in the evenings, then joins us for supper at Magnolia Bend. Oh, God—I know something has happened to him!"

Marie poured Jasmine a cup of coffee. Placing the china cup and saucer in Jasmine's hand, she said calmly, "Jasmine, it's harvest time, and it's not unusual for Mr. Hampton to work late. If you like, we can send one of the stable lads down to his office to check on—"

"Yes! Yes, let's do that!" Jasmine said.

Marie was starting to rise when both women heard a knock at the front door. "Oh, God!" Jasmine cried. "I know it's bad news!"

Jasmine and Marie put down their coffee and rushed out

of the parlor to the front door. Both women gasped as they stared at the two men standing on the gallery. "Oh, Jared!" Jasmine exclaimed.

Jared looked pale and half-conscious as he stared back at her blankly. He was weaving slightly, a bandage splotched with blood wrapped about his head. Next to him stood a tall, spare, middle-aged gentleman, who was bracing Jared with his arm as best he could. Jasmine at once recognized James Hawkins, a local doctor to whom she'd been introduced at Charity's party.

"Oh, God, Jared, you're hurt!" Jasmine continued wildly. Turning to the physician, she demanded, "Dr. Hawkins, what happened?"

Hawkins grunted, half-pulling, half-dragging Jared into the house. "Ladies, I need your help. We must get Mr. Hampton upstairs and into bed at once."

Both women instantly sprang into action. Marie grabbed a lantern to lead the way, while Jasmine helped the doctor assist Jared up the stairs. "What happened to him?" Jasmine asked again as they climbed upward.

"The sheriff found Hampton in the middle of a downtown street, with his horse standing nearby," Hawkins replied. "Looks like someone waylaid Mr. Hampton while he was riding home from work, and creased his head with a bullet. Obviously Hampton made good his escape, but then he fell from his horse after he reached the town square."

"Oh, God!" Jasmine cried, at once realizing that Claude Boudreau must have been responsible. "Will he be all right?"

The doctor nodded as they stepped into the upper hallway, half-dragging Jared along with them. "It's only a surface wound, Miss Dubroc. I had to put a half-dozen stitches on the crown of his head, but fortunately, his hairline will cover the scar. Other than that, he seems to have sustained a beating on his back and belly, but nothing too serious, as far as I can determine."

Jasmine was biting her lip and fighting tears as the four-some turned into Jared's dark, chilly bedroom. While Marie lit additional lanterns, Jasmine and the doctor removed Jared's coat, then gently maneuvered him onto the bed. Hawkins pulled off Jared's boots, then threw a heavy quilt across him. By this time, Jared was sound asleep. "I gave him a heavy dose of laudanum at my office—that's why he seems so weak right now," the doctor explained. "He should feel all right in the morning."

Jasmine thanked the doctor and Marie saw him out. As soon as the two were out of the room, Jasmine collapsed in the wing chair next to Jared's bed. She'd left her shawl downstairs, but she didn't even notice the chill seeping through her woolen dress. She shook silently, tears spilling down her face as overwhelming emotions surged through her.

There was no doubt in Jasmine's mind that Claude Boudreau had been responsible. Damn that blackguard to hell! she thought. She regretted that she had been unable to do more to bring Claude to justice.

Jasmine was so grateful that at least Jared was alive. To think that she could have lost him, before she'd really let him know how much he meant to her!

"Jasmine, are you all right?"

Jasmine turned her anguished face toward Marie, who stood at the portal in a pool of light cast by the lantern she held. At the moment, speech was impossible for her, but she managed to nod weakly to her friend.

Marie stepped forward, her classic face lined with compassion. She handed Jasmine her handkerchief. "Oh, Jasmine! Don't cry. You heard the doctor—Mr. Jared will be fine."

"But he could have been killed—and it's all my fault!" Jasmine burst out, dabbing at tears.

"How is that, Jasmine?"

"Claude!" Jasmine exclaimed, her green eyes filled with guilt and anger. "I'm certain he did this to Jared."

"Well, if he did, that hardly makes it your fault," Marie pointed out firmly. "Look, Jasmine, why don't you go on home now and get some rest? I'll keep an eye on Mr. Jared."

Jasmine shook her head vehemently. "No. I'm staying here until he awakens."

"But the doctor said he should sleep through the night."

"Then, I'll stay here all night."

"Jasmine!" Marie gasped, her luminous brown eyes widening. "You mustn't! What will Mr. Jared's aunt think when you don't come home? I'm sure Miss Charity is worried about you, even now."

Jasmine bit her lip. After a moment, she said evenly, "Marie, please send a servant down to Miss Charity's with a note. Tell her that he had to work late and that the two of us are now sharing supper. Tell her he'll be escorting me home later, and not to wait up for me."

Marie was frowning. "If you say so, Jasmine. I'll write the note at once and dispatch it to Magnolia Bend. But—do you think Jared's aunt will believe this?"

"Well, at least she won't know someone tried to kill her nephew tonight."

"That's true," Marie conceded, her countenance lightening a bit. Placing a hand on Jasmine's shoulder, she added, "All right, Jasmine, I'll take care of it. But you must try to get some rest." She walked across the room and fetched an afghan from the foot of the silk brocade daybed. Returning to Jasmine's side, she placed the wrap about the other woman's shoulders. "You're shivering. I'll send a servant up to build a fire."

"Thanks, Marie."

Marie left Jasmine alone with Jared. He looked more peaceful now. Color was slowly returning to his face, and he was breathing more deeply and evenly. Her eyes lovingly roved over his chiseled face, the thick, curly hair radiating outward from the bandage on his head. Thank God he was alive.

The manservant came up and started a crackling fire, and soon the bedroom was filled with cozy warmth and the soothing golden glow of both the fire and the lanterns. One hour passed, then two, then three. Jasmine was nodding off to sleep when she at last heard Jared's voice. "Good evening, love."

"Jared!" Instantly wakening, she stood and looked down into his smiling face. He looked quite alert, almost normal. "You're awake."

"So it appears," he said, shaking his head slightly and

grimacing. "Although for a moment, I thought I had died and gone to heaven. You're some angel, love. Come give me a kiss."

"Oh, Jared!" Jasmine leaned over to kiss him tenderly, loving the warm feel of his lips on hers. Pulling back, she sniffed and asked anxiously, "How do you feel?"

"Don't ask," he replied ruefully.

"That bad, huh?" She clenched her jaw. "Claude did this to you, didn't he?"

"Yes. Although I'm proud to say that he and his two hired thugs doubtless look even worse for wear at the moment."

"Oh, Jared!" She took his hand, and held it tightly in hers. "Tell me what happened, darling."

He explained how he had been ambushed. When he finished, he smiled at her reassuringly. "Don't worry. I'll get him next time."

Jasmine was horror-stricken. "You can't mean you're still determined to pursue Claude."

"More determined than ever, actually," he interrupted, a grim determination glinting in his blue eyes. "I'm afraid he and his boys really got my dander up this time."

"Oh, Jared! You don't know what kind of man you're dealing with."

"You're speaking of Hank Rawlins, alias Claude Boudreau?"

"You knew!"

Jared nodded. "Murchison paid me a visit on his way out of town."

"Then you know all about Claude's criminal background, how dangerous he is! And you're still determined to go after him?"

"To kill him, actually."

"Jared, that's crazy! You were almost killed yourself tonight, and if something happened to you, I would just die!"

Surprisingly, Jared grinned at Jasmine's hysterics. "Why, Jasmine, I'm beginning to believe you love me after all."

"Of course I love you! And if you didn't already have a hole in your head, I'd put one there."

Then Jasmine paused as a shadow crossed Jared's eyes.

"Would you fetch me a stiff brandy?" he asked. "Whatever that doctor gave me has worn off."

"Oh, heavens! I'm so sorry. Of course."

Jasmine took one of the two lit lanterns from the dresser and dashed downstairs. Moments later, she returned to Jared's bedroom with a tray containing a decanter of brandy and two snifters. "You're joining me?" he asked, lifting an eyebrow.

"I could use a drink," she admitted, and he smiled.

After she had handed him a snifter half-filled with the amber liquid, he patted the empty space on the bed next to him and said, "Come join me, love."

"Oh, I couldn't! I might hurt you!"

"Jasmine, after what I've been through tonight, you'd need a sledgehammer to inflict further injury upon me."

"Oh, my poor love!" Jasmine took her own drink and sat down gingerly next to Jared on the bed. She held his hand and glanced at the bandage on his head, biting her lip as she again studied the small, bright stains where blood had seeped through. "Does your head hurt horribly?"

He took a long draw of the brandy. "My head has known better days, my love."

"Jared . . ." She stared down at her drink, and all at once she was blinded by tears.

"What is it, love?"

"It's just that—I could have lost you!" she sobbed.

He wrapped his free arm about her, scowling as fresh razors of pain lanced through him. "Love, you haven't lost me. You're not about to."

"But you must promise me that you won't ever a-gain—"

"No promises, Jasmine, except for one." Kissing her mouth, he whispered soulfully, "I'm going to marry you and love you senseless for the rest of my life."

"Are you?" she asked in wonder.

"Indeed I am." He stared down into her tear-filled eyes. "And what of you, my love?"

"I'll going to marry you and love you senseless for the rest of your life—if you'll have me, Jared."

"And why wouldn't I have you?" he asked in an outraged tone.

She lowered her eyes. "I wouldn't blame you if you gave up on me. I've doubted you so many times. That is, until—"

"Until?"

"Until today," she said breathlessly. She looked at him with her heart in her eyes. "Oh, Jared, everything has at last become so clear for me. Today I talked with your aunt, and she told me of her visits with my father, of how he really cared about me, after all. And it made me realize that I've held myself back from you in some ways because I always thought my father hated me. I thought all men hated me. But your aunt made me understand that that wasn't true. My father loved me—"

"Who wouldn't love you?" Jared asked tenderly. He leaned over to kiss her again, and this time he nudged her lips apart with his tongue. She responded by opening to him and kissing him back, loving the brandied taste of him, the velvet stroking of his tongue deep in her mouth.

"Oh, Jared," she breathed after a moment. "When I think that you could have been killed, without my ever getting to tell you these things—how very much you mean to me, how sorry I am that I ever—"

He laid a finger across her mouth. The corners of his eyes crinkled with gentle amusement. "Does that mean you're at last through fighting me?"

"Oh, yes, my love!"

He winked at her. "Then, let's make the surrender complete."

Jared took her brandy snifter and set it, with his, on the bedside table. Turning back to her with a sensual smile lighting his face, he removed the pins from her chignon, releasing her heavy locks. He combed a hand through her lush golden curls and drew an unsteady breath. "You've told me you're through fighting me, love. Now show me."

Realizing what he meant, she protested, "Oh, no, Jared, I'll hurt you!"

"You'll love me," he whispered soulfully, stroking her wet cheek with his fingertips. "You could never hurt me."

Watching him lean toward her, she asked, "Jared? You mean here? Now?"

"Don't worry," he told her smoothly. "Who would guess that a savage beating always puts me in the mood for romance?"

"Jared!"

"Why don't you go latch the door, just to be on the safe side." His eyes were bright with need as he added, "You see, I did have quite a scare tonight, and I find I can't wait to make love to you."

Jasmine stood, trembling, as she stared down into his beautiful, ardent blue eyes. "Are you sure, darling?"

His slowly spreading grin took her breath away. "Think of it this way, love. When again will I have you this eager to please me?"

"I'll always be eager to please you, Jared."

Jasmine went to the door and threw the bolt, then walked over to the dresser. Her eyes met Jared's in the mirror, and the intensity of the look they shared again had her feeling weak-kneed.

Across from her, he smiled and said, "I'd tell you to leave the lights on, but then you'd see my bruises."

She whirled to face him with tears in her eyes. "Jared, we can't do this. You're too hurt."

"Oh, yes we can. Now, turn down the lamps." Ruefully, he added, "Actually, love, I'm not sure I can abide seeing my bruises, either."

Jasmine extinguished the lamps and approached the bed in the semidarkness. She heard Jared's chuckle again. "You get to do all the work," he said.

"It will be my pleasure," she replied.

"Indeed," he said.

Jasmine stripped off her clothing in the flickering light of the fire, as Jared feasted his eyes on her glorious curves, her beautiful long hair. She joined him on the bed and helped him remove his shirt. She heard him wince as her hand touched his bruised midsection. "Jared," she pleaded, "this is madness—"

"Indeed, the finest madness of all. Now, hush," he

growled, his voice thick with both pain and yearning. He removed her hand from his middle, pulled it lower, and added wickedly, "You're aiming too high, my love."

Jared undid his trousers and guided her hand to its proper place, and she moaned as she leaned over to kiss him. "I love you so much," she whispered achingly.

"I love you, too."

Breathing became difficult for Jasmine as she felt Jared's manhood growing hard and distended in her hand. "God, it's been so long since we've—"

"I know, my darling. And soon, we'll be together like this, every night—always," he vowed, his voice filled with an emotion to match hers.

They kissed deeply as Jared caressed Jasmine's breasts, and she boldly continued to stroke his manhood. Both were wildly aroused, yet frustrated that they had to keep distance between their bodies to keep from hurting Jared's bruised middle.

Jasmine had to be closer. Looking straight into his eyes, she smiled, then leaned over and latched her lips onto his manhood. He responded in an agony of need. She heard the primal cry rip from his throat and it stirred her to the core. Moments later, she heard him say hoarsely, "Now."

"Now," she breathed back with a smile.

Afraid to touch everywhere, they expressed their love with an ultimate embrace. Jasmine straddled him and he thrust himself into her, hard and deep. She cried out in wild abandon as he thrust higher and higher, then she froze as she glimpsed the expression of stark pain on his beautiful face. "No, Jared, this is hurting you."

"Let me be the judge of what is pain and what is pleasure," he told her fiercely. "After what happened earlier, nothing can ever touch us again, my love. And tonight—by God, I'm going to be close to you!"

Jared withdrew, then rolled Jasmine beneath him, pulling her tightly to him. She instinctively arched upward, wrapping her legs about his waist as he pressed deeply. He felt wonderful inside her, so hugely swollen that she feared she couldn't take him all, but she did. She could hear his mingled moans of pain and pleasure, and knew the position he had assumed must be torture to him. Yet she was beyond fighting him, lost in the wild and wonderful friction of his possession, of possessing *him* in return.

And knowing that he was enduring this agony just to be close to her moved Jasmine as nothing ever had before. After almost losing him tonight, she needed to be close to him, too. He was claiming her totally and fiercely, and it was so sweet. She was obsessed by the thought of merging with him—one mind, one body—and she could only moan, toss her head from side to side, and plead, "Please, please."

"Yes," he whispered back. Quickly he withdrew and pulled her to her knees beside him on the mattress. "Wrap yourself around me."

Realizing what he intended, she protested, "No—"

"Do it," he demanded hoarsely. "Now. Please."

With a low sob of pleasure, she wrapped her arms about his neck, and when he lifted her hips and rammed himself inside her, she moaned and curled her legs around his waist, clinging to him. "Now we're touching," he said in a raw, unsteady voice, "everywhere."

He crushed her breasts against his chest and she pressed her aching mouth into his. The pressure of their joining built. Her flesh throbbed and tightened about him until she was sure she could not endure it. Then the whole world tore apart and there was nothing left but the two of them, consumed in a white-hot flame of purest pleasure.

She was totally limp, completely at peace, as he lowered her to the mattress and collapsed upon her. "I think you must be in agony," she whispered.

"My agony has been assuaged, dear heart," he whispered back, the pain in his voice lightened by never-failing humor.

The pink glow of dawn was spreading across the bedroom when Jasmine awakened to see Jared standing over her, fully clothed. He smiled and said gently, "Jasmine, we must get you home. We've doubtless caused a scandal already, but at least we'll be wed in a couple more weeks."

She stood and donned her clothes, glancing worriedly at his bandaged head. "How are you feeling?"

"Oh, like about ten cannons are going off in my head—simultaneously," he said with a wry smile. Watching her tie her chemise over her firm breasts, he cleared his throat and added unsteadily, "Hurry, love, or I'm afraid I won't get you home till noon."

"Why are you in such a rush, Jared?"

"I told you, love, we must get you home before there's a scandal and—"

"And you can't wait to go after Claude, can you?"

He scowled at her, but said nothing.

"Damn it, Jared, tell me the truth!"

He sighed, brushing a strand of hair from his brow. "All right. As soon as I see you safely home—where you're staying, by the way—I'm heading over to Vidalia to get Jack. He's been acting as overseer on my plantation ever since Mertson went back east. Anyway, once I've gotten Jack, the two of us will hunt Boudreau and his thugs."

"No!" Forcing her arms through the sleeves of her dress, she stepped forward, her eyes beseeching him. "Oh, Jared, please don't!"

"I thought you were through fighting me, Jasmine," he reminded, giving her a reproachful look.

"Not where your life is concerned!" Glancing again at the bandage on his head, she gestured plaintively and said, "Jared, for God's sake, give it up."

He shook his head. His voice was thick with emotion as he replied, "I can't, love. Not after what he did to you."

"Think of what he did to *you*! Of what he might do next! Jared, our whole future is at stake here! Leave Claude to be apprehended by those trained to deal with his type—like Marshal Murchison. He should be coming back to Natchez soon, and—"

"I'm afraid I can't afford to wait, Jasmine. What if Boudreau should come after you next time?"

"He won't—I'll be careful."

Jared shook his head. "Not good enough, Jasmine."

"If you loved me enough you'd give it up!" she cried.

"Jasmine, I'm doing it for you!"

"Are you? Or are you doing it because you value your code of honor above all else?"

He flung a hand outward in exasperation. "Are we back to that again? Are you going to start in about Florence again, as well?"

She shook her head slowly. "No. I can't blame you where Florence is concerned. I understand your feelings about her, and I've come to respect them. It's just that—"

He stepped forward and gripped her by the arms. "Jasmine, when will you believe that I love you above all else, including my honor?"

A tense silence fell between them. Jasmine ached to tell Jared that she believed him already, yet a confusing, persistent inner voice forbade her to say the words. "I love you above all else, Jared," she told him at last. "And I'll die if I lose you."

He pulled her close and pressed his mouth against her hair. "For the dozenth time, Jasmine, you're not going to lose me." Drawing back, he forced himself to smile as he began to button her dress. "Come, love, let's get you home."

# ★ Thirty-three ★

Back at Magnolia Bend, Jasmine received a letter from Marshal Murchison in the morning's post. She ripped it open and read it quickly as she sipped her coffee:

Dear Miss Dubroc,

I've now found the evidence I need in order to convict Hank Rawlins. Two witnesses here in St. Louis—the lady of the evening I told you about, and a former Rawlins gang member—are willing to identify our man and to testify against him once he is apprehended.

I'm convinced now that I have a watertight case established against this scoundrel. I am making arrangements to travel at once back to Natchez to arrest my quarry. I sincerely hope that the man you know as Claude Boudreau is still in the region.

If you should need to communicate with me in the interim, kindly leave a message for me at the City Hotel in Natchez, to which I'll dispatch for lodging immediately upon my arrival in your city.

Until we meet again, let me implore you once more to exercise all caution in dealing with Claude Boudreau.

Your obedient servant,

Doyle Murchison, United States Marshal

Rereading the marshal's letter, Jasmine had to shake her head ruefully. If only Murchison knew that just a few hours before, Claude had almost killed Jared!

Jasmine remained terrified for her fiancé's welfare, especially since she knew that Jared was at this moment again trying to locate Claude. If only Murchison would hurry and get back here! When could she expect him to return? she wondered. Jasmine studied the date on the marshal's correspondence. It had been posted several days past, yet Jasmine also knew that it was a long trip by steamboat from St. Louis to Natchez. She mentally calculated the time the trip would take, and figured Murchison might well be back in town by the coming weekend. She could always check with the City Hotel to see if they'd heard from him regarding his planned arrival date, and she could also consult with one of the general agents in town, to find out when the next packets were expected from St. Louis.

Jasmine figured she would have at least three days in which to keep Claude Boudreau from killing Jared! If she could just keep the two of them apart for that long, then Murchison would do the rest, she was sure.

Should she go to Jared and tell him that Murchison was on his way back to Natchez and planning to arrest Boudreau/Rawlins? Recalling her predawn conversation with Jared, she shook her head grimly. Jared wouldn't give it up. She knew him all too well. He didn't want any help from her or from Murchison. Hadn't he been furious with them both before, when Murchison had interfered with the duel?

No, Jasmine decided. If she informed Jared of the marshal's plans, her action would more than likely backfire in her face. Jared, realizing that Murchison would soon hone in on his prey, would surely be more determined than ever to locate and kill Claude before the marshal could once again intervene.

Thus, Jasmine knew she'd best keep her peace regarding the marshal's planned return. Yet the problem remained—how could she get Jared to back off from hunting Claude until Murchison arrived back in Natchez? She mulled over every word of her argument with Jared earlier that morning, hunting for a strategy.

Suddenly, an idea struck her. Maybe Jared *would* back off, if the notion were put to him in just the right way.

But would that be fair? It didn't matter, she decided vehemently. What would be hideously wrong and unfair would be to allow Claude Boudreau to murder the man she loved! Keeping Jared alive was all that mattered! And by God, she would do whatever was necessary! Jared was the best thing that had ever happened to her, and she'd be damned if she was going to lose him to that villain Claude!

Filled with a new resolve, Jasmine paced the parlor, plotting and scheming. She knew she'd have to get Maggie situated with Charity for the morning. Then she'd be ready when Ephraim came by, as he did most mornings, to inquire of her plans for the day.

Thirty minutes later, Jasmine had donned her cape and bonnet and was standing on the front gallery waiting for Ephraim. She figured her plan had an even chance of success. She'd have to find Claude, of course. That would likely be the easiest part.

The hard part would be deceiving Jared.

* * *

Jasmine convinced Ephraim to drive her to Jared's office Under-the-Hill. The waterfront community was bustling with activity as they rattled past the storefronts lining Silver Street.

Jasmine's purpose in descending Under-the-Hill this morning was twofold. First, she would go see Jared, and try to convince him to stop hunting Claude. Then, she would go see Savannah Sue. Jasmine had a gut feeling that Claude might be hiding out somewhere in the waterfront community. After all, Jared had told her he'd been accosted by Claude at the top of Silver Street last night. And he'd also mentioned that Claude had been in the company of two river rats—which meant that the men Claude had hired must have resembled the unsavory types who often hung out near the landing.

As Ephraim turned the buggy down Middle Street and proceeded briskly toward Jared's office, Jasmine prayed that he would be there. She reasoned that if she had an effective plan for finding Claude, Jared and Jack might well have a better one between them.

In his office, Jared was shuffling through papers as he spoke with Jack. Moments earlier he had come to the same conclusion regarding Claude Boudreau that Jasmine had reached. "If I can just get things set here for the day," he told the other man as he checked over a freight damage claim, "then you and I can hit the streets and hunt down Boudreau."

"We'll nab him, boss," Jack said smoothly from his chair across from Jared.

That's when Jasmine burst into the room. "Jared! Thank God you're here! I must talk with you!"

Both men stood. Jared had paled at the sight of his fiancée; then color again flooded his face. With jaw clenched, he stared at Jasmine furiously. "Jasmine! What are you doing here?" Then, less caustically, he added, "Has Boudreau tried to contact you again?"

"Mercy, no!" she said, stepping forward. "I simply must speak with you, Jared—"

"If Boudreau hasn't been bothering you," Jared cut in as

he strode forward angrily, "then what on earth are you doing out on the streets, woman? Was I simply talking to myself when I told you to stay at Magnolia Bend?"

Jasmine swallowed hard, feeling a flush heat her face as her fingers nervously twisted the tie on her reticule. Jared was slow to anger where she was concerned, but she had really provoked him this time, it was clear. Every muscle in his body appeared tensed as he glared at her. His eyes cut into her like icy blue diamonds.

"Jared, please. I didn't come down here alone—Ephraim's waiting for me outside in the buggy. Can we please talk for a moment?" She glanced awkwardly at Jack, then added, "Alone?"

Jared inclined his head toward Jack. "Jack, if you'll excuse us, the lady is about to explain to me why I shouldn't tan her backside."

Jack grinned. "Sure, boss. I'll wait in the outer office." He nodded to Jasmine and left the room.

Jasmine anxiously studied Jared's coloring and his bandaged head. "You shouldn't be working this morning. How are you feeling?"

"Much better than you'll be feeling shortly if you don't give me a satisfactory explanation for flagrantly defying my wishes," he ground out.

She sighed. "I supposed I'd best get straight to the point, then." She squared her shoulders and plunged in. "Jared, this morning, you asked me when I would believe that you love me more than your honor. Well, there is a way you could convince me of that."

He raised an eyebrow. "Oh?"

"Call off your search for Claude Boudreau for five days."

He laughed incredulously. "Jasmine, you've clearly lost your mind."

"No, I haven't," she said steadily. "If you really want to prove you love me, you'll do it."

For a moment, he merely stared at her. Then he snapped his fingers and exclaimed, "By God! You're planning to go after Boudreau yourself, aren't you? Can you deny it?"

"No."

Jared was shaking his head, his blue eyes incredulous. "I can't believe I'm hearing this! Haven't you any idea how dangerous the man is? Why, you're a mere woman—"

"What makes you think that only men are capable of resolving things?" she cut in angrily. Opening her reticule, Jasmine took out her father's small pistol and held it up by the handle for Jared's perusal. Noting with satisfaction his flabbergasted expression, she continued crisply, "I may be a woman, Jared, but I can use a gun and defend myself. My father taught me to use this pistol when I was younger, and I'm not afraid of Claude."

In a deadly serious voice, Jared ordered, "Jasmine, give me that gun before you do harm to yourself."

She backed off, shaking her head. "No." As he pursued her aggressively, she held up a hand and said, "If I do run into Claude, would you really not want me to have this gun?"

That stopped him in his tracks. He stared at her, totally at a loss.

Seizing her advantage, Jasmine carefully replaced the gun in her reticule. Staring Jared straight in the eye, she repeated, "I'm not afraid of him, Jared."

At last he found his voice. "I believe you're not! But I'll not let you do this crazy thing." Stepping forward and gripping her by the shoulders, he said fiercely, "Mother of God, Jasmine! Would you place your revenge above our love?"

"Would you?" she countered. "Jared, I can't let him kill you! Promise me you'll back off for five days."

His hands fell to his sides and he shook his head vehemently. "Forget it, Jasmine. I won't make bargains with your life."

"Wrong!" she cried passionately. "If you loved me enough, you'd do anything for me! You'd even forsake your code of honor for just a few days. But you won't, because it means more to you than I do!"

He looked stunned. "You're really serious about this!"

"I'm dead serious."

Jared was silent for a long, long moment, scowling at her fiercely. Finally, he asked, "This is the only way I can prove that I love you?"

She nodded.

She heard a frustrated growl rising in his throat. Then, after a moment, he stalked off to stare out the window, his broad back rigid. She heard him sigh. "Very well. You have my word as a gentleman. But beware, Jasmine. You may find the price you are asking is far too dear."

"I know," she whispered as she left him.

After Jasmine departed, Jack came back into the room. "Well, boss?"

Jared turned from the window with a brooding frown still gripping his face. He related to his friend all that had happened between him and Jasmine. "Would you believe that little spitfire intends to go after Boudreau herself?" he finished indignantly.

Jack chuckled. "Well, I can see why Miss Jasmine is riled, boss. After all, she *is* the one that snake threw in the river in the first place. And females tend to get feisty when their menfolk are threatened—like you were last night."

"Still, we can't let her do this."

"No, I reckon we can't."

Jared scratched his jaw thoughtfully. "Let's stop searching for Boudreau—for now," he instructed his friend. "Instead, I want you to watch Jasmine—every minute of every day."

"You got it, boss." With a crooked grin, Jack added, "And don't worry too much about your Miss Jasmine. I figure Boudreau ambushed you last night to give you and her a good scare. Now that he's done his dirty work, he'll hone in and try to collect the money from Miss Jasmine."

"That's precisely what I'm afraid of!"

"What I'm saying is, that lowlife ain't likely to harm Miss Jasmine till he collects. It's afterward that you and me have got to worry about."

"Quite possibly," Jared concurred grimly.

"In the meantime, I'll watch Miss Jasmine like a hawk, but I'm betting she'll be careful, too." Jack's grin broadened. "You know, boss, I've spied her practicing with her pistol behind Hampton Hall a couple times when she didn't think no one was around. If I do say so myself, that little lady of yours is a crack shot.''

"You're joking!" Jared exclaimed.

"Nope. And in a way, she has an edge over us.''

Jared's scowl became murderous. "What do you mean?''

Jack rocked on his heels. "Well, boss, Boudreau won't be expecting no pistol packin' mama.''

Jared's frown was now so deep his eyes were narrow slits. "Would you kindly get out of here and go watch the girl before she gets herself killed?'' he snapped to Jack.

"Sure, boss.'' Undaunted, Jack clapped on his broad-brimmed hat and turned for the door.

As Jasmine climbed back into the buggy beside Ephraim, she had the disquieting feeling that Jared had acquiesced to her demand far too easily. Yet she couldn't afford to fret about that now; her purpose at the moment was too critical.

Jasmine asked Ephraim to drive her to the back entrance of the Scarlet Slipper, hushing the old man's automatic protests. Once they were parked in the filthy alleyway behind the brothel, Jasmine climbed down from the buggy, hurried through the back door, and went upstairs.

Savannah Sue was just stirring when Jasmine knocked on her door. Inside the prostitute's room, Jasmine quickly explained her predicament—how it was imperative that she at once locate the Frenchman who used to visit Florence here. "Have you seen the man around here recently?'' she asked Sue.

"Well, ma'am, I ain't,'' Sue replied, raking a hand through her disheveled hair. "But one of the other girls here had a run-in with a mean character the other day—she got beat up real bad. The poor soul wouldn't tell me who done it to her, but later, Stan the barkeep told me he conjured it might have been that there French feller that used to come around to see Flossie.''

"Which girl did this man beat up?''

"Rosie, the Spanish one. But I don't think she'll tell you nothin' about the lowlife that slapped her around.''

"She'll tell me,'' Jasmine said grimly, "when I tell her

that Jared's life is at stake here. You see, last night, the Frenchman—Claude Boudreau—tried to kill Mr. Jared.''

"Oh flying flapjacks, ma'am! Why didn't you say so in the first place? I'll be deader than a slab of salt pork before I let nothin' happen to Mr. Jared! He's the sweetest, kindliest—well, you know how fine he is, ma'am! Come on now! We're hauling Rosie out of the sack right this minute!''

An hour later, Jasmine returned to Magnolia Bend to find Marie Bernard waiting for her in the front parlor. "Jasmine, what do you think you are you doing?'' the Frenchwoman demanded as she watched Jasmine enter the room. "I came down here to check on you, and Miss Charity said you were out running errands.''

"That's true,'' Jasmine returned evasively, not wanting to involve Marie in the dangerous task she knew she must now undertake.

Marie slanted Jasmine an admonishing look. "Errands, indeed! With Claude Boudreau once again committing his villainry? You know, you're a very poor liar. After what happened to Mr. Jared last night, a blind man could clearly envision your next moves. And have you forgotten our agreement?''

"What agreement?'' Jasmine hedged.

"That you wouldn't do anything without first consulting me?''

Jasmine sighed heavily as she set her reticule down on an end table. She stepped forward and said plaintively, "Marie, Claude tried to kill Jared last night. That changes everything.''

"It doesn't change the fact that we're friends, or the fact that we're in this together.'' Marie firmly took Jasmine's arm, then led the younger woman to the settee. "All right, Jasmine. Sit down, then spill it out. Everything.''

Knowing she was trapped, Jasmine complied.

# ★ Thirty-four ★

Three days later, Jasmine and Marie drove out to the Old Spanish Parade Grounds for a late-afternoon meeting with Claude Boudreau. Jasmine had learned of Claude's whereabouts through Rosie at the Scarlet Slipper. She shuddered every time she remembered what that poor woman had endured at his cruel hands. Later, as Jasmine and Marie had agreed, she'd sent Ephraim with a note to the boarding house where Claude was staying. He'd agreed to meet her today.

Jasmine sorely wished that Marie hadn't insisted on coming along with her this evening. After what had happened to Jared, Jasmine knew she must meet with Claude again. But she hated needlessly subjecting her friend to the danger of being in Boudreau's villainous company.

Yet Marie had insisted that she and Jasmine were in this thing together, until the end.

"Jasmine, isn't that the cutoff?"

Marie's tense voice cut into Jasmine's musings. "Yes." She guided Sugar off the wide road onto a narrow dirt path through the woods.

"Please be careful when you speak with this man," Marie said, gripping her armrest as they rocked down the potholed trail, the crisp branches overhead scraping against the cloth canopy of the buggy.

"Marie, we've been over this a thousand times. I know precisely what I have to do. You just worry about doing your part. Stay in the buggy as you promised. And if trouble should arise, ride like the devil for help."

"Yes, Jasmine," Marie said with a heavy sigh.

Jasmine brought the buggy through the parking area, all the way out into the wide clearing, and halted the horse beneath a sweeping live oak.

Jasmine smiled fleetingly at Marie, then gathered her cloak tightly about her as she headed toward the sunny center of the parade grounds. No one was around as yet. She went to stand on a small knoll. The crisp wind snapped at her clothing and burned her cheeks as she scanned the area for Claude.

Jasmine knew her greatest challenge would be to maintain a cool, unflappable facade. Her plan was complete, she knew; her speech was well-rehearsed. Yet she'd need a confident mien, as well as consummate acting abilities, during her discussion with Claude.

Seconds later, three men emerged from the woods to the south of her. Jasmine's heart hammered as she watched Claude Boudreau approach her, flanked by two husky-looking men wearing cloth caps, jersey shirts, and dungarees. She clenched her jaw angrily. "I thought our agreement was that we'd meet alone!" she called out to him irritably.

Claude gestured to his men to stay behind and approached Jasmine alone. She noted that he had changed his appearance again. His beard had been shaven, except for a bushy mustache and sideburns slanted to his jawline. He wore a gray topcoat, striped trousers, and a beaver hat, pulled low to shutter his eyes. "Just making sure you didn't double-cross me, my dear," he drawled as he arrived by her side, grinning and tipping back his hat. He nodded toward her buggy at the edge of the clearing. "I note that you didn't come alone, either."

"That's my maid, not a hired thug!" she snapped back.

He ignored her comment, brazenly eyeing her up and down. "You're looking quite comely this evening, Jasmine."

Jasmine fought an automatic urge to slap the impudent scoundrel who stared at her so insultingly. How could she ever have thought she loved this evil cad? How could she have let him deceive her? Depravity seemed to ooze from the dark eyes that raked over her. She must have been insane to ever look at him twice! "Let's get down to business," she gritted.

He bowed from the waist, then straightened to smile at her mockingly. "Tell me, are you ready to meet my terms now, Jasmine?"

She turned casually, descended the small knoll, and began to walk, feigning a nonchalance she hardly felt. "I'm ready to meet your terms," she informed him nastily.

Claude chuckled as he fell into step beside her, his boots crackling the winter turf. "I assume you did not like it when I almost killed your beloved fiancé?"

Jasmine shrugged, pausing to turn and stare at him in steady challenge. "That wouldn't have gotten either of us what we want, now, would it, Claude?"

He whistled, looking both shocked and fascinated by her remark. "And just what is it that you want, Jasmine? I had truly thought your fondest desire was to save your precious Mr. Hampton."

"Oh, shut up, you smug villain!" she retorted. "All of this is your fault, anyway. You took all my money, and now I'm stuck living with Jared Hampton's doddering fool of an aunt, who's driving me insane. And Hampton himself only wants me as his unpaid slut."

Claude looked amazed. "But I thought the man was planning to marry you?"

She shrugged. "He keeps postponing the date. Let me assure you that what that liar wants is *not* a wife."

He laughed cynically. "And you are thinking I will do something to remedy this situation for you? Surely you know me better than that, Jasmine."

"Oh, yes, I know you better than that." Looking Claude straight in the eye, she said, "I've decided I'll meet your terms, Claude—fully—with one condition."

"Oh?"

"You and I are splitting the twenty-five thousand."

"*What?*" He howled with laughter. "Your gall amazes me, Jasmine!"

"Does it?" she countered calmly. "Tell me, would you rather have half of twenty-five thousand or half of nothing?"

His expression grew tense and guarded at her words, and his eyes narrowed to dangerous slits. "And what makes you so sure Hampton will give you the twenty-five thousand in the first place?'' Again sweeping her with his repugnant gaze, he sneered, ''Evidently, the man does not hold you in as high esteem as you led me to believe.''

Jasmine flung off his taunt with a gesture of dismissal. ''I'll get it from him,'' she asserted haughtily. ''I've told Hampton I'm tired of being his unpaid doxy, and that he'll get no more favors from me until he suitably endows me. He's growing quite weary of the game, I assure you. And he shall succumb shortly.''

Now Boudreau was shaking his head and grinning. ''Why, Jasmine! If I'd known you possessed such diabolical genius, I never would have thrown you in the river in the first place.''

''That's your misfortune,'' she snapped. ''Well, do we have a deal, you blackguard? An equal split?''

Boudreau mused for a moment, scowling and rubbing his jaw. ''Very well, Jasmine. May I ask what you'll be giving Hampton when he turns this astronomical sum over to you?''

''You may guess,'' she said with a spiteful smirk. Tilting her chin disdainfully, she went on, ''However, I've no further desire to service the man. I'm planning to leave him.''

''Tell me, Jasmine, if these are your plans—if you really don't care what happens to Hampton—then, why include me? Why not simply cut me out of your scheme?''

Her eyes gleamed with anger as she retorted, ''Because I know you'll be skulking about, watching my every move! Because we *both* know you'll never let me get away with it.'' Staring at him with thinly veiled malice, she added, ''When one cannot defeat the devil, one bargains.''

He chuckled. ''Indeed. Tell me, when will this—er— exchange between us take place?''

''Saturday night, aboard the *Mississippi Belle*. She'll be in port at the landing late that afternoon, and she departs at eight.'' Casually, Jasmine went on, ''I'll have my man come around to your boardinghouse tomorrow with your ticket. I'm reserving a cabin for us on the boiler deck.''

Boudreau had been frowning skeptically as Jasmine spoke. ''Wait a minute! You want to meet on a riverboat? I'm not sure—''

"You seemed to find the setting appropriate enough the last time," she cut in with sweet sarcasm. Smoothly, she went on, "Your men may check out the riverboat beforehand, of course. But bear in mind that I'll be watching from somewhere up on the bluff, and I won't board the *Belle* with the money until I see your river rats leaving. Then I'll join you—just me and my maid. Surely you're not afraid of two defenseless little ladies?"

He glanced contemptuously toward Marie in Jasmine's buggy, then laughed. "Indeed, I'm not." For the third time, Claude's lascivious black eyes swept Jasmine up and down, and she struggled not to succumb to the nausea his hated look sent surging through her. "Why, Jasmine, I do believe you're sentimental. Do you wish to conclude our little assignation where it began?"

"Precisely," she said through gritted teeth.

He drew a step closer, and the revolting smell of stale tobacco and soured liquor swept over her. "You remember, of course, that the money won't be enough. I also want—"

"You don't have to spell out what you want," she cut in acidly. "Your terms will be met, Claude. I simply wish to get this over with, to be done with you. And with Hampton, of course," she added hastily.

"Oh, of course," he echoed derisively. "Very well, then. Just so you understand that you're spreading those pearly thighs for me." Even as she glared at him in trembling outrage, he stepped forward and caught her forearm in his painful grip. She could see the dark violence in his eyes as he added, "Bring all the money Saturday night. After you've serviced me to—er—my satisfaction, we'll split Hampton's loot straight down the middle."

By now, Jasmine was so revolted that she could barely hiss out a reply. "As you wish."

"Until Saturday night, then," he said mockingly.

Nodding curtly to Claude, Jasmine squared her shoulders, turned, and left him.

Hank Rawlins smiled to himself cynically. He had obviously underestimated Jasmine Dubroc. She had surprising spirit and cunning. A sadistic thrill rippled through him as he thought of Saturday night, and envisioned himself ravishing her slim body. Pity—they'd be on the riverboat, so he'd have to use a gag to muffle her screams, even at the end. He'd be able to see the terror in her eyes, though, and that would be enough! At last, he'd drink his fill of her, make her beg and plead for the mercy he'd never give! The bitch deserved it for toying with him!

Then, when he finished with her, he'd once again dump her in the Mississippi. This time she'd be dead, of course. And all the money would again be his!

Jasmine also felt self-satisfied. She needn't have worried about being able to fool Claude Boudreau. The man was clearly so depraved, he easily believed she was capable of equal turpitude!

Oh, she was capable of unspeakable sin, all right, but only where Claude Boudreau was concerned! She had several surprises in store for that sadistic swindler!

Jasmine climbed in beside Marie and snapped the reins. Both women were quiet until they arrived back on the main road. Then Marie tensely asked, "Well, Jasmine?"

She expelled a heavy sigh. "It's all set. I think I've gained his confidence and, hopefully, everything will go according to plan."

Marie nodded, then told Jasmine sternly, "Just remember that we're in this together."

"Marie!"

"Oh, yes. I'm going with you Saturday night." With a thoughtful frown, the Frenchwoman added, "It's taken me a long time to realize this, Jasmine, but now I know that you are right about everything."

"I am?"

Marie nodded solemnly. "We can't let Mr. Jared know what's going on. We want justice here, not vengeance. The first thing we must do is go back to Hampton Hall. Mr. Jared owns at least a dozen pistols. We'll find the one that is most like your father's, then you'll teach me how to use it."

Jasmine's green eyes were enormous as she stared at her

friend. "Marie! I thought you were against guns, and didn't you just say we want justice, not vengeance?"

"We do. But if we are to seek justice here, we must give ourselves every advantage. We must leave nothing to chance."

With a half-wondering smile, Jasmine acknowledged the wisdom of her friend's words. Marie Bernard was proving herself to be quite an intrepid ally!

## ★ Thirty-five ★

On Saturday night, Jasmine stood out on the bluff in a small clearing just off the Esplanade, a spyglass in her hands as she stared at the lights of Natchez-Under-the-Hill below her to the south. Behind Jasmine on the roadway stood her horse and buggy; Marie was waiting for her in the conveyance.

A brisk wind tugged at Jasmine's cloak and bonnet and her breath escaped in white puffs on the frigid air. Above her, the skies were dark and clear. The moon was full on this late-November night, and Jasmine found this ironic. The moon had been full on that other night, too—the night this mad adventure had begun. Now the light helped illuminate the *Mississippi Belle* at the landing below.

Fifteen minutes earlier, Jasmine had spotted Claude Boudreau and his two hired thugs boarding the *Belle*. Now, again detecting movement on the gangplank, she raised the spyglass and watched Claude's two river rats leave the boat and walk across the ramp to the landing.

She smiled. Her time had come. Lowering the spyglass and drawing her cloak tightly about her, she returned to her buggy. "It's time, Marie," she said to her friend as she climbed inside, carefully placing the spyglass under the seat.

Marie nodded. Both women were tensely silent as Jasmine

snapped the reins and clucked to Sugar. At last they descended the steep incline of Silver Street into the waterfront community.

What would Jared think if he could see her now? Jasmine wondered as they clattered past the Scarlet Slipper, which was lit up like a meteor and seemed to strain at its seams with the sounds of bawdy music and revelry. Jared would doubtless hang her hide out to dry if he knew what she and Marie were up to tonight.

Jasmine and Jared had planned to go to a concert of the Philharmonic Club this evening, but she'd claimed that she had an excruciating headache, and that she needed to go home to bed at once. Jared had taken this in stride. It seemed like he was being all too indulgent toward her lately.

Jasmine automatically sank back further in the leather seat as they turned down Middle Street. To her intense relief, they passed through the streets unaccosted, and in due course arrived at the landing.

As Jasmine and Marie alighted from their conveyance, an old black man, who'd been slumped on a bench outside a cotton warehouse, ambled toward them and offered to take the horse and buggy to a nearby stable. "You going on the *Belle*, ladies?" he asked, shivering in his tattered old coat.

Jasmine found she instinctively trusted the old man, who reminded her of Ephraim. Nodding to him, she went to pull a small leather bag from the boot of the buggy. Then she gave the black man a generous tip, and thanked him for seeing to their conveyance.

After watching the old man trudge off with the horse and buggy, Jasmine turned with Marie toward the *Mississippi Belle*. The riverboat towered beyond them in white-railed splendor, all lit up, its twin stacks billowing smoke into the cloudless November night. On both decks, hands were milling about, securing freight and assisting passengers. Jasmine sighed as the shrill whistle pierced her ears. Obviously, any passengers from Natchez had boarded by now; the boat looked ready to depart the landing at any moment.

Jasmine and Marie exchanged a knowing, sympathetic glance, then started across the gangplank to the boat. As they walked along the creaking, shifting ramp, Jasmine thrust her gloved hand inside her cloak pocket and placed her fingers on their tickets. She knew that Claude would be waiting for her in the cabin she had reserved on the boiler deck, and that this was their last chance to back out. What would happen if she lost her nerve?

Jasmine mentally scolded herself for such thoughts. She had to go through with this. She had to be brave, and she must make sure that neither she nor Marie got hurt. Indeed, her entire future with Jared depended on her behavior during the next few minutes.

As the two women stepped onto the main deck of the *Belle*, a young man in a dark uniform and black cap came forward to greet them. "Evening, ladies. May I help you?"

Jasmine showed the gentleman her tickets. "I've a cabin reserved for my friend and myself on the boiler deck."

"Of course, ma'am. May I call a porter to carry your bag upstairs?"

"Please, that won't be necessary."

"Whatever you say, ma'am. We'll be departing the landing any minute now, and dinner will be served in the main cabin as soon as we get underway."

Even as the man spoke, two deckhands came forward to draw in the gangplank. Jasmine thanked the man and headed with Marie to the main stairway. She was grateful that they hadn't been met by Captain Rutledge, who knew Jared and who might also recognize her from before.

Jasmine and Marie climbed the main stairway together. Glancing upward to make sure no one was within earshot, Jasmine whispered to her friend, "Remember, Marie, I want you to wait outside the cabin until I call for you."

"Jasmine, are you sure—"

She nodded fiercely. "You *must* wait for my signal, Marie. Otherwise, Claude may become suspicious and our entire plan will be in jeopardy."

"Very well, Jasmine. But if anything should go amiss—"

"I'll call for you at once," she promised.

On the boiler deck, the two strolled past a line of doors to room twenty-seven. At the door, Jasmine paused. Spotting a narrow beam of light spilling out from the transom, she nodded meaningfully to Marie. Marie embraced Jasmine briefly, then stepped back into the dark shadows on one side of the door.

Jasmine braced herself, then gripped the knob. Finding the door locked, she knocked.

"Who is it?" she heard Claude call out.

"Jasmine."

A moment later, he cracked the door slightly and stared at her with gun in hand. Even as she gasped, he glanced about quickly, then yanked her inside and locked the door behind them. "Good evening, Jasmine," he said at last.

Forcing herself not to panic, Jasmine stared at the pistol still in Claude's hand. Though the weapon wasn't aimed at her, the sight of it was sobering, nevertheless. "Claude, will you kindly put that gun away?" she asked him levelly.

To her great relief, he merely grinned and complied, opening his brown frock coat and shoving the gun into his waist. He moved off to pick up a half-filled glass of white wine from the desk and slowly took a sip as he raked his eyes over her. She quickly scrutinized the room. As before, the stateroom was sparsely furnished with a narrow bunk, an armoire, and a small desk. The lighting was low—only a couple of candles on the desk—making Claude's evil purpose quite clear. Within seconds, Jasmine had memorized every detail of the cabin.

Noting that Claude's expression had grown quizzical, she nodded to him and said stiffly, "You might offer me some wine, Claude."

He poured her a glass, handed it to her, then turned to check the door. "Just so we won't be disturbed."

"Surely your men searched the boat before they left you here all alone?" Jasmine asked him with sweet sarcasm.

"My associates had a good look around—as much as they could without attracting undue attention," he replied, taking another sip. "I have found one cannot be too careful in these matters."

He nodded toward the bag that she still held in her other hand. "That the money?"

"Yes." Tilting her chin and staring at him steadily, she inquired, "Shall we get down to business?"

He stroked his jaw thoughtfully, again eyeing her up and down in his brazen, sickening manner. "I rather had in mind pleasure before business. Do take off your cloak, my dear."

"As you wish," she said tonelessly.

With a sudden surge of recklessness, Jasmine downed her wine, then handed Claude her empty glass. He grinned, striding away to pour her another glassful. She turned, laying her bag on the bed, then quickly doffed her cloak, bonnet, and gloves. Moments earlier, she had again heard the boat's shrill whistle, and had felt the vessel rocking slightly as it steamed away from the landing. She figured that the passengers would now be gathering in the main cabin for refreshments before dinner.

Jasmine knew she had better act before she lost her nerve. Her timing here was critical, too. She undid the latch to her leather bag, reached inside, then turned around, her father's loaded pistol in her hand as she faced Claude Boudreau.

"What the hell?" he cried, looking stunned as he took a step toward her.

"Hold it right there, Mr. Hank Rawlins," Jasmine said with a triumphant smile. Watching his hand move toward his frock coat, she added fiercely, "Don't even try it! Get your hands up in the air!"

He froze, his hand still poised near his coat, a muscle twitching in his jaw as he glowered at Jasmine.

"I said, get your hands in the air!" she repeated in a cold voice.

At last, Claude raised his hands. "Why, you double-crossing little bitch! You knew who I was—"

"Indeed, I knew!" Jasmine cut in, laughing bitterly. "And who are you to talk of betrayal, Hank? After what you've done to me, not to mention to your other *wife* in St. Louis, and scores of others?" She backed toward the door, keeping her gun trained on him, not even blinking as she reached behind her with her free hand to disengage the lock. Moving away from the door, she called out, "Marie!"

Within ten seconds, Marie Bernard had dashed into the room with a loaded pistol in her own hand. Her gun was also pointed squarely at Hank Rawlins.

"My God!" he exclaimed, looking flabbergasted as he glanced from Jasmine to Marie. "Women? With guns? What kind of a trick is this?"

"Just shut up and take off your coat," Jasmine snapped. "Slowly."

When he didn't move, Jasmine cocked her pistol and said, "I see you're wondering if I have the nerve use this gun— aren't you, Hank? Well, you see, Natchez can be a rather dangerous place to live. When I was twelve, my father taught me how to load and use this pistol, just in case there was ever any trouble when he wasn't around. I've shot a squirrel or two in my time, even a skunk that got in our garden." She grinned. "And you'd be so much easier to shoot than a skunk, Hank. Don't you agree, Marie?"

Though Marie's face was pale and tense as she stared at their dangerous prisoner, she managed to nod to Jasmine.

"Now, take off your coat!" Jasmine snapped to Rawlins.

Looking murderously at Jasmine, Hank removed his coat.

Spotting the pistol tucked at his waist, Marie said, "Jasmine, let me get his gun."

"No," she said vehemently, reaching out to grasp Marie's sleeve. "Don't go anywhere near him. We don't want him grabbing you and disarming you." To Hank, she said, "Now, remove that gun by the butt with two fingers of your *left* hand. Slowly, or I swear, you're a dead man."

Once Hank had gingerly extracted the pistol from his waist, she said, "Now, place it on the edge of the desk. Carefully. Then step away from it."

Glaring at Jasmine, Rawlins complied.

Jasmine nodded toward Marie. "All right, Marie, you can get the gun now."

Marie stepped forward and picked up Hank's pistol, never taking her eyes off him.

"What's next, Jasmine?" Hank growled, every muscle in his dark face contorted in fury as he stared at the two women.

"Take off your clothes," she said calmly.

"I'll see you in hell first!" he retorted, his black eyes blazing.

"You may," Jasmine rejoined calmly. She aimed the gun at his midsection, then lower. She smiled. "But I promise you you'll die a very slow and agonizing death first."

"Why are you doing this to me?" he demanded furiously.

"Why?" She laughed incredulously. "You can even ask that? After you tried to kill me—and the man I love?" Staring Hank straight in the eye, she said, "I'm doing this to you, Hank Rawlins, because it's high time you discovered what it feels like to be victimized—to be totally humiliated! Now, take off your clothes, damn it!"

"All right! I'll do it." Glaring at Jasmine and Marie all the while, Rawlins quickly stripped down to his long johns.

"Everything," Jasmine said.

His mouth dropped open. "You've got to be kidding!"

"Do I look like I'm kidding?"

Rawlins glanced wildly from Jasmine to Marie. Then, finding no mercy in either woman's expression, he cursed under his breath and began unbuttoning his winter underwear.

Moments later, Hank Rawlins was standing before Jasmine and Marie, naked and heaving with rage. Jasmine reached behind her to open the door, then moved aside, grasping Marie's sleeve and pulling her back, as well. "Now, go out on deck," she told Rawlins.

"Have you lost your mind?" he asked in a disbelieving hiss. "Woman, it's almost December!"

"Go out on deck!"

Rawlins had no choice but to exit naked onto the frigid deck. Jasmine and Marie followed close behind him with their guns trained on him. Jasmine noted with relief that no one else was about on the boiler deck.

Rawlins moved to the railing, then turned to face Jasmine, shivering violently with both rage and the cold. "Well?"

Jasmine paused a moment, scanning the dark shoreline. She smiled as she spotted a familiar cove near Bacon's Landing. Her timing had been perfect! Smiling at Rawlins, she said, "Jump."

"You're crazy!"

"Jump, damn it!"

Muttering obscenities, Rawlins hastily climbed the railing, then dove into the black waters of the Mississippi.

Jasmine moved forward, grinning her satisfaction as Rawlins's naked form disappeared into the river.

"It's over, thank God," Marie whispered from her side, crossing herself as she expelled a heavy sigh.

Jasmine turned to Marie and hugged her friend tightly. Then she laughed until tears sprang to her eyes.

In the cove next to Bacon's Landing, Marshal Doyle Murchison had been sitting in a rowboat with his hastily appointed deputy, waiting for the *Mississippi Belle* to steam into view. "Lordy, I sure hope Miss Dubroc knows what she's doing tonight," Murchison muttered for the dozenth time. "When I arrived back in town late yesterday, she and her friend already had everything planned. I tried going by that boardinghouse on Water Street to arrest Rawlins myself, but that rascal had already moved again. I just hope he showed up for the meeting with Miss Dubroc on the steamboat tonight."

"I'm betting he showed," the deputy said as the river slapped at the side of their yawl. "He wants to collect her money, don't he? Though he'll have a surprise or two in store for him there," the man finished with a dry laugh.

Murchison nodded. "So he will. Miss Dubroc said she'd lure our pigeon for us. She said we had to do it her way, too, else we wouldn't have a prayer of trapping Rawlins—not with his thugs searching the *Belle* before she even departs. But, oh, Lordy, I just hope the girl knows what she's doing!"

Just then, both men tensed as the *Mississippi Belle* steamed into view. Within seconds, a naked man came flying off the boiler deck into the water.

"By God, she did it!" Murchison exclaimed, clapping his hands and grinning as the riverboat steamed past them toward the bend. Giving his deputy a friendly nudge in the arm, he added, "Didn't I know it all along? Everything's going just like clockwork, ain't it, boy? Now, quick. Let's row!"

The two men rowed out to retrieve Hank Rawlins. Murchison knew their quarry wouldn't get far—not naked in the near-freezing waters, and hundreds of yards from shore, to boot. Nevertheless, Murchison kept his eye sharply trained on the man now flailing about in the silvery waters beneath the full moon.

Quickly, the two men in the rowboat caught up with Rawlins, then hauled the coughing, sputtering man up into the boat. Murchison applied the handcuffs to Rawlins, while his deputy threw a coarse woolen blanket over the convulsively shivering man.

"Well, good evening, Mr. Hank Rawlins," Murchison told his captive with a broad grin. "Seems the United States government has a bit of unfinished business with you. Between me and some folks you know up in St. Louie, I'm figuring we'll get your neck stretched right quick."

Rawlins, still coughing and shuddering, was glowering at the *Mississippi Belle* as she disappeared around the bend. *"That damned bitch!"*

"Ah, yes," Murchison laughed, stroking his jaw. "The little lady has a message for you. She told me to tell you she likes stories that end where they begin."

On deck of the *Mississippi Belle*, Marie and Jasmine were still smiling to each other as the steamboat rounded the bend. Seconds earlier, they'd glimpsed Marshal Murchison and his deputy rowing toward Hank Rawlins.

"Justice, not vengeance," Marie whispered to Jasmine.

"Poetic justice," Jasmine added, fondly squeezing her friend's hand.

Suddenly, a stern voice called out from behind them, "Well—good evening, ladies."

The women whirled to view Jared and Jack, standing at the stateroom door. Both men were hatless, dressed in dark clothing. Jared's head no longer sported the familiar bandage of past days.

"Jared!" Jasmine gasped.

"Indeed."

"Evening, Marie," Jack added, his voice full of reproach as he stared solemnly at the woman he loved.

Jack stepped forward and took Marie's arm, firmly leading her off down the deck, leaving Jasmine and Jared alone.

Jared tucked his pistol into his waist, then strode over to join Jasmine at the railing. His frown held a formidable menace that was mirrored in his steely eyes, yet she was too curious about his presence to feel apprehensive. Setting her own pistol down on the railing, she stared at him incredulously and asked, "Jared, what are you doing here? And where *were* the two of you?"

"Jack and I were in the staterooms on either side of yours," he replied. "Captain Rutledge let us drill holes in the walls. Every second you and Marie were in there with Rawlins, we had our pistols trained on him."

"You did? You mean Captain Rutledge knew all about this?"

"Indeed he did."

"But that means that you also knew. How on earth did you manage to hide when Hank's men searched the boat?"

"In flour barrels," he replied with some distaste. "Actually, Jack and I hid on the *Belle* well before sunset. After Boudreau's thugs left the ship tonight, we climbed out and positioned ourselves in our assigned rooms."

Though angered, Jasmine also found herself grudgingly admiring Jared's tactics—the lengths he'd gone to to protect her. "So you and Jack were watching the whole time? You've known everything—all along?"

"Jasmine, between Jack and me, we've watched your every move for the past five days. We even knew that Murchison and his deputy would be waiting in the cove tonight to pick up Rawlins."

"Why—how dare you!" she sputtered indignantly. "You gave me your word you'd back off!"

"I promised you I wouldn't make a move on Rawlins for five days, and I haven't," he pointed out, staring at her gravely. "However, you are another matter entirely." He ran a hand through his hair and sighed fiercely. "Jasmine, it was sheer hell for me just now, watching your confrontation with Rawlins from the next room. I ached to rush into your cabin and break that bastard in two with my bare hands.

Somehow, I managed not to—though if he'd laid a hand on you, I would have intervened, despite my promise to you.'' Abruptly he pulled her into his arms and continued in a breaking voice, "For you see, dear Jasmine, I love you far more than my honor.''

The stark feeling in his voice, in his gaze, touched her so deeply that Jasmine found tears welling in her own eyes as she hugged him back. "Oh, I love you, too, Jared. So much!''

"Now, I should beat you, you wayward girl," he went on in a hoarse, exasperated tone.

She curled her arms around his neck and smiled up at him seductively. "Why don't you just take me back to Natchez and marry me instead?''

"A splendid idea," he rejoined, kissing her.

Jasmine sighed happily. She glanced down the deck and observed Jack and Marie, also locked in a passionate embrace.

# ★ Epilogue ★

On a night a week and a half later, Jasmine and Jared were again aboard a riverboat, this time heading downriver on the elegant steamboat *Natchez* to begin their honeymoon. The two stood at the railing on the high promenade deck, just outside their stateroom, sipping the champagne earlier presented to them by Jared's friend the captain, Tom Leathers. The early December sky was dark and clear, the golden cycle of a new moon shining with bright promise above them. The river beneath was wide and smooth, shimmering with a thousand reflected stars. The only sounds were those of an owl hooting along the forested shoreline and the paddle wheel lapping the current.

Though it was cold, especially up on the steamer's third deck, Jasmine and Jared were cloaked in heavy wool and sheltered in each other's embrace. "To my beautiful bride," he said, clinking his champagne glass against hers.

"To my wonderful groom," she returned as she sipped the bubbly brew.

"The wedding today was so lovely," he went on. "I thought my poor aunt would never stop crying."

"She was happy—just as I was. And am."

"And you got to marry in the Catholic church—just as you always wanted."

"Is that what you always wanted?" she asked him wistfully.

He drew her closer and spoke with a catch in his voice. "All I ever wanted was you."

"Why Mr. Hampton," she said with a smile, "I do believe you've just stolen my line."

Jared leaned over, gracing her lips with a tender kiss. Afterward, he grinned. "Wasn't Jack and Marie's wedding a wonderful surprise last week?"

She nodded. "I can't believe how quickly Jack married Marie after our little adventure."

"You women make us men resort to extreme methods," he grumbled with a frown.

She giggled at his dramatics. "I told Marie she and Jack should wait and have a double wedding with us, but she insisted that that would be stealing our thunder. I think the two of them were more comfortable with the small service at St. Mary's chapel last week. And it was so wonderful of you to give them your plantation house in Vidalia as a wedding gift."

"Jack and Marie will need a house now that Mertson has returned to the east and Jack is overseeing my plantation full-time." Jared chuckled. "I never thought I'd see the day when Cactus Jack Malone would want to settle down like he has. I tried to give him and Marie a hefty chunk of my land, as well, but Jack refused. In time, I'll change his mind. My holdings in Louisiana are so vast that eventually I'd like to divide the plantation and build us a new manor house farther upriver."

She feigned a pouting look. "Well, actually, Jared, I rather fancy your hunting lodge over there."

His eyes twinkled with devilishness. "Do you? I wonder why." With a husky chuckle, he added, "Don't worry, woman. We're never giving up that cabin. We learned a great deal about each other there that afternoon."

The two sipped their champagne in a blissful, shared silence, then Jared said, "You're going to love New Orleans. I'm going to take you everywhere. And, of course, we'll buy oceans of presents for Maggie."

"Do you suppose we could shop for a layette, as well?" she asked him coyly.

His eyes lit with incredulous joy. "Jasmine! You mean— a baby?"

She nodded. "Mind you, it's a little too soon to be certain. But a woman has an intuition about these things. I think it happened the night you were wounded, and we were—"

"So very close?"

"Oh, yes, my darling!"

He hugged her tightly, pressing his lips against her hair. "My love. I'm so happy."

"Me, too," she said dreamily. "In fact, I only have one regret." When he drew back and eyed her quizzically, she said, "I would have given my eye teeth to have actually seen Hank Rawlins's face that night when Marshal Murchison pulled him out of the Mississippi!"

Jared chuckled. "Oh, Jasmine, to hear you laugh about this! Don't you realize how significant that is? Rawlins has lost his power over you, darling! That was one reason I didn't intervene that night when you sprang your trap on him, though it almost killed me not to. I knew you needed to walk through this alone, if you could."

"Thank you for that, Jared," she said with a tear in her eye. "It's a selfless gift I'll never forget. But you must know that I was determined to bring Rawlins to justice not because of what he did to me, but because he nearly killed you."

"I believe you," Jared said earnestly, "because I know just how you felt. I wanted to kill him for the same reason —what he did to you." He scowled down at her. "Still, woman, you don't know how you scared the living hell out of me when you insisted on taking things into your own hands. But you had me over the proverbial barrel. I had to prove, if I could, that I do love you more than anything—including my honor."

Jasmine felt an acute stab of guilt. "Er—Jared?"

"Yes, my love?"

"Um—" she dared to look up at him. "You never had to prove that to me."

*"What?"*

She twisted her fingers around the stem of her champagne glass and avoided his smoldering eyes. "Well, what I mean is, after that night when you were wounded, when we talked and shared so much . . . I never doubted you loved me after that."

"Jasmine, are you telling me that you deliberately deceived me?" he demanded.

Miserably, she nodded. "I was afraid Hank would indeed kill you, and I had to get you to back off, Jared—any way I could."

As he glared down at her, she could hear a growling sound coming from deep within his throat. She stretched upward quickly and kissed him, her lips softly parted beneath his firm mouth.

"What the hell," he said. "I'm mad about you."

Jared tossed their champagne glasses over the side, then scooped Jasmine up into his arms and carried her into their stateroom. Smiling up at him as he set her down on her feet, she said, "You know, the last time I left for a honeymoon on a steamboat, I ended up getting thrown in the river. I'm glad," she finished dreamily.

"You're glad?" he inquired with a disbelieving laugh as he turned to close the door.

"Because otherwise I never would have met you. You rescued me, Jared."

"And I've been yours ever since!" Returning to her side, Jared pulled her close, slapped her bottom playfully, then began efficiently undoing her cloak and bonnet. "Now, you glorious creature—it's high time I turned you into an obedient little wife. I might just start with a kiss." He paused to demonstrate in a leisurely manner as his fingers attacked the buttons on her traveling frock. "Or a nibble or two, right there. . . ."

They explored all the possibilities as the *Natchez* rocked them into the night.

# ABOUT THE AUTHOR

Eugenia Riley is the author of numerous historical and contemporary romances. A native Texan, she is a magna cum laude graduate of Texas Wesleyan College in Fort Worth, a former English teacher and editor of *Touchstone* Literary Quarterly. She lives in Houston with her husband and two daughters.

Ms. Riley is also the author of *Laurel's Love* and *Sweet Reckoning*, both published by Warner Books. Her next historical romance from Warner, *Angel Flame*, will be forthcoming in approximately one year.

Ms. Riley welcomes mail from her readers. Please write to:

Eugenia Riley
P.O. Box 840526
Houston, Texas 77284-0526